IF HE LIVED

Lillian is a woman who feels too much. As a psychiatric nurse, she empathises with her patients: as a mother, she mourns for her lost, runaway daughter. Now suddenly she has a new feeling, that her house, one of the oldest in the small Massachusetts town where she lives with her husband Freddy, has been invaded, violated by some past evil. And then Lillian sees the boy...

If He Lived is a ghost story, beautifully told, utterly convincing and all the more terrifying because it happens now, in our world, to people just like us. It is also the story of a marriage, of a relationship that is tested to its very limits by both forces we can recognise and those we cannot.

JON STEPHEN FINK

Born in the USA, Jon Stephen Fink has lived in Britain since 1978. He is the author of two other novels, *Further Adventures* and *Long Pig*.

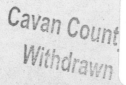

BY JON STEPHEN FINK

Further Adventures
Long Pig
If He Lived

Jon Stephen Fink

IF HE LIVED

V

VINTAGE

Published by Vintage 1998

2 4 6 8 10 9 7 5 3 1

First published in Great Britain by
Jonathan Cape 1997

Vintage
Random House, 20 Vauxhall Bridge Road,
London SW1V 2SA

Random House Australia (Pty) Limited
20 Alfred Street, Milsons Point, Sydney
New South Wales 2061, Australia

Random House New Zealand Limited
18 Poland Road, Glenfield,
Auckland 10, New Zealand

Random House South Africa (Pty) Limited
Endulini, 5A Jubilee Road, Parktown 2193,
South Africa

Random House UK Limited Reg. No. 954009

A CIP catalogue record for this book
is available from the British Library

ISBN 0 09 959971 6

Papers used by Random House UK Ltd are natural,
recyclable products made from wood grown in sustain-
able forests. The manufacturing processes conform to the
environmental regulations of the country of origin

Printed and bound in Great Britain by
Mackays of Chatham PLC, Chatham, Kent

To

Amy Mitsuko

and to

Francis & Maureen
for their friendship and forbearance

Prologue

CLOSE TO three years went by before Dr Marit Sonnenfeld published on the Foy haunting. She had kept her audio and video tapes, notes and conclusions out of circulation, although she let odd pieces of the story strain through during ordinary conversations with her friends. In these moments her mood dimmed, she spoke quietly and seemed to be the captive of her own disturbing thoughts.

Because Marit's closest friends were also her psychology faculty colleagues, the fragments they had picked up from her – half-descriptions of the small New England town, the people who had been visited, the apparition itself – began to drift around academic conferences. Questions from *psi* researchers and investigators trickled in, and Marit let them pile up. Was it true she'd caught the image of a ghost on video, the ghost of a little boy? Was there a family connection between this child and the couple who had seen him? Did both the husband and wife show *psi* ability? Marit wouldn't answer their letters or phone calls, she strictly refused to take anyone into her confidence. On account of Dr Sonnenfeld's high reputation at and outside the University of Pennsylvania the rumors about this haunting took on a tingling glamour.

The letter from Lillian and Freddy Foy arrived when Marit was winding up her research on near-death experiences. That work had been a very long haul, it was true, and when she returned to Philadelphia from her time with the Foys the grind of writing the NDE book still stretched ahead of her. But even after she had put the finishing touches on *Sensing Death* some eighteen months later, Marit balked at going back to the nerve-racking case; evidence of the occurrence she had collected in Massachusetts stayed locked in her desk drawer. Marit's decision (and behavior in general) mystified everyone close to her.

In the end they got their explanation. Her monograph, *A Scientist's Personal Experience of an Apparition of the Dead: A Case Study* (Sonnenfeld, 1984), was printed in the *Journal of the American Society for Psychical Research* soon after Marit's mother died. She'd held off publishing what she knew about the ghost in the Foys' house until Judith Sonnenfeld lay beyond any more earthly horror. It was an act of love that took the place, for some precious time, of obligations to science or to the believing or disbelieving public.

The even deeper truth, of course, was that after twenty years of chasing down paranormal phantoms Marit Sonnenfeld's whole sense of reality had been jolted. Another awareness had come alive in her. Ben and Katy, her two pre-teens, noticed the change in their mother's quietness, that remote darkening behind Marit's already dark, burnt sugar eyes. It removed her from other people in a room and at unpredictable moments it seemed to remove her from the room, too. Sometimes Marit saw her children looking at her and openly wondering where the quiet darkness in her eyes came from; it was good they didn't know yet, Marit thought, and she didn't want to frighten them. To friends who asked her, though, she said it was this: the physical closeness of death rubbing against her.

The Foys had thought they'd called in an expert on the motives of the dead. Well, before Marit's two nights in their home she knew as much about such things as Lillian and Freddy did. But she left there knowing that the motives of the dead and the living are the same, and reason is no shelter from them.

The question Marit started with was also Lillian's first question – What kind of torment was in her house? After listening to the story they began to tell her, Marit's suspicion was that this ghost had broken into the world through cracks in the Foys' marriage.

Chapter One

A HOUSEHOLD rule stemmed from Freddy Foy's attitude to the evening meal. While they sat at the dinner table Lillian's radio in the kitchen had to be tuned to easy-listening music or switched off. Let her listen to whatever she wanted to hear while she was cooking, the heavyweight championship from Madison Square Garden or ice hockey from Canada if she enjoyed that, but once the food was on the table Freddy wanted the atmosphere cleared of the 'grit and grime of the outside world'.

As he leaned over the pot-roast with carving knife and fork, Lillian picked up Freddy's small distress signals. Voices on the radio gatecrashed the dining room, complaining about pesticides in the food chain. She cut them off, sent them sliding away under the all-music station and came back to the table to find Freddy sawing at the little bale of steaming meat, violins crying in the background. The strings sighed and moaned through the creamy harmonies of a Broadway ballad that the whole country was humming thirty-odd years ago, when the Foys were newlyweds.

'The light's just so loud in here.' She wanted him to see her squinting up at the six-bulb wagon wheel fixture that poured brightness onto them as if they had sat down in an operating room to eat dinner.

Without looking up, concentrating on his action with the knife, Freddy said, 'You don't want me to cut my finger off. Am I right?'

'I'd know what to do if you did.'

Now he looked at her. '"Loud", anyway. You can't get away with inaccuracy when it comes to a dose of medicine, can you.' The leaden evenness Freddy dropped into his voice when he corrected a student's blueprint or technique at the drafting table he used with his wife now.

'It's too bright white. We might as well be in the Highway Diner.'

'"Bright", see, that's clear. I can understand "bright".'

'You knew what I meant the first time.'

'I had to think about it.'

Growing up with him, Lillian had watched Freddy become more of the moody soul he had always been. The first summer he was home from Carnegie Mellon, when they would run into each other somewhere around Lawford most afternoons, she noticed that already he laughed less easily. College life must be a place of bruising truths. Freddy used to turn softly quiet when she teased him, usually with jokes about his thinning hair or his march into mapped-out middle age. All playful compliments really, bold flirting, Lillian's attraction to his careful, practical, inward nature, his undramatic decency, qualities as natural in Freddy as ore in the ground. Then something changed in him, something their time together either peeled bare or zippered up, and these days even gentle ribbing would turn him as quiet as a concrete block; he'd pull his mouth to one side, biting the inside of his cheek, screwing down the lid.

Freddy's lid must have been screwed down too tight for too many years. The pressure, when it detonated, had given them a mortal scare only eighteen months ago. It was a 'warning', Dr Mollo told them, nothing as damaging as a full-blown coronary, but the kind of tremor that deserved respect. This house-call wasn't strictly for Freddy's benefit, Marcello Mollo wasn't his cardiologist but a psychiatrist, and Lillian's boss at Mount St Mary's hospital. He had stopped by for an update, for his personal information; the special gift that made Lillian such a sensitive nurse also left her wide open – if anybody took a knock, she took it too. Direct and physical in expression, Mollo said confidentially to Lillian that these shocks can be timely things. 'Morris Bernstein gave me a peek at Freddy's chart. We're in agreement. A lot of men we've seen who've been zapped the way Freddy has come out the other side of it and they're much looser personalities. Much more relaxed about life in general.' They were whispering back and forth in the kitchen. And what about the other ones, Lillian didn't need to ask (but did), how do they come out of it? 'They go very quickly,' said Mollo, shrugging at the crudely obvious.

Her husband came out of it clinging to control. Freddy did the nutritional research himself and worked out a diet that leaned toward cod and mackerel, broccoli, carrots, spinach and rice. 'Tell Dr Mollo I'm doing fine on my Eskimo diet,' he'd instruct Lillian almost every morning. As his strength came back to him, as he began to feel terra firma underneath him and not a crumbling cliff-edge, Freddy's old appetites returned like a flock of wintering birds. Lamb chops then lamb roasts, meatloaf (he shopped for lean hamburger meat, *lean* – it was a word he used as a magic charm), then sirloin tip, pork roasts, pot pies, beef stews, 'solid protein to build me up'.

At fifty-two he had needed animal strength, the strength of a steer to walk back into that walnut-paneled room for drinks with Vernon Mercer and a representative quorum of Lawford Academy's trustees. Freddy's welcome back to campus, that's what Vernon called the party in his handwritten invitation, and as a friend and colleague that was

7

specifically what he wanted it to be. But that wasn't all it was. As the school's Provost Vernon was hosting a post-crisis examination. It felt that way to Freddy at least, when he'd answered for the fourth or fifth time the fourth or fifth combination of trustees' questions about his habits and health. Was he drinking less now? Eating less, eating more? Was he serving a sentence on an exercise bike? Finishing his martini (but refusing a refill), Freddy had stayed till the end, diligently socializing, glad to reassure them all that he was just as keen as ever to move up into administration and just as fit for the workload.

If the heart tremor changed him, it was a subtle change Lillian perceived. Freddy's concentration was narrower and more gauged, it was the patient concentration of a wildlife photographer or model train builder. He would wait out his unofficial probation in the classroom. There, with T-square and mechanical pencil, plotting elevations and floorplans, he was allowed to start again where he'd left off. Now, two years along, his probation was about to be lifted.

Full attention on the pot-roast, Freddy's prim Napoleonic mouth was compressed almost to a bud under the correct tweezered angles of his iron filing mustache. He didn't talk to Lillian while he arranged the meaty leaves of the roast first on the serving dish and then on their plates. With the flat of the large knife steadying a single slice of meat on the serving fork's shallow curve he set aside the darker crusty end-piece for himself and passed Lillian a slice from the pinker interior. Intimate knowledge. One more of the uncountable transparent everyday encounters in a room where they did their living. This house folded them inside it.

And yet when he sat down to eat Freddy unemotionally measured the place against Old Mill House, as if their home's real value was its rating on the property market. 'The Mill's got four double bedrooms, but that's not the main attraction,' he said. 'There's real Lawford tradition attached to it.'

Old Mill House was one of the most famous buildings in the area, one of the best preserved early eighteenth-century stone-built mills, converted into a home for the first Provost of Lawford Academy around the time of the First Continental Congress. It was older than the Foys' patchwork lodge by a hundred years, but its stately history wasn't the feature that tugged at Freddy so mightily. The ancient house was included in the package of his proposed elevation to Deputy Provost.

Freddy spooned out some diced carrots for Lillian and a molehill of mashed potatoes. He offered her his weariness. The small puff of fatigue came from the labor of explaining, again, the entire formal offer made to him by the trustees. In the last couple of weeks Vernon Mercer had pressed Freddy for an answer more than once.

'Why can't they give us until after Thanksgiving?' Lillian asked him. 'It's not a thing you can say yes or no to overnight.'

'I think Vernon's point is that it's been in my lap for enough time. They've got their agenda. There's a scad of politics involved.' He paused, laying it before her. 'Should I show I'm so willing, that's the prime question. They all know, the McCallisters and Pells and the rest of them, I was raring to go two years ago. I don't want to look *grateful*, do I? Their commitment to me has to be as solid as mine is to the Academy.'

'You wouldn't be happy teaching anyplace else. Don't you think they know that?'

'Do they? Do you?' Freddy chewed a mouthful of food in a burst of choppy bites. It had the effect of blocking Lillian's side of the conversation. He swallowed and continued. 'Politics is the essence. Why do you think they're offering me Mill House? Chandler's entitled to stay there until he turns his toes up, but that house is being offered to me. At lunch yesterday Vernon told me they had to spend three hours talking Chandler out of moving his son's family into it.'

She said, 'I don't want to sell up.'

'For the tenth time,' unangered, only emptied of fresh ways to explain it, 'we don't have to sell. We can rent it out. We'll get ahead and stay ahead.'

'Nobody told me we were on the way to the poorhouse.' She saw his mouth bunch up and pull to the side, he was gnawing the inside of his cheek. 'All right,' Lillian said, 'say we rent our house. Pack everything up and move there. I don't know how I'd feel around all that extra space. All those big bedrooms. Four of them, Freddy?'

'There's a fireplace in each one. They don't have to stay bedrooms. I can make one into a sewing room for you. And I can have a library.' Another thought. 'And we could each have our own bedroom.'

'Oh, you know,' she said, giving her words little weight, 'I'd miss this pokey old house. It's ours.'

'May I have the potatoes?' Without waiting Freddy leaned up out of his chair and pulled the bowl across the table. He didn't look at her, bluntly looked away, let his eyes wander over his food.

Without a doubt, though, Lillian was there. Present, an object in his view. Of this dumb fact she was sharply aware. Her husband saw sitting across from him a woman whose femininity had grown broader and more bruisable as she nosed toward fifty. On her feet most of the workday in Molyneaux Wing kept her legs and her back trim; the softness collected in her light-filled, inquiring, observant eyes. At the beginning it was the social daredevil in her that hooked Freddy, Lillian's fearless approachability. The calm pleasure she got out of talking to, listening to, anybody she met simply amazed him; he saw the danger. People abused her interest, that was how Freddy read it, they used her as a receptacle. Maybe it wounded him to imagine anyone else getting the same sense of themselves that he felt so powerfully when he was with her, the thrilling permission to be honest about what he wanted. At the time he was courting her Lillian's copper hair was also a flag to him, and he'd watched it dull to rust brown then slate gray. Plucky against the drag of time, she kept her pageboy hair-do, the style she'd worn first when she was a young mother. Now the drapery around Lillian's face was thinner, the face also thinner. The stranded cheek bones deepened those gem cut eyes. Her pinkish skin, an indoor complexion, carried a dusting of blonde down, and this oversoftening combined with the squarish leading chin conformed absolutely to Freddy's picture of Lillian as wife, nurse, endurer. Whatever troubled her, excited her, engaged her, mystified her, she took it all into her heart involuntarily and confined it there while the rest of the organism plowed on.

'Other people living here, though.' Lillian shuddered the point home. 'I'd see this house every day when I went to work. Probably see them through the windows, walking around inside.'

'Yes, there's that.' The idea didn't horrify Freddy. 'We shouldn't underestimate our *sensitivities*.'

She defended her sensitivities. 'You build up a life in a house. After thirty-one years, Freddy. More than half our lives.'

'That's what I'm telling you. We'd still *own* it. And we won't rent it out to any Mister Magoo who knocks on the door. This place is going to attract people like us. Its historical appeal will.'

The Hoagland place, as the Foys' boxy L-shaped residence was known locally, had been erected as the carriage house of a country estate in the early 1800s. The mansion was burned to the ground in 1867 – by one account an accident with a soup pot, by another, disinheritance flaring into arson – but the coach house survived uncharred. It led a commercial life as a livery stable and by the end of the century it had outlasted most of the neighboring brick buildings, resisting other fires, neglect and property development, modern onslaughts which had ruined many of Lawford's older prettier streets. Its owners juggled a living out of the buckboard, trap and phaeton trade into the 1900s and then, in 1912, the building was sold to the family that gave it its monicker. Samuel Emperor Hoagland added the upper story for his brood of boys and turned the room that was now the Foys' kitchen into the ground-level extension of a subterranean workshop. Hoagland's basement was a beach-head in the northeast United States, an outpost of the pioneer automobile business. It was the first true garage in Lawford parish and between the wars Hoagland and his sons built, sold and serviced their own line of two- and four-seater runabouts. This part of Lawford, the south end of Church Hill, which petered out into dipping lanes, hay fields, a wide shallow creek and woodland, fought off incorporation. It survived on the apron of suburban Mistley, a post-war town planned and planted by businessmen who were cannier or just luckier than Sam Hoagland. Hypnotize Freddy and he'd confess to a fluttering pride in his ownership of the place, a secret identification with the self-taught architect, engineer and independent carmaker who was trampled out of business by Henry Ford.

In the summer Lillian liked to open the kitchen windows to the warm baking smell of earth and grass cuttings from the fields, to the gentle applause of mossy water in the culvert that ran under the road and skirted the house. But now in the colder stiller months the small pleasures of her home were more interior. Days turned and returned (when they weren't muffled in cloud), around the low afternoon light, a parting, an opening between two stretches of russet dusk. On her days off, in the mornings after Freddy had cruised off to school, Lillian could sit at the dining room table (where she was sitting now) and watch through the window undistracted. There was the patched asphalt of Church Hill, the straggling bony trees that came out to meet it, the empty platter of the field behind them, a weak abandoned world. Icy brilliance hardened over it and coated the front hedge and porch steps, lacquered the panes a foot from her face, but inside this house Lillian sat in coal-fired warmth, drinking tea, looking out, settled in.

The dark, when it came early in the evening, sealed them up here.

From her place at the table she saw the two of them reflected in the dining room window, glassy shadows, Freddy and herself framed there eating dinner, cropped as if to make a point about the settled life they had made together. Their history was embedded in the fabric of the house, thought, felt, stamped and hollered, murmured and moaned, vibrated into its wooden floors and beams, its lath and mortar. Lillian took her eyes off the reflection, came back to Freddy. 'You can accept the offer from them but you don't have to accept Mill House. They're the ones asking *you*, you know.'

He jumped on the influence at work here. 'I can hear Mim's voice.'

'Not true.'

'Arthur wanted to stir up some faculty rumors,' he said, greatly annoyed. 'Funny joke. After the trustees do their three-hour medicine dance around Warren Chandler and fix it all up for me, I get up on my hind legs and say sorry, no, not interested. Don't tell me you haven't examined all the angles with Mim and that golf gang of hers.'

'If she knows anything then she got whatever little tidbit it was from Arthur. He's the lord high *priest* of gossip. But she wouldn't talk us over that way. You should know that about Mim.' Lillian kept him from derailing her. 'I'm not moving out of here. I don't want it. The next time you talk to Vernon you can blame it all on me.'

Freddy considered this, stoically. 'All right,' he said. 'I'll live there. By myself, if needs come to must.'

Lillian played along, or turned it into play. 'I'd like to see that.'

'I could do it. I'd move in at night. Nobody in Lawford would have to know that you weren't there with me.' Half-serious, Freddy's mouth tweaked into a half-smile.

She knew (and knew *he* knew) Freddy couldn't survive coming back to a wifeless house for more than a week. After that he started to miss his audience. The household tasks he carried out were one-man shows:

13

picking up the dry cleaning, managing the income and outgo, tackling the home improvements. (The authentic wagon wheel he wired to splash down all that light was only the latest.) This necessary work he performed first of all for Lillian. Daily proof of the lengths (a thousand short ones added together) he'd go to hold up his end of their marriage. All Lillian had to do was stay in her seat.

'I'll let you take my blue striped dress.'

'Why would I need anything of yours?'

She advised him, 'You'll want to make a realistic model of me to put in the window. For a decoy. I've got my tailor's dummy downstairs somewhere, if you want it.'

'I'll need a few more of your personal things if it's really going to look like you're living with me. Your eczema cream and your cornplasters.'

'And make sure you keep two plates on the kitchen counter. Hang my car coat in the hall closet and you'll hardly know I'm not there.'

'That's enough,' he said, calling time.

'And I could do the same thing with your brown suit. Stuff it with mattress wadding and sit it in your green chair. Just promise me,' she pushed the joke a little out of shape, 'we'll talk on the phone once in a while.'

'That's enough,' he repeated, straight-faced.

'The biggest scandal in town.'

'Lillian, now you don't know what you're saying.'

What could realistically be settled tonight? Only their official positions. They chewed their mouthfuls, they fell back on table manners, quietly spoken requests for the applesauce or for milk from the pitcher, they remarked on their tiredness. Music from the radio filled the gaps with a Fred Astaire tune, and safe behind its happy tappy breeziness Lillian said, 'I had that dream again last night.'

'Oh, now, look.' Freddy's mock dismay was over the spoonful of peas he'd just knocked off the edge of his plate. Powerless to block their escape he watched green vegetable anarchy fan out over the tablecloth. 'Never a dull moment.'

As the disappointments piled up and Freddy's old sense of humor soured, Lillian saw middle age cover her husband the way a sandstorm attacks a road. His hair had gone, pitiably, from everyplace on his crown except for the crisp hairline, and this weedy fringe he plastered back with hair tonic. The mix of gray and chestnut threads streaking his scalp gave Freddy's beautifully globe-shaped head the look of a painted Russian doll.

More and more Lillian was noticing that what used to be forceful in him had drifted into mulishness, as though this was part of the physical process of his body's aging. Shoulders, chest and belly bulked out; spilled and slipped weights of soft muscle and softer fat resettled in lumpy mounds at the back of his neck, the spreading gravity of his buttocks. To Lillian he brought to mind something like a statue in a neighborhood park, a figure of forgotten importance, degraded by bird dirt and carved initials. But if you stayed to look past the natural wear and inflicted tear you'd see the old magisterial soul gazing out at you, undented.

She still enjoyed, and warmly, the creeping border of rough hair that edged from his wrists under the rolled cuffs of his cardigan. An unexpected masculine excess which Freddy would try to tuck away, tidy up. Short of taking hedge clippers to the problem (only vanity was less attractive in a man), there wasn't much he could do against an unkempt part of him that sneakily exposed this unruliness. Hairy wrists were not the embarrassment; it was the hint of personal disorder that Freddy couldn't hide or correct. When Lillian saw him absentmindedly plucking his sleeve forward all the reasons that long ago moved her to feel close and safe with Freddy were right there in front of her.

'Why do you think this dream has dug into me so much?' Lillian said, winning his attention back from the runaway peas. 'Wait till you hear how it went. It's one for the record book.'

'That's your area, though.' Freddy was now picking up the peas individually, craning them over into the little corral of the serving spoon. 'Mr Freud and his friends. Mollo's the man to ask, not me.'

Dreams stayed with Lillian, usually without spooking her the way this one did. Dr Mollo's word on the subject was, 'Dreams don't foretell the future, they foretell the present.' The deepest meaning brought to life in a dream might not be graspable any other way. It was, somehow, her own story Lillian dreamed, with riddles to answer, dangers to face down, treasures to bring back, its roots bedded in the reality of the past. Did Freddy know this about her? The first time she tried to tell him about the monkey chained to the hot stove she couldn't grab his interest either. She imagined her words echoing muddily in his head, reaching him as if she'd spoken them underwater.

Remembering the dream for him she said, 'I was coming in through the back door, just normally, and I heard this yapping, this squeaky, I don't know, this trapped animal kind of panic.'

'You should have woken me up, Lil.'

'I looked over at the broom closet, which wasn't there anymore. All the yap-yapping was coming from behind a pot-bellied stove. It's very hot and I'm going over to it to get warm. I'm cold as snow. The latch on the front is unhooked, all I have to do is reach down and tip the door open. It creaks when I do that, when I see the wood burning in there, but the noise isn't from the hinges. It's this *shrieking*. A little organ-grinder type monkey is chained up to the stove. He's chained up by his neck, jumping around, going crazy. I can't do anything to calm him down, but when he sees me, sees who I am, he – he's got these old eyes. Human eyes. I think he wants to say something to me but he can't talk. It's stuck in my head but I can't figure out what the darn thing *means*.'

'That's going back some years, isn't it,' he said, deliberately not encouraging her to go on, 'organ-grinders.'

With the plates cleaned, dried and stacked in the cupboard, Freddy said, folding the dishtowel, 'I just want to finish my crossword,' and patted Lillian's arm on the way out of the kitchen. She heard him in the upstairs bathroom, water running in the sink. A splash on the back of his neck, a smear of soap, rubbing with both square hands. Then around to his face. Sitting alone Lillian thought she could feel on her skin the pressure of electric light in the room, fronts of light pressing against the windows like warm air in a rubber balloon, bowing them out, the walls too, bowing a fraction, warping outward. She sat in the middle of this tidal pull, in the thick, enclosing, twice-breathed air.

Chapter Two

BEING THE parents of a teenage runaway (though Hildy wasn't a teenager anymore, she had been gone for fourteen years) marked them, scarred, bereaved, labeled Freddy and Lillian, each in different ways. Around the first anniversary of Hildy's disappearance, only a day or two after her eighteenth birthday, Freddy weighed the evidence and came to the conclusion that Hildy didn't want to be found. This year-long separation was on *her* head. Legally, she was an independent adult now. Who sent Lillian nonsensical messages, written on scraps torn off of brown paper bags, cocktail napkins and other road trash, mailed from southern and western states farther and farther away. Freddy was not going to let her mire him in hopeless regret. He banned any more discussion about Hildy. No more talk about the tensions, fractures and upheavals of Sixties society, no more theories about her maladjustment, no more sessions with John Early, the detective overseeing Hildy Foy's *case*, and in private or in company no uttering of her name.

18

Freddy's stiff-necked method for coping with the situation fell on Lillian like a polar wind. He was wrapping her in a coat of ice. A double absence from her life then – her daughter gone and the finest part of her husband gone too when he gave up on Hildy. Lillian only had to add her own absence, anything else was the worst hypocrisy. She flit on one of her days off while Freddy was in his classroom. The feeling of great sin came over her later.

Three weeks at the YWCA in Boston and then she sent Freddy a telegram to let him know she was alive and well. The next day she got him on the phone. He didn't ask when she was coming back. What he needed to know, what was fair to tell him, was if she had any plans to return, so he could make plans of his own. (To sell her clothes? Hire a housekeeper?) She'd stomped him when he was down, she'd demolished their marriage, marooned him, and he was notifying her officially.

Lillian let him vent. She heard and believed he was tormented, made sick. But for the next five weeks she lived in a motel only a few miles from Lawford. The night she finally walked back into their house she found Freddy in his undershirt and sagging trousers, standing in front of the gas range, heating a can of soup in a pot of boiling water. Slowly he was falling apart, like an emptied tenement building. She poured the Cream of Tomato into a saucepan, made a rack of toast for them and sat down with Freddy at the round white kitchen table. There they ate, haggardly staring at each other. One of the first things he said to her (he made it a dignified plea) was, 'Are you through with it now? Are you finished with this neurotic attachment to your spiteful daughter?' But Lillian didn't splash hot soup into his face, she didn't pick up her blue suitcase and trudge out of there again. She went upstairs and unpacked.

This ramrod stance of his bewildered her, in light of certain shared knowledge. Both had strong memories of Lillian's stormy junior year in high school – when she had to tell her parents she didn't have the flu: she was pregnant. The baby of that big Irish family was going to have a baby of her own. As Lillian gave them the news, her two older sisters, Eileen and Bridget, stood behind their seated mother and father, bracing them, posed like a Victorian family in front of a camera (or, as she described the terrible scene to Freddy, like the Romanovs facing the Bolshevik firing squad). Her sisters damned Lillian for her selfishness: getting pregnant was a punishment for it, it put Lillian in a sub-category of women and dragged her family down with her, it revealed her ugly secret self. Over and over again they asked her whose baby it was. 'It's mine,' was all Lillian would say. Eileen handed her mother the telephone and said the best thing was to call Father Agnetti – he'd know where Lillian could be hidden until the baby was born and he could set the machinery in motion for its adoption. Then they really saw what kind of female strength they were up against. If she had to, Lillian would move to another town, finish high school and raise her child, unhelped. Her mother and her sisters were set to fight. Not her father. He stood up, tall and orthodox and luckless in his salesman's suit, with crying women on every side, raised his hand for quiet, didn't get it, and sat down again, swamped by his own tears.

It was the first whisper Freddy heard when he came back home for Easter. Nobody wanted to hear about his freshman year at Carnegie Mellon, everybody wanted to tell him about Lillian and the boy (or man!) she refused to name. He saw her at a friend's lunch party and they talked about real things – their obligations to themselves, the urgencies in their lives. Her baby, his career in engineering or architecture. On a date in Boston, coming out of the movies, they walked past a man who was struggling to change a flat tire. Freddy stopped, handed Lillian his jacket, and helped this stranger. With a warm-cold rush Lillian thought, 'He won't last in the real world.' But she wasn't an obstacle to him; she said yes when he asked her if she loved him and yes again when he asked if she loved him enough to marry him. Her parents didn't come to the wedding, though after Hildy was born they congratulated Freddy – on the birth and for taking responsibility like a man. They died believing Hildy was Freddy's child.

So this was the good man Hildy fought. The adoptive father who turned her into the unperson of the Foy family. It never occurred to Freddy or Lillian that telling Hildy, when she was thirteen, about her real daddy (a high school auto mechanics flunk-out long gone from Lawford) was making her a gift of a loaded weapon. And after a little target practice she got to be a snake-eyed expert with it. 'You don't know why I do things. I'm not even *related* to you! You're just this *man* bossing me around, like some weirdo who followed me home.' Only a stranger would have done to her what Freddy did: handed Hildy over to the police.

'I don't have a doubt in my mind', Freddy snapped back, 'that your real father's got a closer relationship with the police than I'll ever have.'

As Freddy told it, Vernon Mercer received complaints from neighbors of Lawford Academy who had seen a 'hippy girl' loitering around the school at lunchtime. Hildy wasn't exactly camouflaged in her tropical fish Hawaiian shirt and overalls (Monday), her ripped jeans and tuxedo jacket (Tuesday), or her frilly summer dress and motorcycle boots (Wednesday), the center of attention on the main steps. It was obvious, the Provost heard, this hippy character was on a mission to hook the entire student body on hard drugs.

When Vernon went outside and saw it was Hildy Foy they were complaining about, he discreetly brought Freddy's sixteen-year-old wild flower to her father's office. 'Does your school know you're wandering all over town?' he asked her while Vernon was still with them.

'Why can't I come over and say hi to my friends?' she said, already feeling victimized.

'Who are your friends?' Vernon asked her.

She ignored him. So Freddy said, 'Is that what you're doing here?'

'Yes.'

'What about yesterday, Hildy? And the day before?'

'*Yes.* I just came over to say hi to Philip's brother.'

'It's a half-hour to get here from Central and a half-hour to get back. Your lunch period's only forty minutes long.'

'Bradley's one of my *best friends.*'

Freddy knew Bradley Fahey. A wily, nervous kid, who was too impressed, Freddy thought, with his big brother's recklessness, overcompensating for the embarrassment of having a father who was the chief of police. The younger Fahey had lately been making some noise of his own, stupid wisecracks in class, lame practical jokes. He was not widely liked. A direct question led Freddy to the first floor bathroom where he found Bradley puffing on a joint. Cocky first, then terrified, he started off pretending he was only smoking an ordinary Kent kingsize and two stoney seconds later he was taunting Freddy with the confession that he'd bought the dope ten minutes ago from his daughter.

In the privacy of Vernon's office Freddy called the cops.

When he came back from there he told Hildy if she could wait five minutes he'd give her a lift back to Central. Then he quoted her, word for word, the story he'd just gotten out of Bradley. Denied, denied! And (bewildered, outraged) denied! Through the window Hildy saw the squad car cruise into the circular driveway and she got up to leave. Freddy blocked the door. 'We'll get through this together,' he promised her. 'Nobody's going to mistreat you.'

They grabbed her in the hallway, two middle-aged overweight patrolmen who had to listen to her shriek at them, 'Gestapo rape!' and 'Make marijuana legal!' as she battled them off with her fists. They handcuffed her, bent her over in a vicious hammerlock and stuffed her into the backseat. In the middle of the attack on her liberty, dignity and person she was enraged by Freddy's tight-faced silence; he wasn't lifting a finger to help her, allowing those uniformed thugs to haul her away like she was yesterday's garbage.

To the neighbours watching from their porches across the street Freddy was a portrait of decent authority indecently pushed to the brink, and finally roused wasn't in the mood to compromise. He had news for them all. As he got into his car and followed Hildy to the police station he felt sickened, revealed, divided against himself. His decent intentions suddenly seemed to him *monstrously* decent, and they'd led him to a climax that was the opposite of a conclusion. ('Hypocrite!' What did Hildy mean, calling him that?) He was sitting with her in the reception area, facing the procedure, because . . . because of a decision he had made without consulting his heart.

They took less than a gram of hashish and an ounce of marijuana from her, plus six tranquilizers. Some horse trading with Chief Fahey ended with Hildy's first offense charges being dropped; Freddy would keep Bradley from expulsion. That night Hildy pretended she and her mother were alone in the house. She looked straight past Freddy. According to Hildy a real crime had been committed all right – against her. Whose law was going to punish *that* criminal? Only her law, and she'd bring it down on his back hard enough to leave a dent.

'Hildy, you're twisting it all around.' Lillian and her girl sat in the kitchen while Freddy slept far away upstairs. 'He talked himself blue with Philip's dad, and that's the only reason you didn't come home with a criminal record.'

'So besides everything else he wants me to be grateful.' Whenever Hildy was on trial she spoke in a trashy drawl, trying to sound toughened up and unreachable. She'd pump up the belligerence, daring a force of compassion just as awesome to blow in and prove her lovable. 'I'd never do that to my kid. Calling the police on her,' shaking her head, lost in disbelief.

Lillian held Hildy's hand and stroked those tapering fingers, amazing replicas of her own. 'Tell you something,' she said. 'I wanted to be a nun. I was totally sincere about it. God's gift to the Carmelites. Until I was fourteen, and then I went boy crazy. I guess it'll be the other way around with you.'

They laughed themselves limp at the idea of Hildy as a jaded streetsmart elderly Mother Superior, but Hildy recognized she was being told that one of her parents, at least, believed her wild-hearted behavior had its spiritual side. So said the note she left for Lillian to find on the kitchen table early next morning. It was the first time she ran away, gone (it turned out) with her motorcycle thief boyfriend Philip to Canada for three weeks. She knew how to score against Freddy. All those days and nights of boiling uncertainty, she doled them out as punishment. Hildy couldn't do anything to keep it from hurting her mother and she was gigantically sorry but the only answer was for her to split.

Later on, when Hildy got herself into the predicament Lillian had landed in at the same age, Freddy was convinced he was the target of her vendetta. It was the second time Hildy ran away. She called from a public telephone, wouldn't talk to Freddy, and cried to Lillian; she'd lost the baby. 'Insensitive pig!' she called Freddy. 'Fascist motherfucker!' It was all his fault! She refused to come home or to check herself into the nearest hospital, wouldn't say where she was or where she was going, hung up the phone and sent Lillian crazy with worry. Where had the girl gone? How could she cut herself off from home, draw a black line through her family? Lillian didn't hear from Hildy for another month.

Let me die out here, let me live out here ... The plain card was

24

postmarked South Braintree, Mass. The next one arrived two months after that from Manassas, Virginia. *A peel against enemas. May his children be orphaned and his wife widowed.* Another one came six months later, forwarded by the landlord of an apartment house in La Grange, Texas. Along with a politely worded demand for the back rent Hildy had skipped out on, he enclosed an itemized bill that covered damage to his property (walls, carpets and furniture), plus twenty-five cents for the stamps he'd stuck on the envelope. Hildy's note said:

You have my permission to ask Father Agnetti to bless my empty bed. He can bless my baby's empty crib too. In the name of the Fever, the Gun and the Moldy Toast. Mom, get Fred back to Mother Church. Confess confess confess you fascist pig! Emotional abuse killed my baby and you know it. Does Mom? I believe some penitence is due. Not from me Fredward. You! Silence is the biggest lie. The worst pain and murder! I'll check up on you. You won't see me again until you stop hurting us.

For the last two years there had been nothing, an empty lake of time. This long silence she inflicted on them wasn't peevish or vengeful. Its content was darkly obscure. Then in the morning on Lillian's day off, in the summer, around the middle of July, Hildy called her mother on the telephone. Their conversation lasted exactly three minutes. It was long-distance. Something had moved her to get in touch.

She said, 'Remember when you used to take me to the bay? Hoopoe Bay?'

Pictures from those days crowded in on Lillian as she closed her eyes against the colorless sunglare caught in the kitchen window. The pink light breaking above Hoopoe Bay. 'You know, Hildy, I do. And do you remember Jimmy and Dexter? We used to go with Mim Cuddy's little boys.'

'I'm standing on my porch and I can see the ocean. I can see seals on the rocks.'

'Where are you, sweetheart? Hildy? Oh, I know I . . . I know how you don't want me to ask you, but I . . .'

She let Lillian realize that this line of talk was only eating up expensive time. In the ragged lull she told her mother that she'd broken her ankle slipping on her own front step but that was weeks ago and now she was bouncing around the house again, 'lopsided, but on two legs'. She didn't ask about Freddy. Lillian thought there was a hesitancy in Hildy's meandering description of the chore-packed days that turned her life into a circus act; some admission or question was being reined in. But about the specifics of her self-exile, not one word.

It wasn't very hard to imagine Hildy's face, the powdery northern whiteness of it that seemed sensitive to roomlight; the vibrant copper hair (*mine, ours*) would be darkening now; her hands propping up her round stubborn head, elbows anchored on the table, while Hildy stared out at her ocean, outcroppings of rock, corkscrewing seals. Or stared at a menu in a coffee shop booth. Or into the porthole of a laundromat tumble dryer. Lillian imagined Hildy walking, loose-limbed, arms and legs a track coach would give his own arms and legs to train, the soldierly amble that said, 'You can't take *me* by surprise, man,' on her way across the hot blacktop of a beachfront parking lot.

At thirty-one Hildy must have crossed the border Lillian reached in her thirties. Up till then you're so busy whirling through youth that anything that happens to you becomes another pebble you flip blindly over your shoulder into some waiting reservoir. Like all of the other ones it drops beneath the clean surface behind your back, and you go on. Then, at thirty, you turn and look for the first time. You see the hoard poking out into the air, the tip of the buried pyramid – and you're penetrated by the astonishing knowledge that a fair part of your life has already been lived. The whole of Hildy's twenties gone, and they had passed by out of her mother's sight. Gone too, all of Lillian's forties. Therefore, no: She wouldn't ever move out of this house, not while time was shrinking.

Chapter Three

WHEN, THE night of Hildy's phone call, Lillian welcomed Freddy home from work with news that the trail was hot again ('Can't Detective Early trace the call?'), he sank into the trick he had of shutting his eyes and talking over her, preventing any comeback. Since then communication between Lillian and Freddy had become more and more symbolic.

For direct involvement, for the sense of touchable human life, Lillian had the company of the rest of Lawford's population. Many times on the bus into work she came close to getting caught staring at other passengers. Years of experience, practice and, it had to be said, sly talent warned her to look away half a second before anyone who felt her intrusion glanced up. They would have been wrong to feel assaulted. Sympathy and gentle fascination linked Lillian to them, those passionless faces so drained under the gangway's fluorescent lights they looked like they had been pickled in skim milk. But every kind of strangeness drummed inside them, emotional storms, shocking desires, no different from her patients at St Mount's – except in one way: these good citizens, normal people, showed they had the strength to contain their wilder thoughts and feelings, or to conceal them. For the time being.

What would a second Lillian Foy see, watching this Lillian with the same benign invisibility? A woman at the end of her forties, passably attractive, who didn't neglect her appearance but did little to push it into the foreground, letting those who'd look find her remaining beauty located in her widely spaced blue eyes which surprised you with their grains of lilac; her long shape wrapped in a Russian-looking black coat, red wool scarf shawled over her head, warmth and color against the dark and cold of these Massachusetts November mornings; a tautness around her full mouth, bare of lipstick, that censored her own strange sense of things. Psychiatric nurses aren't immune.

At her Peck Avenue stop, across the street from Mount St Mary's, all of this was pushed to the back of Lillian's mind. The view she had from there of the hospital's forbearing old brickwork bulk summed up the day's demands and brought them forward to meet her. Where they were welcomed. Patients in, patients out, this one's improvement, that one's back-sliding, new assignments to make, medications and/or therapies started, stopped, rescheduled ... predictably and unpredictably the landscape of Molyneaux Wing could change in a dozen ways overnight, and at the top of every seven a.m. shift, as head nurse, Lillian took the sprawling responsibilities into her personal care.

Going by the clock, night duty still had a quarter of an hour to run. Billy Cooke, manning the desk, with a grateful smile waiting for her, was angling for a favor. He figured he could take Lillian through the overnight report in two minutes flat and then sprint home to eat breakfast with his children before the school bus carted them away. 'Any excitement?' Lillian asked him and Billy shook his dark head, all quiet in the trenches, but the pregnant smile stayed. 'Somethin' outta nothin'.

You'll hear about it,' he said and then quickly gave her the rundown on a new admission, post-stroke with perceptual difficulty, referred by Dr Gertler, scheduled for evaluation with Dr Mollo at eight-thirty. And Douglas Cottle was on another hunger strike. 'Is it okay with you if I duck out right now?' Billy's wool hat was on, his jacket too, hood up. His gloved hand presented Lillian with a clipboard, the pale green pages of her new patient's history.

As she stood there reading it over a thin high voice cracked behind her. 'Boy oh boy! I'm happy to see you're finally here!' It was ten to seven. Billy politely pushed between Lillian and the old guy who made a grab for Billy's sleeve as it brushed by. 'Wait! You're my star witness!'

Tired of repeating it Billy said, 'I didn't hear what you heard, Perry. You tell Mrs Foy.'

'I know what happens,' Perry Gillies nodded at them, unsuckered. 'You'll stick together.'

All Billy had to offer Perry was a bone-tired glance above a bolstering little wave for Lillian. Perry was on fire to deliver a hot piece of news. His pale eyes protruded with it over the sallow pouches and drooping red rims. The twisted tufts, puffs and choppy shapes of his badly combed hair sent out a sleepless energy. This was a notch or two above Perry's typical excitement level. Arms folded, faking patience while Lillian took off her coat and scarf, his fingers spidering in place, he had to hold on to the most justified, sanest grievance ever recorded in the history of civilization. He'd been rankled by a remark he overheard, tossed out by one of the younger nurses. 'It was Laney Strand. Bad behavior doesn't deserve my repect.' He was putting Laney on notice, in absentia.

At the staff review meeting after lunch Lillian planned to ask Nurse Strand if she really did call one of her elderly patients a 'freaky howling coyote'. In-jokes were out. It took ten-tenths of a nurse's energy to break through the thick curtain of delusion; the job is to reach the person who's alive behind it. Apparently, Perry only remembered the two-day old incident at four o'clock in the morning and for the last three hours he'd been badgering Billy Cooke about it. Lillian asked Perry, 'What were you doing up and roaming around so early?'

'Not feeling a hundred percent good,' he said, with a frowning broad mouth. 'It so happens that I didn't want to sleep.' His hair wasn't badly combed, it was uncombable, pressed into the pillow at twenty insomniac angles.

Perry traded on his seniority. He was in his middle sixties when he came to St Mount's for a double hip replacement. He started a conversation with Lillian in the cafeteria one day, toward the end of his physiotherapy; he put his hand on her rear end and humidly whispered in her ear, 'I haven't been with a woman since VJ Day.'

As soon as he could keep up with her on her rounds Perry signed up to do volunteer work in the psychiatric unit. That was fifteen years ago. During their thousand-mile walk from room to room, reception to atrium, year after year, she heard how Lawford parish had bordered Perry's whole life. World enough. 'Never out of work,' he'd say, and then laugh at his thin, brittle arms, at his penguin walk, remembering the body that earned its privileges by manual labor. 'I used to slug my way out of trouble, don't worry. Any trouble I could get into.'

Lillian didn't doubt it. Perry even managed to startle her one morning with the discovery that they 'had a little bit of the past in common'. Sixty years ago Perry worked as a mechanic for the firm of Hoagland & Sons. 'I was a grease monkey for old Sam . . .' replacing brakes, repairing power trains, installing engines right in the Foys' basement. Thanks to Perry the Foys owned a photograph of the workshop, its founder and employees as they were in 1920. Packed into the four seats of a Hoagland Sprite (the automobile's body as shapely as a fat man's bathtub), were Sam Hoagland, his four bow-tied and

Derby-hatted sons, Perry in loose sleeves sitting behind the hard rubber steering wheel and next to him another apprentice mechanic, a burly, sandy-haired seventeen-year-old named Elias Cobb. All dead now, except for Perry Gillies. Right after he heard that Lillian and her husband lived in the Hoagland place Perry fished out the water-spotted black and white picture and gave it to her.

Something shadowy and hopeless began unraveling in Perry during the war. For two years, Forty-three to Forty-five, he resided in the care of the state mental institution. 'I'm the biggest goddamn patriot since George Washington!' he yelled from his window then. The Marines needed his fighting spirit on Iwo Jima! The First Army were doomed without him in France! On the day he was released, the day the Japanese surrendered to General MacArthur, Perry celebrated with a streetwalker in the back of his Studebaker, showed her his discharge papers and asked for a military discount.

Charitably, the eastern state General of the Daughters of the American Revolution took him in and put him to work. Daphne Wootton knew her genealogy, all right, and the family trees of all the most durable clans in the Lawford-Hadleigh-Woodbridge triangle whose founders dibbled their seeds into the local topsoil before 1776. Perry's clan, the Gillieses, had been farmhands, day laborers and handymen for as long as the Woottons had been gentry. So Perry got himself hired as an odd-jobman and was employed at Wootton Hill for thirty years, outlasting his patrons. 'Life's a barrel of laughs if you don't make any plans and if you do it's a practical joke.' That was the attitude that kept him afloat. That, and a servant's inheritance from Daphne Wootton's estate.

He was in Lillian's service now, unpaid auxiliary staff. Perry was rostered to escort patients to and from their therapies or examinations, bring them trays of food when they couldn't get it themselves, he scuttled around Molyneaux Wing on errands for everybody, inventoried supplies, and watched over the art therapy group. His bungalow, owned by St Mount's, sat in a corner of the hospital parking lot. This convenient set-up made it easy for him to clock in at all hours. Since he'd been tramping the corridors there for a decade and a half, the MDs and RNs treated him like a native in a place where they were the colonials, who were usually obeyed, sometimes outsmarted; Perry was on regular duty as an informer, an interpreter of the moods and sign language of people whose sickness was giving the orders. Lillian wanted to show him she was taking his outrage seriously, so she let him lead her to the dayroom.

Rell Mayfield, the woman who had been slandered by Nurse Strand, stiffened up when she saw Lillian and Perry marching toward her like a punishment detail. They stopped beside Rell's wheelchair, Lillian in her pink smock already a calming presence. Perry in his gravedigger's blue workclothes and decaying slippers, with his camel-faced look, only cranked up her dread. He supported himself on the arm of Rell's chair, a sudden move that made her jump. His ruined hands, thought Lillian: gray-skinned, large square-tipped fingers once as strong as three-inch bolts, they seemed to weigh his arms down. He parted his dry lips, offering Rell a concerned smile that only gave him the look of a condescending vampire – gums sunken away from the teeth almost down to their roots, yellow pegs and wedges plugged in at useless angles.

The woman started howling, but not like a coyote. Helpless, human fear, physical fear. You might hear such a forlorn, stricken cry reach across the vacant prairie, only there it would be a cold sliver of the sky itself, a part of the landscape. But in this dayroom, coiling out of an eighty-five-year-old woman in a wheelchair, it was actually eerie. Rell gulped a breath and worked up her cry again. It was more of a whooping now, over the potted plants and bluegray carpet, over the nubby oatmeal linen furniture, against the walls painted the color of a cooked pork chop. Lillian only repeated Rell's name to her, testing for a way in. When her grandchildren had brought her into the emergency room for treatment (as though they were dropping off a TV set at the repair shop, Lillian remembered thinking at the time), the wife had described what was wrong. 'She's starting to scare our kids. Bamma's acting funny.' Snow and static on the football channel. Just let me replace this little electric doohickey and you can pick her up in a week.

Really look at her and you would see the last survivor of her generation, depleted of everything. A big family sucked out of her, made from her blood and her very meat. Look at her. Bone rails for a lap that couldn't balance a child, the reddened, shallow face, loose skin ready for the tanners, her rickety frame covered with a baggy white hospital-issue nightdress, what she resembled most was an antique chair in storage.

Conspicuously on Rell's forearms and dotted around her skin under the collarbone, visible in the demure scoop along the top of her nightdress, were tiny crescents of dried blood. Some of the nicks were fresh and seeping angrily. 'This is new, isn't it,' Lillian said to her, smoothing Rell's arm while she examined the wounds.

Rell listened to her, emotion winding down for a few fragile seconds. 'Oh,' she reached for a sensible reply, 'you think your sheets are clean, that's what you expect.' Rell was straining her face away, neck arching back, fighting against the need for this attention, struggling to avoid the sight of her own damaged skin. She couldn't do it. The whirlpool was up around her waist, dragging her under again. With frantic eyes narrowly closed in disgust and self-protection she stared down at her arm and started to pick at the skin, digging her fingernails into it. 'Help me *do* something, Nurse, *please*. It hurts. They sting.'

Lillian trapped Rell's busy hand as though it were a butterfly on a windowpane, cupped it in hers. 'I know what to do, Rell. Rell? Let me see.'

'They're coming *out*!' The old woman dug in against know-it-all authority. 'You're not going to spray me all over with *insecticide*. I won't allow that.'

Her freckles were frightening the heck out of her. She was coated with them (another onetime natural redhead), and this morning they had all grown legs and feelers. They'd sprung to life as hungry insects invading Rell's body, a horde driven by stupid, prehistoric instinct to infect her, to paralyse, devour. *Unstoppable.* Any discussion ended here. Why did she need to tell Lillian what was happening? Couldn't she see the waves of bugs for herself, swarming out from under her sleeves? Why wasn't any move being made to help her! The howling started up.

'Uh-oh,' Perry said, backing away. 'There she goes.'

'Don't add to it,' Lillian said to him in a hushed voice.

Rell's fingernails were at work, jabbing into her skinny chest. 'They come to where there's filth and dirt.'

Perry avidly agreed. 'She's not lying; they do.'

'I want to know why this', Rell swallowed and said, 'is happening to me.'

The question wasn't far from Lillian's mind. 'You're not so different from any of the rest of us.'

'I know why,' Perry had to say. 'It's obvious there's already been the Resurrection and the Last Judgment. So we're living in the bad world that Jesus, Mary and Joseph and the all-holy whatnot abandoned. That's why.'

'I'm going to talk to Rell alone,' Lillian said to him. 'Can you go unpack the dried flowers for work therapy?' She watched him head down the corridor, heard his slippers flapping against the linoleum. Perry didn't believe that twisted religious theory of his, not body and soul. If he carried around such doom then locked inside him must be some knowledge of grace. The Church knows what this world is, what we are at our worst – crueler than the ocean, drowning out any good. But the Church, the eloquent fact of its lasting presence, is evidence itself that *this* is not *all*. At the heart of everything there is sanity.

Lillian touched Rell's arm. A flash of disgust and horror faded when, briefly, Rell recognized her freckles were freckles and not stinging insects. How senseless, how absurd. Then the horror rushed through her all over again, ambushed her, when some part of her mind comprehended that she was the host to another kind of parasite. Horrified that she couldn't trust her own perceptions, or her own noggin to make sense of them. What to do but howl when you're attacked from within by figments with hammers and axes?

'They leave a little shadow when they go, see that?' Lillian said, daubing the nicks and cuts with antiseptic, bandaging them. 'It looks exactly like a freckle, that's all.' Most of Rell's unbrushed hair was bunched into a terrycloth turban of shocking turquoise. From the slipping fit of the turban's hemline she was shedding split gray hairs, put unkindly she appeared to be molting. Lillian sat with Rell for another fifteen minutes and treated her to a salon-style manicure.

Her granddaughter-in-law wasn't telling the full story when she'd said, for the record, that Rell's howling was terrifying the children. Lillian had talked to the children, too. They were frightened by the sight of a grown-up who had been expelled from the grown-up world. Rell's family had shut her into a room that, before she moved in with her rubber mattress and sleeping bag, wasn't much more than a cramped service porch at the rear of the house. She was barred from using the only bathroom to wash herself (a bucket and hose had to do) because her body odor was so heavy it soured the air for the rest of the day. Lillian had taken Rell's history from her overwhelmed relatives. What were the deeper reasons for such hysterical sadness? For a family's emotional starvation of one of their own?

Beyond the trembling dread and violent mental pain of these people

Lillian found moments – more than moments – of calm delight. Douglas Cottle was occupying his usual spot, crumpled into the overstuffed chair that he dragged, every morning, in front of the patio doors. He sat there to keep his eye on the leafless, upcurved, beseeching branches of the emaciated chestnut trees outside. In fine weather Lillian sat with Douglas on the grass below, in a ruckus of birdsong.

'It's freezing cold out there today,' Lillian said, bending over him to get his attention. The high, hollow sky was washed with very clear icy light. It didn't look like Douglas could be torn away for any kind of conversation this morning. 'Is it all right if I interrupt you for half a minute?'

'My energy,' Douglas answered her, through a tight mouth. 'Need to save it.'

'You need to have it to save. I heard you didn't eat any dinner last night.'

'Fasting.'

'You can do that, Douglas, all right. Until lunchtime,' she said. 'Then we'll have a talk over spinach salad.'

She got a faint shake of the head from him, temperamental agreement. Douglas was one of Lillian's younger patients, only thirty-two. He had been an ornithologist. In his chair he had the look of a consumptive or the polio-crippled son of some great house. Bent in on himself, chest first, then meatless shoulders, loose arms, hands clasped between his knees, and with such an expression of mourning a black armband wouldn't have been out of place. Flawless in its way, his cool blanched skin was laid over sharp features. Scrawny jaw and chin, his straight unlovely nose, all jutted out under overhanging fronds of blue-black hair.

Douglas lived in impressive defeat. When Lillian sat with him outside they didn't talk very much, they listened to the birds' solos,

37

duets, ensembles. Douglas heard them singing in ancient Greek and he gave Lillian on-the-spot translations. The meanings weren't clear to her but the words were beautiful and they rode on a flow of such unashamed feeling that sometimes, Lillian thought, it was hard to see it as an eruption of mental illness.

'They put sauerkraut on the menu. I took a bite before I realized what I was eating, so I need to fast until it goes through.'

'Think it will be through by lunchtime?'

'By then. Yes. I think so.'

'We can have lunch together.'

'Not sauerkraut.'

'No. Spinach salad.'

'Spinach salad sounds like sauerkraut if you say it fast.'

Douglas combed the Bible, the I-Ching and Hindu wisdom texts for passages which proved that nine-tenths of the food we eat is poison to our system. We can survive, simply – on distilled water, purified air, rye grass and sunlight.

A little after eight-thirty Lillian found Dr Mollo in a whitely lit examination room with their newest responsibility, Bertha Orban. Mollo sat in a chair opposite hers, knee to knee, her left hand sandwiched between both of his. He was aware of Lillian standing in the doorway but he didn't break eye contact with the heavyset old woman. Mollo's purpose here was to acquaint his head nurse with the situation.

As if he were describing it all to Bertha, his considerate attention still on her, Mollo said, 'We've got Bertha with us, Mrs Foy, because she's recovering from a stroke. She's doing very, very well. Except for some impairment to her left side.' Mollo's quick permission brought Lillian closer in. 'Her left paralysis isn't where the thing stops. It's opened out into left blindness.' Holding up his ten scrubbed, stumpy fingers Mollo said to Bertha, 'Whose are these?'

'They're your hands, Doctor.' Her voice was slack, the lisp thick.

Mollo asked her to raise her right hand shoulder high. 'Thank you. Lower it, please.' Then he picked up Bertha's left hand, held it between his as before. Lifting it a little off her lap he asked her who it belonged to.

She was sure. 'You.'

'How can I have three hands?'

Bertha fell back on logic. 'Three arms,' she said, 'so three hands.'

The world stops performing according to old assumptions, it boots them out of the shared reality and look how these people fight their way back in. They want to make it easy for you to share theirs but the truth is Dr Mollo doesn't have three arms and birds don't sing in ancient Greek.

Mollo stood, excusing himself from Bertha's company as though he had just finished a beautiful meal at her home. A head taller than the doctor, Lillian looked down into his assertive, intensely intelligent eyes, angling for his attention. A stranger might mistake the intensity there for impatience; he was never impatient, only way ahead of the game. The full beard Mollo sported he kept trimmed very short, just enough length to the grassy charcoal whiskers to keep from looking grizzled. Above it his gray-flecked Calabrian hair, gentle waves on top that poured themselves into energetic iron-brown wavelets at the back, expensively barbered. In his shoes he made five-foot-one, with a tennis player's proportions and by the way Mollo carried himself, erect, on the balls of his feet, you could see he had the same competitive stamina. When he was at Yale he'd captained the rowing team. His colossal confidence would make an averagely built man seem hulking, bigger than the ideal human male should be. Mollo's wife, Sandy, a real fashion plate ten inches taller than the doctor, told Lillian once that the practice of psychiatry for him was a means to another end. What did Sandy think that end was? She'd let Lillian know as soon as she figured it out herself.

As they were leaving Bertha Orban's room Lillian asked if there would be any chance of a few private minutes with him later on. 'I'm really up against it today,' Mollo said. 'Can you save it for our session tomorrow morning?'

'What session?'

'You break-a my heart.' Italian disbelief, desperately praying hands, desperately fake Italian accent. 'Our anniversary. Didn't Sharon remind you?'

Lillian had received a note from his admin assistant. She'd read it and instantaneously forgot all about it. 'My two days off are mid-week. Then I'm on call Saturday.'

'Okay. We'll have to do it next Tuesday then.'

'I'd really appreciate a little time with you today.'

He made a calculation in a hurry. 'Come by the office at seven.'

Three or four times during the day – on rounds, at the Monday staff meeting, passing by the nurses' station – Dr Mollo spoke with Lillian, and he said nothing to make her think he couldn't keep their appointment; he didn't refer to it at all. The lights in his outer office were still on when Lillian got there a few minutes after seven. The room was empty, Sharon had gone home, the inner door was shut and locked. He might have been stuck in an allocation tug-of-war on the sixth floor, or possibly he was in the cafeteria drinking a late cup of coffee. Lillian sat down, decided to wait.

She used the time alone, unrushed, to mull over the short version of the monkey dream she would give to the doctor. As she silently rehearsed how and what she'd tell him Lillian knew (and this shook her a little) that she was prepared to tell Mollo something about the dream she didn't tell Freddy. Specifically, that she was naked in it and the warmth from the stove spread across her belly and the tops of her bare thighs, it pulled her closer to the light and the shrieking.

What kind of insight was she after? On the other side of the small waiting room was Dr Mollo's up-to-date collection of medical journals, systematically displayed on slant-backed shelves, just like a newsstand. The wall was shingled with magazines. A smattering of covers had Marcello Mollo's name printed under a bold headline; another of his papers published, reviewed, debated, featured, praised. Lillian scanned the titles for twenty minutes, then left for the chapel.

That was where Perry Gillies caught up with her. He was twitchy, agitated, stiff-jointed, his cogs slipping. They stood together outside the chapel door. Perry started scratching under his unbuttoned shirt. 'That Rell brushed her red ants all over me. Been itching all day.' This joking around was an excuse. The shirt hung open. He unzipped his trousers.

'Cover up and I'll listen to you.' Lillian gently bullied him. 'Come on, close it up. You're not Jungle Jim.'

Perry said, 'I can't keep my thinking quiet.'

'This is something new? Nobody around here has ever had to guess about your opinions. What did you say and who did you say it to?'

'No, I'm leaking from here. Bad ideas are bubbling up in the mud.' He wiggled his fingers beside his head to show Lillian where the mud was stored. 'Somebody'll use 'em against me. Sure. Hold me responsible. They'll get me with it, my own hearsay.'

'Is there a particular person you've got in mind?'

'It so happens that I do. Anybody who knows I'm here,' he said. 'I want you to say a rosary for me tonight. One a night, from now on.'

'I always do. For St Mount's and all who sail in her. Perry Gillies included.'

'But a special one, Mrs Foy. I feel like I need – which is, I'd like to have some good words from a good person put in for me.'

41

Inside the small white room that was lit softly from its corners, the oily smell of wax from the rack of candles, the papery smell of hymn books on the table by the door, the truncated cherrywood pews, among these fixed points Lillian knew where she was. The first rosary she said was for her vanished daughter, for Hildy's safety and happiness, also, as ever, for her return. She dedicated a second rosary to Freddy, a third to her raft of patients, and finally a fourth to Perry, for his ailing spirit to be consoled.

The rhythm of the words she repeated let in a gust of welcome from the constant Presence there. At the heart of everything, there is sanity. This presence, this unseen order, existed at St Mount's, in the daily work of untangling confused minds, separating what seems to be from what is. There is an invisible dimension that involves us, webs us together, we're ingrained in it the way prayers are ingrained in silence, our small pasts in history. Coming out of the hospital chapel felt to her like emerging from the trunk of a tree into the light and air of full consciousness.

Chapter Four

AS LILLIAN arrived at her front door, digging in her bag for her keys, deep blue evening saturated the street around her. The porch light shining amber in the nook of the eave was a proxy welcome. Freddy installed it for Lillian, he said, for her safety and peace of mind. The lamp was triggered by the sound of footsteps, so when the house was empty it would look like somebody was home. Indoors, the blue darkness spread through the rooms. Flicking on the kitchen light didn't sweep away that chill, in fact it was just then she felt a nervous ripple pass through her, a sense that something in the house had been disturbed. As if the furniture had been knocked slightly out of place.

Setting the dining-room table she was softly jolted again, this time by something as present and physical as she was. In the space around her chair she walked through a block of freezing air. She could step into it and back out again, it had definite borders and dimensions. With the flat of her hands Lillian followed its round edge, she could puncture its surface with her fingertips. A draft from below or above? No, this

43

coldness was simply hanging in the middle of the room. She slid the chair out and stood on it, ran her hand over the low ceiling, which felt warmer to her touch. She was standing in a column of distorted air, a yard in diameter, sandwiched between ceiling and floor. Here was a household repair job for Freddy to go to town on, with dropcloth and level, plaster bucket and trowel. A day at the beach for him.

Something else was out of kilter. Through the aroma of roasting chicken the air in the kitchen was flavored with cigarette smoke. Somebody must be in the house, she began to think. That toasted-paper odor was strongest around the door to the basement. Hildy used to sneak her smokes down there, tobacco and the other. Freddy lit up his after-dinner cigarettes there too, when he was quitting the habit.

Beyond the larger of the two basement rooms Lillian saw, from the foot of the stairs, the stocky bulk of the coal-fired boiler, its orange glow leaking against the back wall, and she heard its throaty breathing. She checked over the double row of cardboard boxes, all stored safely, unransacked. She inhaled the oily dampness of workrags and tools, the heavy dampness of earth. Hildy's belongings were warehoused here, and the cartons of outgrown, outmoded clothes, broken appliances, ugly, preserved china plates and statuettes, Freddy's and Lillian's hoard. A burglar wouldn't escape with much of a haul from this vault.

Under the boxes oil stains on the concrete floor appeared to be oozing. No – moving. Lillian followed the activity with her eyes – a carpet of black gravel on the move, dully glinting here and there in the strained light. She bent at the waist for a closer look and saw that the wavering dark mass was a colony of insects, beetles, small and black, hundreds of them fanning out across the floor but pooling under a damp spot in the wall near the storm doors. Not carrying contamination, they were contamination brought to life.

Half an hour later, when Freddy came home, Lillian was busy

scrubbing the kitchen. His first words to her were, 'What's my army blanket doing over there on the floor?'

Lifting the olive drab bedroll out of his way she saw the tactic had worked: no overspill of bug life was pushing through the gap at the base of the door. Freddy headed down the stairs ahead of her, armed with a flashlight, and when he reached the bottom step Lillian said, 'We're under attack.'

'Wonder what they are.' The fascinated entomologist first, before the concerned homeowner. Freddy, experimentally, squashed a few of the slow-moving insects, shiny carapaces splitting like nutshells under his shoe. 'After the exterminator's been down here we should call in an archaeologist.' He stood in one spot, blandly casting his eye over the inventory of their accumulated past, smiling faintly. Possibly Freddy was struck by the posthumous look of the half-lit room, a crowded, ignored, thrift-store open burial.

'We ought to rummage through all those cartons,' Lillian put to him. 'I'm not on call this Sunday. Or next Saturday.'

'Yes,' he said, raking the flashlight beam over the wandering insects, a searchlight over a dazed crowd. Then the light landed on the damp gray stain, about the size of a dinner plate, a foot or so above ground-level. 'They're coming from there,' Freddy showed her. 'Or digging into it. There's a hole in the plaster.'

'Did you mean yes this Sunday or yes next Saturday?'

'What?'

'I've been talking to you, Freddy.'

'I heard what you said.' He scattered twenty beetles with a sweep of his shoe, knelt down and angled his flashlight at the sifting pore in the wall. 'You said I never listen to you.'

Lillian sat down with delicacy on the wooden stair, tucking the spread of her dress underneath her legs. 'I smelled cigarette smoke when I came in here before.'

'Somebody was in our basement?'

'You haven't been sneaking down for a smoke?'

'I'm on the witness stand now, that it?' Freddy sniffed the air, investigating. 'I don't smell cigarettes. And the last time I had one in my mouth was ten years ago, Lillian, in front of you. I know what this is about. Asking permission.'

She might as well try to wrestle a pillar of Jell-O. Freddy waded back to the row of boxes, bellied up to them, and occupied himself with the vital work at hand. What there was to do, he did. In his element Freddy was masterful. He stood with his back to the boiler, fists on hips, studying the situation, gathering himself, then he tilted into action. He started by embracing one box at a time, straining his humped back, hoiking the load to the middle of the floor.

'Dinner will be on the table in fifteen minutes,' Lillian said, leaving him to work. 'Pace yourself, kiddo. It's not a one-day job.'

'A little insecticide, some fungicide, some insulation,' he answered, telling himself, 'move nine-tenths of this junk collection out of here and I can make it into a nifty private den. My getaway.' He saw it all, as he flicked his fingernail under the curling crust of white paint and plaster, webbed and scaling. 'Sand the walls, dry out the damp, slather some treatment on here. My underground headquarters.'

Not only did Freddy scrub up energetically before dinner, he changed out of his suit and into his gray overalls. Between bites of food he scribbled a floorplan on his napkin, in ballpoint, thinking through the details out loud: describing the skylight he would install and the duct system for passive ventilation, talking without a break and without noticing that Lillian was sitting at his elbow instead of in her usual place across the table. So, reluctantly presenting him with another home repair challenge, she reported the freak draft funneling into the dining room.

Lillian guided him to it, poked her arm into the area where an hour earlier she'd felt the refrigerated air. It seemed to be there only faintly now, faded the way a shout fades in the distance. Freddy couldn't feel any difference at all. But he was in an active mood. He came back from the kitchen with a lit candle and traced the edges of each window with the flame. No breath of winter hissing in through them. Freddy's activity exhausted Lillian tonight. As he went back to work on his basement restoration, she screened out the noise with radio music and drifted upstairs to the bedroom. The pair of empty twin beds made her think of two rowboats immobilized on the flat silt of a dry lake.

A drop of condensation started out, hesitated, rolled down the snout of the bath faucet. Another one broke free, swerved through the chicane of bluegreen patches where the metal was corroded, the brass gone rougher than sandpaper; the tub was antique. Her bareness in the water made Lillian think our exposure didn't end with that, at naked skin. Other nakednesses prickled underneath. It came to her that she was daydreaming. The face that came floating back to her belonged to a woman who had turned up first in the emergency room two days before, shivering all over, terrified that she was about to die from a drug overdose. Her name was Greggie, a thirty-year-old woman mistaken for a doped-out teenager by the police. Until Lillian did a little digging the officers were convinced Greggie's ID was fake. It was the first thing Lillian saw in her smallness and dulled anger, the stray girl.

Drama roared on the surface. Thin and spiky, anemic, dehydrated, color seemed to be drained even from her hair, which had been stiffly yanked into a feverish topknot days ago. Greggie's face had an unfinished look about it, all its features blurred, waxy, waiting for the fine work of definite lines that would decide its character. Her blue jeans hung like sails around her legs and on top she wore a dirty pink sweatshirt decorated with eagerly sparkling loops of rhinestone that spelled out Do You Think I'm Sexy. Lillian was touched by the stutter of gaps in that fizzy come-on where, in twos and threes, rhinestones were missing. 'I forgot what I took,' her voice in slurred panic, trying to answer Lillian who stood over her while another nurse syringed a blood sample from Greggie's arm and Dr Kaplan checked the dilation of her dazzled, apprehensive eyes. All of a sudden Greggie remembered which narcotics she'd swallowed.

They weren't dealing with a heroin addict here, it was an attempted suicide, by means of half a bottle of codeine cough syrup and a handful of Tylenol capsules. She told Lillian from her ICU bed later that she thought she was closer to death when they were pumping that charcoal milkshake into her stomach than when the Halotussin kicked in. The more Greggie felt under observation the less willing she was to talk. Lillian's questions about where and how she was living, relations with her family, whether she'd tried to kill herself before, whether she was lonely or grieving, sleeping at night, drinking, constipated, sounded sinister to Greggie and she feared for her physical safety. She begged Lillian to tell her straight – did the hospital want to know these things so they could classify her, clear her for the euthanasia program?

All this medical commotion, maximum activity, Lillian was thinking, was concentrated on this wounded girl, who saw how much power her weakness was giving her. Her desperation, her sick soul, made everybody jump, made detachment impossible, immoral; she excited their humanity or forced it out of them. To save her. Greggie had done the trick of transforming herself into a wanted child. Attention overflowed toward her and kept her visible in the visible world. If she lost her agony she'd lose her stake in life – then she'd be sucked into the vacuum: where her voice melts into her bones, the features of her face unmake themselves, she is evicted from Creation, worse, she is *uncreated*. That was the death Greggie saw waiting for her, she'd had a premonition of its power to wipe her out of human memory, she would be eaten by God, dumped into the universal nothing as if she had never been alive.

'She'll be over in the ICU for another thirty-six hours,' Lillian said to Billy Cooke that first night. 'Labs for liver damage are back and it doesn't look like she's got to ask Santa for a transplant. The suicidal ideation has a history, this wasn't a spur of the moment thing.'

'You sell your house yet?'

'Who said we were selling?'

'I heard you were movin' up to the north side.'

'Where on earth—?'

'Then Perry's been makin' up stories to get me goin',' Billy said. 'Me and Paulette want to get off of Wignall Street.'

'All I said to Perry was that Freddy's giving me a migraine over it. He wants to move. I don't. I'm very attached to that house.'

'But if you start thinkin' different about it, will you give us a call before it goes on the market?'

'Well, we're staying put.'

Greggie's case wasn't at the top of the agenda at Lillian's next staff meeting. Douglas Cottle had a visit from his mother that didn't end in a fist fight. Rell Mayfield's freckle-bugs were a torment to her again and her nightly howling was tormenting everybody else. The art therapy group had stopped making Immortelle bouquets. Perry was assigned to pick up a new supply of dried flowers from the wholesalers but nobody had seen him around the unit lately. Nobody had walked the hundred feet to his bungalow either, to find out if he was malingering or dead.

'Do that after your med rounds, will you Laney?' As Lillian jotted the note on her checklist, Perry flapped into her office on a mercy mission. 'You were supposed to get those immortelles from Mr Corban.'

'I know. I'll get to it in a minute. My tire's flat. I mean, my battery's dead. The guy came over and charged it up.' It didn't matter to Perry that nobody in the room believed him. 'You know that girl? The one who just got out of the ICU? She's in 421?'

'Greggie.'

'She really worked herself up.' He elaborated. A black canvas bag had been confiscated from her and she wanted it back or else she was going to sue the hospital. 'She was sitting up. She signaled at me through the door,' pleaded Perry. 'What would you do? Walk away like nothing was going on?'

In a procession of two Lillian and Perry walked along the corridor to Greggie's room. He presented the bag to her, rescued from the Lost and Found. Greggie ordered him to stay with her as her 'official legal witness' while she inventoried the contents. She was alert and talkative, panic snuffed out, and the grandfatherly gallantry Perry was showing her kept her calm. Lillian left them sealed in quiet conversation, Greggie falling into her life story with the words, 'I always knew I was special on account of how other people treat me . . .' Perry moved to the bedside chair, ready for a long session, his frayed corduroy slippers tucked underneath him, elbows on knees, hunched forward, listening, nodding.

Ten minutes later an orderly grabbed Lillian away from the telephone. The girl was tearing the place up. Greggie was out of bed, wrapped in a sheet like the Statue of Liberty, backed against the wall, fending off anyone who got near her with the spindly metal stand which still held her saline drip. 'No! N-no!' was all she shouted – at Lillian, at paunchy, scurrying Dr Kaplan, at nurses and orderlies bottlenecking the door. Between shouts she was snarling, dripping saliva, stabbing with her harpoon into the menacingly shrinking space around her. 'No!' They were up against a hunted, cornered, doomed creature wildly drowning in fear.

Eight hands landed on Greggie and held her down, first on the floor then on the sheetless bed, an Aztec sacrifice. Lillian at one end and Dr Kaplan at the other buckled the four leather cuffs on her, jerked the straps tight. In the doorway behind her Lillian heard Perry cheer them on. 'I'm in favor!' he barked out. 'I *vote* for that.' As soon as the Haldol took Greggie under, in the battlefield stillness, Lillian asked Perry what on earth made Greggie go to pieces like that.

'Let me try and reconstruct it in my mind,' Perry said, on hand to help, everybody's determined and unhumble servant. 'It was a normal talk, going normal. Then she got worried.'

'About?'

'Some object was missing out of that big bag. Some lucky charm. I told her don't worry so much. If somebody stole it right out from under you how lucky can it be?'

'You think that's what upset her?'

'I was talking sense. Trying to calm her down. Keep her flying straight and level, but boy, did she start saying all kinds of goofy things! First she got scared that Dr Kaplan was coming back to put her to sleep like a stray dog. I tried to calm her down but she argued with me. She was sure about it! And she was sure about another thing. Before you turned the gas on her you were going to use her body without her permission.' Perry gave her a soft choking laugh, with a blinking glance at Greggie lashed to the bed. 'For copulation experiments.'

'Oh, Jesus.'

'I know. You couldn't argue with her.'

'And then what?'

'So I didn't argue anymore. Then she went off like a firecracker. Bam! Boom!'

His only motive, he told Lillian (making it sound like the single most noble and beautiful thing he'd ever done in his life), was to take the hypertense hyperventilation out of Greggie's paranoia. He knew how it felt when you couldn't trust your own ideas. So he reassured her, with confidence based on long years of personal experience, that she wasn't crazy: yes, she was completely right about Dr Kaplan's designs on her body and her life. Oh, Lillian saw in one clear flash exactly how it went. '*They do whatever they want with patients in here,*' Perry would've told her. '*It's a chamber of horrors! I've been trying to escape for twenty-five years!*' Reverse psychology that backfired, he was sorry as hell, but he was standing before her with a clear conscience. But Lillian knew, from the same long experience, that Perry's motives weren't so pure. This was entertainment for him, pumping up the emotional gasoline and striking a match. You're surprised to see it in an eighty-year-old man, the window-breaking vandal, quick eyes that hid the leer of a sadist.

Greggie was still strapped down when Lillian left for home at seven. What is it about me, she wondered, am I so unprotected? I don't reach into them, they reach right into me, beneath my skin, they bite into me ... When she undressed for her bath Lillian noticed the marks on her arms and calves. Now the heat had seeped out of the bath water and she was still examining the brick-red bruises, in cold alarm. Cases existed, she'd read about them, seen photographs – a Sicilian woman who produced Christ's cross in bloodstains on her arms and chest, Christ's wounds in her palms and on her forehead. The fingerprints of Heaven or the breakout of her private hysteria? On Lillian's wrists and above her ankles she was collared with explicit welts, as though she'd been scalded there with hot metal straps. Or as if she had sucked up that girl's searing, tender, futile desperation, shackled all day to a hospital bed.

When Freddy saw her come out of the bathroom wearing her long-sleeved nightgown, he asked Lillian if she wanted him to turn up the thermostat. 'I'll do it,' she said, went downstairs, counted to ten and came back up.

Chapter Five

As a thirteen-year-old expert on fashion Hildy had needled her mother something rotten about this cambric blouse. She called it Lillian's 'Three Musketeer shirt', its collar high, long and pointed, its front bibbed and ruffled, its sleeves puffed from the shoulder, pleated and gathered tight into floppy lace cuffs; too swashbuckling for a psychiatric nurse, for a woman who rides the bus to work. A period piece in more ways than one, from a period in Lillian's womanhood when dressing up still carried a vaguely romantic charge for her, a blush of anticipation no matter how unspectacular the event. Hildy should have been intrigued, and mouthwateringly, by the surprise glimpse of a looser, independent, daring side of her sturdy mom's personality which hinted at Lillian's younger years. But this morning in her Three Musketeer shirt, her straight, plain charcoal wool skirt and schoolmarmish high lace-up shoes, she aimed to make a specific impression on Dr Mollo. 'Attention, now,' the costume said, 'I'm here as promised, dressed for important work.'

True enough, although the basic reason Lillian worked her outfit around that blouse was that its cavalier cuffs would hide the strange marks on her wrists, angry as sunburn, still there three days later. A dozen different causes could lie behind it, allergy to some natural or synthetic fiber, psychosomatic sensitivity of her skin; misinterpretation and misleading clinical implications would be as likely as an on-the-money diagnosis. Why invite the interest? And thinking pragmatically for a minute Lillian decided it was the wrong day to worry Mollo with the notion that she was susceptible to suggestion, internalizing intense emotions of her own or, even worse, of her patients.

The doctor's interest in mental abnormality (*oddity*, his own fond Believe It Or Not word for it) was the interest of a librarian in a trove of books. You only had to glance at the corkboard in his office, collaged with snapshots of children and grown-ups, to see what they got out of their time with Marcello Mollo, MD, PhD. For addicts, alternatives; for schizophrenics, containment; for aphasiacs, coherence; for the paranoiacally deluded, reliable education. A cynic might see the showcase of photographs as a running total of Mollo's bouts in the ring against disease and impairment, a trophy wall, a record meant to be more of a testimony to him. Lillian's opinion was that, up to a point, a cynic would be right.

Before he named it for her, Lillian didn't think of her colored hearing as an oddity. Sounds, especially music, taking on shape and color didn't interfere with her ordinary working perceptions. Two days a week Mollo did independent research in the area of human cognition and questions Lillian had been answering for him were at the root of his study. When she heard the squeal of skidding tires did the 'spray of silver needles' she saw in front of her resemble any other abrasive sound? In her first session a year ago she described the rumble of African drums as 'dark-green and brown waves', a Bach harpsichord piece coiled out as a 'deep blue ribbon with stabs of mint green'.

Through her headphones today she heard the squealing tires again, and the African drum chorus, and the Baroque harpsichord – and without thinking about it Lillian described them all to Dr Mollo with the identical words.

'Very wonderful,' said Mollo, in gratitude and approval. The two of them were sitting at opposite ends of the curved sofa in a room adjoining his office. Like the carpet and walls the few pieces of furniture were in desert tones – reddish earth, sandstone, mineral browns. Roomlight was low, from one lamp, and it enhanced the mood of informal formality. Unless that came from Mollo's posture, short legs tucked tight against the sofa's front, body swiveled to face Lillian. He thought he looked relaxed. 'How would you like to try something new this time? You'll be the first one, how about that.'

'*How* about that.' Lillian was ready with her fullest candor. 'An adventure for me.'

'Good. For me, too.' He was up, hands busy with the small stereo system, cueing up a cassette, testing the volume then checking the recording level on a second tape machine. Finding a spare bit of fabric on Lillian's blouse for the clip-on mike was not a problem. 'Try not to move around very much, it picks up everything. All right,' Mollo said, standing away from her as if she were about to explode. 'You're going to hear a longer piece of music and I want you to tell me what you're seeing all the way through it. Can you do that for me?'

'It'll be hard to shut me up.'

'Would I want to do anything like that?'

'Some people do.' Out popped the truth. She saw her hands folded chastely in her lap, the lace cuffs spilled limply forward.

'If you already know the *Symphonie Fantastique* this might not work so well.' Lillian shook her head; she didn't. 'Fine. We're in business. You'll hear the second movement. Before I put it on for you, tell me about your black screen.'

The tape recorder was running. Lillian said, 'It spreads out in front of me, in three dimensions. Like a square of the night sky ...' A slow, warm, lapping pulse rose inside her, following the surges of double basses and cellos, advancing and retreating underneath, visited by harp strings above. 'Thick colors, low, flat waves in front, they're burgundy red and – oh, rose color. Those are big, globby pearls on top – they're royal blue, dropping down ...' Her eyes stayed open watching as violins glimmered in with the start of the waltz. 'Particles of light, red-gold flakes sprinkling into the black ... They're melted together now—' pulled out of the gliding melody, 'into a red-gold kind of scarf, turning, a scarf underwater. So much is going on in the background, I can't describe it all at the same time. Oh, it's very beautiful, this music.'

'Concentrate on what's appearing closest to you, Lillian. Tell me what's dominating the screen.'

Mollo stood still, didn't gesture with his hands, limited any interference in the air. He didn't need to worry. Lillian was inside the waltz as the waltz swirled through her, colors dancing, she was performing for him by being who she was, out loud. 'Pearl shapes too, different from the harp, clearer blue. The blue you see in stained glass ...' Alto flutes unwound the string of round notes that she didn't know was the Beloved's melody, swept into the dance, embedded in it, lifted by it, tangled in the vines of violins which finally released it again ... and the dance spread apart, held itself back, held its breath to adore this single beauty ... 'Crystal blue, the clearest, the purest blue, oh it's ...' Lillian couldn't say any of the words that rolled through her head during the galloping finale, because she was holding her breath to hear it, to adore it. The music got to her, physically. The expression she wore when it finished fell somewhere between ravished and dumbstruck.

She fished out a little gold pen and a notepad from her purse and held them out to Mollo. 'Will you write down the name of it for me?' Underneath the title he wrote – Berlioz, Hector. French 19th C. Taking the paper from him Lillian said, 'I bet he was a redhead.'

He let go of a crisp astonished laugh. 'As a matter of fact . . .'

'Can I sit here and listen to it again?'

Lillian saw things Mollo couldn't, past the transparent colors, she met the emotion with an intensity that was hers alone to feel. Now she listened to the music with eyes shut, night sky all around her, the hollow blackness of the universe. Solaced. Pleasure as full as this hardly entered her life anymore. Not at home where, lately, Freddy hemmed her in one minute and crowded her out the next. Not at work where every atom of her attention was under constant demand. But this twinkling waltz, even in its regular looping three-four orbit, flowed, overflowed with elemental freedom. Lillian had a memory of it. Withdrawn into herself and in the same caught breath flung out into the sky. This feeling rinsed through her before, when she was a sixteen-year-old girl riding on the back of Rick Hamilton's motorcycle, riding the pure velocity, air rushing in her face, whipping her hair around, summer air across her skin, her bare arms, over her legs under her dress, the ground flying backwards. Untied . . .

Dr Mollo, somewhere out in the dark, clicked the cassette back into its plastic case. 'All right?'

Lillian nodded, opening her eyes, almost tearful. 'I've never heard such a beautiful . . .' Her words ran out.

'It's very emotional stuff. High Romantic,' Mollo said. 'That's why I picked it.' He sat next to her and said, in a tone that came close to sounding off-the-record, 'Was that different? Did it trigger anything else the second time you heard it?'

'Oh, you know what? I pretty well ignored my colors then.'

'I didn't know you could do that.'

They were puzzling it out together, digging toward the heart of something obscure and true. Their conversation was a little bit

58

liberating, it took them a fraction of a step closer to the separate knowledge they each were after. On her way out of Mollo's office Lillian asked him brightly, 'How do I compare to all your other oddities?'

'You're an uncommon type.' Stated as a compliment, delivered with a brisk smile.

'There must be ones who get stronger colors than I do.'

'Sure, but it's the way you tell it.' Then he took the question seriously. 'I mean it's how you're affected, how it seems to me. As if somebody's rubbed your senses with a cheese grater.'

'Oh my gosh, that comes through? I was hoping I just had a sixth sense, was all.'

'Let's say five-and-an-eighth. It's supersensitivity, one way or another.'

'My antennas, meep-meep.' Lillian wiggled a finger from the top of her forehead. And this summed up the main question on her mind. Are the borders of ordinary reality sharp and clear? Where are they? I feel the cold more than Freddy does. Do we have a word for whatever goes on outside the general agreement? She said, 'Are the colors there but most people can't see them or am I just making them all up?'

'Oh, your colors are *there*, it's a real perception. You don't imagine, you *see*. Which is not the answer, it's the riddle. For instance, think of this. Flowers show off their pretty colors to attract bees so the flowers get pollinated. Red roses, yellow daffodils, so on and so forth. But a bee sees in the ultraviolet. The colors of the flowers he sees aren't the ones we do. So, you tell me – what's the real color of the flower?'

This was good to hear. Dr Mollo was confirming Lillian's own non-scientific opinion. She was on the right side of the line between intuition and delusion, between intense emotion and (Freddy's word), irrationality. These were working definitions she used every day! How else could she handle Perry's obsessions, Douglas's diet of water, sunlight, grass and alpine air? Here was delusion *de luxe*. Textbook cases! If her own perceptions were defective, the beliefs based on them perverse, Lillian would recognize the symptoms. And if her mind was too far gone for that, wouldn't somebody around Molyneaux Wing (say, the chief resident) notify her of the fact? No, if anything, fierce human longing for her missing daughter was the true measure and guarantee of her mental health. And the same could be said for her growing clairvoyant sense that Hildy was reaching out for her too, from somewhere.

Chapter Six

LILLIAN CAME out of there dully troubled. This was where she fell down (accusing herself, all the way home), living closer to the surface than she'd realized, her rawness laid open to Dr Mollo. Or was she being unkind to herself? What a talent she had for mortification of the spirit! Always the backlash after a burst of feeling – and no wonder, her mind was ripe for it, dammed up the way it had been with thoughts about Hildy.

Strained and quiet, she ate with Freddy. Over their bowls of peach ice cream she startled him, confused him, by coming out with, 'If you feel something you should say what it is.'

He laid his spoon on the table. 'What's put such a fateful tone in your voice?'

'My tone?'

'All right.' He tightened, braced himself. 'I'm listening to you.'

'I don't want you to listen. I'd like it if you talked.'

'Like in a spy movie,' he said lightly.

She wasn't going to be kidded out of this. 'Why do I get the feeling I've walked in on you in the men's room when I want to say anything about Hildy?'

'Is this about me or her?' He was trying to keep up. 'Or does it have something to do with the kind of day you had?'

She said, 'I think you live in a room without any windows. But in the world outside, you know, where I am, serious things are going on.'

'Did you hear from her again?'

'I . . . No. Summer was the last time.'

'Then *what* are you talking about?'

'Remember when Hildy lied to us about going to North Carolina with Philip? You locked her in her room. She smashed her hand through the window, crying her head off. "I'm not a criminal! I'm not a sinner! I'm not a slave!"'

'What's made you think of that?' Freddy needed more information. She didn't have it for him. 'Round and round. You're dragging it around with you again – you think!—but it's dragging you, my dear.'

'It's right here with us, that's right,' Lillian said.

He found his argument. 'How much sympathy can you lavish on somebody who soaks it up like a sponge and doesn't give a drop of it back? Every single time Hildy fell down a hole, who pulled her out? Over and over again! I was there with a rope – money, excuse notes for school or I jumped down into whatever hole it was *that* time and pushed her out, with her muddy shoes kicking me in the face. It's an endless thing. This is more of the same.'

'You want to know how different this is?' She took his hand, gripped it and wouldn't let Freddy pull away from her. Full of affection she said, 'For your sake, your sweet sake, kiddo, I choked down the worst of my loneliness and all my worries about her. As if it was a natural thing for me to do for you, to let Hildy matter less and less. I almost tricked myself into accepting that's how things are. That's finished with.'

62

'Does that change anything?'

'In here.' Lillian tapped her breastbone. 'Both of you canceled me out. Hildy ran away as far as she could go and you made up your mind about how long I could go on caring. We kept asking each other, 'How can she do it? How can Hildy blank us out of existence?' I couldn't imagine such a thing because that's something I couldn't ever do. But you can do it. Blank her out of life. So that's why I'm asking you, it's what you can tell me. How is she doing it? You're the one who can tell me.'

Through most of that Freddy attempted to interrupt her, cocking his head back, blinking his eyes shut, repeating, 'I always . . . I always . . .' until he broke in with his full defense. 'I always put you first, isn't that what I do? I put you before me. Before Hildy, yes – guilty! And to do that I push past our little problems. So I won't get stranded! Now you've heard my true confessions, *in toto*. All right, Monsignor? Haven't you seen me carry all this on my back from the very beginning?' Chubby hands open, lifted to the sky, holding up this house, these years, their entire lives, and since nobody else volumteered to applaud his heroism Freddy bitterly applauded it alone. 'Who protects *me*?'

Lillian regretted the tug-of-war, slept badly, woke late the next morning groggy and leadenly grateful for her midweek day off. The hangover from her squabble with Freddy wasn't a hundred percent regret, though. Another symptom, it was further proof of some change pushing through, a tremor sent ahead to prepare Lillian for the arrival of a vast illumination. Whatever this turned out to be, she was sure it came out of a sense of time emptying away. Doesn't a mother see in her baby girl a fresh version of herself as a woman? She sees the part of herself that moves into this generation's world, how the girl will be a woman with men and away from them. Her earliest meditation on Hildy. If she had been the mother of a son, Lillian wondered, would her craving to help be any different? To feel the depth of the impression he makes in any event in his life, to explain whatever she can understand about how the world hits back. This is the help any child wants from its mother, isn't it . . .

These thoughts slid over each other as Lillian opened the mail box and stood looking back at the house. Winter sunshine smacked the roof and walls, clear, bright and cold: a mean trick. At this hour the broad sky held a shell of slick light, mountainous white clouds, and in the hedges a sparkle of bird music, the full display of a spring day. But sunlight landed on house, ground and skin without any warmth. Hollow, heatless light. There were November days that looked and felt exactly this way eighty, ninety, a hundred years ago, when no one alive knew anything about President Reagan or Disneyworld, the Second World War, satellite TV or TV dinners, Marlon Brando, *Valley of the Dolls*, rockets to the moon, the Boston Strangler or Larry King. Our house was here then, with another world around it. People who haven't been born yet will be living in the Hoagland place a hundred years from now (or will they call it the Foy place then?), and under the same pale blue sky, in the same November weather, at noon, someone standing on this spot might feel the same quiet chill about our vanished time and the vanishing of theirs.

The tinny clang Lillian heard when she closed the low chain-link gate jostled her inner stillness, it cracked as hard as a sonic boom. In that second she was aware, starkly, that the stillness wasn't hers, it was all around her. The birds had stopped singing, the air was silent, the ground was still, the sky frozen, the mood of the weather changed, deepened, suddenly overshadowed. It was a strange solitude because Lillian wasn't alone in her front yard. She saw the boy walking away from her along the hedge, a schoolboy, carrying his books over his shoulder slung together in a leather belt. The wide flat brown tweed cap he had on was a surprise, Lillian was used to seeing kids his age

64

(nine? ten?) topped off with a baseball cap twisted around backwards. Maybe he wasn't a local boy.

He did seem to know where he was going, though. Lillian trailed after him, quick enough to catch up, but when she swung around into the backyard he had slipped out of sight. Not into the street, and unless he'd sprinted across the lawn and vaulted over the fence, not into the Patricks' jungle of scrub and weeds. A few more, slower steps brought her to the place he'd gone. The back door hung open. Lillian stood in front of it for a few seconds, listening. A loud drumming came from inside the house, a spitting, splashing, hammering rush she tracked down to the kitchen sink. Both faucets were opened up all the way, the hard white tube of water foaming into the drain.

With the back door closed and the torrent in the sink shut off she could hear water rumbling from the faucet in the downstairs bathroom, and with that shut off she could hear another stream angrily pelting away in the upstairs bathroom too. A dry leafy odor wound through the house, the trace of cigarette smoke again. Lillian's concentration was lucid, sharpened once she understood she had an intruder and had better face him. *What are the possibilities here?* She silently listed them as she went up the stairs. It might be a burglary or childish vandalism, or truant mischief, and if it came to a physical confrontation, all right, Lillian had handled uncontrollable children before. And this one, from the glimpse she got, looked like he was on the small side, even if he was also cocky enough to break into a stranger's house and leave taunting proof of his crime. It was common for homes to be violated with more personal, altogether nastier messages, Lillian recalled reading, fecal puddings squeezed out onto coffee tables and carpets. When she cornered him she could threaten the boy with the police; she could give him a sharp lecture about private property and march him home; she could be outraged, or charitable. She knew one thing, whoever this boy was and whatever he was doing, he had to be told in a loud voice that he didn't belong here.

From the top of the stairs Lillian had a view into the bedroom. She didn't go any further. Something she saw stopped her short, a gem which made the whole intention clear. This was unraveling as a crude practical joke, with Freddy as intended victim. In front of the bedroom doorway, planted so nobody could miss them, was Freddy's pair of silver military hairbrushes. They were a wedding present from his sarcastic (and late) uncle Nelson, stashed away in the basement for the last twenty-five years. Freddy felt mocked by them (as Nelson, also bald at a young age, knew he'd be) as soon as their bristles began raking out dead clumps of his hair. A sadly obvious target, Freddy's baldness, perfect for a nasty-minded schoolboy to attack.

She carried the silver brushes into the bedroom and called from there, 'All right, sonny. Olly-olly-in-free.' The faucets in the bathroom poured out hot and cold water into the sink and bathtub, the only reply she got. The room, the house, filled with a hush when she shut off the running water. The boy was nowhere around. He wasn't hiding under Lillian's bed or Freddy's, he wasn't crouching behind the door in Hildy's old room. Real fear only began spreading through Lillian when she knew that something unreasonable had entered there too, trouble she wanted to spare her husband.

Chapter Seven

LILLIAN WAS beginning to feel like a spy in her own life. 'I read an article today,' she lied to Freddy. A survey of discipline patterns in public and private schools, she told him, heavy on statistics but light on down-to-earth detail. 'Do you get more problems with your younger boys or the older ones?'

'Freshmen try things because they don't know me. Seniors try 'em because they think they do,' he said. Then, 'Usually just once.'

'You stop it then and there? Whatever they're doing?'

'I had a boy last year, a senior, who turned in a rendering that his father drew for him. This man was a professional architect. Either the boy was going to flunk or the whole class was going to get an apology from both of them, *viva voce*. Well, they came in, *père* and *fils*, a real court martial.'

'How's the semester been?'

'Nobody pulled *that* stunt again. That particular keelhauling was *legendary*.'

The web of possibilities kept growing new edges, taking Lillian in ten directions at the same time, keeping her from sleep. One thought should have struck her sooner. The boy must have broken into the house a week ago, smoking cigarettes in the basement, prowling around. Does this make sense? While he was down there he found Freddy's hairbrushes, by sheer luck, but he didn't get the chance to plant them anywhere because he heard Lillian clomping around upstairs. He could have sneaked out through the storm doors. And today he sneaked back in to finish the job. A determined little boy could have done that, nursing his plan (and his grudge, if that's what it was) for days. Freddy might have overdone the discipline this time, and unfairness from a grown-up can slam a child sideways. Children have vivid and mighty ideas of justice.

Unless this didn't have anything to do with Freddy at all. For the first time Lillian wondered whether the prank was aimed at her. Somebody's son or little brother watching her at St Mount's, what would he have seen? If he'd been one of Rell's grandchildren he might have seen Rell shrieking about her bugs and Lillian standing over her, tormenting the old woman with painful medicine. Or did Greggie come into the hospital with a young boy? If he'd been there he would have seen Greggie in hysterics and Lillian strapping her down to the bed for worse torture. But no children were wandering loose around Molyneaux Wing, not then, not that she could remember. The facts were scant. Stitching them into a story that ended at gushing faucets and silver hairbrushes felt the same to Lillian as finding animal shapes or presidents' faces in the vacant bulges, folds, hollows and tissuey vapors of clouds.

Heavy headed, eyes sewn shut but the darkness behind them energetic, she lay in bed half-conscious and half-dreaming. It was as if Lillian had fallen through the mattress into a vat of black marbles, the rattling dark sliding around her while she sank. Her arms and legs were somehow folded into uncomfortable angles, her knees rubbed sorely against each other, she came drifting up again, out of sticky sleep. Her uneasy eyes opened on shadows pushed into her corner of the bedroom, from the unclosed curtains, and in front of them she saw the large red digits of her night-table clock, signposting the hour, one fifty-five a.m. Drowsiness clawed Lillian under again, the pool of black clacking marbles closed over her head and softened into the border of a dream. This dream was made of noises, sounds she knew – a shovel digging damp earth, a trowel spreading mortar or plaster, light machinery clinking: it was a chain ratcheting over the teeth of a gear, metal grinding, silver-gray, and it stopped with a curt red-orange chirp. Fragments of pictures drizzled in, she caught jumpy flashes of the rim of a wheel, a coil of hemp rope, thin, crisp paper burning. Every sound, everything Lillian saw was pierced with emotion which bled into her, touched her with the shock of helplessness, angry surrender, a cold pang of isolation, dangerous knowledge.

Hazy daylight was all that morning had to spill into the room. Lillian was exhausted, as if she'd been trapped in a screaming argument all night. Freddy was standing in front of the bathroom mirror, knotting his tie. In the peaceful ordered unchanged physical world.

Looking over at her he said, 'It's seven-fifteen. Or are you off today?'

She didn't move, she lay there like an invalid under the thickness of her blankets. 'What day is it?'

'Thursday. All day.'

'No,' she said. 'I'm late.'

'If you can get dressed in five minutes, I've got time to drop you off. Want to ride in with me?'

It took more strength than Lillian had to prop herself up on her elbows. She dropped back onto her pillow. 'You woke me up in the middle of the night.'

'Me? I was dead to the world,' he said. 'How did I?'

'All of that clunking around downstairs. What are you doing, digging a tunnel to China?'

Freddy buttoned up his cardigan, avoiding the obvious fact that Lillian was having a bad time. Let her keep this invisible struggle of hers from breaking out, please! He gave her a befuddled look, a comic frown. 'I came up here after I graded that pile of drawings. Oh, and I finished my basement plans. Was I drawing too loud? I used a soft pencil.' Trying to joke her out of whatever kind of mood had invaded her. The gag fell flat. 'Something's wrong with our pipes. Maybe that's what you heard. I banged on them with a wrench a couple of times in the kitchen.'

'What's wrong with them?'

'I can fix it. We don't have to call in the cavalry. We've got rust coming out of the kitchen taps.' He patted her foot, prepared to be considerate but not indulgent. 'Come on. I'll give you a ride to work.'

Lillian was going to have to look after herself. 'Oh, you know what, Freddy, I think I'll take one of my sick days. I need to sleep.'

'What did you do all night instead?'

Chapter Eight

AS DIRECTLY as his controlled language could get across, Freddy was telling Lillian he didn't want to be burdened with a real answer, and he didn't have the energy to embark on a journey up the Amazon in search of one either. Under it all she was Lillian the Brave, wasn't she? Lillian the Trouper, Lillian Redux. It was the strength of hers he loved above everything else, her bent for working out problems by herself, without making them his.

'I've never felt like such a magnet for little uproars,' she said. 'Such exhausting days. So many in a row.'

'You're bound to get them like that once in a while.'

'It's just the surprise of it, flattening me out.'

'KO'd. You need a day to yourself,' Freddy prescribed. And predicted, 'One day of tomato soup and toast and you'll bounce back like a rubber ball.'

Under it all she was close to fearsome knowledge. Terrible things were happening to her – *to* her, and some underground fracture was slowly splitting her off from anything safe and familiar. Begin with the red welts on her ankles and wrists, the strap marks. Next, the boy parading (prowling?) through her house. He had carried a mood in with him that was still here with her. There was the house itself. Insects in the walls, rust in the pipes, a pocket of freezing air coming and going in the middle of the dining room, one disturbance after another, the old fabric breaking up. And in spite of the point-blank warning she'd leveled at Freddy he still had nothing to say, nothing to ask her.

'Enough of this.' Lillian made this pact out loud with herself after Freddy left for work, sitting in the empty kitchen with her third cup of tea. Rain, stabbing down early in the day had thinned out almost to a mist. Water sheeted the slope of the asphalt, slanted and dropped off into the culvert, the peaty canal flowing into Mannings Creek. Under the spit and dabs of rain Lillian heard the chevroning stream spilling past her basement wall. Was the house, the old wood, trembling? Lillian felt it tremble around her, the walls and floor unsteady, she was in the cabin of a ship in a mud-colored ocean. Enough of this.

The banging noise started the minute she'd come downstairs. She had been ignoring it for an hour. The shake of a window in its frame, wood against wood, a natural sound to hear in a scampering wind. But the shallow thuds came regularly, with beats and pauses. Before Lillian went outside she tracked the banging to the wooden storm doors. Of course: this was the boy's route out of the house; he'd left the doors loose behind him. In the backyard the small landscape held a stricken quiet, visited by the weightless fall of rain on the grass, the grainy skitter of it along the gravel. Lillian stepped there carefully, a housebreaker's footsteps on the way to the wide dark-green storm doors. Both hands on the handles and she couldn't budge them half an inch. From this Lillian understood, in the space of a breath, that the boy had come back, he was there at that minute trapped in the basement. Maybe he'd never left the house at all. Good. She'll keep him where he is until he answers a question or two.

With dreamlike slowness Lillian repeated the short walk she took in her dream, and where the broom closet should be, there it was, and not a pot-bellied stove. No suffering squalling monkey, and she was still wearing all her clothes. But expectation stitched a hook in her stomach and gave it a twist when she reached to unlatch the thin overpainted door between the kitchen and the basement.

Downstairs the two square rooms had been cleaned and cleared by Freddy. Preparing the ground for his renovation work, he began with those storage boxes. Lillian guessed twice as many had been lined up there a week before. The floor was swept, the remaining boxes clustered in the middle of the room, a stack too short to hide a crouching boy. She went straight past the tidy brown island of cartons toward the deep alcove where the boiler squatted. 'You really pushed your luck coming back here,' she called over to him and it felt like she'd just spoken those words to herself.

Except for the breathy noise from the core of the boiler the room was still, and except for a box of Freddy's old shoes, a spooled garden hose and a broken rake it was empty. Lillian's mind was clear, her thoughts flowing. He couldn't have gotten out by sneaking around her; even if he'd pulled that off she would have heard him going up the stairs and squeaking open the door to the kitchen, she would have heard him walking overhead, as he'd heard her. The short flight of concrete steps ending at the underside of the storm doors only denied her the other (the last) possibility. Freddy kept them secure with a pair of padlocks, top and bottom, and Lillian jiggled each of them, held their locked pretzel weight in her hand. Right in front of her the two keys that would open them hung safely on their brass hook. If that, then this: something had loosened inside her, something clear and vital had gone cloudy, gone wrong.

73

She lay on the living room sofa, hands tucked between her knees. Lillian slept gratefully and didn't dream.

Hours later she woke in the dark of evening. Her shoulders ached and her head hurt. Freddy sat at the kitchen table, leaning over a bowl of soup. She asked him what the time was and he answered, 'I thought the best thing was to let you sleep. You looked completely tuckered out.' He only turned his head toward her, the look on his face was strained and secretive. Lillian felt the air on her lower arms and the meaning of Freddy's distant gentleness quickly hit her. The sleeves of her sweater had hitched up halfway to her elbows, so he must have seen the welts on her wrists. But he only said, 'I made some Cream of Tomato. Do you want me to bring some over there?'

'I'll eat it at the table,' she said as she sat up, and tried not to make a show of brushing down her sleeves.

The look he gave her, that camouflaged look . . . as if he'd found her lolling naked on the cushions, or laid on a mortuary slab. It was an expression that stripped Lillian of any defense. While he stood at the stove warming the soup, she peeled back her sleeves to see what he'd seen there. The rashes, the welts, had changed. Changed shape, not healed. They had narrowed, darkened, deepened. The same bruising braceleted both wrists. Her skin was purpled and numb under the rough imprint of a thick strap, viciously tied.

Freddy watched Lillian spoon the soup into her mouth. He said, 'That's a good sign. If you've got an appetite.'

'I'm not coming down with anything,' she said between spoonfuls. 'It was tiredness, that's all.'

'You sound better. Rested.'

'Freddy, what did you do with our things? Those big cartons downstairs. I've got whatnots packed away that I didn't want you to throw out.'

'I just cleared out some old clothes of mine and a crateload of broken appliances. Is that what's worrying you? Well, I repacked our valuables and your old dresses. And Hildy's collection of junk, too.'

In a muted voice Lillian said, 'I guess it *is* junk.'

'That was a way of saying. All I meant was miscellaneous.'

'You're really getting to work down there.'

'I feel energetic,' Freddy said spunkily and, he hoped, infectiously.

'Me too.' She captured his tone, forced some reassuring light into her face, some strength into her voice. 'Have I been worrying you?' She held his hand, shook it. 'I was overtired, work-tired, but I feel much better now. By tomorrow morning I'll be as normal as peach pie.'

'Well, I believe you,' Freddy said. 'You're the authority.'

Chapter Nine

FOR PEOPLE who are sure they've never faced a ghost the questions are the same as for those others, who are certain they have. Is it made out of my dread or desire, solitude or a confusion of memory? Is it outside in the world the way I am or have I seen into an existence beyond this one? Are places haunted or are people? You are forced to wonder whether your senses can be more intricate and intense as easily as they can be clouded, whether the enfolding layers of your assumptions about physical reality can drop spectacularly away and show you what is real underneath it all, timeless truth. Could a figment do this? A ghost comes to you with the power to communicate the nature of death, and so it silhouettes the nature of life; it is the filmy distance between them. It is human essence: this is what we are at heart and in fact, individual spirit not sagging meat and calcifying bones, not chemicals but consciousness – a life-hungry soul fills each body to the fingertips and shapes a single lifetime. If we are anything, aren't we the history of our choices, mistakes, accidents, motives and memories?

Can a soul be anything but that? Questions as old as humanity, and when it's your turn to ask them you find yourself circling back to the simplest, unanswered ones. Why do ghosts come to some of us and not others? Why do they appear at the moment they do?

Afterward, Lillian's mind would be swimming in these riddles. But in the minutes before, her sleep was neither deep nor troubled, her gauzy thoughts were calm, released, floating away from her like breath sighed into glacial air. A chill lay across the upper half of her body, she felt it through the plaid flannel of her nightgown and it woke her. Somehow her blankets had come untucked, they were slanting off the bed. Lillian's first thought was that she'd slept through the thirty double-beeps of the alarm clock, but it was hours before she had to get up for work. The red digits on the dial told her it wasn't quite two in the morning. Freddy was asleep, his round heavy back turned toward her in his bed a few feet away, not disturbed by the weak grunts of panic in the room with them, torn into the air, which rattled Lillian awake.

She saw the boy crouching in the gape of the bedroom doorway, stripped to his longjohns, cramped in an awkward posture with his arms twisted and stretched backwards, tied together at the wrists. He seemed to be balancing on his bare feet like a bird on a shaky twig. And with the same desperate concentration Lillian focused on him, he stared back at her wordlessly asking, *What are you doing here?* The same silent question flaring in Lillian's head at that trembling instant.

He was there in front of her with the force of disclosure. This visit didn't have a thing to do with Freddy, with any joke or theft, its purpose began and ended with this eruption of the young boy's suffering. Suddenly Lillian was hit with the pure revelation of his face. So this was what he looked like! Tallowy skin composed around dark, slightly almond-shaped eyes, drawn into crescents by his frantic appeal, crushed under thick eyebrows, a burden on that smooth oval face, a size too large. His charcoal black hair was used

77

to being combed and parted but instead it scattered back from the rough hedge of his hairline, shaken loose, crazily splayed out. Bent double now, he wrenched his neck upward, to keep Lillian in sight, his whole victimized expression said, *I don't understand what's happening to me* – he wanted an explanation from her of the terrible, unnamable secrets that he had stumbled across too soon. *Is this what you adults allow? Is this what you do?*

The mood he brought on, the emotional currents he stirred up, invisible before, broke the surface in his solid shape. *Terrible . . . terrible.* A hemorrhage of raw feeling channeled from him to Lillian, connected them, and as it did she felt pushed to the edge of a seizure, in the grip of vertigo. A booming wind rose, battering inside her ears or outside the house, she couldn't tell. It pounded, swelled, sank, rushed at her again, carrying her closer to him, to his mouth working to form words Lillian couldn't hear but could understand; the boy was pleading for her help, and mercy.

The fluttering pressure in her chest felt gigantic. She couldn't speak, move her body or turn her head away, she couldn't close her eyes on the sight of this lacerated, brutalized child, fighting for safety which was beyond her strength to give him. His mouth hung open, an astonished silent cry escaped and in the next few seconds (minutes? breaths?) sleep flooded over Lillian, blanketing her and the struggling boy under vast darkness.

The alarm clock sparked to life as it did routinely, at six, shaking Lillian into a wholly familiar morning. Since she usually had to be ready for work before Freddy did, the custom was for him to let her into the bathroom ahead of him. But she stayed in bed, wrung out, and as she lay in the alarmless quiet a shadow slid across the window pane, gray and transparent; Lillian felt it before she saw it, as though a hand had swept over her eyes. A departing, emotional presence that left behind a tense absence. When she tried to sit up a cloud of nausea cramped her stomach and she said to Freddy, across the space between their beds, 'I think I'll just go in for half a day today.'

Somehow the hub of it all was in this house. She watched her husband perform the monotony of his morning habits, rubbing his face with both wide hands, stuffing his bluewhite feet into his bedroom slippers, following his heavy footed track to the bathroom, actions all his own, repeated ten thousand times. Seeing Freddy there, hearing him, her *sense* of him (she was getting closer to it now) meshed into his undeniable reality. In the same way Lillian could describe the sensation she had of that unreal boy, as real to her as Freddy was.

Washed, shaved, putting on his shirt, stopping to look from the bathroom doorway, Freddy found Lillian had slipped down under her blankets again. He said, in his classroom voice, 'You're not going to let me down, are you?'

'Oh,' she answered him, 'this is about you.' She saw his lips draw in, he'd been misread, wrongly accused. Lillian nudged him with a weak, cancelling smile.

Freddy rubbed the back of his neck, distressed. She had underestimated his power to be concerned. 'I don't like to see you down in the dumps, Lil. If you're overworked all I can do is say all right, rest up, stay in bed until your stamina is a hundred percent. You dropped a hint but I don't know if my guess is right, if there's less to it or more, and I end up thinking there's something I ought to be doing for you that I'm not doing.' After all, Lillian was a nurse and she knew when she was ill. Freddy was only deferring to her out of respect, not neglect. He sat himself on the edge of her bed, hands folded, prepared to listen.

She said, 'I'm awake. I'm up.'

'Do you want your tea and toast in bed? Say the word.'

'Nothing like that.' Then, considering Freddy's care as much as her own, 'You don't have to handle me like an invalid.'

'Is that what I was doing? "Handling"?' He sounded injured,

rebuffed. 'Maybe my bedside manner is totally amateur, but if you don't tell me how you're feeling how am I supposed to know?'

'You're right. How are you supposed to know?' His talk was an intrusion, it short-circuited her connection with the boy, the memory of him started to sputter. 'Just let me lie here quietly. In Boot Hill.' Lillian closed her eyes on Freddy and reassembled every detail she could recall about the strange visit to fix it in her waking mind. She wouldn't let herself be robbed of him; she wasn't ready to dissolve this mystery in the acid bath of Freddy's logic. And whatever sense he was going to talk, Lillian knew that her realism touched deeper levels than his. What returned to her as she remembered the charged air and the boy's churning desolation was his need – distinct, overpowering – for her to stay there with him, to join him in his tragedy.

If she'd had this strange experience a year ago Lillian would have hurried over to Father Agnetti. He would have had a few useful ideas about it. At the end of his life he acquired the look of a biblical patriarch. But she was drawn to the old priest most of all by his slant on her work, his curiosity about her patients. From physical and mental tics to suicidal ideation he interpreted psychological sickness to be a purging of the soul. He broadened neurosis and psychosis for her into a matter of spirit. At his funeral Lillian was the lay member who spoke for the St Mary's congregation, eulogizing Bruno Agnetti's equal love of scientific and religious enlightenment.

Of course, the transfer of affection to his replacement was never going to be automatic. Father Terhune, twenty-nine years old, didn't make it any easier for Lillian by inviting everybody to call him Tim. Or Timbo. He did this from the pulpit on the Sunday of his investiture. Lillian traipsed to Mass less often these days and avoided confession altogether. On the other side of the grille (impossible to force the picture out of her mind) there sat a casually friendly towhead priest whose depth of human experience could be read on his face in two seconds.

His listened to Lillian alertly, nodding his head, mm-ing, oh-ing, as she laid out the pieces of her story, beginning with the first time she saw the boy outside her house. Here and there she interrupted herself to remind Terhune – Tim, Timbo – of her twenty-five years' work in psychiatric medicine; if she was a little bit unsteady, well, she had a right to her glass nerves after the berserk ordeal of the night before. Fingers pressed to his lips, saying nothing but giving her jabby supportive nods, he appreciated that Lillian knew when a vision was a delusion and that she wouldn't waste his time with her questions if she thought they could be better answered by Dr Mollo.

With his head inclined toward her on the thick stalk of his neck Terhune wore the serious expression of a mechanic estimating repair work on a front axel, beginning to understand what Lillian wanted from him. She was down there in the thick of it and he was far enough outside for his judgment to be sharper, but they both believed that a human soul survives death, has life beyond the body . . . Sure of his ground, he asked her to single out the clearest impression she had of the boy. 'Let's look at it. Tell me again. What comes back the strongest?'

She didn't have to dredge it up, she'd been pierced by it. 'His pain, his physical pain. The creation of it was a purpose in itself,' she said precisely, with grim confidence. Now she had a question for him, and her tone didn't change. 'Can ghosts be sent by God as messengers or do they come with messages of their own?'

Terhune laughed softly to himself, prickly embarrassment fighting against his sudden appetite for frankness. 'I don't know if we can say for definite what was there. Whether it was a ghost of some description. The world's full of strange things.'

'And strange people.'

'Amazing people. If God wants to get a message to any of us, I think He sends it direct through our conscience. Why would He need a ghost to deliver it?'

'I was hoping you could help me figure it out.' The poky office was stripped of Father Agnetti's belongings, and this suggested an answer to Lillian. 'Maybe it depends what the message is.'

Terhune admitted the possibility with a little flip of his hands. Her eyes were on him again. Finally, he gave in to her. 'I think it's all kind of far-fetched.' He was in touch with firmer ideas, he made it his subject now. 'Wild interpretations are coming from everywhere. I'm sure there are serious people out there who've got serious things to say but those aren't the ones you hear. You hear about guardian angels and miracles, spirits from Atlantis. It's the Middle Ages all over again. I'm not', he plausibly noted, 'putting you in that category.'

Nevertheless, Lillian got the idea that he wasn't going to be happy until he talked her out of her backward belief. 'I never saw anything like that before, Father.'

'I know, it must have been a shock. But don't you think it's too easy to jump from some kind of experience you don't understand to supernatural explanations? Why don't you tell me if you see it again.' Then, as if he were writing out a prescription for tranquilizers, Terhune jotted a few lines on a piece of his letterhead stationery. He folded it in quarters and put it in Lillian's hand. 'Samuel Johnson's opinion of the whole ghost thing.'

She folded it again and fit it into her coat pocket. Terhune was disappointed. He expected her to open it in front of him so together they could enjoy the moment when a powerful intelligence shakes the loose pieces into place. Lillian was glad to deprive him of that hokey pleasure; she didn't read what he'd written down until she was in her seat on the bus into Lawford. Under her breath she said, 'I could find this in a fortune cookie.' The note read, 'All argument is against it, but all belief is for it'. That deaf dumbhead Terhune! Giving her the gift of the one thing she already knew – for godsakes, that was just exactly where her confusion *started*.

Chapter Ten

BILLY COOKE warned her, 'I'm dead on my feet, okay?' – so Lillian didn't have the tiniest doubt that she owed him double for covering the first three hours of her shift.

'Me too,' she said.

And won his quick delicate worry. 'You got to quit goin' out to nightclubs and all those wild times.'

'Well, first my boyfriends have to stop kidnapping me.'

'You'd let me in on the big bad secret if I asked you direct, right?' Billy said.

'You know me. You wouldn't have to ask.'

'That's what makes me think I oughta be askin'.' His face held as still as a Benin mask. Billy wouldn't let her get away with such a sweet dodge.

His hard kindness caught her. 'I'm all right, Billy. I got smacked with a migraine last night and I woke up seasick this morning.'

'Man, they're killers. Yeah. You're okay, though. You're back?'

'Let me at 'em.' She leaned her head to read the top page of Billy's overnight report. He let her take the clipboard from him.

Then with a mellow grin he picked up the stack of folders waiting for Lillian's attention. Billy gathered them up against his thick chest, hugged them in his heavy dark arms, teasing her a little with the amount of news she was about to receive.

Greggie the would-be suicide had been released into her boyfriend's care and she was now an out-patient contracted to keep a twice-weekly consultation with Dr Kaplan. And everybody was having problems with Perry Gillies. Billy had plumbers in half the day on Wednesday, floors awash with overflow from the bathroom. Perry was in there when the flooding started, with every tap jammed open, every toilet backed up.

'He said it wasn't his fault. He didn't do nothin' to nothin', he said.' A claim Billy didn't believe. For two days Perry kept himself awake by tanking up on black coffee, and he wouldn't leave the unit. Agitated one minute, arguing out loud with nobody, the next minute defeated, collapsed and morose. Between the two extremes he'd be pestering the staff for the only piece of information that mattered to him – the exact time Lillian was going to be back.

'Where is he now?'

'We got him home,' Billy said. 'Found him conked out on the floor in the atrium. Guess his little legs couldn't do any more laps.'

At lunchtime Douglas Cottle had to talk Lillian through his new theory of nutrition. His old ideas about food were wrong, they were insane ideas, he admitted. Air, grass and H_2O is a diet for cows! Humans, every week, need to eat their way through the spectrum. 'Today is Thursday. I'm eating in the violet.' Lillian ordered a regular lunch for him and went down to the kitchen to supervise the coloring of Douglas's tuna fish, vanilla pudding and milk. The boiled red cabbage didn't need any work.

She took her lunch break later than usual, but she didn't eat. Lillian used the time for research, first in the book store across the street from the hospital and then in the library. As she picked through the row of books the way she would search for a ripe melon, Lillian was thinking how much this is like having a strange disease. If someone would tell her it was a known quantity, the trouble had a name and a history, that it flared up in people with a particular predisposition, then she'd know how to respond. But the selection of anthologies, personal testaments and sorcerer science covering psychic mysteries and semi-religious revelations stacked in the Paranormal/Occult corner of Pickwick Books pretty much made Father Terhune's case: in this area wild claims burn up all the breathable air. *The Umbradine Prophecy*, *The Conniston Horror*, *The Lie of Mortality*, she skipped over the tawdriest titles, those hammy quivering swoons decorated with ghostly hands bestowing gifts of prismatic light, shimmering humanoid figures descending from the pink ether, *Death Before Life*, *Your Ancestors Want to Speak to You!*, the shelves were jammed with simpleminded twilight trash being peddled as the highest wisdom. Was this the true face of her own baffling encounter last night? Self-conscious, belittled, she left the store empty-handed.

She knew she should have ridden the bus all the way into town and begun her research at the public library. Even though the old building, mapped with soot, was crunched between a department store and the *Tri-City Intelligencer*'s glass-fronted offices, it stood with a gaunt formality at the back of its elegant stretch of greenery. The double lawn and the clean concrete walk kept city noise at a distance. In the spring you'd see people sitting on the square-backed wooden benches, eating their lunch under the walnut and chestnut trees, but in this noontime chill the benches were deserted. The lumpy overcast, the cold, encouraged Lillian indoors and brought back a memory of her college life, crossing the campus to spend whole days plowing through card catalogues, roaming the stacks, cracking the textbooks. Here she was now, diving in again.

The titles were less welcoming than the ones she ran across in the book store. She leafed through *Parapsychology: Its Relation to Physics, Biology, Psychology and Psychiatry*. She found *Human Personality and Its Survival of Bodily Death* easier to absorb but too abstract for her purpose, and *Cases of Appearances of the Dead, Vols 1–5* only helpful as a digest of experiences as frightening and obscure as her own. *From Anecdote to Experiment in Contemporary Psychical Research* was valuable for one reason alone: its bibliography led her to the work of Marit Sonnenfeld.

The opening sentences of Sonnenfeld's autobiography, *The Secret Life of a Parapsychologist*, caught Lillian with their peppery directness. They were the words of a questing spirit solidly attached to Mother Earth: 'I know there was a time when I believed in the possibility of life beyond death. If I concentrate hard enough I can almost recall the passion that drove me to prove it was true.' Skimming the pages Lillian found a fair statement of the problem she was facing. 'Anyone can concoct a theory about restless ghosts. The trouble, as always, is how to separate good theories from bad. All such theorizing starts from the same point, with the idea that somewhere inside us we carry an indestructible version of ourselves. This part is unique to each human being, experiences the world through the body and, usually, disappears back to its source when the body dies. In truth, the assertion is a deeper question about our mortality and unknowable past: do we come from mud or God, do we return to mud or God? And, more precisely, can the inanimate world be imprinted with single, personal outbreaks of tragedy? A good theory will narrow down the possibilities, guide our imagination and predict what we will find. A bad theory mollycoddles us, it points in a broad direction and allows us to think that anything we can imagine is possible . . .'

Sonnenfeld's sober, adroit and disciplined approach to the depths of the subject gave Lillian a concrete hold on it, a ledge of reason that kept her from dangling. As she read at random through the book, her confidence in its author rose, and even warmed. From the freshman days of her academic career Marit Sonnenfeld only wanted to know one thing – what in the world is really there. She talked about her 'crazy fear of wishful thinking'. As a defense against it, she designed experiments to study telepathy, clairvoyance, precognition and psychokinesis and brought what she learned to her investigation of hauntings.

Lillian glanced up from her reading to let the flitting ideas settle. A picture was beginning to take shape. She could remember two times – no, three – when she dreamed about Hildy the night before she heard from her. Two postcards and that phone call in the summer. Would Sonnenfeld say it was clairvoyance or precognition? And the strange boy, how did he open up all the faucets, leave Freddy's hairbrushes on the hall floor? Psychokinesis? What would Sonnenfeld make of the stigmata on Lillian's wrists and ankles? Was that a case of telepathy? She scoured the index for some hint, some advice.

It struck Lillian that the author of *The Secret Life of a Parapsychologist* and *Psychic Investigation: A Guide to Principle and Practice* recognized the connection between the way we think the world operates and the way we perceive other people. The one depends on the other. When she was younger, Sonnenfeld wrote, she would camouflage her shaky confidence by backing friends and strangers against the wall (sometimes literally) with inflamed overcomplicated arguments, a habit of mind and heart which scared off anyone she wanted to attract. The admission touched Lillian. A person who faced herself so honestly and revealed what she saw without a qualm deserved a measure of trust.

In her book jacket photograph Marit Sonnenfeld appeared accessible, assured, not yet in her thirties when the autobiography was published. Her small-boned oval face presented itself without make-up, framed by baroque bunches of springy black curls which just brushed the shoulders of her endearingly frumpy cardigan. Her cheeks formed a wide parenthesis, the crescent crease in one of them was the shadow of an unsuppressible smile at herself, tickled to pose for the camera. Lillian read a soft irony there, the expression that would rise into Sonnenfeld's face whether an idea of hers was proved right or wrong.

Hers were the only two books Lillian checked out of the library. She slipped them into her coat, one in each big pocket, to protect them from the rain.

Under the damp navy blue scarf a grandmother's face looked back at Lillian from the staff room mirror. The upper half of her winter coat, heavy and shapeless, genderless, added to the portrait in the frame. Lillian had seen war photographs of such women, refugees on European roads, toilers, saddled like pack mules, figures of pointless pity. Without her coat and scarf she came back into our decade, fluffing out the flattened strands that made her head seem pinched in the middle, brushing down her dress-sleeves. Alone in the room, eyes lowered, Lillian turned her wrists up into the light and bent them back from the hem of her cuffs. Overnight, the welts had faded, they had almost healed. All she could see there was a pale pink band, the strength of a blush; but before she left the privacy of the staff room Lillian felt the places with her fingertips, expertly, doubting the returned smoothness, the surprise recovery, then finally believing it.

She didn't see Perry until evening (he knew where she would be), laboring down the hall toward her as she was on her way into the chapel. He looked sickly, shaky, disheveled, and when his splayfooted walk brought him close enough she saw a new sign in his face. His long lips were dry and cracked and the cracks were threaded with dried blood, and the hard set of his eyes clamped over some kind of rising drama. 'Wait a second, Mrs Foy,' he said, breathing through his mouth. 'Can you give me some time?'

'I knocked on your door at about four-thirty. I guess you were still asleep.'

'I couldn't keep my eyes open anymore.' This perturbed him. 'You can fight it off for a day or two, then it weakens you out.'

'You shouldn't deprive yourself of what you need. Douglas isn't eating, you're not sleeping, it's a regular epidemic.'

'Don't count me in with that sad sack. He eats plants and grass, there's something wrong with him,' he said, corkscrewing a finger at the side of his head. 'He doesn't know a lot. But with me it's the opposite. I'm eighty-one years old,' Perry gave it a harsh stress, his voice clenched. Unwilling to say any more.

'Is that what's at the bottom of this? This no-sleep kick you're on?'

Perry's shoulders drooped a little. Lillian felt the tension break as he unclenched and said, 'I'm not a worthless man!'

'No, you're not. You *know* that. What happened? Did you forget?'

'The other night, when I shut my eyes . . .' He tugged at his loose workshirt, tugged it open. Lillian drew it closed and buttoned it for him. She held Perry's hand as he started again. 'What did I do wrong, y'know? I volunteered to fight in the war, I wanted to go! Now there's retaliation against me.'

'No, from where? From who?'

'From spite! You don't choose what's necessary. You see it and you do it.' He was attempting to be impressive. It was as if he had blundered into the moral universe and for the first time in his life he had to advocate, defend, justify. Left too late, and now it was imperative.

'When you're attacked, you fight back. Fighting back isn't a criminal deed. It's – what do you call it, for safety . . .'

'Self-defense.'

'It's self-protection when you fight back. I don't know any Thou Shalt Not about that, God doesn't persecute you for fighting for your country. To restore normality!' Despondently he said, 'I shouldn't have lived so long.'

'It's a hard habit to break.' Lillian felt Perry gaining strength from her attention. Leaning on it, anyway. 'You're a veteran.'

Bolstered a fraction, limply pointing at the door to the chapel, he said, 'Are you on your way in or did you just come out?'

'Want to come in with me?'

'No. Please . . .' he said. 'Say a double rosary for me, Mrs Foy.'

'Maybe if it's that important it should come from you.'

He moved away so Lillian could step past him. 'I've got to work up my courage some more.' She stood still though, with the feeling that Perry had something else to say. 'I want to tell you I'm very scared at the moment. I know something. I'm dying. You understand me?'

Yes, Lillian thought; because he is in contact with the fact of it, he can feel its grip around his joints, thickening in his lungs and around his heart, slowing him to a stop. A man as old as Perry would have seen the slow approach, watched the shadow close in on him and take the shape of his own face. She wanted the world to be kind to Perry. 'Who'd want to be eighteen all over again? When you don't know anything.'

'I remember. I don't want my young days back. This is different,' he said. 'This is persecution! Attacking me in my sleep and this is not fair. Whereby dreams are being forced on me two nights in a row.'

'What kind of dreams?'

'Rotten ones. The worst, poison,' stumbling for the words. 'A boy is there. Tied up. Wrapped up in barbed wire or something, it's hurting him very bad. And he's crying to me, but what can I do? I can't do anything. He's getting hit and so on, he can't stop crying, you understand? People are burning him with cigarettes. It's the worst thing to see, it's my worst fear.'

The scene he described arrested her. 'What people?'

'How do I know? Jesus, Jesus Christ.' Perry began to sob. 'Is anything lower? A little kid, tormenting him like that . . .'

She let Perry lean on her arm as she walked him back home, without letting him guess that his touch was comforting her, and his eighty-one-year-old bones were holding her up.

The soul of a dead boy? No: an explosion of her colored hearing. A figment? Some kind of emotional spasm? Why should the same figment visit her house and Perry's sleep? How to hack her way to the root of it, that was what Lillian had to decide. On the bus going home Lillian was traveling too fast, faster than she could think, and even felt the heated air around her tightening, claustrophobic. Two stops after she climbed on, she climbed off and started walking. How much more of this was she strong enough to carry alone?

Looking up through the slow rain as the street began to slope upward she saw that her route had taken her the long way around, past Lawford Academy. From the sidewalk Lillian saw their blue Ford in Freddy's parking spot abutting the main building, and remembered Fridays he stayed late to chair the weekly faculty meetings. Inside the modern square arch of the entrance (the annex was the only twentieth-century architecture on campus), Lillian heard people talking, a broth of echoes spilling out into the flat corridors on both sides of her. Assured, manly laughter, tones of agreement, overlapping invitations, the meeting had just broken up.

In Freddy's office she seated herself on the short wooden bench reserved for visitors. Soon, Freddy trooped in with Arthur Cuddy and a tall, youngish man Lillian didn't know. Arthur dropped out of the conversation as soon as he saw her there, greeting her with his trademark, 'Hell*oooo*,' and following it in, leaning his big body over to deposit a kiss on Lillian's cheek. 'Do you know you're soaking wet or is this a trick to get a free drink out of me?'

'Which one would you believe?'

'Neither,' he complimented her, affectionately.

'I was just saying,' Freddy said to Lillian as though she'd been in the meeting with them, 'before Vernon spends that money on a swimming pool he'd better decide where the extra cash is going to come from for the upped insurance every year.'

'So there's another reason he should invest in the star,' the young man rolled his head, chuckled. 'Oh man!'

'What's this?' Lillian asked them.

'Oh, it's Vernon's headache,' Arthur explained, 'so of course it's ours. Mrs Hyland left the school—'

'Emily Hyland died last week,' Freddy took charge. 'Hyland Chevrolet? She left us a hundred and sixty thousand with the catch that we have to build a swimming pool for the school *or* erect a fifty-foot tall red, white and blue neon star on top of Cox's Hill. Right behind us. Oh, and the star lights up red whenever there's a traffic fatality.'

Arthur said, 'I'm voting for the star.' Before they fell into the swimming pool/neon star debate all over again, as courteous as a knight Arthur turned to Lillian. 'You haven't met Chris O'Dowd, have you.'

O'Dowd nodded, uncomfortable in the spotlight, and raked his finger nails through his thin white-blond hair, neatening it in Lillian's honor. Freddy picked up the slack. 'My wife, Lillian,' and to her he said, 'Chris is taking over my drafting classes.'

'If the boys will let me,' said O'Dowd. 'They're real devoted to Freddy.'

As if suddenly realizing, Freddy said to Lillian, 'Why aren't you at home, for goodness sake?' Turning back to O'Dowd, 'My wife doesn't usually go slopping around in the rain.'

'I stayed with a patient, and I thought . . . I wanted to ride home with you, that's all.'

'Did Freddy tell me you're at Mount St Mary's?' O'Dowd asked her, tilting his head a little to the side.

'In the psychiatric unit. Did he tell you that?'

'I better watch my Freudian slips around you, right? Or else you'll find out I'm a crazyman and throw me into a rubber room.' Friendly enough right off the bat, bridging the way with his little knowledge. The look O'Dowd gave her dripping headscarf was half-serious and fully sympathetic. 'It must be very tough work.'

Freddy tugged a couple of tissues from a box behind his desk and passed them over to her, with a small comic sigh. 'Oh, Lillian. Look at you.' Then he said to the men, 'We'll save that drink for some other night.'

A knot gripped and held inside Lillian's throat. She had the feeling she looked idiotic. An orphan of the storm. The signal that reached her was that her bedraggled shape had put Freddy on the spot. She saw he was shedding discomfort like an odor. 'It's been a draining day,' she said.

'Come with us for a drink,' Arthur said brightly. 'I'll get Mim to meet us at Giuliano's.'

'Thanks, Arthur,' she said. 'Not tonight, no. I'm a little worn out. Fighting off a chill.'

Freddy had his coat and gloves on. He patted Lillian's damp shoulder. 'Let's go home. Come on. Let a smile be your umbrella.'

Chapter Eleven

FREDDY'S BASEMENT den, even while it was being built, gave him the kind of private contentment he was looking for. He kept himself down there at work on the renovation until bedtime every weeknight, trundling tools and supplies in through the storm doors, trailing electrical cables along the stairs from the kitchen. Busy with new necessities, out of Lillian's company. Over meals Freddy spoke to her as though she'd shattered his concentration and he only seemed completely present when he was bringing her up to the minute on how the building work was coming along. The impression Lillian got was that he wanted her to look forward, as he was doing, to an easier time when his sanctuary was finished and they would hardly have to spend any time together at all.

All right. She had her own project to accomplish. Lillian had Marit Sonnenfeld's books to absorb. On the weekend Freddy's nonstop manual labor came with a bonus – it was going to tucker him out and he'd be in bed by nine o'clock, under deep layers of sleep five minutes later. The sadness of it!—that Lillian wanted to watch for the ghost boy, make all of her preparations, behind Freddy's back.

That is, her preparations to understand and accept. Would he come to her again? The question itself was a measure of his importance to Lillian. Even after only a few days she had to exert some kind of effort to hold him still in her mind. Yet one memory was constantly there – the emotion he'd twisted into her, and pulled from her, too – clear, crushing grief. The cause of the boy's grief though was cloudy, unless it was the same as hers: a reminder that death is coming, that this life ends. If the boy didn't come back Lillian was afraid he would disintegrate into fantasy, break up into glittering particles and hang like buzzing static in the air.

From time to time Lillian's eyes came up off the page she was reading, she found herself marveling at the keenness of Sonnenfeld's perceptions and the personality at the heart of each small revelation. Lillian read and re-read this passage, eyes lifted between readings: 'My mother looks at breakdowns in life, all the failures and imperfections and something inside her "knows" that she is not seeing the whole picture. According to my mother (and a variety of ancient wisdom texts) the world we call "real" is no more than a stage on the way to a perfect existence beyond the here-and-now. Of course, she may be correct, if believing is seeing.' For her father, a District Circuit Court judge who faced the brutalities of this world on a regular basis, any ideal human condition was boldly imaginary. The law was like that, he taught her, an 'ideal in harness', in practical service, carrying us over a rutted torn-up crumbling road. He kept his skepticism for the law's jugglers and acrobats who argued their cases in front of him, emotional creatures pleading to define what's true. 'Our house', the young parapsychologist wrote of her secret life, 'was full of discussion, opinion and jostling arguments.' Lillian took all of this as a declaration that nothing should be hidden, a frightening but, to her at his moment, thrilling thought.

In the living room where she sat drinking cups of black coffee, with Marit's autobiography open on her lap, Lillian heard the heavy cartons scrape as Freddy shunted them around the basement floor. The sound raised a fine spray of color above the page she was reading, aqua-blue fringed with silvery white like the fan of water shaved off the surface by a skidding water-ski. It had the effect of magnifying the print, and the magnified words held her deeply in the story Marit told of her first brush with a ghost:

After one semester of very discouraging results from my *Ganzfeld* experiments, I began to question whether I really believed in the thing I was looking for. At this low-point my thesis adviser introduced me to his twenty-six-year-old cousin who had come to Rhode Island for the summer. Georgia Love was casual about her psychic talent, it was as common in her family as blue eyes and black hair are in mine. Her mother, two aunts and her eighty-eight-year-old great-aunt, she told me, all shared a telepathic receptivity which they called 'the vision'. Her aunt Kate had even been the subject of *psi* studies in the 1960s (Landreth, 1963, 1964; Zoeger, 1968).

'It's like a breeze coming off people,' Georgia used to say. 'And everything about their life blows toward me, straight into my mind.' The 'sitter group' I organized (four other psychology t.a.'s, Georgia and myself) met three nights a week for twelve weeks. Our ouija board sessions produced a few surprises that we rated 'above chance' and we felt encouraged. In that confident mood we moved into all-night seances.

On a humid, overcast July night, in the dark of the new moon, we chose a grassy clearing in a corner of the Caseville cemetery. The dead seemed to be huddled around us, listening, under the cluttered branches of the pine trees and that heavy black sky. My fingers were on the planchette with Georgia's and before I could take a breath, with a force we had never felt before, it spelled out the name Edward. Then a second name, Mears. Georgia's eyes closed and her upper body leaned back. She repeated the name, as a question first, and then as an answer.

How could I be sure the *mood* wasn't taking over, separating us from our surroundings? In my diary that night I wrote, 'I had to overcome the fear by letting go. To show myself I could know what was there if I only faced it, *whatever* it was.' Calmly, Georgia said to me, 'I don't feel very well. I feel cold.' I put my hand to her forehead, it was damp and cool. 'Somebody is laughing,' she said. None of us were. 'I can't see his face. He's as old as Daddy. He doesn't want you to see his face.' Georgia sat forward, opening her eyes. 'He's coming.'

We all looked where Georgia was looking. For minutes we held as still as the pine trees we were staring at. The air was quiet, hanging over us. Then there was movement under the branches, over the patch of brown grass twenty yards away. I had William James's words ringing in my ears, *the treacheries of uncertain light . . .*

We agreed to write down our eye-witness reports before excited talk in the group contaminated the evidence. Around the table in a coffee shop we read our notes out loud. The cold that Georgia felt earlier we all felt then, as five of the six accounts agreed, detail for detail. Georgia's was the most complete and vivid. She had seen a human figure emerge from the shadows under the trees, a 'tall man in dark clothes'. He moved left to right, stopped, then moved away in the same direction. She said there was something about 'Edward' that reminded her of Abraham Lincoln, and two of the others noted independently that he was wearing a nineteenth-century frock coat (Sonnenfeld, 1977).

I read out my page of notes last, and it took no time at all. I had not seen anything there. My lack of belief was blamed, my detachment. Any kind of doubt, no matter how deeply suppressed, might close off the route the dead use to reach us. We argued the theory until sun-up. Maybe Georgia Love's real psychic gift was her unhampered power to believe.

Let Marit come and ask Lillian. Lillian understood the gestures that needed to be made to show she was willing. For whose sake? The dead boy's – for him. In the back of her mind this invitation she made, to let him in and end any doubt about his reality, came close to proof of it in itself. She thought, Put yourself in his place. Wouldn't you hope to persuade a confused mind of the plain fact of your existence? Lillian had to satisfy herself; the boy would want that, wouldn't he, to see a display of faith in him before he took her any deeper into the reason he had appeared in her life.

The home-made 'motion detector' was only a length of kitchen string with a row of feathers stuck to it, red antique feathers plucked out of Hildy's thrift store boa. While she was trying it on a diagonal between the door and the vanity table Lillian tried to ignore the imaginary conversation she was having with Freddy. Tonight he'd say, 'My God, Lillian. What now!' 'It's by the book,' she'd answer, 'a scientific book.' 'Science from when? The Dark Ages? It's right in front of the bathroom. You want me to trip over it and break my neck?'

When the string was anchored and taut, Lillian followed the next recommendation in Sonnenfeld's *Principle and Practice*. She made a diary note of the feathers' motion (if any) in the room's unhaunted air. On a pad on her night-table she wrote, 'Draft-proofed bedroom. Feathers hanging still.' Besides the feathers on the string Lillian set up two thermometers, one on the night-table, another on the floor near the place where she'd seen the boy before. It was settled, she had taken the dare, invited him back, and sitting up in bed she waited for him.

Worried that even with the caffeine buzzing warmly inside her she still might drowse off, Lillian moved to the plump, upholstered chair facing the bedroom door. Across the room's terrain of patchy shadow her eyes took in every angle and curve, glanced over the lines of the solid objects around her. The colonial spindles of the bedposts, the limp line of feathers, the comb-like shadow they threw on the carpet in a watery square of weak gray moonlight, Freddy's porpoise shape under the swell of his blankets, rising and falling on each slow breath. All of it was hers, in a way, Lillian had secret knowledge here. She said to herself, 'This is how it looks when I'm asleep,' falling into distraction, close to sleep. Then, jerking her head up, she forced herself sharply awake, her eyes wide open.

First she saw the moon through the window, through a fracture in the crust of cloud, and she struggled to remember if she'd been dreaming. Something had startled her, a noise or a voice. But the silence around her had steadied now. She half-remembered what she'd heard, a human sound nudging the silence apart, a small sound – *ma*. The feathers weren't moving, the air was still, but a pungency had wafted in, the sickly, oily odor of melting rubber. Alert to it, Lillian worked back to the most likely source: it must be seeping up from downstairs, some material Freddy was using in the basement, left too close to the boiler. With pictures of fiery catastrophe whirling in her head she made a move to get up and go see. Only, her legs wouldn't lift her. She felt the chill on her ribs, on her shoulders and neck, on her face, it gathered Lillian inside it. Staring at the thermometer next to her, she watched it sink to freezing. All together, gently, the tips of the thin red feathers bent up, as if they were riding a steady breeze, caught in a current flowing toward her. Behind them Lillian's bedroom doorway held a slanting, pale amber, archaic light.

A word was frozen in her throat, an agony of alarm, trapped in a hard breath before she could cry it out to Freddy. And she knew that tearing pressure in her chest, Lillian had felt its grip before, the shearing pain of loss. The boy stood at the foot of her bed. How beautiful he was! Trustful, as he looked slowly around the room (but not at Lillian), and undefended. He was dressed in the clothes he had on when Lillian saw him outside the house – flat cap, knickerbockers, neat shirt and short jacket, and his schoolbooks dangled from his hand, slung together

101

with a brown belt. Lillian tasted tears in her mouth and felt them rise, steaming behind her eyes. He was unhurt now, his bones unbroken, his skin unscarred, but soon, soon, she knew, he had to tumble into disaster. Finally, he turned his face toward her and the calmness of his expression confirmed what Lillian knew. And even more, he was there to tell her what mattered most of all – she was reachable.

'Lillian. Lillian, dear?' Freddy was calling her from the other side of a sheet of early daylight. She saw him bending to sit on the edge of her bed, still in his pyjamas, feet bare. He must have just woken up. A few strands of hair stuck out from his scalp at sloppy angles, and blinking a little to clear his eyes he passed a hand over his wide brow, over the uneasy creases put there by this new unknown trouble.

'What's going on?' Lillian said dully, without focus.

Into her open eyes he asked, 'Are you awake now, Lil?'

The feathers and string were collapsed in Freddy's hands, looped around his fingers. He knuckled his thumbs along it, fidgeting it through, like counting beads on a rosary. 'What's going on with this?' he said, laying the idiotic handicraft on her lap.

'It's a piece of scientific equipment.'

Freddy's mouth sphinctered, he was skeptical. He was looking at his wife slumped in her chair, apparently exhausted and obviously talking nonsense, nightgown hitched up to her knees, bathrobe untied, her arms slackly hanging over the chair's sides, her legs sprawled, as if she'd been dropped through a hole in the roof.

Lillian handled the loose coil, brushed her palm over a few of the red feathers and thought, I did do this. And then: I did see him. 'What an amazing thing,' she said to Freddy.

'That's a good word for it. I can think of a few other ones.'

Her beaten voice didn't go very far to relieve him. 'I'll tell you what I think I know.'

'Please, yes.'

He was going to hear it all from the beginning, if she could see exactly where that was. 'About a week ago I found a strange boy in the house.'

'You didn't know him, is that what you mean? And he broke in?'

'Yes.'

'How did he get inside?'

'The back door was open. But I'm not sure that's how he did it.'

'Jesus, Lillian. Who was he? Did we get burgled?'

'He turned on all the water in the sinks. It just looked like a prank to me.' She smiled, remembering. 'And then he laid out your old military hairbrushes in front of the bedroom door. Then he disappeared.'

Freddy went quiet and looked away toward the door. Anything else he wanted to say could wait. Her whole story had to come out first.

'He came back three nights ago. He came in here while we were asleep.'

'You must have been awake if you saw him.'

'Yes.'

'Why didn't you wake me up?'

'I started to,' she said. 'I tried to.'

'But he stopped you?' Freddy's stiff anger with her was the temper of a parent whose toddler had wandered into a busy street. 'He could have done anything he wanted to us. Didn't you think of that? I was here, wasn't I. Why didn't you say something?'

'Nothing came out when I opened my mouth.'

'This happened three nights ago? Finally I'm hearing about it. Did you call the police?' Lillian shook her head. 'Did you tell Mim?'

'I'm telling *you*, Freddy. I couldn't tell you before I was sure of what I saw.'

'Either a boy broke into our house, into our *bedroom*, or—. Is that what happened or not? A boy from the neighborhood?'

She straightened herself slowly in the chair, gathered her bathrobe

103

and her thoughts. When she spoke her voice sounded calm and strong. 'He's a dead boy. He's a presence in this house. Don't stop listening to me – please, Freddy.' The agonizing memory of him, Lillian's memory of the lonely unpitied torture he brought to her surged over her as she thought, This is true and I'm saying it out loud, bringing it into the daylight world. Now the fear stabbed again. Convincing Freddy, she understood, drawing him inside the circle, was something the boy wanted. Influence as real as death, stronger than death, and as clearly as she saw Freddy sitting there Lillian saw she was frightening him. Could there be any doubt about it now? Before she said any more she moved over to the bed and squeezed next to him, her arm around his wide soft back. 'I think he died here. Each time I've seen him it's been clearer, I don't know how.'

His dry throat cracking, Freddy said, 'What are those feathers?'

'To see if he has any effect moving in the physical sphere.'

'That isn't you talking.'

She knew what he meant. 'It isn't Mim, either.'

'One small blessing.' His quick, unintentional harshness stopped her. Finding a little patience, he said, 'Did you talk to anyone about this? At the hospital?'

'The second time he was here, after I saw him tied up and in pain, Freddy, in so much pain, I went and spoke to Father Terhune.'

'You'd tell our local mad monk that you've seen a dead boy walking around our bedroom, but you'd hide this piece of news from me? Why?'

'Because I didn't tell him that,' Lillian said and let her arm drop from Freddy's back. 'I just kept it to general questions about ghosts and whatnot. A priest is supposed to know about things like suffering souls.'

'Oh,' he said, temporarily defeated. 'It's a Catholic matter.'

'He's in agony, *agony*. I know it and I can't shut him out. Is that a

Catholic thing? You want me to forget I saw what I saw here?' She gave Freddy a chance to say yes, to show her she was appealing for help from the wrong person, but he didn't say a word. 'Something has started, something is different. You feel it? A change.'

Freddy picked up the thermometer lying at his feet. Lillian told him what she'd read in Sonnenfeld's book, held the volume in front of him, the ballast of scientific authority, and informed him that when the ghost boy was there the temperature dropped from forty-nine degrees to thirty-two. He didn't feel the room get any colder during the night, he said. Then he asked her, 'Is he here now?'

'No. He left.'

'All right. Tell me again. Can you remember when it started?'

She had invited him to touch her and Freddy had made the reach, it felt that way to Lillian. She traced backward through the appearances, signs and sensations, how the boy squatted half naked and trapped, the sudden odors of tobacco and rubber, the rope marks mimicked on her wrists and the wider ones on her ankles, and a painful fear began to coil in Freddy's gut. He studied Lillian's face – could he see any change in it? This was the woman who waved to him from the kitchen window when he drove off to work in the morning, the woman who chaperoned him through the end of his youth and these long middle years, who managed a solid career (in mental health, for God's sake!), a woman of maturity and normal, predictable reactions, not a Nervous Norvis, and inside the expected limits, as far as he could see, she was happy. Freddy kept watching her. Was her face thinner, were her eyes deeper in their hollows, more fervent? He saw the unkempt wisps of hair curved toward her mouth, one or two stuck to her underlip (did she notice?), a spreading emotional heat in her cheeks. Now Freddy made sense of the fear that was pulling at him – he was afraid because it *was* this woman saying these things. Everything he was hearing from her, he was sure, must be a bizarrely coded message, telling him – what,

105

exactly? He was looking at her the way he'd gaze out at a landscape, into a deep canyon or thick forest, trying to seize details remotely familiar to him. Lillian had puzzled her way back to the beginning, to the monkey dream, and she was about to tell him she was naked in it, but to make it clear that he had stopped listening Freddy interrupted her with 'If you want to say something, then just say it to me. What's going wrong, hm?'

'Well, I have to do something,' she said urgently. 'Right now, most of all, I want you to help me understand what it is, all of this.'

'I'm trying to understand you, that's what I want too.'

'Understand *me*?'

That string-of-feathers contraption! Tell me there was no psychological meaning in that thing! It was a barrier, a criticism, a complaint, a voodoo line strung between her side of the room and his, a spell she cast against him, a sign of unhealed grievance. It was the eruption of a family crisis. A defect in her, a mania or phobia, buried under her regular habits of work and homemaking finally had overpowered her. The bad juices were flowing. Like mother, like daughter; earlier for Hildy, later for Lillian. Or this was the form a simpler horror was taking in her, the shattering reality of days and years passing. Freddy wondered if between the two of them, she was aging faster. His heart felt unmoored, as swollen as the Hindenberg, about to bulge through his chest. He hunched forward, elbows planted on knees, a pose of serious concentration, believing it might only be his concentration that was holding him there in one piece.

Lillian was telling him, 'I tried to be honest with myself. What if I imagined every one of those things, how would I know the difference?'

'This bed is real. Leprechauns are imaginary.'

'Look out the window a minute.' Both of them looked. 'You see the telephone pole on the other side of the street?' Freddy nodded his head.

'You see two birds sitting up there? One on the top wire and another one on the pole?'

'Yes, Lillian.'

'Me too.'

'And do you remember the first car we bought after we got married?' Freddy was still staring through the window. He nodded his head. 'The Plymouth. Tell me what color it was.'

Freddy obeyed. 'It was a two-tone. Pink and white.'

'I remember it too,' Lillian said. 'Somebody else, somebody at the hospital dreamed about the boy. The boy came to him too.'

'A *mental* patient?'

'No. Perry Gillies, remember him? He gave us that old photo of our house. From when he worked here for Sam Hoagland.'

'Gillies?' But he wasn't even *trying* to place Perry. Freddy stood, defying the terrible sadness that turned his legs to cement. A final thought had wormed into him: he was out of his depth. And yet his strength (it took a physical effort) could only sink him deeper. Minutes earlier, the same strength kept him from asking Lillian about the objects in the hallway. Pointing at them, resisting no more, he said, 'What are those supposed to mean?'

Whatever they meant to Freddy, the pair of white satin pumps with their mother-of-pearl silver-edged buckles delivered a body blow to Lillian. The boy was telling her, with intimate tenderness, that he saw into the concealed parts of her life, he knew what she knew, and not only that these were the shoes she'd worn with her wedding dress. They were a remnant, as the boy was a remnant, of a day that separated past from present and present from future – bringing them to her (how? *somehow!*), he called her name, he took her back to the ceremony in St Mary's and forward through every heartbreak and happiness Lillian knew in her married life until this moment.

'Oh my,' words no more than croaks as her tears escaped, too messy for her to stop. 'Oh my.' She let herself weep and hugged the shoes to her chest, slipping down against the doorframe, ending up cross-legged on the floor. 'Oh my.' For a little while she felt alone in the room and cried without covering her face. But the molten outpouring didn't last. The shaking, the leaking tears, the twitching lips, she brought them all under control and arthritically faltered back to lie on her bed, face down, curled around her white satin shoes, also around the fearful knowledge that Freddy couldn't row her to safety.

He was afraid of this too. There was only one nurse in this marriage, and she was unwell; only one teacher and he was stymied. So, leaning on the virtue of his frank relationship with the practical world, Freddy arrived at a decision.

From her bed Lillian heard him downstairs on the phone. She called to him, asked him who he was talking to. A pause. Then Freddy called up to her, 'Arthur, that's all.' And even though he'd dropped his voice she heard Freddy say into the phone, 'Lil's feeling low. Maybe we can all cheer her up with some championship gin-rummy.'

Chapter Twelve

LILLIAN EXPECTED, and pretty much hoped, the rain would stop Mim and Arthur from making the fifteen-mile drive over the lightless country roads that moored Woodbridge to Lawford. It had been rattling down out of a grim sky for two days and nights, turning the air hard, the streets slick and the ground into a muddy, pebbly stew. The curtain strung across the end of fall had split top to bottom and winter was ripping through. Was Freddy sure the Cuddys still wanted to go out in this treacherous weather? Maybe she ought to call them, Lillian volunteered, catch them before they got into their car. 'Pish tosh,' says Freddy, her English butler, a snack bowl in each hand.

It wasn't for their safety's sake she wanted Mim and Arthur to stay at home, but for her own. After her demanding day at St Mount's Lillian was afraid she might crumple under the strain of pretending gin-rummy would shut out whatever was menacing her, whatever form it was taking tonight.

'Do we have to keep these in here?' Freddy asked for information, tapping one of the small cardboard boxes with the buffed toe of his loafer. Both boxes were carefully packed with tied clumps of dried flowers, brittle bouquets of pale violet, indigo, coral and burgundy red buds, each bunch mournfully gathered at the waist with a black ribbon. The harvest of Molyneaux Wing's art therapy.

'I'll move them into the kitchen,' Lillian said.

'No, no.' He was quick, two steps ahead of her. The first box was under his arm when the doorbell chimed, sending Freddy off on that tangent, smoothing down his hair with his free hand, the correct and official greeter. 'Is that Mim Cuddy, the Woodbridge beauty queen?'

Mim's hair looked newly sheared and colored, a boyish haircut that added a peppiness, her face as fresh as a college kid's. Black wool capris, narrow at the ankle. Powder blue mohair sweater hanging down to her knees like a work of art. Taking one of Lillian's hands, then a catwalk step back, Mim posed à la Flamenco saying, 'Let's bring back the Beatniks.'

'I'm breaking in a pair of bongo drums,' said Arthur.

'Where are they?' Freddy asked him. 'We could have a jam session.'

'Right now they're dangling from my rear-view mirror.'

'He's such a rebel,' Mim said, tugging on Arthur's tweed lapel.

He could be photographed as-is for a quality menswear catalogue, presenting more than wearing his suit. A heavily built man, round backed, propped up on stocky thighs, his chin luxuriously embedded in a rubbery lap of fat, but wholesome fat, a buttery layer of it under his smooth skin, like a woman has, or a seal. Beneath the soft pink chin (shaved and cologned), a bright red moiré silk bow tie. 'My raspberry to the weather,' he bragged to Lillian.

They were coddling her; they had dolled themselves up for the visit. Arthur, the diplomat from the Court of St James, and Mim the planky Arizona ranchgirl. The unfenced openness of the western desert – she was its emblem as it was hers; Mim knew what creatures lived under the rocks: scorpions, tarantulas, diamondbacks. And they all had to be flushed out, lured out, pestered out into the open.

'Gin.' Mim wasn't bluffing. She spread out the majestic run of clubs, four to ten, Jack, Queen, King, in easy triumph.

'Flabbergasting!' Freddy leaned out of his chair to give himself a better view of her winning hand, the heavy curve of his stomach dented by the edge of the table. 'Caught me with Fort Knox,' he woundedly congratulated Mim and sat back down to tote up the points on his scorepad.

'It's in the genes,' Arthur said. 'Dexter's been trying to get me into the futures market. He gets it from her. "It's just like some big hairy casino, Dad!" Did Jimmy Hoffa's father have to listen to this kind of propaganda?' A shrug as he let Freddy add his forfeit to the total. 'Thirty-four from me.'

Freddy's small eyes swiveled toward his wife. 'Lil? Points?'

'Thirty-eight.' She showed him and he double-checked, tapping the loose cards with his pencil.

As Arthur dealt the four corners of another hand Freddy said to him, 'It doesn't take a Rockefeller to make a killing on the stock market. If you've got the talent for it you shouldn't let it dribble away. Dex is your son.'

'My talent is dribbling. I come from a proud line of dribblers. My ancestors were dribbling all over the British Empire when Wall Street was a swamp and a pewter mug store.' A wedge of white blond hair slipped down over Arthur's brow. He shook it back loosely into place. 'The Cuddys were even on the wrong side of the American Revolution.'

Freddy wouldn't believe a word. 'You can fight your genes,' finger wagging, pushing his opinion with his advice, 'but you can't win.'

111

'No,' Arthur said, 'the stock market is about as comprehensible to me as particle physics. The gambling genes definitely aren't mine, they're Mim's.'

She freely agreed. 'Straight down the maternal line. All the best things get passed down that way. Like male pattern baldness.'

Stage whisper, from Arthur, 'Her mother taught her how to play Texas Hold 'Em when she was six.'

'That's the tradition, mother to daughter.' Mim fanned her cards like a pro, fingers closed on that shell-tight arrangement.

'If it's a female trait, well,' Freddy answered for the men, 'it definitely skipped the Birneys.'

'What about my mother's quilt store?' objected Lillian.

'Sure, it came damn close to bankrupting your family, didn't it. The business gene skipped Hildy too, as far as I remember. It must be recessive in your family.'

Mim expected Lillian to come up with an answer, to punch back, and when she didn't Mim calmly testified, 'That's not the Hildy Foy I used to know, Fred. She never took a vow of poverty or went around shouting property is crime. That girl always had some action plan up her sleeve. Remember one summer? She was going to buy land in Nova Scotia and build a log cabin to live in. Hildy, Dexter, Phil Fahey and Jessica Buckman. What was it? They wanted to buy Army surplus Jeeps, paint them psychedelic and sell them off.'

'That's right,' Arthur teased Freddy, warmly. 'I don't know what you're talking about. Your girl had vision. I had to pay Wharton thousands of dollars for Dexter to learn about niche markets.'

Lillian gazed hundreds of miles north. 'Nova Scotia. She had everything plotted out. She got pamphlets from the travel agent.' A blink, a shake of her head to clear the distraction. 'I wasn't going to tell her to quit being unrealistic.'

'What's unrealistic anyway?' Mim asked generally.

'That time,' Lillian recalled, 'there was a problem with raising enough money to pay for the Jeeps.'

'But it was easy for her to make black market money when she wanted it.' Which was where and how Freddy wanted the conversation to finish. 'Are we playing gin? Arthur's draw, I think.'

Lillian said, 'It wasn't the money. It wasn't the drugs, the pot or whatever she was selling then. It was all one thing. Her gutsiness. That's right,' she said, against Freddy's shutting eyes. 'All she wanted to know was how the rules got to be the rules. She had a very strong sense of honor about herself, that's what it was.'

Freddy's reply was, 'You don't have to defend her anymore.'

The four friends could hear the weather battering at the sides of the house. As a wing of rain shaved the kitchen window Mim said, 'Something in them is you. That sounds dumb to say. But there's something else – it was there in Jim and Dex, some mood underneath you can't really identify. A part they bring with them.' She turned her head, her sculptural jawline, exploring the thought. 'Hildy was as fearless as an astronaut.'

All the magic had gone out of gin-rummy for Lillian. Holding onto eleven cards she drove Freddy quietly insane by taking a hundred years to discard the extra one. Instead, she went on, 'Even with all the antagonism Hildy still wanted us to approve of her. Her whole fight was getting us to see every kooky thing she did from her point of view. Sometimes I got in there,' giving Mim a puzzled smile that said, But as for the impossible times . . .

Mim said, 'Take it as a compliment. It was her kind of respect, giving you credit for being able to see all the way down to her real motives. The morality of whatever it was, that's the part that mattered to her.'

The talk finally uprooted Freddy. 'If nobody wants to play gin let's fold this hand. Let's fold the game, all right?' He spilled his cards face up on the table.

Cutting through the strain Arthur leaned over the side of his chair for a look into the box on the floor by Freddy's feet. 'I recognize those bouquets. Do I?' He angled an unsure glance up at Lillian.

'What else could they be this time of year?' she said. 'I've loved that story since I was a baby. All the sadness of it.'

'Only you, my dear, would fall head over heels for the sadness.' Freddy didn't mean to sting her with his little laugh. 'Why *is* that?'

'It's so sad it's beautiful.'

He shifted in his chair. 'It's a waste of emotion, isn't it. Save your pity for actual tragedies. The kind you see stretchered into the hospital day after day.'

'When I think about it I'm amazed I've got any feeling left in me when I get home, but I do.' Then Lillian found her voice. It was sharper than she'd thought it would be. 'So what if the Immortelle story makes me feel something. And so what if it isn't exactly true, plenty of things like it have happened. *Do* happen. The spirit of her story is true. That's what touches people, Freddy.'

'I missed out on so much in Reindeer, Arizona,' Mim said. 'Arthur, you told me it was a little boy who got murdered.'

'In the Hadleigh version,' he told her. 'Where I grew up it was a stable boy who ran away from his sadistic master. The old guy caught him, broke his neck and dumped his body down a well. In colonial days.'

'Oh no. In Lawford,' said Lillian, 'we heard it was a little girl. Six or seven years old. Killed by a foreigner out on the Hadleigh road in the 1800s.'

'There were newspapers.' An academic point Freddy needed to make. 'They had broadsheets in colonial times. And the *Intelligencer* has been going for a hundred and fifty years. All this time and nobody's bothered to dig into it? Come *on*.'

'Did those stories make the news?' Arthur wondered. 'Probably went around town as a rumor. Like the vanishing hitch-hiker.'

Freddy jumped on the example. 'Exactly! Mortal fear plus loneliness – *boom* – that's what you get. Forget colonial days! *Cave men*, I'll bet, calmed each other down with stories that explained everything they couldn't understand. And who doesn't mind being told, daily evidence to the contrary, that there's, say, justice in the world or life after death? People want to *believe*. Or sometimes *not* believe, if the facts are too ugly. So the Immortelle story starts out as some terrible tragedy, somebody's son or daughter gets murdered, and then what? Secondhand it's a mystery, thirdhand it's a rumor and before you can say boo it mushrooms out into supernatural hokum. Oh no, this one isn't a sad demented crime like hundreds of other ones, which by the way tell you something you don't want to hear about how things are. Random and meaningless, our out-of-control world! So what do we tell ourselves? A story about revenge from the spirit realm. We get a twisted kind of comfort from that idea. How can you accept the murder of a helpless child? It's practically impossible, beyond our powers. And so, look: here's one who got strangled by a maniac but she isn't helpless. She isn't *dead* dead, either. She comes back once a year. We want her to, for us, for *our* sakes.'

'It isn't out of insecurity,' Lillian replied, excluding Mim and Arthur. 'She's reminding us what's inside besides flesh, blood and bones. The strength of that little girl's soul! Can you imagine it! Her life got ripped away but she wouldn't let go of it, she just won't let herself be lost and forgotten.'

'Wait, hold on.'

'I'm talking about the grip of her spirit, Freddy. A soul that can reach through—'

'Wait a minute. You think souls are separate things, separate from us, like this pitcher,' which he nudged with his index finger. Eyebrows lifted to ask permission first, he tilted another vodka gimlet into Mim's glass. 'What's the Immortelle's career total? She came back and killed the Frenchie who killed her. Fine. What about the other hundred and sixty or seventy? One a year, she mows them down. For a little girl she's got a hell of a taste for vengeance.'

'She's not vengeful,' Lillian said. 'Father Agnetti used to tell us she's attracted to suffering souls.'

Freddy rolled his eyes in a slapstick appeal to Arthur, who was no help at all. Like a large white-crested bird Arthur watched the struggle from above and only swooped down to say, 'Socrates proved the immortality of the soul, didn't he.'

'On the same night he swallowed poison, if I remember the story,' Freddy added. 'When he was under a little last-minute pressure.'

Lillian glowered at him. 'Freddy's got the same explanation for every spiritual thought or holy vision. It's all wishful thinking. Anything out-of-this-world—'

He intercepted that line of talk. 'Dead is dead. Your brain stops thinking and your body stops feeling. If your life was miserable then your misery stops. Pleasure, holiness, selfishness, stupidity, kindness to dumb animals – it's finished. Gone is gone. The rest of the population keeps rolling without you. It's natural. Humanly necessary.'

'If dead is dead, what did I see upstairs?'

'Oh, Lillian.' Freddy's spread hands did his pleading. *Don't*, they said.

Mim asked her, 'What did you see?'

'Drop it, please, Lil,' Freddy said.

But she dared him, 'Explain my wedding shoes. How did they get there? And your hairbrushes.'

'I never saw my hairbrushes anywhere. You told me you found them on the floor.' To Arthur, his ally, he said, 'She forgot she left her shoes outside the bedroom. In the middle of the night though, in the middle of a dream you wake up and remember. It can blur. Whatever you've got on your mind blurs – am I right?—into one nonsensical idea.'

'No. It was the boy, the dead boy.'

'You saw a ghost here?' Mim tugged Lillian's sleeve. 'In your bedroom? Don't *lie!*'

'What an *amazing* thing. Did you try to communicate with him?' Imagining the weird meeting excited Arthur's honest attention. Freddy had to glance away at the ceiling, jaw clamped, to keep from saying to him, You don't believe ghosts are real things – not you! 'My sister saw one when she was at Wellesley,' Arthur chipped in. 'Audrey was up late one night studying by herself in the French House kitchen. She looked behind her and there it was. An old woman sitting in a chair by the door, reading the funnies. She ignored everything Audrey said to her so Aud went back to her Balzac. Two seconds later she looked around again and the chair was empty.'

'Where were the saner voices and cooler heads?' Freddy begged him on behalf of the last living reasoning member of the human race. 'Ask yourself why the first thought in her mind was, "Holy hell – a ghost!" All alone in the dead quiet, with God knows what else she was thinking about or reading right then that might have been agitating her, you can see how it happens.'

'It didn't frighten her at the time, that's what frightened her. Audrey asked around, described the old woman to everybody but nobody had seen her before. Anyway, a few days later she found a snapshot of her in an old French House scrapbook.' Arthur chewed an ice cube from his drink and said thickly, 'She was the cook there in the Thirties. *That* scared Audrey for real.'

It had taken this long for Lillian to puzzle out an answer to Arthur's question. She said to him, 'I don't know how to describe it, but we communicated – something, somehow. It was like being inside a cloud together, an emotional cloud, and while I was in it I could feel whatever he was feeling.'

'What do you remember? What did it feel like?' Mim asked her.

'Helpless. Beyond help. Confused. Torn away, cut off from his life. He can't make any sense of what's going on, it's all pouring in on him. Hurting him.'

'Physical? You were in pain?'

'No, he was. I knew he was, I could feel him feeling it. And I felt him crying out. To *me*. He knew things about me, that's how it felt, both of us were alone and he wanted to come to me . . .'

Freddy didn't sit still to hear the reprise. From the kitchen where he kept himself busy mixing a new pitcher of drinks, he followed the rise and fall of her inflections; he knew when she was telling the Cuddys about the strange boy's first visit, then his appearances in their bedroom. In our bedroom, *ours* for godsake. Someone extra in it now – who, in spite of being dead, is more of a presence in it than I am! Tonight Freddy's nose was rubbed in the stuff that proved how meager his influence was in this household. As if in the last fourteen years he'd had the power to command or prevent anything much under his own roof.

Arthur needed to call Freddy's name twice before he got any response. Then he prodded him, 'Did you see him? This boy?'

'No,' Freddy told everybody. 'Definitely, I did not. There wasn't anything in the room to see.'

Mim wasn't surprised. 'No, well. You've got to be sensitive to see ghosts.'

'I slept through it.' There was more than self-certainty in his reply, there was pride. 'Both times.'

Aside, to Mim, Lillian said, 'You know, I've been reading about that.' She jumped out of her chair with a sudden spurt of energy, more than she'd had all evening, and left the room.

Freddy knew what she'd gone after. For half the morning and most of the afternoon Lillian didn't budge from the living room sofa where she sat reading those library books. The power of the supernatural! You bet, over his wife! He doubled back through the kitchen and switched on the dishwasher; its shivering growl covered his exit. Out of the Cuddys' view and hearing Freddy blocked Lillian's way. In a tense whisper he accused her of breaking her promise. 'They'll misinterpret the whole thing. Can I tell you how it looks? Like you're putting your anxieties on display. They won't understand.'

'What won't they understand?' The question challenged him and for a second or two shut him up. 'I don't know if *I* understand what's going on. Do you?'

Freddy stayed pessimistic. 'I do, yes, I think so.'

'In case you haven't noticed, Mim and Arthur are intelligent people. They're our friends. And I'd like to hear somebody else's opinion, if that doesn't break any rules.' The look she gave him, accusing, wronged, unappeasable, Freddy had not provoked in her for many years.

'Can't it wait? Talk to Mim tomorrow. Just don't drag it out in front of Arthur.' As much with an appeal to common sense as with his two hands he tried to pry the books away from Lillian. 'You know what he'll turn it into. The king of gossip.'

'Such a trial being married to me. I should apologize to them. It's a crying shame you're married to a wife like me.' A frown, an unafraid shake of her head. 'This isn't about you. They don't *care*.'

She was back with the Cuddys ahead of Freddy who made his entrance from the kitchen, wiping his hands with a dishtowel. Arthur blurted, 'We could get your ghost on the front page of the *Intelligencer*, I'll bet.'

'Don't you dare.' An order from Freddy, not a joke, which he fixed with a hard little smile. 'No, Arthur. It wouldn't do a lot for our property value.'

'I think you're wrong there,' Arthur said before he was distracted by the copy of *Psychic Investigation: A Guide to Principle and Practice*.

'Listen. She's so clear on this.' Lillian read from Sonnenfeld's autobiography in a voice of sturdy conviction, standing in for the author. "'My first attempt at a hypothesis led me back (irrelevantly, from a scientific point of view) to the borders of religion. Do you begin with the assumption that ghosts are the separated souls of people who once lived, personalities liberated from the body by death who travel between the material and non-material worlds? This was the starting point for my predecessors in parapsychology a hundred years ago. The idea is not obsolete. One theory to come out of this early line of thought suggested that emotional sensitivity, intense empathy, might act as a pathway connecting us to a region of existence beyond our own. In this view the content of human feelings associated with trauma or merely the catastrophe of dying must be especially powerful . . .'" Was there a number Lillian could put to the crowd of lives and deaths she'd nursed in her time at St Mount's? How many beds multiplied by how many days in twenty-two years? Many hundreds up to today's, she thought, and today's drills into her deepest of them all. Or was she opened up the same way each time? "'Departed spirits then, and sometimes those of the living, come through to us psychosomatically,'" she read on, less firmly, tripping over the last word. "'They reach us from the inside out, touching our psyches first. It would be the brain, in this case, which in turn produces sensations, just as a film projector throws pictures onto a screen . . .'"

'I can follow that,' Mim nodded, letting the idea settle in her mind, neither accepting nor rejecting it yet.

A faint quivering attacked Lillian's cheek. As Freddy watched, her face seemed to shrink into itself; suddenly it was so small. She brushed her forehead with the edge of her long hand. 'Got a headache. Sorry.'

'From the morbid atmosphere,' Freddy kindly explained to her.

On her feet, Mim asked him, 'Aspirin in the bathroom?'

Lillian waved off her stupid pain, an apology for hogging the spotlight. 'I can cope.' But they all noticed a change in her humor. When she spoke she sounded dazed. 'He came *here*. He came to *me*. Why would he?'

'Maybe he was a patient of yours once.' Mim's idea.

'But what was in this creature's mind,' asked Arthur, 'why did he decide to come out of the woodwork so close to Immortelle night? That's where the investigation ought to start.' It's possible Arthur was clowning, or sweetly considering Lillian's certainty, but the tricky seriousness in his bare, geisha-white face put Freddy on guard.

He insisted, 'Don't call it a creature, Arthur.'

'Let's say it was—' Arthur fished for a reasonable description, 'a vision. Lillian can tell the difference between a hallucination and a vision – can't you, Lil? As a professional?'

She said, 'I saw a boy in my bedroom.'

'Obviously there's a reason,' Mim supported her. 'Yours or his.'

'Obviously this conversation has become totally inane.' Freddy's tolerance snapped. Chin tucked in, doubled, he said to Lillian, 'You don't sleep so well at night.'

'Because of what I saw.'

'And this doesn't help.' Freddy waved Sonnenfeld's book at her. 'It supplies all the nutty reasons you need to believe in ghosts and angels; and why not devils too, while you're at it. It's playing around with your fear, working on it.'

'Ghosts don't frighten me,' she said.

'Human fear, I'm talking about. Fear we're nothing after we're gone. Which is much scarier than the idea that we weren't any-thing before we were born. This is it,' Freddy gestured at the air, where the flowing, physical, unrecoverable moments had escaped. 'This is all.'

Lillian reached over and took charge of her copy of *Psychic Investigation*. 'It's not neat and tidy. That's what rankles you. I'm not saying I know what it is. I don't know and neither do you. You slept through it.'

Protectively, Mim rested her hand on Lillian's back.

'Should have called off tonight.' It was the right thing to say, the correct feeling to have, except Freddy didn't feel it.

Half to herself, Lillian said, 'It's been a terrible day.'

'What was it, honey?' Mim asked, leaning down.

'Does every family find its own way to self-destruct?' The dreaminess was not Lillian's usual style. 'You can't put a fence around every danger in the world. Children get sick, they're reckless. But you don't *add* to the danger. It's the most normal desire, you keep them safe. That's in the blood, buzzing around the blood as fierce as the itch to have them in the first place.' Directly to Freddy, 'That's all the Immortelle story is about. It's saying – don't forget it, life is sacred.' Then, to them all, 'Isn't it just like a fable? You tell them to put their shoes on and get out there, but you hate it when they go because it's the beginning of the time when you're a lot less use to them. And they know it before you do.'

The men mumbled agreement and let her talk.

'A baby boy came into Emergency this morning. We heard about it at lunchtime. News like that doesn't sit still. He was three months old.' Lillian couldn't control the quivering in her cheek; a shudder spread to her underlip, and her face colored. 'His mother's boyfriend killed him. I knew her, the mother. She was in overnight a week ago. Crying for help, shrieking. Scared out of her skin, you know, we had to strap her down. So much life in her that she wanted to kill. Turns out Greggie had a child at home,' a bitter tightness in the lips, 'and now she's got one in the St Mount's morgue. Before I stopped at the chapel tonight I went down to see him. I needed to look at him, Greggie's dead

122

baby. And touch him. Then I knew, I mean *I knew* what he was: the left-overs spat out by something really and truly wicked.' Lillian had dammed back her tears at the hospital, even in the chapel as she pit her prayers against this obscene tragedy and tears boiled behind her eyes, not one drop shook free. But she cried out her despair now, in the face of tonight's homey pleasures, Freddy's arrangements, the company of friends. 'Such a small life, you know? Just turned into a *thing*, a dead blot lying there. Greggie told me her fella couldn't get the baby to stop crying. Three months old and he was "undisciplined", that's what Greggie said. She said, "Like her mother." The *force* he used on her, my God! What a he-man, who can murder, who has the power to finish off a life he doesn't like. Well, he was crying for milk or because he was dirty, he wouldn't stop and wouldn't say what he wanted, so that man picked him up by his ankles and swung him smack into the wall. Crushed his skull, cracked it into three pieces.' A sourness bloomed in Lillian's throat, and a spreading heat in her own smarting head.

It was Freddy who spoke first. 'The police pulled him in, I hope. He's in custody?'

'He'll plead temporary insanity. Ten seconds of insanity, a mosquito bite. Not guilty!' was Arthur's verdict. 'You know, Lillian, you might be taking care of him in your ward at St Mount's six months from now.'

Mim stretched her arm across Lillian's shoulders. 'Come with me, okay? Let's go into the bathroom for a minute.'

'Sorry,' Lillian was shedding apologies again, 'no, look. I'm all right now. Broke the party up, didn't I. What a mess.' She limply wagged her unoccupied hands, then put them to work sweeping up the scatter of cards, rebuilding the deck.

With no more than a confidential narrowing of the eyes and minute tilt of the head Mim pried Lillian loose. Freddy watched them go upstairs, Lillian being led away like a lame animal.

'Lean your head for me. No – forward.' Mim made use of the strong even light reflecting from the bathroom mirror. A fingertip search first, then gentle touches with the folded corner of a tissue at the beads of blood, dark condensation, blood as dew on Lillian's scalp. The crest of her hair was wet with it.

'What is it?' From that angle Lillian's face was reflected back to her, behind the webby curtain of her disarranged hair-do, its bones coming to the surface, its skin clay-pale, exhausted, mortal. Her nerves had stopped singing; Mim, fussing over her, held her in the tenderest bond. A bond with Greggie's baby (his head no bigger than a softball, sutured the same way), with the nameless spectral boy, with Hildy, with bewildered Freddy, with the living, the swept away, all of them. A human soul arrives mature and complete, it makes a claim on life, on earth, among people, and once it's attached here, to us, it is attached forever.

Mim showed her the stained tissue and said, 'I can't see where the cut is. Does it hurt anyplace?'

'My head aches.'

'I think it's stopped bleeding.' A finger-width at a time, combing the damp hairs apart, Mim uncovered a trail in the undergrowth. Three crooked ridges where blood had wept through the pores. One thick seam from the back of Lillian's head to the crown, where it forked and sent two branches to her forehead. 'Jesus, Lillian.'

Guided by Mim, Lillian touched one of the vein-shaped phantom fractures. In the room below she heard Arthur and Freddy talking, short phrases back and forth that reached her almost as vibrations in her bones. *No, never a self-centered person . . . Depressing work . . . It would depress me . . . Maybe a little heavy-hearted . . .*

Certainly Lillian's description of the dead infant was in Mim's mind, but she made a less direct, less mystical connection between its wounds and Lillian's. Her talent, *her* sensitivity kept Mim in contact with things as they are, here, on the mundane surface of the planet. Thinking such injuries might be caused by someone's fingernails being scraped across the skin, she said, 'Honey, did Freddy do this?'

'Do? How?' The question, the striking seriousness of it, pumped a laugh out of Lillian.

'I know,' Mim said, shaking off the idea right along with her. 'I can't imagine it, really. But weird stuff happens. You know it better than anyone. Who's immune?' Her voice dropped to a whisper, husky with care. 'You'd tell me if he did anything funny.'

'Arthur's probably asking him the same thing about me.' She leaned her head back into Mim's hands. 'I'd tell you.'

'You know you can come to us. For any reason at all.'

Lillian smoothed the sides of her hair. She was aware – the way we're aware of hunger or sexual longing – of some knowledge forming in her, something now unsealed. 'I know it with my heart, all of this is leading up to a change. The boy. The thoughts I've had lately about Hildy. There've been other things. Something out there is coming in. It's an overpowering feeling. Remember the last time anybody saw me in such a dizzy condition?'

'When Hildy left.'

'Freddy didn't know what to do with me then, either. It's too hard for him to see me needy. It unsettles everything he thinks is settled.'

While Mim was downstairs fixing her an ice pack, Lillian heard the three-way conversation, the huddle of voices grow quiet, selfconscious. She'd persuaded Mim not to tell Freddy about the blood; whatever ad-lib lie he was getting from her down there, Lillian could cover by blaming her cave-in on general exhaustion. When Mim came back with a bowl of ice water and a wetted cloth Lillian was lying on her bed.

Mim asked, 'Do you want me to stay with you?'

'Five minutes and I'll be down. I just want to rest my eyes.'

Chapter Thirteen

WHAT WOKE Lillian twenty minutes later in her darkened bedroom was the noise of the Cuddy's car starting, tires slipping in the muddy gravel and then driving off. Freddy was busy cleaning up the dining room and kitchen, rinsing the glasses, switching off the lights downstairs. When he finally came up to bed he stood at the door to check whether Lillian, still in her clothes, was asleep. He asked her if she wanted fresh ice for her cold compress.

'I'm all right. My headache's gone,' she said. 'I just want to go back to sleep.'

'You're tired out. Of course you are.' His simple card game plowed under by babble about the supernatural; the peaceful rhythm of chat, drinks and snacks broken by the cheering story of a mutilated baby; every heartfelt intention, any chance he had of helping Lillian recover her famous strength, sabotaged.

'Can you get me my nightie? It's hanging up in the bathroom.'

'It must have taken a lot out of you to completely wreck the evening. What did you think you were doing?'

Freddy's mood itself was an accusation. Like a rubber hammer on the side of her head, his words as he spoke them thumped into her and brought back her headache. She answered, 'I thought I was unwinding with my friends.'

'It would've been less embarrassing if you just danced on the table in your bra and panties. It was unfair', said Freddy, leaning over the bed in shadow, a slab of opinion about to flatten her, 'to spill out all that creepy talk. Communicating with a ghost in here, all the rest of it. You made them very uncomfortable.'

As if she'd blabbed a bedroom secret. 'I embarrassed you, that's what you're saying.'

'You frightened me.' He paused. 'Didn't you see them squirming?'

'No. You were the only one doing that. They took an interest, Freddy, a serious interest in the books I'm reading. They were trying to understand, same as me.'

'What they were trying to understand was *you*. There's a limit to things you can let loose on your friends. Or don't you think so anymore?'

'Mim and Arthur were engrossed.'

'They were doing what they could to make you feel better.'

'They did, they helped.'

Her criticism jabbed him. 'Isn't that what you've got to do at work sometimes? With the fragile ones. You go along with them a little, pretend the nonsense is real until they snap out of it and they can look at whatever the hell problem's in front of them without panicking.'

So that was the charge against her. 'I'm intact, you know. I'm not infected, I haven't picked up a dose of paranoid delusion from any of my patients. What I saw was real enough to take a hold of me, and pretending it *isn't* won't change anything.' It was their argument about

128

the Church, a repeat performance. 'The world goes on without you, and while you're asleep. Bees see in the ultraviolet, did you know that?'

'Are we going to have a sensible talk here?'

'I wasn't afraid to tell you about the boy I saw – the ghost, or *whatever* he is – but your first idea was, "Uh-oh, Lillian's going off the rails." Instead of thinking, "I've known this woman for thirty-five years and she isn't some hysterical creature who sees monsters in the dark." Why don't you trust me as much as I trust you?'

'Because all the time you're busy delving into the spirit realm and expecting your daughter to knock on the door, everything that really matters in your life, what's here in front of you,' laying his hands on his chest, embodying solid reality, 'all the unexciting things that prop up your life start to fade out.'

'I'll keep my secrets, then. I'll be dishonest with you. Is that what you want? I tell you – don't I? even though you hate it?—whenever I hear from Hildy. Should I stop? Should I insult you like that?'

He shook his head slowly, heavily. 'You were angry when she went. With her, I think, and with—' Freddy rolled his small eyes, taking in the cosmos, *'things*. Hildy wasn't here but I was. So you got angry with me. That was all right. Upside-down, but I didn't think it was completely crazy. When you came back home I knew it would be better for us – yes: without Hildy here. Because so much less of my time and energy was going to be spent keeping you two from hurting yourselves. Now it's starting all over again. I can't explain what you think you saw—' She propped herself up on her elbows and wanted to speak, but Freddy cut her off with pleading tenderness. 'What you *did* see. I know it wasn't a ghost because it would be a miracle if ghosts existed. That's a fact of life. And one more fact of life is that Hildy isn't coming home because *she doesn't want to*. Have you heard anything from her recently?'

'No.'

'No. No?'

'I said.'

'It's just that whenever she mails you a scrappy note or you get one of her crackpot phone calls, you walk around in a trance for days. You're hardly here at all. What comes out of it? More silence on her side and deeper disappointment on yours. It shreds you.' He held his body still; his movement toward her was in all that he had to say. 'I think this thing with your ghost boy is some kind of longing. Like in a dream. Doesn't a dream bring out your strongest fears or wishes or whatever? I'm not pretending to be any kind of psychological expert but isn't that the mental process?'

'I can see her, Freddy, so clear in my mind, talking to a little bunch of her friends, monopolizing the conversation, or eating a hamburger, walking to the market. All right, you can say she's only in my imagination but the fact is,' Lillian used his word, hit it hard, 'the fact is my daughter is alive somewhere. I can't do what you can. Time doesn't mean anything to me. Hildy is like me. We're connected, it's involuntary.'

'Tell me what possible difference it makes *what* Hildy's life is like. The product of God knows what kind of experience. You can't even say for sure why she calls you up. To ease your mind? To taunt you? Inside her head is a tropical jungle! How much does she ever tell you? Where she is, how she survives, or has she ever said she's sorry for torturing you year after year? It's an imaginary existence, Lillian, she might as well be orbiting Venus. She keeps you on the rack and every damn time she gets in touch she pumps up your insecurity. So it isn't hard for me to fence her out. She's a stranger now, a grown-up woman who's been out of this family almost as long as she was in it. You and I are here, we're still together here and we can have what we can have. Or is she going to deprive us of that?'

Some luminous moment had arrived. It had been on its way for –

how long?—its light surfacing across the soft bulges of Freddy's face. A climax of a kind. Since the last phone call from Hildy he felt the pressure wave riding the horizon and now the full force of the change it carried was on top of him.

Fighting back, he said, 'She lives with the consequences of her actions.'

'No – with the consequences of *yours*.'

'I didn't *wrong* her! When she went to live in that midden with Philip Fahey, in that shack, like a Welfare case, she humiliated herself. And us too, while she was at it. She had a choice and that's the way she went. Under-age or not. We agreed we couldn't put her under house arrest. You knew we'd accomplish nothing by dragging her back home, where she *did not* want to be. Good Christ, Lillian. The Academy boys knew about her.'

'What could they know?'

Freddy reclaimed his hard honesty, his virile pact with the said-and-done. He said, 'More than you did, my dear.'

That last terrible year had been marked by a lull in communication between Hildy and her mother. The frisky childhood years, it seemed, were a run-up to this, as if payment was due for the babbled confidences, to be taken out in silence and separation. Where Hildy could hammer out the shape of her life. (How do you carve a statue of an elephant? The elephant is in the stone. Cut away everything that doesn't look like an elephant.)

Freddy and Hildy waved white flags at each other. They visited, on her territory and terms, every couple of weeks. Lillian received reports from him, and nobly respected Hildy's rights and distance. She was sure the foundations were planted, the essential principles and cautions were in Hildy's kit: she wouldn't drug herself into a permanent stupor, she wouldn't settle for Chief Fahey's boobish son Philip, but come hell or high water she'd establish

131

who she was and how she'd live exclusively through the force of her character.

From what Lillian could piece together, Hildy had been pregnant for two months before Freddy was secretly informed of her condition by Philip's father. A quiet father-to-father talk in the Chief's office. Philip had gassed up his police surplus Harley Davidson and was last seen crossing the Canadian border with a female passenger (not Hildy) at Brattleboro. In a fury of concern, mixing blame and remedy, Freddy went to gather Hildy up; they fought; tears on both sides, she sent him home; Lillian was allowed in to hear from Hildy's mouth she wanted to keep the baby, and her voice jittered (with courage? not-yet courage?) when she said it. The way to give them both the best chance, Lillian argued, was for Hildy to move back home. A plan Hildy turned down flat, as a step backward into childhood. Strong tears on both sides, Lillian left her alone.

The next time she heard from Hildy it was from that roadside phone booth, the first of her strained, weird calls. In this one, at least, the purpose was clear. She told Lillian 'everybody's been spared', she'd miscarried. Lillian fought with Freddy until her throat was red-raw, but Hildy was still a minor and as her legal guardian he had to set the wheels of the law turning. Apparently, Hildy had been on the road for five days already. For the brief time when abiding would have brought her daughter back, Lillian couldn't stop the police from chasing her further away.

She said, 'Hildy was humiliated by you.'

'I don't know what to do with you. I'm being honest, Lillian,' and he looked pretty well baffled. The stupefied look that spread out from his stiffly widened eyes was a bluff, though. Underneath it was a sheet of dread, a nakedness, compromised agreement: she might be right. 'That's the truth, I'm at a loss.'

* * *

132

The etheric body, many researchers conclude, is electrical in nature, Freddy read. The vehicle of consciousness. The astral body appears post mortem. Ergo we must have his astral body running around upstairs. Or not running around. Did Lillian say the boy was tied down? The astral light exists between mind and matter, corresponding to Myers' metetherial. Visible. It can be moulded by thought. Ours. Lillian's. In the psychic world according to Dr Sonnenfeld an individual may project and inhabit an astral body which might not resemble that person's physical self. A forty-eight-year-old woman then, Frau Doktor – do I have this right?—might project a vision of herself as a young boy, tied hand and foot, suffering. Clothing and accessories are created ad hoc.

Study the problem from every angle. Freddy thumbed through the chapters of *Psychic Investigation: A Guide to Principle and Practice* and read randomly, with softening antagonism. *Problems with Evidence of Survival of Bodily Death, Fame and Cases of Hauntings, Anomalies of Imagery and Perception, Anomalies of Judgment and Belief, Anomalies of Recognition and Recall.* If the house is well insulated, timber, floor-boards, beams and stair-treads are prone to crack, areas close to any source of heat first and then at structural intervals across the room. Joints. Seams in the wood. The sounds can mimic a trail of footsteps. He sat in his unfinished basement den, his back against the sweating damp-beaded wall, surrounded by disorder, under a worklight, its aluminum housing hooked on a nail temporarily banged into a half-exposed upright beam in the groin of the room. He sat on the strewn floor, legs straight out, in his dark blue coveralls, elastic waistband puckered across his belly, a child with a charcoal mustache, Freddy in his playpen of plaster dust, wood shavings and mortar crumbs. On the other side of the square room, on his side of the archway, the boiler breathed, warmly huffing. From the storage room beyond he heard the flat clatter of rain falling on the storm doors. And that was all.

Streams flowing beneath buildings conduct sound. Lambert deduced it was a stream (engorged in 1885 by the River Chelt) rushing under the Despard property that caused the weird events there. The ghost seen by Rosina Despard arose in her imagination and her terrified reports of its appearance planted it in the imaginations of other 'witnesses'. The haunting ended in 1886, when the Dodeswell reservoirs were constructed at the headwaters of the Chelt, starving the stream to a trickle. There it is: balance. An engineering solution to the mystery. My approach.

Freddy thought, The tyranny of the invisible – anybody can claim anything exists in it! Is it a good thing or a bad one to have an imagination? The great scientists, architects and artists, where would we be without their imaginations? Without suspension bridges, rockets to the moon, polio vaccine, the Ninth Symphony, *The Bridge at Arles*. Without the H-bomb, phrenology, sex in advertising, heaven, hell, sin, witches and ghosts. The imagination of cranks and kooks, of false belief and disorganized thinking. How do you know when you're imagining the real and when the unreal? Engineering, of course! Tests. You've got to know which questions to ask. Hence, experts.

On a closer reading, Dr Marit Sonnenfeld seemed to be less strident than Lillian, and Freddy was having this silent dispute with her because he couldn't argue directly with his wife anymore. He compared his emotional withdrawal from her to retirement. From the ring, from the fray, from the industry. He started to eat his meals in the school cafeteria or at Giuliano's. He slept in the spare bedroom, which used to be Hildy's, down the hall from Lillian. To wash, he used the bathroom downstairs. Secluding himself from Lillian was a choice not an outcome, urged by his feel for balance; the same (and as powerful) as the choice he'd made to marry her. And yet the physical withdrawal felt overdue.

Nine years ago Freddy removed himself from her bed, to apply his passionate energies in other directions (you see, my dear? you agree?). Into his teaching, his home improvements, community campaigns, his local public life. If at home he had taken on the look and role of weekend janitor, that was all right with him – now it was a fulltime job. Here in the basement, in the middle of his renovation work, he came to think of himself more as the caretaker of a historic dwelling. Freddy and Lillian Foy's layer of history, theirs. In his igloo, amid the dirt and disorder and undone work, Freddy had plenty to accomplish. The swollen creek, brownly frothing and heaving over the rim of the culvert, had spread its reek into the old brickwork, which in patches was decayed to the texture of wet breadcrumbs. Through the powdering rot of the wall, through the small crags and peelings he probed the damage done to the innards of their house.

He slipped Sonnenfeld's book out of sight when Lillian surprised him by coming downstairs. He sat on it. (Frau Doktor had nothing to say about invisibility, about a man and a woman, say, alive at the same time, in the same place, who fade in front of each other's eyes, daily paler and paler. So the wife can see solid objects through the husband's shape.) She had not come down to talk to him, but spoke to Freddy as if he weren't actually there. 'I knew', she said in a drowsy trancelike voice, overtired or overcontrolled, 'this was leading up to something important. You just dismissed it. You belittled and ignored it. Well . . .'

A drop in temperature gelled the air as Freddy saw Lillian busily distracted by a task of her own. She tugged a suitcase from under a bundle of wool blankets. Her ancient college suitcase, heavy blue fabric, plastic-coated, slender bevelled pine ribs for support across the lid and back. Freddy said nothing, only watched her as she fished through the cardboard boxes labeled Hildy/Clothes, Hildy/Knick-knacks.

'But I was right,' Lillian said, folding a sweater into the gaping

135

suitcase. 'Hildy called me tonight. She'll be coming in tomorrow morning and she wants me to meet her at the bus station.'

'What are you doing, Lillian?'

'She asked me to bring a few of her things. Stuff she misses. She's been living in Oregon. That's where she's been for five and a half years. The Northwest. Betty wouldn't make it all the way across the country, so she's on the bus.'

'Betty?'

'Her little sports car. You know how Hildy is. She's got to personalize everything in the world.'

When she closed it the blue suitcase was about half full. The inventory didn't take her very long to assemble, the selections seemed to be random. Or were her hands *led* to each of Hildy's belongings without Lillian needing to look? The powder-blue high-school sweater with its navy and gold varsity letter (Hildy wore it against leopard skin print or black leather halter top to irritate Central's bouncy, clean-scrubbed cheerleaders). The thrift store cocktail dress, black chiffon and black sequins. The Basque beret spangled with bowling team badges: enamel, silver, gold plate, brass. The Mexican jacket, red with spidery black brocade in the shapes of cacti and sombreros. The waistcoat made out of a cheap tapestry, a cartoon of dogs shooting pool. The rosewood inlaid jewelry box – bar of quartz crystal wound with gold thread, fossil nautilus shell, string of agate beads, more enamel pins – just the flash of it before Lillian repacked it and in those swift seconds Freddy itemized every treasure the box contained.

All camouflage. He saw through to her real errand. To grab that roomy square suitcase, not for Hildy's belongings, but to pack her own. Freddy was watching Lillian go.

Like a third footstep it dragged and knocked against the lip of each upward stair as it swung from Lillian's two-handed grip. Freddy was an audience, exempt, *excluded*, from the action. Had the telephone really rung? Whether it had or hadn't, Lillian was now on her way somewhere. Causing the smallest disturbance she could. She didn't want him to talk her out of it. 'What should I tell the boy?' Freddy said out loud to the vacated basement, silence accumulating around him. To taunt, to insult, to curse, these things weren't in Lillian's make up. But the door she pulled shut sent down a swearword for her: *frack*. Which left Freddy alone with her choice, her withdrawal, her going, Lillian's going.

Chapter Fourteen

DISRUPTION IN her homelife was turning into disruption in the psychiatric unit. Possibly it was the other way around. But wherever the string of upheavals had its start, Lillian's thoughts this morning were flying in both directions. Covered or not, her jagged unscheduled absences were felt hardest in Molyneaux Wing by the in-patients. After she missed Bertha Orban's self-care evaluation, the old woman would not go into the shower-room with her, and accused Lillian of hiding her true identity; something that, very reasonably, Eva Braun would do. Douglas Cottle clammed up on her at breakfast when Lillian broke it to him that she wouldn't be around at lunchtime, even though she knew what an important day Tuesday was, the top of his cycle, when he was eating in the red end of the spectrum. Her stutter of attendance might also be leaving an even more serious impression on Dr Mollo. Last week Lillian sent Billy Cooke with her case notes to Rell Mayfield's discharge conference. Caring less for patients, more for herself – it could be interpreted that way, and worse: twenty-five years as a highly empathic, a gifted, psychiatric nurse, and now she was on the verge of burnout. In spite of all this Lillian stole one more daylight hour for her own sake. If it was a measure of her state of mind then it told anybody with a heart she had her human priorities exactly right. She was going to see Hildy again.

On summer afternoons, with sunshine bleaching the air and scouring the sidewalk outside, the interior of the Tri-city bus terminal is locked in bitter polar twilight. Its half-enclosed atmosphere has a permanently dull tint, darkening toward shades of clay and charcoal at night and brightening to pale ash during the day. At the edge of winter, as it was now, the dense sky itself might have descended into the building, carried on the breath of an ice cap. Lillian swam into the slanting gray chill from the overheated, modernized ticket office, out of the hard metallic white splash of bare overhead fluorescent tubes, into the high-roofed concourse where a dozen silver buses shuddered, sighed in and groaned out.

As wide and long as a broad city block, the area paved for the temporary relaxation of raddled travelers was dotted and dashed with picnic tables; round ones, rectangular ones, heavily painted with flesh-color enamel. Here pedestrians flowed in and pooled in this sump before being piped away. Thronged with them, the strip of asphalt had the appearance of a dockside and brought to mind history-book photographs of European immigrants packed into customs halls, families clumped together like barnacles.

A pigeon flapped in low over Lillian's head. She felt the down-draft from its wings puff against her hair. She touched the shuffled strands, felt their thinness. Do I look so much older? Too hopeful? Unprepared? Drymouthed she walked along the row of tables where Hildy told her she'd be waiting, approaching each one with the feeling she was about to be given some important news.

A large man in a dark tweed coat, his acre of back rising slowly from his bench at the next table, squeezed himself free, arms held out, luggageless, in greeting or appeal. When he moved away Lillian saw the tumble of red hair, then the cheek, nose and chin of the young woman waiting there. A small boy, five or six years old, fidgeted next to her on the bench, plucking at the shoulder of her yellow rainslicker. The woman stood, glanced around with her immigrant's eyes. Held open that way they made her look like she didn't speak the language, deciphering what she could from the expressions on strangers' faces. Under her shiny coat she wore a Mexican blouse, embroidered parrots and maracas, and underneath that a black skirt that showed her bare strong unshaven legs. On her feet, hiking boots. On her head, a rose patterned scarf knotted under the chin babushka style and losing its hold on the sheaf of red hair. Dyed, iodine red. Mexico by way of Murmansk. She was raw knuckled, Lillian saw, used to doing her own carrying. A backpack, bulky enough for an expedition up Everest, was propped against the table.

'Hildy?'

She turned. The wide face, the pink-tinged skin and, God in heaven, the unstoppable sea-blue eyes. She didn't speak to Lillian but to her little boy, pivoting him gently by his shy reluctant shoulders. 'Ezra,' she said, 'say hello to your grandmom.'

'Hello, Ezra.' Lillian waited for permission to move any closer. Holding herself back was a feat of strength, her whole body shuddered with an ache to touch him, to complete the connection, and then this peace would be real. Hildy's small boy in the cavernous world – her grandson. 'That's a fine old name.'

'Ez's a fine old soul.' Hildy said to him, 'Aren't you, Nat King Cole.'

'I'm *not* Nat King Cole. I just *like* him.' Bolder now, Ezra came out with, 'You're my *other* grandma.'

'That's right, sweetheart. I guess I must be.'

For a minute – longer than that – the two women held each other. Lillian's hand slipped down to find Ezra's head and she brought him into the huddle. They let go, this threesome, when the boy's muffled voice broke in on them. 'I can't breathe.'

It was her own life Lillian was entering again, *allowed* to enter (she felt this as soon as they sat down, facing each other across the public picnic table), and to re-occupy the place of her eviction. From this place Lillian asked her, 'Is Ezra's father here too?'

'Oh,' as if Hildy needed to concentrate on her answer, 'no.' And combing Ezra's thick hair (darker, the red of redwood) with her tapered pink fingers, she said, 'We had some troubles with him. They're all over now, right Ez?'

'You and me,' singsonged Ezra, rehearsed each bedtime, 'wild and free.'

'Orville and Wilbur. Two Wrights make an airplane.'

It all had the unanchored, free-form obscurity of her phone calls and postcards. Hildy's deeper message was unchanged. I'm in control of this – my information, your questions – it will be what I permit. Their visit had limits too, rules which Lillian had to pick up as they went along. Aside from any issue of secret knowledge there was a purpose coming through Hildy's angled posture, her bursts of attention: she didn't have time to waste.

'Ez told me a real funny thing yesterday. Tell Grandma Foy what you said last night.'

He gave her a puzzled squint. 'When?'

'When the lady's radio was on. The mariachi music.'

For the big money, he remembered. 'I saw confetti!'

'He saw colors?'

'He gets it from us, Ma. Has it stronger than I do.'

Lillian said to him, 'I see confetti sometimes too. And ribbons and

141

all kinds of shapes and colors when I hear music.' Shy again, overtired, Ezra retreated, burying his face in his mother's lap. 'The strangest things have been going on at home. Such strange events.'

Hildy caught Lillian's anxiousness. 'Between the two of you?'

'No, honey. Freddy's like always. Getting a little cranky, that's all. A little more closed off.'

'That doesn't sound very strange to me.'

'Maybe I'm exaggerating it. See, I knew you were coming home. He thought it was something I just wanted to believe. Freddy's way of dealing with it all was different. He didn't think we'd ever see you again.'

'I'm sure that's what he wanted to believe.'

'Because he didn't want me to be let down,' Lillian said mildly. She fought against saying too much, as if feeding a small wild animal from her hand; an abrupt move, any excitement, could scare Hildy back into the forest. 'There's so much I've got to tell you.'

'Tell me,' Hildy said, tilting her head half an inch to see the clock behind Lillian. 'I want to hear.'

'Would you believe me if I told you we've got a ghost in the house? Honest to God, I've seen him. Three times.'

'Ma, seriously?' A fresh burst of attention. 'I used to think I wasn't alone there when you and Dad went out. But I never *saw* anything. You saw it, Ma?'

'A boy, a little boy.' She whispered it, not wanting to frighten Ezra, who was listening to the conversation now. 'And one of my residents at St Mount's, he had a dream about a boy just like him at the same time. He knows our house, I mean, Perry worked in it when it was Hoagland's garage. What do you think that adds up to?' Was this a safe subject? Lillian heard herself speaking too fast, unchecked, without thinking. She ached to ask her why she had stayed away all this time, but for some reason was about to tell Hildy how much Marit

142

Sonnenfeld reminded her of her own fearless, curious daughter. Her mental flow was seizing up. Lillian felt incompetent, suddenly clumsy. Not knowing where to start, now she didn't know where or how or whether to stop, and went on just trying to keep Hildy in focus. 'Mim and Arthur think I should dig into it. They're good friends, the Cuddys, we're still close. Dexter's gone into investments. Making a big noise in New York. Remember Dexter Cuddy?'

With much gentleness Hildy said, 'I don't care about Dexter Cuddy. We don't have a lot of time to be together. I've got to make my connection soon. I wanted you to know Ezra and Ezra to know you. I needed to talk to you, Ma. To say some things before I leave.'

A decision had been made for Lillian and she wouldn't struggle against it. Better accept what Hildy was offering. This felt familiar. This old routine. It was Hildy in the flesh, all right, holding forth and holding out at the same time. Pay attention, life is about to be compressed, sped up. The moment took on the quality of a dream rushing past her. 'I brought your things. Found them all.'

'You're a peach.'

Ezra popped his head up. 'Grandma Foy's peach color and Grandma Ellis is cloud color.'

'Is she?' Lillian's hungry glance went to Hildy.

The daughter held her mother's hand. 'I wanted to say . . . I want to say I'm sorry. I know it's not enough. I'm sorry for that, too. I meant to come home. After a couple of weeks. But it just never worked out to be the right time. A different life started happening. It made new claims on me, basic ones I paid off or dodged or whatever, but I was making my whole life from scratch. Away from here I could do that. It got easier.'

'Hildy—'

'No, wait. I did think about you. Especially after I had Ez.'

'Why didn't you tell us you had a son? A husband?'

'Eric and I never got married. And, oh,' she had trouble condensing the whole soap opera into a plain explanation, 'after Ezra was born I went a little . . . I don't know, Ma. My hormones, my strength went. Up here, too.' Hildy tapped the side of her head. 'Eric didn't help. It's all okay now. He sends money. What is it with the men we choose?'

Avoiding any answer, Lillian opened her purse and took out an envelope and placed it in front of Hildy. 'It isn't a lot.'

Hildy said, 'If it's from Dad, I don't want it.'

'It's from Grandma Birney. Your inheritance. She died in '81.'

Hildy counted the money, eleven one hundred dollar bills. 'We can use this.'

'You and Freddy.' Lillian buckled a little, and didn't care if she was straying out of bounds. 'The two of you lock me in a vise.' She rubbed her eyes, and with fresh energy she said, 'We never wanted you to be a different person. We knew how you'd turn out, as long as we could see you coping with your choices. While we knew where you were.'

'*You* never wanted. *You* knew I wasn't extreme or destructive. That was never Dad's attitude.' Then she captured Lillian with a blunt surprise. 'It started with him, that's what I've been waiting for you to understand. Dad and I only agreed on one thing – neither of us wanted to break you up.'

'Break us up? Break me – how?'

'Ma, you and I did too much for him. You still do, don't you?'

'It's a question that . . . it doesn't mean anything to me.' Lillian was aware of the gathering and parting crowds in the station, the straining force of the bus engines. Her composure was disintegrating.

'You've got to concentrate on yourself, Ma, separate from him. I hear you in the way I talk. It was how I kept you with me.' It had the sound of a plea. 'It's an accident who you're born to, but I don't think it's accidental that you're born. Didn't Grandma Birney think that? Don't you?'

144

All of the important answers were still fogged, any chance of clarity was slipping away. No, Hildy refused to help her understand. All Lillian felt was a slight sucking emptiness in her stomach, the sensation of dropping through the gray air. 'Come home,' she said. 'Can't you catch the same connections tomorrow?'

'Ezra and I are going to England. Buses, planes, trains and boats. Complicated arrangements.'

So now Lillian had to live with this. Hildy leaving again, to put an ocean between them. 'When you ran away I called your name up the chimney. Four or five times a day for, oh, weeks. Shouted it up there, into my megaphone, for you to hear me wherever you were.' She was falling back now, into absurdity. 'Freddy caught me at it. Thought I was off my rocker.'

Impatience seized her, and Hildy said, 'I never let Ezra's father load any demands on me. Not the way Dad always did with you. I can see it. He hasn't changed. Nothing has. You have the heart and he has all the ideas. The decisions always go his way.'

'He wanted us to move out of the house.'

'If it's not what you want, you don't have to allow it.'

'I told him no, I wasn't going. And he dropped the whole thing.'

'So that was all? It just ended there?'

Lillian wanted to correct the record and say, No, it – something – started there, a churning motion. But she was after specific truth from Hildy, so specific truth was what she gave her. 'I've been having a rough time with him. He's sleeping in your room. We aren't talking very much.'

'I *made* Eric talk to me, I forced my way in. He didn't even know what he wanted himself until I got him talking. Saying the words. It was uncomplicated, leaving after that.'

'I'm married to Freddy. What do you want me to do? Should I go and live with Mim and Arthur?'

145

'No, Ma. What I want is for him to trust you with his faults and secret feelings as much as you trust him with yours. Pry him *open*.'

'My darling, you don't really know what a white knight Freddy's been to me.'

'Right, uh-huh. His one unselfish act. Marrying you. I think the other side of a white knight is a common ordinary bully.'

'That's not Freddy.'

'What did he tell you – what did he say when he found out I was pregnant?'

Lillian recalled for her, 'He was sick when he heard. Sick at heart. Full of worry, of course. Out of love, you can't deny that.'

'No, he bombed me with love, for sure. He called it love and used it to bully me. You know what he said to *me*, first thing? He said, "I feel emasculated." Then, for two weeks he was coming over every day, twice a day. Trying to brainwash me.'

Groggily, Ezra asked, 'What's brainwash?'

'It's repeating and repeating things to somebody,' Hildy taught him, looking directly at Lillian. 'If you don't think like they do and they want you to think what they think, they keep on hammering at you until you're weak and tired. By then you'd do anything to stop them from saying those ugly things to you. You hate the sound of their voice.'

'Oh,' from Ezra.

'Freddy said what things?' Lillian asked her.

Ezra was awake, alert. 'Can't you put your fingers in your ears?'

'Ez, can you go over to that Coke machine and get us a drink?' Hildy doled out the coins and let him march off.

'He shouldn't go all the way over by himself,' Lillian said, suddenly made tense.

'Ma, it's twenty feet. He's a very independent kid.'

'But the crowds of people. Everybody's bigger than he is.'

'He's smart. He bites.' Then, 'Didn't Dad ever tell you how he was helping me cope with my little problem before I left?'

'He didn't think you'd run away from us.'

'He hurt me, Ma. And he hurt you. You don't even know how. He owes you an explanation – he does, not me. For the sake of his conscience, at least, if he doesn't think he owes you anything. Maybe he should break the habit of a lifetime and have a heart-to-heart talk with Father Agnetti.'

'Oh, we've got a new priest now. Father Howdy Doody.'

'Then let him do it without help. Unless he can't make the jump.' Ezra came back, tightrope walking, balancing three red cans. Hildy hugged him. 'Maybe you have to be a mother to understand. What if I didn't just run away? What if I'd been killed in an accident?'

Help me, Lillian thought. She is my daughter. Why did she come back here – to stir up the mud? to tear me loose? My head aches. Let her tell me. She understands what I need from her. Hildy, the same Hildy. She saw her daughter's eyes lift, her mouth open, about to speak, but her face froze instead. Lillian swiveled around to see whatever it was that had arrested Hildy, asking, 'Is it time already?'

She saw Freddy on the other side of the station, keeping his distance, in his moss-brown car coat, clutching his gloves. Was the calculating approach of a bully in his walk? A bully's sarcasm in his reined-in smile? No. It satisfied Lillian to have him with her; her calm face guided him, invited Freddy to join them.

'Freddy, meet your grandson, Ezra.'

'I'm glad I found you,' he said, sighing relief. 'You don't want to go anywhere, Lil. Come on now, this is totally crazy.'

Something was crazy. Lillian turned around to the shock of sitting there alone. Freakish empty space where Hildy and Ezra had been. She got up from the table before Freddy reached her and fled, pushing against the cattle-slow crowd. The Boston bus was in one direction, the New York bus in the other – if Hildy were on her way to England wouldn't she head for an international airport? Kennedy or Logan. Lillian called Hildy's name, her eyes raked the bobbing faces, expected to see the color of Hildy's hair, a flash of her yellow rainslicker in the shuffling jostle. But, no – not a trace of her. Vanished into a parallel dimension. Or hiding in the restroom. Or already aboard her bus.

Freddy couldn't follow Lillian into the women's room but he was waiting outside when she shot through the door. From gate to gate he tailed her, up and down the clogged lines of passengers, out into the exit lanes where she stood whipped by the noise and lead-heavy smoke from exhaust pipes, then wandered across the rubber-streaked pavement, then raced toward the Boston bus as its doors accordioned shut. He kept her in sight as Lillian walked alongside it staring up into each tinted window, following it as it backed out of its parking bay, in the shaking air. Freddy tugged her away two seconds before another bus brushed past her on her blind side – and if he hadn't been there who knows how it would have ended up.

If Freddy hadn't been there. Lillian's thought, exactly. 'She came back. I told you she was coming.'

'Yes. Yes, you told me.' He steered her around the flesh-color tables, toward the exit.

'She talked about you.'

'Hildy did?'

'Tell me what she meant, Freddy. She said you hurt her before she left. She said you hurt me, too.'

He was slow to answer. 'Sounds a little vague. I'm not sure what that remark means. Where's your blue suitcase?'

'Hildy took it.'

'I see. I thought you were only bringing her clothes in it. You let her take it?' Freddy looked around the waiting room as they passed through it, wired with suspicion, as if he expected to see a stranger

148

sneaking off with the thing. Somehow (and this he'd bet on), Lillian had been tricked. The premonitions, the harbingers, the upward reach of mother love. 'What happened here, Lillian?'

'I know,' she said, in some kind of sympathy, 'you can't understand.'

Therefore, silence from her. Therefore, Freddy knew he wouldn't be absolved. Openly (here it was) she blamed him for losing Hildy. And she blamed him for refusing to believe her when she swore to him Hildy was coming back. Therefore, separation. Worse was on its way. Because, dangerously, Freddy still didn't believe her.

Chapter Fifteen

ALONE IN their bedroom, the presence of Freddy's neatly made, empty bed kept Lillian awake. What was required now, to repair things? She had censored herself before. Long ago she'd stopped plaguing Freddy about the Church, the solace of confession, repentence, heaven, the other, yes, she had the self-restraint. All right – to do: live with what is here. Good. A solution that dragged her around to the question behind it: what *is* here?

A puncture in the silence and the silence leaked away. A faint sound traveled through the house, a human sound. Sobbing. Her eyes went to the doorway. Sobs came in surges and lulls, but the boy wasn't there. Lillian prodded her feet into her slippers and followed the sound into the hallway. From there she could hear it was coming from someplace downstairs. Isn't this what he does? Didn't he get her to follow him into the house before, to follow the trail of gushing faucets that led her from room to room, to his first sign and disappearing act?

In the kitchen the sobbing was louder, but it wasn't coming from there. The door to the basement was tipped open and the exhausted, draining cries rose and broke below. From the landing Lillian saw an angle of lamplight, light that gouged the smaller box of the second room out of a rockface of dark. The sobbing went on, unaware, unstoppably. Crumpled in a corner, pressed against the basement wall, it was Freddy she found, shoulders hunching on each plump sob.

When was the last time he'd let her hold him this way? In her arms tears Freddy might have sealed in before dripped from the pinched corners of his eyes. Purging tears. He tried to speak, lips gummed with spit, but his mouth and tongue were strengthless, flabby, overpowered. So he showed Lillian what had done this to him.

His worklamp lay on the floor, and reaching it on his knees he held it up in front of a wide gash in the wall. At first Lillian thought she was looking at a spot where Freddy had chiseled away the old plaster and exposed rotten brickwork underneath, but the bricks were gone and she was looking into a shallow cavity. Freddy pointed at the humid porridge of earth, gravel, rusted iron shavings and shrapnel, he dipped the worklamp closer and she saw broken layers of black oily strings and globules, shreds of rubber tires. It had the look of a garbage dump, and then of an ancient burial.

Water seeped over a snaking shape Lillian recognized as a human backbone. The smooth, half-covered bowl at one end was the back of a skull. The clear seepage, small, industrious veins of it, carried off particles of dirt, cleaning the vertebrae, the occiput. One arm wedged in the mud, was twisted back against the spine, and she took the lamp from Freddy to see, looped around its wrist bones, the shriveled remains of a leather strap.

Chapter Sixteen

NOT SINCE Samuel Emperor Hoagland and his sons were rolling out their Sprites and Nymphs had the big square yard been so full of automobiles. An ambulance, headlights burning, was backed up to meet the storm doors. It squatted there heavily with its own rear doors split open, gaping, waiting to receive its cargo. Nosed in next to the ambulance at a careless angle was Detective Early's Oldsmobile, which was penned in by a blue and white squad car on one side and the coroner's station wagon on the other. Both the squad car and the ambulance still had their chase lights flashing. Any of the Foys' neighbors whose midnight sleep had been broken by the commotion would be looking through the thin fall of rain, an exciting view from those upstairs windows, as strange to see as a flying saucer using the Foys' backyard for a landing pad.

The men, seven of them, colonized the two basement rooms. At times it seemed to Lillian and Freddy that they had become bystanders, trespassing on property they didn't own anymore. The activity around them was slow, collective, and went on under the open storm doors. Now and then a haze of rain drifted in, wetting the cement steps. Behind it the police radio crackled and hissed, unnoticed or ignored by everybody except the Foys. Detective Early, the coroner and the photographer knelt beneath the little crypt and its relic, studying the find; the two paramedics waited to be called in, one sitting on Lillian's washing machine, the other on her dryer; the two uniformed officers idly peeked under the odd loose corner of the odd cardboard box. Lillian complained about this to Det Early who apologized to her and then, with a flicking gesture that the patrolmen understood and obeyed, sent them to stand by in their car.

'We're going to have to be here for a while. I'm sorry about the invasion,' Early said to her, sympathizing. 'But there's the fast way to do this and there's the right way.'

'Something remarkable happened yesterday. I was going to call you to tell you all about it,' Lillian said. 'And here you are anyway.'

'Something to do with this?'

She didn't know how to answer him, and made a stammering start. 'Well, that's, I wish . . . What I want to tell you is Hildy came back. I saw her at the bus station.' Lillian's chin lifted, implying that proof was now delivered.

Interested, Early replied, 'You saw her. Did you talk to her, Lillian, or did you just see her walk by?'

He asked this without skepticism and for her sake, so his question didn't insult, didn't offend her. From their first meeting with him on the winter morning when John Early guided them through the business of listing Hildy as a missing person, the Foys only had to ask and the detective would tell them how things stood. His deliberate effort to avoid mystifying them inspired confidence, or if not always confidence, then courage. Lillian noticed how Early presented himself, and not just to them, as an example of worldly control. The attitude, adhered to like a creed, worked for him in his youth when he boxed as a college middleweight. Approaching retirement age his body was still lean and flexible, his gray hair still razor cut, his intentions still precise and visible. Of a piece with this he believed the most effective way to handle ugly news (something he did every working day) was to deliver it at the necessary time without hesitation. By this Det Early showed he respected your strength, and this helped you bear the unbearable. The factual world owned him. Shear away the dramatics of any crime scene, any loss, and the investigator's job was plain: uncover the connections. That one ambition was written plainly in the tautness of Early's manner, across the strain in the muscles of his neck, the shaven planes of his cheeks, pinpointed in his narrowly placed gray eyes, in his patience with the forensic procedures.

'Tell me what happened when you met up with Hildy,' he said to Freddy.

'I didn't see her. Lillian did.'

'She's been living in Oregon,' Lillian told Early. 'Now she's on her way to England. With our grandson. The two of them going off there on an adventure, like Wilbur and Orville Wright.'

'I'm sorry she's not moving back to Lawford,' said Early. 'I'd enjoy seeing what kind of a woman she grew up into.'

Lillian said, 'A beautiful one. A strong one.'

'I don't doubt it.' Early held her eyes for a second. 'Anytime you want to, come down and we'll close Hildy's file officially. With a ceremony and a celebration, and you can fill me in on everything you found out from her. How old's her boy?'

'You'd better clear a couple of hours, there's a lot to tell.'

Early excused himself from the conversation with a nod and a terse smile, then joined the coroner by the wall. Frank Wilhoyt had run the coroner's office in Lawford parish longer than Lillian had been at St Mount's. Father Agnetti counted him as a close friend and Dr

Wilhoyt with his scratchy voice, read from 1 Corinthians at the priest's funeral. Some of the words floated back into Lillian's head. *I succeeded as an architect and laid the foundations on which someone else is doing the building.*

Kneeling next to Wilhoyt, Early said to him, 'Maybe we can dig from the top and lift it out. What do you think?'

Freddy advised them, 'That's our dining room floor above there.'

'Okay,' Early said, 'we'll have to go into it from this angle.' He stepped back out of the way to let Wilhoyt's young assistant spread a plastic dropcloth on the floor directly under the opening.

The assistant, whose name Lillian didn't catch, performed his work with deep concentration. A tension sat on the surface of his expressionless chubby face. Too young to be doing this job, Lillian thought. The two men, senior and junior, began excavating the grave with small trowels. Dr Wilhoyt directing, coaching, attending to two obligations at the same time – the evidence and the rookie's instruction. Occasionally he'd brush away the loosened soil, reveal more of the skeleton and point out a detail that would snag Early's attention and Early would lean down for a closer look.

'Looks like we've got to cut out some more of your wall, Fred.' Early extended his arm toward the crowbar lying by the concrete steps and it was handed to him by one of the paramedics. 'Doing your heavy work for you,' he winked at Freddy.

'I don't mind that at all. Any help appreciated.'

Still wearing his suit jacket the detective chipped at the hole's edges, doubling its width with only a few solid strokes. The old mortar and plaster powdered away and stopped at a course of bricks. The brickwork curved inward a couple of feet above Early's head, the beginning of an archway. Below, in the raw dirt, the skeleton's feet were exposed, pressed outward, the soles flat against the destroyed wall and, like the wrists, bound together with a curling strip of leather.

155

'Gary, come on in here and get a shot of this, please.'

Early made room for the photographer who maneuvered his weight slowly, thickly, encumbered by his heavy wool coat. For a fraction of a second the camera flash bleached the entire wall, the wash of pure white light peeled back the smothering shadows. Proof. Another flash, with the viewfinder framing the ankles, the small feet.

In a whisper sounding close to respect for the dead, Early ordered another photograph to be taken. 'Get a good close one of the ligature.'

A third flash, confirming, recording the physical evidence.

It was a shameful discovery. Against Freddy's fascination, the other men's etiquette, their professional attendance, shame was what Lillian felt. For this disgrace, this abomination. She stifled an urge to apologize. In the past she had counseled the maimed and crippled patients who were ashamed of a missing limb or disfigured face, and freed them from the self-torturing idea that their damaged flesh was a burden to undamaged people. At this moment though, Lillian couldn't talk herself out of the thought.

Stopping to examine, to record, starting to dig again, it was four a.m. before Wilhoyt was prepared to remove the remains. The two patrolmen returned to the basement and added their faces to the tight semi-circle gathered around the dropcloth. His assistant at the lower end and Wilhoyt at the upper, they reached under the mud-stained bones and tried to lift the thing out in one piece. Mud packed the chest cavity, cementation which held the spindly structure together; mud caked the pelvis and allowed the rookie to cradle the bent legs. Wilhoyt gave the word, but when they moved it the arms and legs came apart at each joint.

'Wait on't, wait a minute!' Wilhoyt barked. 'Let's get what's stuck together down on the floor.'

Together they lowered the small ribcage, spine and pelvis, and the skull with its teeth all clogged with wet earth as if he'd tried to chew his way out of the grave. As the two men collected the disarticulated bones and began to stack them next to the torso Early asked if they could arrange the complete skeleton the way it had been buried. This they did as well as they could. When they were finished Early added a third length of warped and shrunken leather, sifted from the loose soil, which connected the loop at the wrists to the loop at the feet.

Photographs were taken, the last from directly above. Lillian's heart became choked with the same cold cloud of sadness and the failure of hope she felt when the boy appeared in her bedroom. His silenced struggle lay embedded in her, her nerves were webbed with it; all that was left of him had frozen into a fetal pose, his arms whipped backward out of it, not an object but a presence. And this presence spoke to a part of Lillian buried so deep within herself it hardly seemed to be her there at all, she was spectating the rush of fear, the rising violent shocks. Hildy felt it when she lived here, she said, she'd had a suspicion she was never completely alone in the house. When she was the boy's age. He had lain like this, ten feet underneath their dining room floor while daily life went on upstairs, a fourth resident, occupant of his own quiet room. For how long?

Lillian heard Freddy ask, 'Can you tell if it's a child?'

When Wilhoyt shook his head the wiry strands of white hair he'd combed protectively over his eggshell scalp waved loose. 'Could be a midget, but I don't think so. I won't know much until we get it back for a thorough looksee.' He clawed away the concretion of mud that filled the bowl of the pelvis, then glanced up over his shoulder. 'I'd say you found a boy buried in your cellar.'

Early stepped over the dropcloth to stand next to Freddy. 'When did you start working down here? D'you remember?'

'About three weeks ago.' He kept his eyes from Lillian. 'It's going to be a den.'

'Must've been a hell of a jolt when you ran into this.'

They looked down at the thing they had unearthed. The knees sharply pulled up, the arms wrenched behind. A vision of Bronze Age bodies came to Freddy's mind, the corpses dredged out of peat bogs, a violent act and its secret primal night breaking through to ours – in the company of our electric lights and central heating we could be dragged backwards this easily into the days when we lived by trading joints of meat for strings of cowrie shells. One thought joined Freddy and Lillian then: wherever the boy had lived his life, his death was here, and that human fact bridged any number of unknown years.

'Some kind of a week you've been having.' Detective Early spoke to the Foys, gathering them out of the way while the plastic sheet was doubled over and the boy's muddy bones were stretchered out to the ambulance. He chatted with them about Hildy while the grim excitement ebbed away, until all the other men had gone, into the fragile light of morning.

Awake since midnight, by the time she had to dress and leave for work Lillian was emptied out. She had not gone back to bed; she wouldn't have rested, let alone slept. During the couple of hours she sat with Freddy drinking coffee in the kitchen, he pestered her for details of the reunion with Hildy. What did Lillian ask her, what did Hildy say? On the tail of that he wanted to hear everything she could remember about the three times she saw the dead boy. In other words, to supply him with solutions, but the first and last questions went on circling around them: who is this boy? Why has he come to Lillian?

To add to Lillian's troubles, Billy Cooke was openly cheesed off at her. Whole days, half days snatched at short notice left him with too many nurse's reports to digest, too many treatment schedules to juggle, sudden gaps in the shift he had to plug. The sour expression of Billy's protest waited for Lillian on her desk, in the shape of the area's general condition. Paperwork stacked up like a sinkful of dirty dishes.

She didn't run into Billy that morning. He had signed off shift after thirty-two hours on duty and he'd persuaded Rose MacKinnon from Geriatrics to take over the second half of his rotation. 'He said if I didn't,' Rose had to tell Lillian, 'he'd be ready to check into my unit by morningtime.'

An unexcitable woman of Lillian's age, who always stood with her reddened coarse skinned hands politely folded in front of her, Rose also reported that one of her residents 'got stirred up' when he got Perry Gillies for his breakfast buddy instead of Lillian. Douglas Cottle was now on a yellow-food-only diet. And Perry, cranky and uncommunicative, was causing problems in the unit among staff and patients, leaking foul discontent.

Laney Strand went with Lillian to the dayroom where Douglas sat in his overlarge armchair, a tray of uneaten breakfast on his lap. The kitchen had sent up two bowls of corn – one creamed, one regular – a square of cornbread, half a lemon and a cup of butterscotch pudding. 'My compliments to the chef,' he said, bouncing his spoon on top of the pudding.

'This isn't Maxim's of Paris,' Lillian warned him. 'And I'm not Marcel the maître d'.'

'It's as thick as rhino hide! I can't even break it with the side of my spoon! It's just wrong.' He demonstrated this to her.

The problem was Douglas didn't expect to see Lillian so embattled, so deeply strained. She'd tucked her hair back behind her ears (one less distraction she had to cope with), which lengthened and narrowed her face, made the bones prominent. Her brow hooded her eyes. Those lilac eyes showed a dullness, an internal wear. Color too, Douglas saw, had gone from her lips, which also seemed flattened somehow, thinned by a strange pessimism.

'Are you really and truly upset about your pudding?' Nurse Strand at her most nursely.

He shrugged, then ignored her, and then kept the discussion open with a shallow sigh.

'He missed me. I know.' In Lillian's reflection in the patio window Douglas caught her attempt at a smile, one that accepted blame.

He moved the cup of butterscotch pudding to the back of his tray, the creamed corn to the front, and the regular corn next to the creamed corn; the cornbread he exiled to an upper corner while his other hand reached for the pudding, and concentrating on this game of Chinese checkers he said, 'I don't see any good coming. I'll never get out of here. When I get old I'll still be here, right exactly here, in this chair, and you'll be gone.'

Lillian said to him, 'If you think being here isn't the best thing in the world, I'd say that's pretty good. That's saying there's a life you want to get to outside.'

The bare branches of the chestnut tree waved to Douglas through the window. 'Where will you be?'

'I won't be going anyplace. Unless I win the lottery.'

'Did you win two days ago?'

She was bending down to give him a hug when an odor from Douglas's lap swirled up to meet her. Lillian tugged Laney Strand's arm, led her a few steps away from Douglas and kept her voice low. 'Why hasn't he been in the shower?'

'What's his day?'

'*Every* damn day, Miss.'

'Teresa sat in on his last case conference. I didn't. I don't know what your schedule with him is. How could I if I haven't been in on his weekly reports?'

'You can *smell* what his schedule is.'

'Uh-huh, well. There was nothing in his notes that said he had this problem. And when he was with his evening group nobody said one word about it.'

'Listen to me. You're responsible for what you haven't done as much as what you've done. Have I made my point?'

Laney's reserves sank to nothing. She stared at the floor, gnawed her lower lip, then, a hundred percent professional, asked, 'After you sign off the morning medicines can we re-fix up a definite time for student assessments? Since you weren't here yesterday Dr Mollo said to postpone them.'

'Yes. Yes.' One issue settled, satisfied to take up the next, Lillian said, 'Come talk to me after your break and we'll post a time.' Then she turned quickly to Douglas, as to a neglected guest, patting his arm. 'And we'll get you into the shower, all right, Mount Vesuvius?'

Using his knife and fork Douglas had peeled back the pudding's hide and he was scooping wobbly spoonfuls of the curdy dessert into his mouth. 'They cook too much loose food for me. Talk to the kitchen, Mrs Foy. Tell them I require more grain from the brown end of the spectrum.'

On the short walk from the dayroom Laney Strand carefully prepared Lillian for the strangeness of Perry's decline; at the task of observation she hadn't completely failed. 'Borderline anomie,' was Laney's hawkeyed summary. His volunteer work was patchy, but he spent more and more time around the hospital. Between aimless treks up and down Molyneaux Wing he sat in a hard plastic chair between the elevators. He gave Billy Cooke a straightforward reason for this: 'Guard duty.'

Which was where and how they found him. Lillian was aware of a disquiet, a splintered attention, in his red-rimmed rain-colored eyes: a shape made by events had become visible to him. Nervous and thin-faced, his hair plastered, crushed, twisted, blown by winds of who knows what storm, Perry waited. Pinching the droop of his dewlap, he waited to be covered by the dust of the earth.

'I hear you've decided to ruin your health,' Lillian's greeting. Perry didn't answer her.

Laney said to him, 'We want to keep you working here until you're at least a hundred.'

'Twenty years?' Perry wondered at her, fretfully. 'With you?'

'I'm going to have a private talk with Perry,' said Lillian, and sent Laney to supervise Bertha Orban's hot bath. Alone with the ailing old man she said, 'Guard duty?'

'I've been threatened.' His eyes widened for a second. 'It's god-damned unfair.'

'Who threatened you?' No reply from Perry. 'Threatened you how?'

He said, 'You can make a mistake. You're allowed a couple in eighty-one years, am I present and correct about that? The Pope understands. Mistakes, I'm saying, not sins. *He* must've made a mistake before he got to be infallible, right? Otherwise, how would they *know*?'

'The thing of it is you don't know. You make a choice about this or that, little or big, and somehow you've got to square it with what you've been taught. Other times you end up squaring what you've done with what you've been taught. I think you can make a mistake both ways.'

'Write a letter to the Pope, Mrs Foy. See, you understand the issue. I mean, I deserve grace, I deserve it like anybody else. Nobody deserves to threaten me.'

'Who did this?'

Perry waved the question away. 'Some kinds of mistakes dog you forever. Maybe that's the category I'm in. You know why I didn't shave? On account of yesterday I looked into the mirror and I didn't

162

see how I am now. I saw the sixteen-year-old wrestler. That was me, once was.'

'Want me to get Father Terhune to come see you?'

'Who?'

'Father Tim.'

'He's not qualified. I'd talk to Father Agnetti.'

'He . . . you remember. He passed on.'

'That's what qualifies him.'

'Talk to me, then.' Lillian wouldn't let him hide, she'd follow where Perry led.

His reply to this was a faint tilt of the head, measuring his effect on her. 'Nobody thinks they're a rotten person. Whatever you do, you do it for the good. Some people you fight and other ones you help. Sometimes you fight other *countries*.' He paused to check whether this was registering with Lillian. 'You fight with the Church behind you and because you're a patriot. You don't have to march over there to be in a war. Terrible things happen. But if you fight for a good reason then they should judge the reason.'

'That's what I try to do.'

'What about when you come up against a devil? He can look like anything. A pretty girl. A guy who gives you a dollar. A little schoolkid so to say, or some other camouflage. What do devils do? They wreck our lives, and spit on our grace. That's their whole purpose, to spread crime and lies, riots and discontent.'

Quietly, Lillian said, under control, 'Did you dream about the boy again?'

'He threatened to choke me with a goddamned rope!' Perry's voice cracked and suddenly tears – of miserable anger, persecution – drizzled out of him.

'Was it in our house? Hoagland's place?'

'Here, in here! I was in bed, all safe. All safe.' He calmed

163

himself with large, slow breaths, as though he were swallowing water.

'Did you hear stories when you worked there? About the house?'

'That old time is stronger to me now than last week is. Everybody I knew was so sure of things. We didn't sit around.'

'Was there some kind of feud? Between the Hoaglands and another family? Some fight over money or property, I mean. Some bust-up.'

Perry's concentration was split and wandering. The dark that filled him when he shut his eyes molested him and the sight of his dead-end room was a torment. 'Help me. Give me a pill to keep me awake.'

'I won't let you doze off. I'll keep you talking. Tell me about old Lawford. How it was when you worked at Sam Hoagland's.'

'Those were very clear times. Even the wops who worked for other wops for a nickel an hour, they were happy to be here. Then you get the troublemakers who wouldn't be happy if the whole world was a millionaire. In nineteen . . . they agitated—'

He cut his reminiscence short. He saw Dr Mollo before Lillian did. 'Perry, may I borrow Mrs Foy for a minute?'

'After she gets me my pill. I need it for real.'

'It's on its way,' Mollo promised him, and he said to Lillian, 'I've started him on Halcion and Procardia.'

Perry hoisted himself out of the chair. 'I can't wait around all day. Got people to see.'

Lillian took hold of his arm, felt the wickerwork cordiness inside the sleeve of his shirt. 'Stay here for a minute.'

But he pulled free. 'I've got to help Dr Gloria in OB.'

'He really ought to be scratched from the auxiliary roster,' Lillian said, her eye on Perry shambling down the hallway. 'His balance, I mean his mental balance, is a little precarious now.'

'Why would that be?'

'He's convinced he could die any day. Death is chasing him down.'

Mollo said, 'He told me he's afraid to go to sleep.'

'Did he mention the recurrent dreams? They terrify him; they don't seem like dreams.'

'No, he didn't. What are they about?'

'All I know so far is he's dreaming about a little boy who wants to strangle him with a rope.'

'His death looks like a little boy. To each his own,' said Mollo, not unkindly.

'I'll talk to him some more. Get to the bottom of what's really frightening him so much.'

With a hint of courtliness, a soft tilt of his handsome head, he said, 'Do you think you're completely able to get into that at the moment?' He was studying Lillian's face, her dull skin, the small filigree blooms of broken capillaries on the ridges of her cheeks. 'We need you in A-1 shape. The floor's been hectic lately. You're here, you're not here.'

'It's been a rough couple of weeks. I'm back on the beam.'

The problem from Mollo's standpoint was the half-knowledge he had about the excitement overnight at the Foys' house. Odd fragments of the story were being passed around the unit, first of all by Laney Strand, whose husband was a patrolman on the Lawford police force. It was a private and personal matter, though, and Dr Mollo was less interested in the details than in the kind of toll it was taking on Lillian. 'How's life on the home front? How's Freddy?'

'Feeling energetic. Remodeling our basement.'

Mollo followed up her answer with an analyst's silence. And then, 'Did I hear there was some commotion up at your house last night?'

Lillian felt some internal structure weaken, come loose slightly, like a bracket from a wall. She was managing her troubles badly. She wanted to say, 'Work is what I need. I need to be here,' but she felt pinned under the weight of Mollo's pending judgment. So she gave him the minimum. 'They swore us to secrecy. Poor Freddy. He dug up something historical and he thinks it's going to make him famous. I told him wait until the Lawford Historical Society tells us what it is. They'll get the credit for it, the scholars.'

'What sort of thing did he find?'

'I really can't talk about it. I'm not allowed to.' This wasn't enough, she was still caught in Mollo's silence. 'Something phenomenal did happen. I saw Hildy. She came back. My daughter?'

'Sure – Hildy. To stay? That's fine news.'

'No, well. I spent half an hour with her. She's on her way to England. But I saw her, anyway. And my grandson.'

'Out of nowhere? Or did you know she was coming.'

'I had a little warning.'

Mollo scratched at the side of his grainy beard. 'No surprise you're drained. All those clanging emotions. At least it's a blow-out and not a slow leak. I don't want you worn out.' He added, 'For my own selfish motives,' and perked up. 'I've got a new toy to play with. A graphic computer. I'd like to try and duplicate the shapes and colors you see. We'll play some music like we did before, sit you in front of this computer screen and create everything right there. You just tell me when we've got it right. Then I can see exactly what you're seeing.'

'So I won't be so special after that.'

'Twice as. Rest up for your computer debut. What's your rotation this week? You're off when?'

'Tomorrow and Saturday.'

'Take today, Lillian.'

'No, I've got a million things to do. I can't be off the floor for three days. Everybody will forget who I am.'

'Positively not. This time there's a contingency plan.'

'Since when?'

Lillian had been overruled. Mollo reassured her with a squeeze of her arm. 'Go home, okay? Relax your mind.'

But mental peace was a reward as remote as sainthood, and when she left St Mount's that day Lillian didn't go home.

In the first years of the century the *Intelligencer* ran as a sixteen-page weekly. Reporters were fielded to cover fires and elections, crimes and trials, families of local prominence, national events and issues as they affected life in the towns of Lawford and Hadleigh. Lillian had no method for her research, no hypothesis to point toward a hidden structure or to lend a structure to the known facts. Parked in a carel at the back of the public library she could concentrate her attention and pour her energy into this project. She sat below the tall windows that let a soft, blanketing light fall across the brown room. Facing the box of artificial brightness that separated her from the other readers, Lillian combed through microfilm copies of the *Intelligencer*, beginning with the rough dates she knew in the history of the Hoagland place. January, 1912 was the start of Hoagland & Sons' golden decade, the inaugural year of their automobile business, the year they built their subterranean workshop.

On an inside page of a July edition she found a story celebrating the production of the first Hoagland Sprite. Plunked in the middle of the columns of marching band prose was a pen and ink drawing of the car and a portrait of its majestically bearded chief engineer and prophet, Samuel Emperor Hoagland. This was seven years before Perry Gillies started work for him as an apprentice mechanic: the date in the corner of the photograph Perry had given the Foys, the one that showed him grinning in the driver's seat of a Sprite, was July 4, 1919. *They agitated*, he said to Lillian, 'In nineteen . . . they agitated.' He was telling her about his apprentice year: '19.

Lillian was panning for gold. In the August editions, nothing. In

September, the same. In October occasional stories of labor unrest began to appear more frequently, with more dramatic emphasis. The tone of the *Intelligencer*'s editorials was shrill, its line implacable. A righteous, palpitating, chest-beating defiance of foreign influence fluttered under the headlines. She read:

Bolshevik Plan for Conquest of Country . . . The United States of America, to whose shores these immigrants fled, is now the object of their hatred! . . . THEY PLAN to take four-year-old children from their parents and raise them in State Dormitories . . . THEY PLAN to *outlaw* football and baseball and *outlaw* the worship of God!

Reds Pervade Northeast . . . Police in Durham raided an anarcho-communist cell in a Murry Street hotel. Nightwatchman Paolo Camioli was arrested . . . six other Italians . . . materials useful in the manufacture of time-detonated explosives . . . workers' association social evenings disguise red meetings in Woodbridge, Hadleigh and Lawford . . .

Citizens on Alert for Reds . . . Teachers from Lawford's Central High School signed a pledge to fight any malevolent influence by informing authorities of telltale outspoken criticism of our American government . . . Principal George T. Dence said, 'Bolshevism is a theory devised by Satan . . . the most innocent face can mask the most wicked purpose.'

Armed At All Points Against Red Menace . . . Led by haberdasher Lewis Strand of Lawford, residents manned roadblocks to halt Bolshevik agitators . . . Shotguns, rifles and pistols were proudly displayed as tokens of ultimate resistance to the alien forces of anarchy . . .

Dr Henry Longbough (in fact, a predecessor of Dr Mollo at Mount St Mary's) wrote in an article published by the *Intelligencer* in November, 1919: 'Communism, anarchy and libertarianism are expressions of the same mental sickness. Such perversities arise from a damaged view of the world and society. It is a deluded vision which presents the natural world of predator and prey, competition and profit, family and nation, as material elements manipulated by an elite for the benefit of the chosen few. With this, too, comes the false belief in a perfect tomorrow which may be gained if today's giants are slain. Over-emotional types such as Jews and Southern Europeans are especially prone to appeals of this kind and in many cases go on to infect their offspring – already susceptible through genetic pre-disposition – with the tenacious illness.'

A small item tucked into the bottom corner of the front page of the November 10, 1919 edition snagged Lillian's eye as the librarian whispered to her, 'Closing, please. Winter hours.' On the 8th the nine-year-old son of Italian immigrants, Adamo Bartolotti, disappeared on his way home from school. In a public-spirited appeal for witnesses the *Intelligencer* printed a map of the boy's route. The heavy black line began at Lawford Grammar School and continued up Cox's Hill, doglegged at Wignall Street, crossed Dedham Lane and turned down Church Hill. The trail went cold there, where he was last seen by sisters Dora and Sadie Nichols, walking past their front window. The boy's parents, Gianfranco and Rosalba Bartolotti, said Adamo was a happy boy and a good student who dreamed of flying an aeroplane like his hero Eddie Rickenbacker. Adamo had never made any trouble for anybody or run away before.

Chapter Seventeen

ALONG THE rising curve between the bus stop and the Foys' home only three other houses shared Church Hill. The two-story, roughly barn-shaped buildings sat foursquare on broad grassy lots and looked out over the hay fields, as they had for more or less a century. The last threat of convulsive change in the neighborhood came (and went) half a dozen winters ago when the Foys, the Nicholses, the Johnstons and the Dences banded together to petition Lawford parish council for modern streetlamps. Chairman of the action committee, Freddy Foy, resigned in disgust (read: defeat), fobbed off by one sub-department manager too many. So the 1930s lamps remained, a lonely pair of fluted gray granite pillars, each mounted with a six-sided fez of textured glass. Only one of them still worked, bravely pumping out its landmark light at the sidewalk's first bend.

The short stroll from the bus loosened Lillian's concentration; in the sharp air and rural quiet, under the windless unclouded night sky, its scatter of pale green stars, she moved past her neighbors' doors like a visiting spirit. Lights in the windows, cars in the driveways, clothes-lines, mailboxes – the human traces as persistent as any blind force in nature, as the elm, oak and chestnut trees here, their roots as thick as Lillian's arm, rupturing the old concrete in places. The latent, the permanent, breaking through. This thought had arrested her before, walking toward her house in the dark, seeing the peaked roof's silhouette against infinite night: standing on this spot a hundred years ago, this is what she would have seen – the past became visible to her, and present. In 1919 it might have been the view the Bartolottis had as they arrived at Samuel Hoagland's door to appeal for any scrap of knowledge about their missing son.

Water chattered in the culvert, Lillian's shoes scraped loudly at the mud and gravel spilled into the street, but she heard those sounds in the distance. Present and absent, her perceptions floated somewhere ahead of her. From where she stood Lillian could see Freddy in the kitchen window. He half-squatted to read the temperature dial on the oven, lifted himself on his thick legs to adjust the heat under a saucepan and then sat vigilantly at the table. For a few seconds Lillian had the sensation she was imagining what she saw. Then she stepped inside and the plain reality hit her as soon as she shut the front door: the fragrance of dinner warming (last night's beef Stroganoff), the watercolor of Hoopoe Bay (in autumn) on the entry wall, the Early American maple furniture and her husband's wing chair arranged in the living room, traces of the Foys' life, hovering in history.

'Lil? Lillian?'

'Hi-ho, kiddo.' But her voice dragged, pitched low.

Freddy came out of the kitchen to meet her. 'I found some swordfish in the freezer but I wasn't sure it would defrost in time. So I decided against it.'

She kissed his sweatered shoulder. 'Let me sit for a minute. My stomach feels a little funny.'

'The Stroganoff was in the refrigerator. I'm reheating what was in the casserole dish.'

'You have it. I'll just have a bite.'

'A tough day, hm? I can see it there,' touching the corner of Lillian's mouth, 'and there,' the corner of her eye.

'I owe my poor body two nights' sleep,' she said, sliding down into a chair, her coat still on.

'It's the outrageous price of your job. Traumas are the norm, they're what you wake up to every day.'

'Today I got off light. Only a minor wrestling match with one of my residents.'

'Who won?'

'Two-Ton Douglas Cottle.'

'Which one is he?'

'What Douglas doesn't know about passive-aggression isn't worth knowing.' She leaned forward onto the table, cushioning her head on her arms. 'He peed on a bath towel. I asked him why and he said he wanted to help us.'

'How did he figure that?'

'He said if he peed on the floor, somebody would have to mop it up with a towel, so Douglas decided he'd save us the trouble.'

'That man doesn't belong in St Mount's, he ought to be in Congress. Draft him for the next election.'

'I only worked a half-day anyway,' said Lillian. She turned her head so Freddy could read her jumbled feelings – wounded resignation, guilty relief. 'Marcello ordered me home.'

'Are you saying he suspended you?'

'It's his way of showing he cares.' She raised her head, rubbed her swollen eyelids, propped her slender face in her hand. 'Just look at me.'

Freddy received this as a slap. So he did look at her, trying hard to see the evidence Mollo saw. 'You left work this morning,' he established, 'but you didn't come home?'

'What do you think? That I've been wandering around town with a Dixie cup and a wet rag, washing windshields at traffic lights? I used my time, at the library. When I started in on it I didn't know what I was looking for, but I knew I was on the right track, going back through old *Intelligencers*.'

'Go on, what did you find out?'

The real story she told him was hers: the electric charge that began as a glow in the pit of her stomach then hummed into her veins, reached through her arms and legs as she got closer to Adamo Bartolotti. 'A nine-year-old Italian boy disappeared on his way home from school. Right out on Church Hill was the last place anybody saw him.'

'When was this?'

'In 1919. November eighth.'

'That's Early's work you're doing for him,' Freddy said in broad admiration. 'So let him ruin his eyesight chasing down the rest of the details. How about that?'

'I'm going back tomorrow. Maybe I can find out what happened to the poor Bartolottis. If there was a search. Don't you want to know?'

'The hospital didn't let you off work so you could wear yourself out even more.' At the stove he stirred the dark-red liquid in the saucepan, with full concentration. 'Are you allowed to drink mulled wine?'

'I've got a prescription for it.' She laughed and held up the flat of her empty hand to show him. 'See?'

In the cold months Lillian usually made the drink for them. Freddy oversugared it, the heavy red wine's flavor barely surviving his enthusiasm for cinnamon, cloves, ginger and lemon peel. Tonight this fussing over her was the first stage of his effort to understand, an opening. Setting the spice-fragrant steaming glass in front of Lillian he said, 'This is part my fault. Your situation.'

She sipped at her wine, lowered the glass to the table. 'Hot,' she said, quietly. 'At least you didn't call it my "condition".'

'*Our* situation, I should've said. Ours. I make it too much work, don't I. For you to talk to me.'

'I don't expect you to turn against your own ideas. If you suddenly told me you saw a ghost in the bedroom and you were getting wild premonitions about Hildy, to tell you the truth, as a *professional* I would have had my worries.'

'You're a natural listener, Lil. Not me. I was born with a defect. I'm deaf in a special way. You know how some deafers talk? Too loud? Because all they can hear is their own voice vibrating around inside their head.'

'Honey, it would've scared me, too. "He's coming apart, he's escaping, it's a breakdown." That's how it probably would've looked to me.'

'Not as my girl. As a professional, maybe. Not as my own girl.'

This was true. 'You never wanted me to turn my back on my beliefs. I've loved you for being that kind of husband.'

'I know I should've been . . .' He gave up, glanced away, cleared his throat with a shallow cough. 'The day after you told me about your ghost boy I made a phone call from my office. I was fighting off such painful thoughts. I sat there trying to figure out where this bizarre thing came from. If I've changed in ways I can't tell or I haven't changed at all. Maybe I haven't learned a single thing from living with you for thirty years. I didn't know which questions to ask first.'

'Who did you call?'

'I got through to a Dr Lustig at Boston Memorial. He was extremely considerate. Gave me twenty minutes of his lunch hour. I called myself Charlie.'

'And what was my name?'

'Tina,' said Freddy. 'Lustig got very intrigued when I mentioned your line of work. Also about Hildy, leaving us so young. He started using words like "projection" and "compensation", comparing you to other cases. I couldn't take that. It was all theoretical, of course, on the telephone and all, but I couldn't listen to him anymore, I just hung up.'

'Instant psychoanalysis. He should have his own radio phone-in.' Her resentment took more energy than Lillian could spare and it quickly drained out of her.

'Was it disloyal? That's how I felt afterward. But it was a cold bath, Lil, it opened my eyes. I know I made you face it by yourself – all that sense to make of such confusion, *alone*. I was no help.'

'You thought you were helping me.'

'Before Hildy was born I thought one thing I had was moral strength. Strength of heart. For you to count on and admire. It shrank, that's what I think. Into something harder. Before she left us – oh man, my stupidity! I laid such demands on her. I ran her off.'

'She ran away from both of us.'

'When she was a little girl and the three of us were together, we were a family, weren't we? That's how you remember it, that's really how it was and not just the way it is in my mind?'

'Fred, this is masochism. Is there some other reason you're doing this?'

He had been led to the border of a harsh territory, where every root and rock was exposed. It would take strength to survive there, to make it through and be welcomed back. But Freddy didn't cross over. 'You're right, this isn't helping. Here's what. I'll take care of the house. You can sleep for a week if that's what you want.'

'I've got my research to do downtown.'

'Maybe I can turn up some material on it in the Academy library. I'm pretty sure there's a Bayliss Whitney history of Lawford and

175

Hadleigh. I'll stay late and forage around the stacks. That'll keep me out of your hair.'

'That's not what I want. I'm used to bumping into you.'

His glass rested between his hands on the table. He opened them to Lillian and said, 'I'd like to move back from the spare room. You think that would be all right?'

The light chore of moving the down comforter and Freddy's pillows from the second bedroom only needed one pair of hands, but Freddy and Lillian pitched in together. He was playful with her, unfolding the blanket after she'd neatly folded it, teasing to win her attention. The incubating virus of regret, very likely, had broken out into this slaphappy fever. Lillian welcomed it, malady and all. He had come to her with worried eyes, with questions, and for the first time in her memory Freddy didn't conceal his uncertainty. All this since he dug Adamo's bones out of the basement wall.

Behind him, through the door, Lillian saw the light in the hallway change. Daylight changes this way when clouds crawl over the sun, all the shadows merge. The boy, dressed in his neat school clothes, moved past on his way to their bedroom. The dead aren't dead forever, Lillian thought. She didn't say a word to Freddy. Tonight, if he was able to, he was going to learn that.

'Load me up,' he said, and she stacked the square bundle of pillows and comforter on his willing arms. He returned the gentle hug she gave him before they went into the hallway. With her hand on his back she guided Freddy, chaperoned him toward a revelation that would give him new questions to ask, a sight that would change everything.

Their bedtable lamps could be lit from a switch by the door and when Freddy snapped it on both light bulbs fizzed, popped softly and blew out. In the dim slanting light from the hall he laid his bundle on his bed, saying, 'No crisis, no crisis. Spare ones in the kitchen. I'm on the job.'

Was it the weakness of her vision or of her memory? Intensely alone there Lillian felt queasy with doubt – did she see him a few seconds ago or didn't she? There hadn't been any ghostly tampering with the bathroom light, or with the faucets either. She filled the sink and stroked her face with the clean warm water, bringing an end to the day. Then, sitting in her slip at her vanity table, smoothing on her night cream, Lillian made a pledge to herself. From this minute she was going to attend to her health and more to her physical appearance. Have her hair cut short, like Mim's. Eat to gain back some weight, reverse this famished look. In the mirror she caught sight of the bones and the thin freckled skin between her breasts, the lusterless eyes of a hostage. An older woman can't carry this kind of leanness without looking used up.

A stir in the air broke her out of this drowsy contemplation. Even in the early days of their marriage Lillian was sensitive to the airborne ripples Freddy made when he entered a room, the spreading wave of his skin scent, the smell of sunheat on sand (as she interpreted it) clean, human. It was Freddy's name rising to her lips as she swiveled around and saw Adamo behind her, standing still in the hovering light of the doorway.

Most of his clothes were gone. He stood shivering in his skivvy shirt and baggy underpants, besmeared with mud. Slowly, as though obeying an order, he lowered himself onto his knees and then doubled over. Against an invisible weight pressed on his neck Adamo forced his head upward, defiant, determined to keep his eyes on Lillian. To be sure she was watching. Knowledge shackled her to responsibility: she knew his name now and the day he died. His pain was clear to her – not only the the ache in his shoulder joints as his arms jerked back, or the strap biting into his wrists, but the stab of the moment Adamo knew he wasn't going to get out of this. Disbelief drowned his black eyes. Now his head was pulled back. Lillian saw small ulcers on his soap-white throat and chest, each the diameter of a fingertip, and she inhaled the smell of tobacco smoke, felt heat against her face. *This loss persists, the blasphemy of it*, abrupt intuitions hatched out of these physical sensations, together the truth of the thing she was witness to – the torture and killing of a child.

Her eyes were clamped shut when Freddy found her curled up in the brocade chair next to her bed. She gripped the bunched folds of her slip, the peach fabric creased into fan shapes under her knuckles. He knelt, to hold her then with one frantic arm flung around her shoulders, the other one across her tense drawn-up legs. He cradled Lillian as if he'd plucked her from the water just seconds from drowning. Here was the necessity; this is what he had the power to do. The gentleness in his voice, its searching tenderness, was almost lovesick. 'Lillian, sugar. What is it, huh?'

She opened her eyes, bravely.

Freddy said, 'Is he here? Do you see him?'

By the door, in his school clothes again, Adamo stood unhurt. *This is what I was*, he seemed to be telling her, *and you saw what they made me*.

Freddy followed Lillian's rigid stare. He concentrated on the indoor twilight framed in the bedroom door and after a moment he said, 'He's a small boy. Small for his age. In those old-time trousers. What do you call them?'

'Knickerbockers.'

'Knickerbockers. Yes. Dark-colored.'

'Brown tweed.'

'That's right. Dark brown. And he's got black hair, it's a little messy.'

'You see him there?' She couldn't say Adamo's hair was messy, but he was hovering on the edge of clarity, more shadow than shape.

'He's looking at us,' Freddy said. 'The same way we're looking at him. What's he doing?'

'Do you see him? Tell me the truth, Freddy. Or do you just think you can. Don't try to help me this way.'

Getting to his feet, he said, into the stillness held in the doorway, 'Can you talk to us?' Then, softly to Lillian, conscious that his question might offend the boy, 'Does he hear us? Can he understand what we're saying?'

Chapter Eighteen

IT STRUCK Freddy that the active assistance he'd been providing Detective Early was somewhat underappreciated. On his third visit in two weeks to the station in Mistley he planned to press the detective for overdue answers to the riddle that was carried out of his basement wrapped in a plastic sheet. After all, Freddy had located the birth certificate of Adamo Bartolotti and duly delivered a copy of the document to Early along with the *Intelligencer* story dredged up by Lillian. Adamo was born on August 14, 1910; he was nine years, two months and twenty days old when he disappeared. Where had this concrete information led the community's police professionals, that's what Freddy wanted to know. He was entitled. Early had repaid his initiative with a scrap from the forensic pathologist's report: the bones had been in the ground for more than fifty years. Freddy left there feeling dismissed and certain Early had by now learned more than he saw fit to declare.

The drive into town from Lawford Academy played hell with his mood. Snow mounds muffled the roadside, piled against tree trunks and telephone poles like surf by Atlantic winds. The brief thaw that followed tricked Freddy into freeing his tires from their chains and in last night's freeze the drenched asphalt grew gray bus-length blisters of ice. At two stoplights, one after the other, he lightly rear-ended the same station wagon. The woman driving it must have thought the man thrashing his arms around in the blue Ford behind her was out to fill his lunch hour with a little car-jacking.

To add to all this, Freddy couldn't find a parking space close to the station. For three blocks he leaned his thick weight into the cold returning wind, Russian-style hat squeezed down tight, bare fingers clutching his overcoat's collar. At the last corner, where kerbside basins of grimy slush had refrozen, Freddy's shoe came down on the brittle crust and filled like a toy boat with black water. Frustration and obstruction, obstruction and frustration, the patsy of officials, plaything of the elements.

The two-story brick building wasn't built for comfort. Lawford's jail since Civil War times and Mistley's since the 1940s, its small-town municipal style was updated with each refurbishment but never refined. Marbled graygreen linoleum, laid in square tiles (the occasional corner gouged from the tarry glue), paved the lobby area. Posters promoting bicycle safety and drug awareness called out to Freddy from a glass-fronted case on the wall above the row of plastic chairs, where no one was waiting. The tall counter Freddy leaned against, dabbing a finger to ring the brass domed bell, was solid wood trapped like a bug in amber, forgotten under ancient coats of varnish.

Det Early wasn't back from lunch. This bit of news Freddy received from Early's son, Richard. Fifteen years a patrolman, on his father's advice he accepted promotion to sergeant, stopped chasing burglars, drunks and stolen vehicles and came indoors to handle the public who needed handling. From his clean-featured squarish face you got the feeling he would rather persuade you to drop that tire iron/beer bottle/assault rifle, but if you wanted to turn a test of nerve into a physical fight he'd beat you to the punch. Strong forearms forested with brown hair, shortsleeved uniform even in this weather. In Richard you had a snapshot of his father in younger years. And that impression prompted Freddy to start airing his complaints the minute Richard Early appeared at the desk.

'I'd appreciate it very much,' said Freddy, self-control on show, 'if somebody would tell me how pictures of my basement and that poor boy's remains got into the newspaper last Friday. Do you know anything about this?' He pulled the folded *Intelligencer* out of his coat pocket and laid it in front of Richard as if playing a card in a gin game. 'They haven't published my letter to the editor. But they'll print a picture of our private business without our permission.'

'My dad's going to be back in half a tick. He'll be able to lay it all out for you, Mr Foy.'

'If he does, he better make it believeable.'

'I'm positive it wasn't anybody's idea to cause problems for you people. The very opposite, I think,' Richard said in all sincerity.

'You know what? Three days in a row we had to chase reporters off our property. One fella said he came from a radio station in Brockton. That's a hundred miles away, for Godsake. Another pair of smart alecks wouldn't stop banging on the door and when I opened up they made it sound like I owed it to the world to let them inside. Next thing we know they're trying to pry open the storm doors and break in.'

'They'd be committing a crime, simple as that.'

'It's very bad for my wife. She was resting at the time. And between these newsrats and the cars cruising by day and night, she's not getting the peace she needs. Neither of us are. Fortunately that time our friends were over for a calm evening of gin rummy, so they chased them off.'

There wasn't much point, Richard decided, in this delaying action. He conceded, 'As far as I understand it, my dad thought it'd turn out worse for you folks if we said, "Bones? What bones?"'

'Why did you have to say anything to anybody?'

'Are you and Mrs Foy on good terms with your neighbors?'

'We wave hello from the car. Lillian does. They wave back.'

'Right. We took phone calls for a week. They all wanted to know what we were doing out at your house and who got put into that ambulance. They were thinking all kinds of things.'

'Worse than what it was?'

'We're getting into my dad's territory.'

'Are you saying you don't know?'

'It broke him up a little bit, what he saw. The crime of it. And this is after a long time of looking at the worst things people do to each other.'

Here was the son talking. Freddy asked him, 'How about you?'

A quick, deferential shake of the head. 'It takes a certain type of individual to go into being a detective. I don't want to know everything, I guess.' He gave Freddy an example: 'Dad said when he saw those human bones dug out of your basement, for a minute or two he wondered if it was your daughter.'

'He thought *that*?' A sickening heat flamed in Freddy's chest. He felt it rise, felt the color in his face change. 'How?'

'That's what I mean. He couldn't help it.' Richard waved away the ridiculousness of it. 'He's hardheaded and he can come up with all kinds of possibilities, then he eliminates them one at a time.'

Repelled, astonished, Freddy took a step back from the desk. 'He knows what kind of people we are. He's known us for fourteen years!'

'Sure, of course. He eliminated it in a minute or two.'

'Lillian told him she saw Hildy the day before. Didn't he believe her? Your father seemed happy for us, really thrilled.'

'I'm sure he was.'

Purse-lipped, hands folded on his lap, Freddy sat motionless in the vacant row of white plastic chairs. Motionless because mortified; his mental gears, stripped and spinning, simply failed to grip. When Early came in just a few moments later, stamping snow from his shoes, Freddy blindly waited to be acknowledged.

The detective greeted him with a serious smile, and received only the seriousness in return. 'Come on into my office,' he invited Freddy. Early held open the door to the stairway and let him pass through. Respectful treatment, then. The dignified picture Freddy intended to present was only flawed by the lisping squish of his one wet sock.

In the privacy of his small office Early said, with gentlemanly delicacy, 'We can do something about that. Lay it on the radiator.'

'It's not as bad as it sounds,' replied Freddy. 'I can't spend much time here.'

'You're a little hacked off at me, aren't you. I suppose you've got a right. Mas o menos.' Easing back in the swivel chair Early stretched his arms, stroked his freshly cut hair, sat ready to be blasted.

'Did you expect them to show any consideration, any discretion? They didn't leave it at pictures of our home. The *Intelligencer* gave our address, our names. It's *immoral*.'

'It wasn't the worst thing that could've happened.'

'You *told* them. It was immoral! These self-appointed, self-important opportunists come by and if we don't answer the door they look in our windows. Our privacy's at stake. Why did you let that happen?'

'First off, stories were already going around. I'd rather not repeat them, but if you'd like to hear—'

'Thanks. No.'

'So it was way better if the real stuff came from us, officially.'

'Richard explained that to me.'

'Second, Gary says they didn't get that photograph of your basement from him. There was some mix-up in the lab or something. I'm checking into it.' It was an apology bordered with realism. 'Should I send a patrol car out to you?'

'God, no.'

'I agree, Fred. It'd only make things worse. How is Lillian?'

'She's been back at work. It's good. She's very energetic. I'm meeting her for lunch. Can I tell her you've turned anything up about the Bartolottis?'

The manila file lay on top of all the rest of Early's paperwork. He flipped his glasses open to read from it. First, he said, 'Going back into the records, this far back, I mean it's two-three generations ago. You read about what happened and it's mostly words on a page. But since I actually looked at what was left of that boy,' he clicked his tongue, 'something else, y'know, hits you. People do cruel and crazy things. That's what we do. We invent bubble gum and whatever, light bulbs, airplanes, and we make up reasons to fuck people up. Pardon the language. The variety never fails to amaze me. We're what we've always been, no change since Cain. We're goddamn geniuses, aren't we.'

'What did you find out?'

'They gave up on the case in July, 1920. As far as I can tell nobody made more than a minimum effort to look for the boy. A handful of witness depositions. All together you couldn't fill two sides of one piece of paper with them. Anyway, huh. The victims, the bystanders and the bad guys, the ones who knew, the ones who didn't, there's no difference between them now. Except for that mechanic who worked for Hoagland. The guy you told me about? He's in St Mount's?'

'Perry Gillies.'

'Him. He's what – somewhere in his eighties.' Early handed the loose page of Perry's deposition to Freddy. 'You can read what-all he remembered seeing at the time. I'd be surprised if his memory's improved in sixty-five years.'

'Does it say in there why they stopped looking? Some reason?'

'By some oddball coincidence, Mr and Mrs Bartolotti were deported in July 1920. I infer from that the official reason was To Hell With It. Sure. It wasn't enough of a sorry story that their boy vanished off the face of the earth. You and Lillian know how that's got to feel. But Judge Okrent shipped them back to Genoa and they just weren't going to live long enough to find out what happened to Adamo.'

'Why were they deported?'

'Oh, the court order's crystal clear about that. They were anarchists. *Philosophical* anarchists, their lawyer wanted the Immigration department to understand. As opposed to the bomb-throwing kind. Some help he gave them. And there's the end of the trail.'

Freddy said, 'But they must have tried to find out about him. He was their son, the Bartolottis' youngest son. There were letters, maybe. Something they might've written from Italy?'

'Official records, that's all.' A thought, then Early said, 'Some facts you can discover, other ones you can't.' His resignation was both professional and philosophical.

Accept all of it and be free. The surge of freedom Freddy rode out of Early's office flowed from paired moments: with Lillian, when he accepted the reality of the boy's ghost, and this one with Early, when he accepted the limits of what can be discovered. That was the gift – along with the Xerox copies of the Bartolottis' deportation order – he hurried across town to give to Lillian. *Freely*. How many times before, memorably with Hildy, did he disguise the concrete facts, deflect bombshells? Only because Lillian's Catholic sensitivities turned every practical issue into a moral test; family decisions were the size of the sky and funneled to a point that pressed down on her head – judged in all things, brave Lillian, her soul (and her husband's, her daughter's) dangling between the marshmallow clouds and the roasting pit. Today Freddy could deliver the unadulterated truth and see her relieved of doubt, satisfied in this one single thing, at least.

He got to the library in a headachy hurry, with twenty minutes salvaged for their lunch. By the look of things Lillian didn't want to use the time for anything as irrelevant as eating. At the long table under the high clear windows, she sat with her books and notepad. Some lay open, others in stacks of twos and threes, all of them had pages marked with strips of notepaper. Freddy watched her as she read and wrote, then sat in the chair next to hers without interrupting her. It was hard to say which – Lillian's week away from St Mount's or her enthusiasm for research – had a greater effect on her health. You couldn't deny she looked better, pinker, than she had for a long while. She was winning back her beauty; it smoothed her tall forehead and the girlish arch of her neck, it settled in her wide mouth. She sat erect, in her pale blue pleated dress, the dark blue belt drawing Freddy's eye to the inward curve of her waist.

Freddy reminded her, 'It's twelve-twenty. Want to go to Giuliano's for a chili con carne?'

'Oh, you know what? I'm not hungry,' reaching a hand to his face, without looking up. 'Been working.'

'Me too. I've got some things to show you.' Freddy unfolded the papers Early had given him.

She took in the information and said, 'I'm not surprised.'

'Did the newspaper say anything about the Bartolottis?'

'I got sidetracked. South Braintree,' Lillian said, but as a question or an answer Freddy couldn't tell. 'We're thirty miles from South Braintree.'

'Closer to forty.'

'Something happened there, remember? Around the time the Bartolottis had all their trouble.'

At the top of the notepad Freddy read a date next to two names: N. Sacco and B. Vanzetti.

Lillian opened one of the books and tilted it so Freddy could read the page. 'See when the robbery was? Two men murdered, on April 15, 1920. And two Italians arrested for it on May 5th. Rosalba and Gianfranco Bartolotti were deported in July. Hundreds of other people too.'

'It doesn't have anything to do with our boy. It can't,' he said. 'He was missing in November.'

'But the *times*, you understand? I think about how rough it must have been on them and I just feel sick. The suspicion, the unfair blame. Adamo and his family had to shut up and take it, that's all.'

'It says in the official record there, the court record, they didn't deny being anarchists.'

'Isn't that why they came to the United States?'

'I'm not saying they deserved what they got. But being an anarchist with a foreign accent isn't the best way to fit into Lawford, Massachusetts.' Freddy raised a defensive hand. 'I'm just stating the obvious.'

She had something more to read to Freddy, from a page near the end of the book. 'They're so tragic, these words. Vanzetti wrote them, listen: his final thoughts. "Fellow workers, you have fought all the wars. You have worked for all the capitalists. You have wandered over all the countries. Have you harvested the fruits of your labors, the price of your victories? Does the past comfort you? Does the present smile on you? Does the future promise you anything? Have you found a piece of land where you can live like a human being and die like a human being?" My God, the anger those ideas churned up!'

'You can imagine. But it's a jump to think the Bartolottis got targeted too. What were they?' Freddy skimmed the court order and learned that the federal government had swung into action to deport a day laborer and a laundress.

'Yes, who had glorious hopes for their son.' Lillian held Freddy's eyes with hers, channeling her own vision through them. 'It's the fall semester, 1919. Adamo's in fourth grade. Every day he sees his father digging ditches or hauling garbage for ten cents an hour. And Gianfranco sees his American son growing up in a place where he can be equal with anybody. Adamo loves his papa. He believes him when his papa tells him that in a perfect world a day laborer would be equal to anybody. And Adamo says this at school, on the playground to his friends, to his teacher.'

'Let's assume that.'

'We don't have to assume it. It's a fact.'

Freddy mused. 'I can remember a time when we didn't know there had ever been anyone alive called Adamo Bartolotti. It's amazing to me how much about him we know for sure.'

'I still don't know what he wants,' she said, troubled.

'Give him time. He'll find a way to let us know.'

'Tell me what you think of this.' Lillian separated a few neatly handwritten pages from the moat of scrambled papers in front of her. It was the final copy, Freddy saw, of many aborted versions. While he absorbed it she gave him her reasons for writing the letter: Marit Sonnenfeld is the kind of person who'd be touched by Adamo's story; the feeling Lillian got from Marit's books was that not only as a parapsychologist but as a person she needs to know what lies behind ghosts, telepathy, et cetera; like themselves, she is an enemy of self-delusion. 'She's an expert. She knows things about hauntings we just don't.'

Neutrally, Freddy said, 'It's a very intelligent letter.'

'Good. I think she'll answer it.'

An expert in the field of psychic phenomena – Freddy had to

189

agree – might lead them to a greater part of the truth. The thought made him uneasy. Who was Marit Sonnenfeld? Couldn't she just as easily lead them into the murk? It also rankled him that Lillian enclosed with her letter the page from Friday's *Intelligencer* splashed, sensationally, with pictures of their house. **Grim Relic Buried in Lawford Couple's Cellar**.

'Will you sign it?' Lillian asked him. 'I think it should be from both of us.'

Chapter Nineteen

MARIT SONNENFELD'S mother, Judith – a self-enlight-ened, delicately made woman of sixty-three – collected bits of esoteric wisdom with an artlover's passion. From Jung, mandalas; from Campbell and Cassirer, universal myths and symbolic forms; from Castaneda, *brujo* magic; from the Egyptian Book of the Dead, the human heart weighed on the scales of truth; from the Tibetan Book of the Dead, the cycle of rebirth. *May I know the body to be impermanent and illusory.* She devised her own crash course and in the space of nine or ten months Judith was reciting verses from her favorite *bardo* instead of saying hello or goodbye. It took work to keep her off the subject.

According to Marit's father, Walter, this enthusiasm really kicked into gear around the time Judith began volunteering her time at Laural House, an AIDS hospice attached to the University of Pennsylvania Medical Center. The occasional complaint about her was whispered to him over a whiskey and soda by this senior consultant or that trustee, retired men like the judge, whose deeper concern was for Judith. At any rate, the grumbles weren't dramatic and were thinned out with gratitude from the family and friends of the deceased. His wife (Walter heard) counseled and advised the dying, whatever their race, creed or religion, with a collage of the afterlife she invented more or less on the spot. It was the certainty behind Judith's clear-eyed promises, her raw persuasiveness, that eased any fear, regret, revulsion. This was her message: all the religions, all the sciences, everything we know about atoms, stars and the web of nature points to one reality: all existence is in a perpetual state of transformation. Transformation! Obvious to any reasoning, emotionally whole mind . . . With the monotonous exception of her daughter's.

Why didn't Judith know Marit was on her side? What else had her career been but a dedicated, even fiery, scientific pursuit of the paranormal! So many years of investigation – into telepathy, psychokinesis, remote viewing, hauntings, sensitives, precognition, astral projection – and at the end of it no substantial evidence of any miraculous phenomena. Nothing, as her father would say with some authority, that would stand up in court. Yet in the wake of such human disappointment Marit had been led into what might be even more essential research. In the Near-Death Experience one of two things is true: either the soul travels to the brink of its afterlife, or floating free of the body and into the tunnel toward the light, hearing the voices of the dead, seeing their faces, the glimpse of Heaven, are all just the sensations and threshings of the dying brain. Marit avoided the topic with Judith.

Without saying much they cleared the dinner dishes, cached the left-overs in tupperware tubs for Marit to take home with her. Upstairs the television was on, a movie distracting Marit's two children, its sound drifting down faint as dust into the quiet kitchen. They sat together at the table with Marit's growing file of three-by-five cards. A new one was going to be added tonight; more than one if she could keep Judith's concentration from wandering. Before this all of her recipes were libraried in her memory, but now Marit was setting them down, an oral history in more ways than one. Brisket to knedlach soup, borscht to matzo brei.

'Potato latkes.' Marit titled her clean card in ballpoint. 'How much of what and when do I mix it in?'

'Why didn't you watch me cook them ever?'

That voice. Grinding out the hard edges of her words, dragging out those flat Philadelphia vowels, hammering them flatter with that nasal tone – which could twist a compliment into a criticism.

'Mom, I did. It didn't sink in, that's all. I couldn't follow you. You did it all by instinct.'

'By taste. You've got to *taste* it. All the *time.*'

'I will. I remember you skinned the potatoes and shred them up. And you rinsed them.'

'In cold water. Rinse out all the starch. Until the water's clear. Put in a handful of flour. Maybe an egg.'

'Maybe?'

'Put in an egg and some salt. Some cinnamon and some sugar. If you want to you can fry a little onion and put that in.'

'A handful is what – three ounces? Six ounces?'

'Depends how many potatoes. Marit, listen. How about if I make them next time you come over. You can watch. Take notes.'

'Because I want to write it down now.'

'What's the hurry?' Judith's question hung in silence between them. She said, 'He met that person, that Denise, at his gym?'

'That was his story.'

'I saw her, Joel's new girlfriend.' Disgust, as much for her ex-son-in-law as for his ice maiden Mainline debutante, boiled across her face. 'Skinny like a racehorse. He doesn't know that adorable behind of hers is going to spread out like a hot air balloon.'

193

'He told me she's got a life wish. Was Joel that puky about me?'

'She was buying shorts in Milson's. I don't think she knows how to cook either.'

Marit tapped her pen on the card. 'Can we get back to this? I want to know how latkes work.'

'Your problem is you've got to perk your life up.'

'Things are perky enough for me.'

'I mean you're not *inspired*. Where's the thing that connects you to the higher planes? Surveys and books can't get you there.'

'At this moment you know what inspires me? Hearing you tell me the secrets of your potato pancakes,' Marit said, gently serious.

Judith wouldn't accept this; it was not enough. 'You should talk to those people.'

'No.'

'Explain that to me.'

'It's Bosco the Clown all over again.'

'No, darling. It isn't.'

'Why weren't you proud you had an eight-year-old who *knew* that an old man in a clown suit couldn't cut Mrs Bobroff in half with a saw? Not at the same time she was giggling like a wino and blowing kisses to everybody.'

'You ruined it for the other children.'

Marit asked herself, almost out loud, what new stupidity had poisoned her judgment. The first mistake was showing the Foys' letter to her mother. The next mistake was to expect it to have any effect on her other than the one it had. Namely, Lillian Foy's detailed first-hand account of the boy's ghost and her sense he'd come to her *for a reason* only set the seal on everything Judith already believed about life after death. Was it too dumb to hope she'd notice the hunger in Mrs Foy's descriptions of this lost, restless, wronged, dead child's spirit? In a word, yes. The letter, the whole story, should have been a bright mirror showing Judith how we raise emotion into fantasy, the accident of birth and the unbelievability of death into certain knowledge about our fate. There's your transformation. Judith didn't see any of this in Lillian's six-page letter; where Marit saw spaces, Judith saw shapes.

The price for today's rotten judgment was a conversation Marit did not want to have. She said, 'Doesn't it suggest something to you that there's a story about it in their local newspaper?'

'In my opinion they sent it to show you they aren't making anything up.'

'All it means is they found a skeleton buried in their basement. Wouldn't that spook you?'

'She says they found it *after*. And by the way, in the newspaper – did you read it word for word? It doesn't talk about a ghost.'

'People invent stories, Mom. So bewildering things make sense.'

'You look at it.' Judith rummaged through the clutter of magazines on the kitchen counter. Her small oval reading glasses hung from a rhinestone chain around her neck. She used both hands to put them on. Marit saw a shakiness in her thin fingers. 'On the earthly plane, our lesson is how our bodies are flimsy shells. We only need 'em for the experience before we move up into the Dharma-Kaya. It's obvious', she said, bringing the *Intelligencer* tearsheet to the table, 'this boy's soul is stuck in the Chonyid Bardo. In my opinion. He realized he doesn't have a body anymore and now he wants one.'

'So he's a Buddhist Catholic.'

'It's the same for everybody,' Judith said. 'Can't you tell how hard it was for this woman to write to you? She isn't running into the street and shouting her head off about it.'

'Let's say she's genuine. I'm not saying she isn't. But it's not my field anymore.'

'She wrote to you because of your work. She respects you. You can tell her once and for all. Use your science, ease her mind.'

Coming down the stairs Ben and Katy were knocking into each other, going 'Hic! Hic!' pretending to be drunk on Kool-Aid. 'I can't troop off to Massachusetts. They're out of school for three weeks.'

'What's the matter they can't stay at Joel's?'

Which reminded her. 'He'll be here in a few minutes. He's got them for the long weekend.'

'Look at me. You're just digging for excuses now.'

'Want to hear the other ninety-nine? My sabbatical's over in January. I've got to have my NDE material collated by then. My real work.'

'It's not how you were before, when you started.'

Marit replied, 'I didn't know then what I know today.'

'No, you were braver then.'

Instead of answering with, 'So were you,' she said to Judith, 'Sometimes it breaks your heart to let go of glorious ideas. It takes some bravery, too. Don't you think?'

'But you said this could be a genuine ghost.'

'These *people*, Mom. I said they seem . . . With these things you've got to take a real hard look, close-up. Who knows?'

'You can't know from here.'

'Right.'

'You have to go there to find out.'

'Someone will, but not this little piggy.'

'This is the one that'll *prove* it – *this* case! All the pieces are *there*.' Judith coolly confronted Marit with the plain facts. 'Here's the thing of it. You don't want to go and see. You don't want it to be true. Because then I'd be right.'

'I've got to get Ben and Katy ready,' Marit said, getting up from the table. She called to her kids.

'Black pebbles on one side, white pebbles on the other.'

When Marit looked at her, Judith sarcastically mimed a set of scales with her hands, see-sawing into balance. Her mother, Anubis,

Heart-Weigher, Egyptian God of the Dead. All of Judith's physical traits were passed on to Marit, and this twinnish similarity clutched at her in moments like these. The flamboyant gypsy curls – Marit wore them too, but stopped short of the headband, the paisley chiffon scarf that reined them in. On Judith the skyrocket trails of smoke-black curls were boldly theatrical. A wig, true, but not exactly a fraud. Her real hair was like that before it started to fall out, fried and shriveled by chemotherapy. The cancer that had eaten a third of her stomach seemed to be reaching up to claw flesh and muscle from her face. There the skin was losing its grip, thinning. She held her face at an imploring tilt, a tactic Marit grew up imitating, handy whenever she was faced with mutiny or lame argument.

Her mother with her 'earthtime experience' and 'multi-dimensional consciousness of frequencies', her *sangsara* and astral planes just drove Marit crazy. And way past crazy, into heartache, every time Judith repeated (to solace them all), 'Death is the moment of highest spiritual truth.'

When silent refusal was what she got from Marit, she said, in sad anger, 'All your intelligence, everything you know, and you use it to deny, deny, deny.'

The competing racket at the front door turned out to be Joel arriving, being mobbed by Ben and Katy. His arms hooking them in, their faces raised to be kissed. As if the forces had landed to liberate them from enemy occupation. The children's act didn't get to Marit so much anymore; it would be her turn to be buried under their avalanche of affection when Joel brought them back home. She saw it was a tactic, this overplayed joy, to shame and punish both parents at the same time. Public humiliation, not the worst way for a couple of broken-up kids to retaliate. Marit had seen less mature behavior at conferences from squabbling emeritus professors.

Joel's greeting to her: 'You have anything to tell me?'

'Not much,' she said. 'Minor transportation trouble.'

'At least it's minor.'

'Can I use the T-bird for a few days? My red thing's in the shop. Tony said I'd have it back by today, but . . . He had to order some special part they didn't have in stock.'

Katy was pulling on Joel's overcoat pocket. 'Daddy, are we going now?'

'Yeah, right now, Sailor.' He pried her hand free.

'Right now means talking and talking,' Katy reminded him.

'The thing is,' said Joel, 'Denise has got it.'

'Can't you get it back from her?'

'I'd do that if I could, Marit. Except she's got it in Atlantic City.'

Hanging on the open door, Ben asked his dad, 'Are we going to Atlantic City?'

'Let me finish talking to your mother.' Joel felt his pocket for his billfold. 'I'll rent something for you. Put it on my Am-Ex.'

'Good. Fine. Can you call Tony or Al before you take off? They've got loaners.'

'It'd be better if I just get it from the Hertz on Franklin.'

What wasn't a negotiation? When she met Joel at Penn, a tall, underfed, nervously foot-tapping pre-law prodigy, the sudden steadiness of his handshake made Marit think of her father's solidity. And then his honey-colored hair, trained and trimmed, made her think of nobody else. After Walter met him he, Walter, told Marit it was his impression that Joel lacked any real interest in people, and it would be a surprise if he continued into criminal law. Walter still had the silver dollar he won from Marit when Joel jumped ship (the first time) and leaped onto ITT's corporate law team. The second time, when he left Marit for his physical fitness trainer, Walter let her keep her money.

Conspicuously, Judith hugged Joel. Her hands around his neck,

198

no finger or thumb without its silver ring. 'Is Marit giving you a hard time?'

'Never,' said Joel.

'I don't believe it. She can't appreciate anybody else's ideas,' Judith buttonholed him like a drunk. 'She won't make the first effort.'

Flushed out of his study by the mob of voices, Walter stood between the open sliding doors and met Joel with a formal, 'How are you?'

'Crackerjack, Walter.'

'Well, fine.' Which could have meant 'so what' or 'too bad' just as easily. In front of his grandchildren, Walter tried to be more welcoming to Joel. If the two men had been there on their own Walter would have shown him the kind of courtesy he'd extend to an attorney in his courtroom. Coming from the old jurist now, from that long-framed desertless patriarch (in retirement Walter had let his strong white hair splash and ripple over his ears and collar), the arm's-length treatment was a sentence beyond hope of appeal. Joel was clear about Walter's feelings and acknowledged them with a deft nod and a broken smile. This too was an effect of Walter's persuasive presence, the calm overseer who arrives to insure a quiet climax.

'Say 'bye to your mom . . .' But Joel was saying this to the back of Ben's head as the boy pushed past him, racing Katy to the car.

Judith stayed planted at the front door, ice-flecked wind lapping into the house, waving until they'd driven away. Marit tried to bring her inside, failed, and hugging herself against the glassy chill's edge she asked Walter if he would give her a ride home.

'Why don't you stay here tonight. With your mother and me.'

'I can smell snow,' Judith said. 'Every human soul is a snowflake first.'

Marit's face was buried in her father's shoulder. She softly moaned, 'Because your wife is making me insane.'

'How about a drink first? Then I'll take you home.'

'You're both bullies.'

Walter's study smelled of woodsmoke, leather bound books, newsprint. Pine logs burned in the small fireplace between twin bookcases that ran wall to wall, floor to ceiling. Consecrated mainly to biography and history, the lower shelves loaded with oversize art books stacked horizontally. There were volumes there, in the same places, Marit knew by color before she could read. The bottle-green binding, the gold-lettered black, the maroon and the marbled blue, even a few of the original book jackets punctuated the rows. Walter got impatient with the paper covers, the way they'd slip off when he held the book to read at chest height. Marit sat in his armchair facing the cherry-wood desk she used to hide under, her sea cave, her forest tree trunk. Now her father was pouring her a malt whiskey, with branch water, the way he taught her to drink it.

He said to her, handing Marit the thick-bottomed glass, 'What did she get you fighting about? In the kitchen.'

'It's the usual thing now, isn't it: my stupid resistance, her dress rehearsal for immortality. Don't you get that feeling with her?' Marit sipped at her drink, felt the warmth of it melt into her. 'It's not like talking to somebody who's actually there, while she's becoming one with the universal consciousness.'

'Judith has her reasons.'

'They're good ones. Only they're taking her away from us faster than the cancer is.' She saw Walter's lean grooved face slacken a little, his mouth loosen, but he didn't speak. 'Katy said to me, "Grandmom's teaching me how to visit her after she dies, in the golden dimension."'

'I can understand how that might make you lose your temper with her.'

'I didn't start it, Dad. Anyway, no: Katy's a little girl. At her age fairy stories help her make sense of the world.'

'I don't think age has anything to do with it,' Walter said.

'Katy's world is so *small*. She isn't supposed to know about big stuff like *time* — that it just goes on burning up, picking off the ones you love one by one. The terrible reality is going to hit her too, soon enough. But there's something worse in everything Mom's saying. It's as if she can't wait to fly out of our lives. What difference does it make how things are between us now, because we'll all be together again soon, and forever, in the golden dimension.'

'What your mom's doing looks pretty resilient to me. This is the first time any of us has done this.' Walter leaned back against the edge of the desk, his long back erect, monumental, above it. The fire's light colored his cheek, the back of his hand, his hair. 'The kind of pain she's facing we just can't know. Can you get right up inside it? Looking into the dark from the edge of her life? I know I can't do that. I don't think it would make things any easier if I could. She needs me on this side.'

Marit said, 'It's where she needs to be too. Close to us.'

'We improvise all the way along.' Walter finished his drink and moved, pulled by a thought, to the chair next to Marit's. He said, 'I never stole a single thing. Not once in my life. Not a pack of chewing gum when I was a little kid. You know why? It wasn't because I carried around some notion of honesty, not in the shape of a great ideal written in the sky. I didn't steal because I knew I wasn't a thief. That was the truth about me, I found out.'

'You believe in the law.'

'Inspired guesswork.'

'A murderer could say the same thing.'

'Well, the difference is I'm guessing about what we owe each other, to make life more livable.'

As Marit sat up to kiss him she saw Lillian Foy's letter on his desk. She pointed at it. 'That's what we were fighting about. Why did Mom give it to you?'

201

'To render my opinion in regard to the plausibility of your correspondent,' Walter smiled up at her. From the hardening of Marit's small oval face he saw this answer needed a little elaboration. So he came clean. 'To talk you into going.'

'How much has she talked *you* into? Dad, you know why she wants me to do this—'

'Let's see if we're talking about the same thing.'

'—For the same reason she wants you to think it's a good idea.'

'Being?'

'Our seal of approval. She wants me to certify it. They both do, Mom and Lillian Foy. If this haunting is real, if this ghost genuinely exists, then et cetera, et cetera. What difference does dying make? I want Mom to know it *makes* a difference. There's a fact you don't need science to certify!'

When Marit's breathing sounded calmer, Walter said, 'Remember what the oncologist told us in May? He expected her to be gone by the end of the summer. So these months and days . . .' Walter shifted in his chair, crossed his long legs. When Marit was five or six years old he took her to Washington, DC. In his lawyer days. Walter was arguing a case in front of the Supreme Court. At the Lincoln Memorial Marit took a long time gazing up at that giant of humane wisdom and said to Walter, 'Daddy, it's you!' This broke through to Marit now.

Perhaps it was the expression on Lincoln's face (as she remembered it), so like Walter's in the struggling firelight, the concentrated hopeless passion of a deathwatch. She said, 'You can reach her, can't you? I'll help you. Help me do it, Dad. We can pull her out of this tangled-up trance she's in. Then we can say what we need to say and know she understands.'

'She's a warning to you, isn't she,' he said, 'of what we revert to when everything reasonable and rational gets stripped away. It's not a reasonable thing that Judith has to die.'

'Doesn't that tell us what we have to do? To make her life more livable? I walk in the door and the first thing she tells me – does Mom talk to you about this? – the first thing on her mind is the program of her funeral. Extracting promises from me. I'm supposed to get her death horoscope done. It's going to decide whether she'll be buried or cremated. And who should be invited to her funeral dinner. Did she tell you this? Where people should sit, which songs we're going to sing. They're in *Tibetan*. Did you know she wants to be there *sitting up* at the head of the table?'

'If that's what she wants, she'll have it.' Walter picked up the letter that was lying on the desk and handed it to Marit. 'What would it take to look into this?'

'If it's nothing?'

'Let's start there.'

'One day. Two, maybe. You can usually turn up a lot just by having a conversation. The idea is to eliminate all the extraneous possibilities.'

'What if there's something you didn't expect to find?'

'I'd stay longer. Examine more,' she told him. With a caution. 'Nobody is even sure what a ghost *is*. It's all cliquey disagreement in the *psi* community. For a hundred years it's been the same ideas running into the same objections, round and around. What good would it do Mom if I came back and said it was a case of psychosomia or the power of suggestion, for instance, or headlights bouncing off a bathroom mirror? I won't lie to her about it.'

'No, honey, you've missed what I'm saying. Don't go for her sake. Go for yours. You don't want to be pushed away from her? I'll tell you how to get in close. Treat this ghost case seriously. Go into it with the same seriousness you save for your other work. How can you tell what's going on up there? From here, you can't. *Whatever* you come back with, you'll end up so much closer to her. I'm talking about how she feels right now. Her thoughts and questions, her stabs at answers.

Tell her you're going to do your goddamndest to find out if it's a real live ghost that's spooking Mr and Mrs Foy.'

'Can you take my weight?' Against his half-mumbled complaint and a burlesque groan, Marit dropped herself onto her father's lap. She could bully her loved ones too. 'Mom doesn't have your subtle knack. She tried to shame me into going.'

'Did she? How?'

'Amazing. With Bosco the Clown. Here I am practically thirty years later, letting her down the same exact way.'

'Not so,' Walter dismissed it, shook his head. 'Funny, we were looking through the album last night. We've got snapshots of that party. One of you protesting in front of the top half of Lena Bobroff. Your anatomy lecture.' He held onto Marit's hand, kissed it. 'You were the most magnificent thing.'

Chapter Twenty

In TOO many ways Marit's trip to Massachusetts was an evasion. It began to feel that way to her on the long drive from the airport. Instead of tackling Joel on the subject of his rushed plans for Christmas with the children (why skiing? why *Austria*?), she was here. Instead of digging in and arguing it through with her father, winning him as an ally, Marit was here. Apparently, confirming her mother's opinion of her: here she was again, riding into opposition against any claim, armored in 'questions, questions, questions'. Judith's harsh view of Marit (the harshness was a recent thing) was that for her knowing the truth was secondary; what really mattered was the chance to exert an influence of her own. So, the larger business was about Marit herself. Was the larger business of radium Marie Curie's character? Instead of framing the conclusion of her NDE study, she was driving into the dark blue late-afternoon winter shadows of Lawford, Mass., concentrating on inferior problems.

And here, in place of the transparent shapes and noiseless sounds of home, the unfolding view imposed itself on Marit. The surface of this small town had something to say to her, inside information about the people who lived in it. On the main road leading her into Mistley she drove past cleared fields and straggling woods, then the landscaped headquarters of Dynotronics Data Systems, copper-colored glass walls that marked the area's foothold in the future. Then, a loose collection of older buildings strung along the straightening road. The expedition deeper into the countryside had Marit thinking of a descent in a diving bell. But between Mistley and Lawford the undersea canyons were colonized by common American settlers – a Burger King, a Walgren's, a pastel-painted car wash, a Greyhound bus station, and somewhere near here she must have crossed into Lawford because she drove underneath a banner, yellow letters on red advertising 'Lawford Days, Dec 17–23'.

In the narrow residential streets, ice paved the flat front lawns. One of them, behind its knee-high chain-link fence, was mobbed with plastic ducks, geese and Dutch windmills. Even Lawford's eccentricities were small and embraceable. What was it, Marit wondered, that had the strength to chase Lillian Foy out of her privacy? (She could put the same question to herself.) If there was a clear answer for both of them it lay in the single question every other one echoed: what unknown thing is waiting to be accepted?

Marit re-read Lillian's directions to the Bluebird Motel while the attendant pumped gas, washed her windshield, checked her tire pressure, made himself noticeably helpful in just about every way he could. The oval patch on the breast pocket of his coveralls was embroidered with his name – Kenny. High school age, dark hair pulled back in a pony-tail, Kenny walked and stood with a confident slouch. He was slouching against the car door while he waited for Marit to sign the credit slip. Along with her receipt (and a slow look at eye level), Kenny handed her a complimentary bunch of dried flowers.

'From me to you,' he said.

Without looking at it Marit dropped the tiny bouquet onto the passenger seat and said, 'The Bluebird Motel? Am I anywhere close?'

'You bet, you bet. A lady in distress.'

'No, just in a hurry.'

Kenny pointed at the empty intersection. 'Left at the lights, first right onto Hoad and you'll see it. It's got a big bluebird for a sign. You're visiting somebody for Christmas?'

Marit started her engine, revved it. 'Thanks.'

'Are you going to be at the Bluebird till the twenty-third?'

'I doubt it. Thanks for your help.'

'In case you are, those flowers are for your bedroom. Y'know, for hanging on your door.' Maybe they were a promotion gimmick, but Kenny looked skewered by Marit's glassy lack of interest. She picked up the whisk-broom dry stems, looked at the garnet-sized pink and purple flowers. Kenny said, 'Don't want the Immortelle to get ya. I'd never forgive myself.'

'Who'd that be?'

'Little baby dude? Comes into your bedroom?' He grabbed his throat with both hands and made choking noises. Finally it hit him that Marit didn't have any idea what he was talking about. 'Are you from Australia or somewhere?'

'Thanks for the flowers.' Marit pressed a smile and pulled away.

She didn't hear him call out, 'My name's Kenny!'

The Bluebird Motel was a shrine of post-war optimism. Behind the homey office (a wood fire burned in a flagstone fireplace), eight separate cabins huddled around a semi-circular driveway. The room was cold. Firewood and kindling waited in the grate. A nesting routine, Marit thought, lighting the newspaper under the dry pine logs, watching the fire catch like a climber on a rockface. Before the room had warmed up she was on the phone to the Foys. She spoke to Freddy who told

207

her he'd made an eight o'clock reservation at their favorite restaurant for an authentic Italian dinner.

The bird-boned, elderly bartender at Giuliano's told Marit he was a friend of the Foys, had been for twenty-three years. 'Beautiful together,' he said, tilting his head in admiration. 'Combination of the president and Florence Nightingale.' Twenty minutes early (she had no trouble navigating the route Freddy carefully described for her), Marit used the time to sip a Scotch in the half-lit bar. From her booth she had a clear view of the entrance, and beyond the bar, which was divided from the restaurant by a plastic partition made to resemble stained glass, she could see some of the crowded tables. The clack and clatter of plates, the unselfconscious seashell murmur of public conversation, the lunchroom odor of pasta steam, the punctuating thump-squeak of the kitchen's swinging doors, the middle-aged waiters in their white shirts and short red jackets beetling around the diners, all this was here, going on out of Marit's sight and hearing, outside her consciousness. Multiply that by tens of thousands of restaurants, by millions of bartenders, waiters and diners whose existence you will never enter, whole lives way out there at the distance of ideas. There's your unseen world. Isn't that wonder enough? Ten days ago she didn't know Lillian and Freddy Foy existed and in a few minutes Marit would see their faces, hear their voices, they'd materialize out of the story in Lillian's letter.

The Foys came in at eight exactly. Both of them had dressed up for the occasion (for her or for Giuliano's, Marit wasn't sure) – Freddy in dark suit and tie, Lillian in a long woollen dress, undecorated by any jewelry. More retired sportswoman than Florence Nightingale; Freddy less president than middle manager. He carried himself toward Marit as a one-man delegation, round-shouldered and bottom-heavy, but moving with a lightness which surprised her. He shook her hand with delicate pressure. His welcoming words were slightly blocked and thickened by the peppermint he was sucking.

Lillian gave her husband room to take the lead. The grip of her handshake, though, was surer than his. It was her decision to ask Marit to come see them. Even so, Marit read in her a discomfort that crackled just below the surface. Perhaps facing Marit now she thought, in Marit's place, she wouldn't take such a woman seriously. Her narrow face was tensed, the fine curves of her eyebrows hardened by more than Freddy's dancing excitement. Anxious, maybe, that a diagnosis was already in progress.

'Tony says our table's ready,' Freddy said. 'Or we could have a drink here before we sit down. Whichever you'd like.'

'I'd like a gimlet, I know that,' Lillian said.

Freddy aimed a finger at Marit's empty glass. 'That's a Scotch?'

'It was, yes.'

While he waited for their drinks Freddy chatted with the bartender. He told the old boy, glancing back at Marit, that she was one of Hildy's out-of-town friends. Where was it written that scientists weren't allowed to be pretty, weren't permitted to wear so much black with so much style? The corkscrew curls, blue-black, were longer than she wore them in her book jacket photo. Her expression, its sharpness, was softened in person with nerve and humor, both there in the attention she gave Lillian when she listened. Her glance avoided nothing and when Marit spoke she used her eyes – exclamation points, accent marks – to push her words across.

Moseying back to the booth, Freddy picked up the thread of Marit's and Lillian's easy conversation. Only three hours in town and already Marit was finding her way around Lawford. Lillian said to Freddy, 'That boy at the Texaco tried to make a pass at Dr Sonnenfeld.'

Marit shook it off. 'It wasn't so terrible. He made me feel exotic.'

'At the Texaco . . .' Freddy was reaching for a face, a name. 'On Frisbee Road? Near your motel?'

'He had a pony-tail. And a gold earring. A real teenage street pirate.'

'Yeah, Kenny Westholme. I've got his little brother in one of my industrial drawing classes.' Freddy slid heavily onto the bench seat across from Marit, with a wince of comic disgust. 'Kenny's going for the Olympic record with the girls around here.'

'In that case I won't be flattered.'

Lillian asked her, 'Are you all right at the motel?'

'It reminds me of summer camp. Except for the temperature. It'll take a bonfire to heat up that room.'

'It's an old building,' Freddy said, knowledgeably. 'Not as old as a lot of the places a few streets away. Old for modern. It's got a history, though.'

'Ask Kenny Westholme.' Lillian held in her laugh, only let out a sniffle, until Marit joined in, full-throated.

Freddy ignored the whole joke. 'Our house is almost a hundred and seventy years old, but even that's not ancient for Lawford. We'll show you the Old Mill House at the Academy. Boy, that's beautiful. From the 1680s.'

'Ours is well-known, too,' Lillian put in. 'A landmark in its own way.'

'Does it have a reputation for being haunted?' Marit asked the question casually, as a tourist might.

'I've never heard any stories,' Lillian said, looking at Freddy for corroboration.

Freddy shook his head. 'It was the first car garage in New England. Around the First World War.'

The tidy canvas bag Lillian had with her was brought out onto the table. She knew Marit's time and patience with them was not inexhaustible. On top of the file of photocopied evidence was the sixty-year-old newspaper story about Adamo Bartolotti's disappearance. 'We'd like to know what you think of all this.'

'Let me read this later,' Marit said, skimming the page before putting it aside. 'We'll take it all step by step and see where things lead, all right? Maybe you can introduce me to the other people who were with you when you found the skeleton.'

'I found it,' Freddy said. 'I dug it out of the basement wall.'

'And this was before you saw the little boy in your house? Or did you find it after?'

Lillian answered. 'After.'

'We're not a couple of screwballs, Dr Sonnenfeld. Not the crazy kind of people you probably meet in these situations.'

'I didn't come up here to prove you are. Anybody can be deluded. Sanity's no protection against mistaken beliefs. Neither is intelligence or even the willingness to investigate what you're sure is true. Some things people believe – sane, smart, educated people – because *not* believing them is too much of a sacrifice.'

Matching her strength atom for atom, Freddy said, 'And that's true on your side, too, isn't it.'

'Are we on different sides?' She asked Lillian, 'In your letter, what did you tell me you wanted out of this? If you want me to perform a scientific ceremony that stamps your ghost with the official seal of approval, well – .'

Freddy nodded in rapid agreement. 'I didn't believe it at the beginning either.'

'She didn't say she doesn't believe us,' Lillian said to him.

'I know that.' Freddy released a pent-up breath. 'When Lillian told me what she'd seen – two, three times she saw this boy – I said she should get some rest. She wasn't sleeping well, she told me that. I said it could be a hundred other things, not a ghost. I held out.' His direct

211

eyes, he hoped, their steadiness, supported his honesty; Freddy was as serious about the factual reality as Lillian was, as Marit was.

'What did you think was going on? Before you saw the boy yourself.'

'Before?' Freddy shrugged. 'I had a different outlook before.'

'I need to get all the events clear in my mind,' Marit said; information for Freddy, but her glance passed to Lillian. 'The first time you saw him he was outside the house.' Lillian nodded. 'Then he walked in through the back door? Who did you think it was?'

The Foys traded brief, secret smiles. She said, 'I thought he was one of Freddy's boys. Getting back at him. A practical joke.'

'Has that happened before?'

'No,' Freddy confirmed.

'And he didn't look like anybody you knew, Lillian?'

'I didn't see his face until the next time. When he came and stood next to my bed.'

Freddy was toying with the loose bundle of toothpicks bunched in a shot glass in front of him. Shuffling them between thumb and index finger, eyes lowered. Marit didn't intrude. She asked Lillian, 'Do you have any children?'

'A grown-up girl. Hildy is living in England.'

A little hotly, Freddy jumped in. 'Do you have any?'

'Ben and Katy. Almost teenagers.'

'High times ahead,' he warned her.

'Was it a rough time for you?' asked Marit. 'With Hildy?'

He frowned. 'Average rough, I'd say. Hildy is about your age. You remember those days. All that anti-war go-go-go. Those rock concerts.'

The talk started to blow past Lillian, she was stuck in her own dark place. 'What's happening to me?' she said in a voice so small, so constricted by a tightening fear, that Marit didn't hear the question.

Until Lillian put it to her again, pierced her with it. 'What is happening to me?'

She startled Freddy. He covered her hand with his. 'I'm in this too. It's both of us.'

So Marit asked them both, 'Has anything else happened in the last two weeks? Anything since you wrote to me or anything you left out of your letter?'

'No,' Freddy said.

'One thing,' Lillian said. 'My chief resident wanted me to take some time off. I didn't want to. I can go back on my regular rotation whenever. It's this tiredness I haven't been able to shake.'

'When did you start feeling tired?'

Lillian thought back. 'We had our friends over one night to play cards. I got a headache and Mim went with me to get an ice pack. It was the strangest thing, Dr Sonnenfeld.'

'You had a tough day at work, didn't you,' Freddy reminded her. 'It's understandable.'

'They brought in a baby, dead. Terrible,' said Lillian. 'Killed. Her head was smashed in. And when I got my headache, Mim saw my scalp was bleeding, like somebody cracked my skull open.'

'*What* happened?' Jolted hard, shocked he was only hearing about it now, Freddy struggled between nervous anger and embarrassment.

'I'm sorry, kiddo. Didn't know what you'd think.'

Marit said to him, 'You didn't see it?' Freddy shook his head. She asked Lillian about the first time she saw the boy come into her bedroom. 'How did you know you weren't dreaming?'

'It was obvious,' Freddy answered for her. 'You could feel him in the room.' He looked straight at Lillian and said, 'You could feel him. The way I'm sitting next to you right here.'

No, Marit thought, the Foys aren't lunatics or publicity hounds. But they held a secret between them and this was their advantage

213

over her. To break into it (that was what they were asking her to do) Marit needed to assure them her mind wasn't closed, just as the Foys needed to assure her their minds were just as open. 'I wish I had your certainty,' she said. Against their secret she had her expertise, her strictness. 'You read my books, you wrote to me. But did you look at John Taylor's work? His books are usually on the same shelf as mine. No? Well, if you'd've written to him instead, this would be a whole different discussion.'

'How?' Lillian asked.

'He thinks a ghost is part of the mind that can exist outside the body. It can move around in the physical world. An energy field, that's what Taylor thinks it is. I used to run into him at conferences and annoy the heck out of him with the same grisly old arguments.'

A little sharply, Freddy said, 'Which are?'

'If a ghost is physical then it reflects light. So when one appears, everyone there ought to see it at the same time. This doesn't always happen.'

'I was asleep the first two times. Didn't Lillian make that clear in her letter?'

'You won't find absolute agreement, that's what I want you to know.' They listened to her, settled into silence. 'I'm close to people, personally close, I mean, to people who believe each of us has a spirit inside us. Invisible energy that remembers everything we've done or that has been done to us. It's made of memory and consciousness, everything we've known and felt. It's not a physical thing like this glass or that wristwatch, we don't – *can't* – know it with our senses. But it reaches into us with telepathy. From the *inside*. All right. Then you run up against definitions of telepathy. Is it actual thought-pictures you're tuning in to or shared human emotion? Some people can be saturated with emotion. Squeeze them and it oozes out in the weirdest ways.'

Lillian said, 'Which idea do you think is correct?'

'It's an open question.' Marit spread her hands in front of her, showing her openness. 'I'd like to know.'

'We're not fraudsters,' Freddy pointed out. 'Or screwballs wasting your time. You don't think we are.'

Marit's eyes told him he was right. 'Look at it from my side. If you were crazy or out to trick me or use me, what else would you say?'

A laugh detonated in Freddy, tight hacking laughter that fully, rib-ticklingly appreciated her point. 'It's like hearing your voice on a tape recorder,' he said. '"Is that *me*? I sound like *that*?" From where you're sitting, I know you're starting from scratch with us. It's easy to forget that. You haven't lived through all this.'

After dinner, back in her motel room, Marit wrote in the journal she'd started to keep: 'When a camera is pointed at you, you can't help feeling the obligation to pose or perform. F. is more prone to this than L. He waved a bread stick like a baton when he talked. His possession of the facts dominated hers – stiff, forced, exaggerated. 'Lillian wasn't sleeping very well . . . I didn't know what she was telling me at first . . .' Defending her. Protecting her from me. Made L. squirm a little (F. did). She is more deeply disturbed by the events, Adamo's story touches her – it overtook her slowly. F. gulped it down whole. He wants to convince me. She wants me to know what she knows.'

Chapter Twenty-one

EVEN THE weather was the same, Lillian noticed. She commented on it to Marit, figuring the fact was helpful, as they stood together outside the house. The same sky at the same time of morning, but today the sharp air collected a dust-soft rising whiteness from the folds of snow covering the field, bordering the house, helmeting the gable above the front porch. 'Show me', Marit said, 'where you were standing when you saw the boy.'

'By the mailbox. I just closed the gate, so I was – no, a step over to the right,' Lillian directed her to the spot. 'I didn't hear him walking up or anything, he was just there all of a sudden.'

The fence she pointed to was low enough, Marit guessed, for an ordinary child to climb over without much noise or strain. She handed Lillian the tab end of her tape measure. 'Now show me where he was standing.'

Thirty-one feet away, in the corner of the narrow yard, Lillian stopped her backward walk. 'Do you want me in the picture?'

'Not this one. You can let it go, that's fine.' The tape measure's thin metal tongue lapped back into its spool, competently ignored by Marit while she made a rough sketch of the yard in her notebook. This can be done, these things can be known, and I see this place, these relationships, freshly. Lillian looks and remembers, she can see what isn't here. A physical map of metaphysical events, nailing them to the ground. And if the events are unreal, what will this map show? From the place Lillian remembered standing when she saw the boy in his white shirt and knickerbockers, his long brown stockings, with his books slung in a leather strap, Marit clicked off several photographs: the two streets, the front of the Foys' house, the ghostless patch of snowy ground where the chain-link fence cornered the yard. She handled the camera efficiently, with practical skill, and no less her pen and notebook, her tape measure. Tools for collecting. And a demonstration of her control, an ability she employed naturally, the way a carpenter can spot and hammer a nail. 'I'm glad you could take time off work,' she said, walking over to join Lillian. 'You won't let me miss anything.'

Lillian adjusted the scarf she wore, Rosie the Riveter style, against the cold, tugging the edge down on both sides. 'If you can't expect understanding from a psych unit, who can you expect it from? I'm on leave this week. They've been terrific with me.'

'What do they know about your mystery guest?'

'Nobody at St Mount's even knows I wrote to you. Let alone you came. My friend Mim, I didn't even tell her.'

'Not me, no. Your other visitor.'

'Him?' Lillian attached a smile to her fresh, abrupt understanding. 'They all read the newspaper. Everybody wanted to hear how Freddy opened up the wall and found what he found. I told Mim and Arthur about Adamo. So four of us know. Five,' she said, including Marit.

Silently, Marit also included Walter and Judith. Seven. 'They must

217

have seen the kind of strain it put you under. It can't be like anything else, digging up a skeleton in your house.'

'Tell you the truth, I've been a little tired out lately. Lately,' she said, weighing it again. 'Since the summer. I've had my daughter on my mind.'

'Did something happen this summer?'

The two women were strolling now, along the side of the house above the trickling culvert. Conversation came easily to Lillian, she opened herself to this chance to talk. 'When she called me in July it was the first time I talked to her in two years. She's so unpredictable. There she was on the other side of the country. Now she's on the other side of the ocean. You fill up the distance with all kinds of imaginary beasts. Rational, irrational, it's all the same worry.'

'A person only has to walk out of the room,' Marit said, 'and you start imagining them. Where they are, what they're doing, thinking. What stopped you from calling her?'

'She's got her own way of doing things. Hildy knew how I felt and if she wanted it to be different between us then she had the power to do something about it. She had to *want* to call me up. Then it would mean something. Finally she did.'

'But it took two years.'

'That time.'

It was still a live issue, the rift and the unbreakable attachment. Marit had a mental picture of mother and daughter as two sandstone pillars, tall and stark under the star-wheeling night sky, motionless under the sped-up arc of the rising and setting sun, for thousands of days and nights. Unrecapturable time.

'He went around here to the back door.' Lillian was a few anxious steps ahead in her bulky caramel-colored winter coat, her stiffly tied scarf above it like a flower bud on a thick stalk.

218

Catching up, Marit asked her, 'Have you seen him here again?'

'No. Each time it's been different. I got the feeling he wanted to lead me toward something. I don't usually leave it open,' she said as they came into the backyard.

Marit shot a few pictures of the wide-open door and the lightless kitchen beyond. Inside, Lillian showed her how the faucets streamed, how the rattling water in the downstairs bathroom led her along Adamo's route through the house. But Marit called to her, lagging behind, 'The basement is down these stairs?'

Clattering back across the brick floor, Lillian said, 'Don't you want to record everything in the right order?'

'Let me take a look at what's down there. All right?'

No one had cleared away the mound of loose earth, mortar, plaster, lumps of damp brick. The gash in the wall, a ragged wound gouged by an enormous claw, remained untouched; no one had been down here since that hectic, crowded, extraordinary night. In the face of Lillian's promise to have John Early send copies of the police photographs to the motel, Marit perched, crouched and leaned in to take her own set of pictures. From the stairs, then moving closer, from the arched partition between the two rooms, on her knees in the spilled dirt to get her camera up into the hidden grave. She found the infill was mostly rubble, chunks of rock, concrete and brick honeycombed with pockets and channels where cold air drifted and pooled. 'What's directly above us?' she asked over her shoulder.

'Our dining room.'

'The cold spot you found, it was in the dining room. Above here?'

'Yes, uh-huh. Maybe we should measure, to locate the exact place.'

The frost in the ground penetrated the basement. A soft plume of Marit's breath joined the air inside the opened wall. She took off her field jacket and ducked her head into the widest part of the opening, and when her small, narrow shoulders followed, Lillian thought she was going to crawl all the way in.

'But it's gone now,' Lillian said. 'After we found him, after they took him away, the cold spot went too.'

Emerging, clicking off her flashlight, Marit said, in dry amazement, 'He was buried back here for so many years. While life went on upstairs.'

'He would've been my grandfather's age, if he lived. He could have had a family of his own. I think Adamo suffered because of his parents.'

'Who doesn't?'

'It was very bad for immigrants around here then. They got singled out. Adamo didn't think he was so different. He said the Pledge of Allegiance, he was an American. The Bartolottis might've told him the world is this or that, warned him men exploit weaker men, that selfishness is all around him, but I think he wanted to judge people one at a time. He was intelligent, I know that, and with a soft heart. Maybe he had to go and see for himself if his parents knew what they were talking about.' Lillian hunched her shoulders, against the surrounding chill, against the thought: 'I guess they did.'

Really, Marit thought, this woman had a gift. To fathom the heart and mind of that dead little boy – and to pull Marit along with her, some of the way. It brought back the memory of a documentary film she'd seen on television. A forensic pathologist set up camp in a Guatemalan village to examine the remains of Mayan Indians allegedly massacred by a military death squad. As the white-haired, cowboy-booted Midwesterner studied the bones and wounds and rotting clothes, slowly identities emerged. A teenage girl named Raimunda, her six-year-old sister Concepción. There were photographs of the victims, as they were in life. Seeing them, sitting in her own safe home a million miles away from Guatemalan death squads, Marit fought off a wave of hopelessness, rising to meet the gasps and sobs of the survivors. Lillian was bringing Marit closer to the boy, to her idea of him, and Marit pulled against it; she was not going to be led from here into the presence of a ghost. She reminded Lillian, 'There's still a lot left to determine. I don't know what I don't know yet.'

'But don't you ever get inklings? And follow them? Some kind of inspiration about what you're looking for?' She said this sure that Marit did. 'I see it every day at work. When staff listen to a patient it's not all by-the-book diagnosis. You look *in*.'

'I'll bet you're grateful for MRIs and X-Rays. For blood work. For every kind of physical test.'

'To confirm what you suspect, sometimes.' This wasn't resistance from Lillian, or argument; it was an offer of a way in. 'Think of the worst thing people can do to each other. You don't have to have the exact facts to know it's true – it's happening right now. The most perverted, cruel thing.' Lillian looked at the broken wall, the disgorged rubble, remains of remains. 'You can see good exists, and order, by the lack of it. Because I know things don't have to be this way. The day after we found Adamo I was in the chapel at St Mount's. It's the opposite of this.' A jut of her chin at the dirt and disorder.

'Is that your husband's picture of the world too?'

'You should ask him.'

'Is he a strict believer? I get the impression he's somebody who has serious beliefs.'

Out of a fluttering laugh, private and warm, Lillian said, 'How can you believe, Freddy says, how can I believe in heaven and hell and God-is-good when the Virgin Mary chooses some Portuguese peasant or those children in Yugoslavia to convey her message to the rest of the world. They're supposed to be an example of humility before the

221

majesty of God. But look, he says, there they are in *Life* magazine and on the CBS Evening News getting more attention than the Pope. A tiny village nobody ever heard of before, making a fortune on instant souvenirs.' A thought escaped, too easily. 'Freddy isn't comfortable looking in, that's all.'

Upstairs the set of military hairbrushes and Lillian's white satin wedding shoes were laid out by the bedroom door, waiting for Marit to find just as Lillian found them before. They had been left there by the living this time. Describing how she'd found those sentimental objects there on the floor Lillian urged them into Marit's hands, as though touching their solid reality would bring her closer to the supernatural event. Relics of more than the Foys' marriage now. When they reappeared, Lillian told Marit, the shoes and the brushes seemed powerfully part of her and powerfully strange too, as if pieces of the moon had been left for her to find.

The curtains were drawn, smothering the roomlight, to give Marit some idea of how the bedroom looked in the dead hours of the night. 'I was lying in bed when Adamo was here. That one's mine.' The dry fact of their separate beds shoved Marit with a soft force. And shoved again when Lillian said, 'Freddy was asleep, with his back to me.' She moved – without needing to be cued, helpfully – to the place the boy came out of the dark bringing his tragedy to Lillian, and for a few seconds the same kind of intense quiet ringed them and held the whole room still.

'Can you remember what Freddy said to you, first thing, when you told him there was a ghost in here?'

'He was worried about me.'

At their dinner Freddy had dominated their conversation, correcting small details in Lillian's version of events, *whatever* the events – courtship and marriage, parenthood or the haunting. Marit sensed he was capable of unintentional abuse, she could picture his broad face and small mouth slackening, his worry taking the form of disappointment and reproach. 'Worried how?'

'It frightened him,' Lillian said. 'To see me frightened.'

'He stifles you a little bit.'

'No, it can look like that to an outsider. I don't know what I'd say to him if it was the other way around. I doubt if he'd even tell me; he'd want to solve it for himself. And not disturb me.'

'He must have made you think you were disturbing him with it, that first time,' Marit suggested.

Lillian's replies were coming less easily. She was concentrating hard but the sharp focus of her expression, arms wrapped around her middle, the posture of an adult about to explain something complicated to a blundering child, already said, *Stop. No further down this line.* Her face stayed turned away from Marit, light dusted the side of it, filling in the thin cheeks, leaving her eyes in shadow. Before Lillian spoke her hands made a jerky preamble, impatient with herself and the situation. Breaking through the tricky stillness, she said, 'I just want to understand the ground rules. You want to know about Freddy and me. All right. I'm not offended, Dr Sonnenfeld. You're making your judgments, I understand that. I do the same thing with my admits at the hospital every day, ask the relatives every kind of personal question. I know, it's necessary, and no matter how reassuring you try to be it's a pretty severe procedure.'

'Do I owe you an apology, Lillian? Tell me if I do.' She waited to be told, but Lillian didn't say yes or no. 'All my questions are the same question. It's the one you're asking too: why is this happening to you now? Three questions in one.'

'But you're going in the wrong direction.'

'Unless I can see something you can't.'

'I'm only saying I know you need to see what's in the background, and we're *giving* you the background. But you're ignoring it, all the research Freddy and I did.' Her throat started to redden, to blotch with insistence. 'Did you read the papers I gave you? What do you think of them? This is connected to a little boy who was actually alive, Dr Sonnenfeld, and he died in this house. I know his name! You see that? We have to find out about Adamo, about *him*. Do you see that?'

'Yes, I do,' Marit said automatically. The glimmering thing she saw was this: Lillian wanted her to care about Adamo as much as she did. To feel the weight of the grief, the danger's closeness. 'I'm going to consider everything. We won't leave anything out. Inch by inch, all right? Let me nail down the what-is before I go plunging into what this might be.'

Partially keeping the thought to herself, Lillian said, 'I must be attracting him somehow. Is that possible? Have you heard of such a thing before?'

'It's different each time.'

'Can you help me find out or *not*?' This was an appeal she made, fearing it might be useless. A grim sadness had taken up residence in her face, dimming and narrowing her eyes; whatever menace had moved into her life had found a place waiting for it, and now it was in her keeping.

'Ask me a question I can answer.' Inside, Marit faded a little, thinking she'd bullied the woman. A builder was what she was, not a wrecker. She'd slipped today. Her witness-interviewing technique, unused for too long, showed the bad old signs of gangbusting confidence and shoot-'em-up judgments. The purpose may be the same but this wasn't what Lillian practiced, not what she was used to in *her* profession, and Marit's brand of hard-eyed curiosity only complicated their relationship; Lillian didn't know how safe it was to respond, all along she'd thought she had been talking to an ally.

So Marit listened with clean attention. If it was important for Lillian to tell, it was important for Marit to hear. And to record on her pocket tape recorder. It was important to talk with Perry Gillies 'while there's time'. Perry was in his eighties and in crumbling health. Dreams he'd had about the boy, Lillian began to believe, terrifying ones over the last few weeks, were versions of Adamo's visits to her. Perry's affection for Lillian had the color of dependence, she presented it that way, unsentimentally to Marit, and hers for him was more detached but constant, sharing so much history. At St Mount's together for fifteen years, and sixty-odd-years ago Perry lived and worked in this house. At the end of this conversation Marit wrote one line in her notebook. 'L. may not know how much she knows.'

What had opened her up to let Adamo in? On her slow drive back to the motel Marit tried to picture things from Adamo's point of view. What would a dead child want from Lillian Foy? She was in the world, where things could be done, where human will could have an effect. She was a grown-up with a touchable heart. A nurse. A mother.

The courtyard was webbed in the blue hues of dark when Marit pulled in. Snow had started to float across on a light wind, loose scarves of it caught and twisted in the air, settled dustily on the shingles of her cabin. The telephone rang as soon as she was inside; Mr Bouzoukis, the manager, had a message for her. He couldn't tell her any more than what he found on the message pad, he apologized, but his son had been minding the phone and all he'd written down was, 'Dr Sonnenfeld's mother'. Cold alarm swam through Marit's blood. Dialling her parents' number, hearing the phone ring too many times. That stupid irresponsible Bouzoukis! Didn't he think it made a difference to know whether the message was *from* her mother or *about* her?

It was Judith's voice, not her flat greeting from the answering machine, Marit heard then. 'I was meditating,' she said. 'I didn't hear the phone. I'm here by myself.'

'You called me?'

'After my lunch. You were with those people?'

'With one of them. At their house.'

'How many discoveries did you make?'

'About the ghost, none. About the Foys, one or two. An extraordinary thing is happening to Mrs Foy, for real. That's a discovery.'

'Don't decide what it is in the first five minutes. You sound like that, in the way you said it.'

'Mom, you remember when you came to the university that day? That diploma I earned? A PhD, Mom. Believe me, I know how to—'

'In those days you weren't so prejudiced. Anyway, I want to tell you what to look for if it's an astral haunting. Probably electrical discharge hangs around in the areas where the spirit appears. And sometimes you can see an aura. Is she seeing the aura or the whole person?'

'You can help me by taking care of yourself. I'm sorry I interrupted your meditating.'

'So it happened now, so never mind. This matters more. I don't want you to ignore invisible evidence you can't pick up on a Polaroid snapshot.'

'I don't use a Polaroid. I haven't even started monitoring yet, Mom, so please – you don't know what you're talking about.'

'One thing I know. You went up there because you promised your father. You're just exploring around the edges, for show, and not really going into it. You're putting on a show.'

'My car is in the garage, my kids are with Joel and his airhead girlfriend, I've got my NDE conclusion to write and I'm hundreds of miles away in a motel, in the snow, in Massachusetts, *and* I'm staying until Monday. What kind of a show does that sound like to you? Tell me, please, Mom, because to me it sounds like the Jerry Lewis Muscular Dystrophy Telethon!'

'I don't want you to be there because Dad twisted your arm.'

'How can I say it so you'll believe me? I'm here for the right reasons.'

Mrs Sonnenfeld's brainy little girl! Too brainy to be open about her motives. As always, she's following her own plan, everybody get in line behind her, what's good for Marit is good for all the rest of you. Bravo and encore! Coming from Judith, her old sour song, the ballad of Marit's flawed character sounded flat and stale. Still it unhinged her and hours later sent her into angry sleep.

Chapter Twenty-two

PERRY SHUT himself in his bungalow. His absence on the floor was noticed but not recorded by Billy Cooke, and if it weren't for the outcries escaping through Perry's bedroom window, heard by an orderly on his way across the parking lot, nobody would have checked on him at all.

Billy found him in bed, dressed in his stale work clothes – the pink St Mount's smock over his blue shirt and trousers – open-eyed, exhausted, in the grip of some flattening sickness. Perry didn't talk to Billy Cooke, he only made a noise through his dry, tightly pressed lips that sounded like 'brrrrp-brrrrp'. He'd been keeping himself awake with doses of benzedrine, stolen from the pharmacy. Dr Mollo confiscated the bennies and warned Perry about the balance of prescribed drugs he already had in him to deaden the pain, aid his kidney function and his stomach's work and to encourage his colon, all those organs independently quitting on him.

The world was disgusted with Perry Gillies and now it was

shrugging him off. In a wheelchair they moved him into St Mount's where Dr Gertler found him a room on the Geriatrics floor. From the other side of the pain in his gut another impulse, not his own, moved against him, sent from someplace invisibly far away and invisibly close. Death was in motion toward him. Its cold heat made luminous every moment he had lived, every choice, every plan, his meager gains and gifts, every face he knew, each detail mountainous when it came to him, and yet added together, eighty-one years of moments, gains, losses and the rest amounted to his vanishing smallness ... So don't make a meal of me! Look at the box I ended up in! Let me go, and go in peace. *Ite, missa est . . .*

He stared at the blank back of the door where a blur of light collected on it. The light spread and hardened, became human. Perry felt a steepness as he looked, it raised him or raised the bed under him, lifted him toward the boy. The sight of Adamo choked him – those large beetle-black eyes, his scraped and gouged skin, his filthy underwear – and then it sparked a burst of Perry's hate. Adamo caught the blunt force of it and his mouth opened, hanging open without forming words but words came out of it. Through his bones Perry heard what Adamo said, words spoken without use of breath, vibrating inside him, clawing him there. Adamo stared back in something like famished awe, as if Perry was the dead, come to wrestle him into the dark. 'I'm just a little boy.'

'What was I!' Perry thought he said this out loud, in his cupboard-sized bedroom, with its gray-green metal locker, his sink, his chair, his windowless cell. 'You don't belong here! The hell I'm suffering for *you*! You want to see me in my coffin, don't you! Is that all you can do? It's pitiful!' Refusing the shame along with the destiny. 'You can't dictate to me,' he said and with as much effect as saying this to Death itself.

Adamo moved closer to the bed, moved by his own need, to break Perry's alliance with life. His small body was naked from the waist down. Dirt covered his legs, formed crusts, darkly filled the creases of scrapes and gouges on his skin, human dirt mixed with oily dust from the ground. He climbed onto Perry's bed, he sat at the end of the mattress without touching Perry's feet, and then crawled toward him, to be held in Perry's arms, to be comforted. And lying down there, Adamo shuddered through him, ribcage through ribcage, legs through legs, the weight of a shadow pressed through the spaces in Perry's body.

A grab at the lanyard dangling above his head snapped on the small reading light. Its whiteness spilled across the bed, its edges fading quickly in the empty room. Perry tilted himself on one hip to find the warm wetness under him had bled through and colored a patch of the sheet brown, staining it with latrine odor, his sick man's smell.

The phone call at six a.m. jerked Marit out of a dream about her children. While Lillian was explaining the urgency to her, making apology, Marit's thoughts were still stumbling over the half-remembered picture of Katy following Ben down a manhole and disappearing under the asphalt of Henry Street. She asked Lillian to go over again what she'd said and the pieces of information slowly stopped knocking and spinning against each other, and settled into clear meaning.

'He begged me to come in and talk to him,' she was saying about Perry. 'He had a terrible night.'

'What kind of terrible?'

'Perry told me the boy was in his room. And Marit,' Lillian said, 'Adamo was with me too.'

'Did your husband see him?'

230

'No. He asked me what was wrong, you know, I couldn't go back to sleep. So I just said my stomach felt bad. It did, too. This time it was different. He spoke to me.'

'The boy did,' Marit confirmed. 'Do you remember what he said?'

'He never did that before.' It was interpretation she wanted, uncertainty was the root of her fear. 'He told me he was just a little boy. As if that should protect him.'

'What from?'

'From me.'

Under his own steam Perry cleaned up his bed and himself. The heavy sour odor was trapped in the curtain-darkened room, lying in the air like humidity. He was dressed when Lillian and Marit let themselves in, sitting on his bed. His eyes were bad, his mind taken over by his trouble and the hope of relief Lillian was bringing him, so he barely noticed Marit. She stayed back, outside the ragged oval of reading lamp light, and she heard Perry plead to be believed.

'I can count to a hundred, I know my ABCs. This is my left hand,' he said, lifting it, showing her, 'this is my right hand. My name is Perry Craig Gillies. The President of the United States is Ronald Reagan.'

'I know you're not making this up.' Lillian held both of Perry's hands, held them still.

'You're sitting right where he was.'

She was next to him on the bed, sitting sidesaddle, her long form blanketed in her dark wool coat, leaning into the light. Two arcs of hair unclasped themselves from her scarf and crowded her face. With a gentleness that surprised Marit, Perry touched Lillian's chin, raised it so he could look at her. More than that; to be received by her, unjudged. She was the crack in the dark world where light strained

231

through to warm him, clear light to direct his steps. He didn't have many more to take. Marit saw deep exhaustion, life exhaustion, in his raw eyes, the whites dipped in mercurocrome, his chapped mouth also red, thin and wide, in permanent doubt, pulled downward at the crusted corners, the weight of frank disappointment there, and below on his throat the flappy skin of the very old, badly shaved days ago, white bristles and longer hairs in clumps on his Adam's apple and straggling under his jaw; his limbs with no power in them, the bundle of cords that held their tension had gone slack, loosened at the center. Perry spoke a few more words to Lillian which Marit couldn't hear. Then he stopped himself and raised his eyes over Lillian's shoulder to take a look at Marit.

'Who's that there?' he asked Lillian.

'She's helping me,' Lillian said and turned a little to open the circle to Marit, introducing her to Perry as 'Dr Sonnenfeld'.

'My name's Marit,' she told them both. 'Hello, Perry. Lillian said you saw something in here last night. I'd like to know what scared you so much.'

Perry ignored her. 'What do you need help about?' he asked Lillian. 'I'll help you. Billy told me you left and for all I knew you were gone for good.'

'How far away could I go?'

'Billy said the North Pole.'

'I came back for you. Marit came all the way from Philadelphia. She wants to find out what the boy wants from us,' Lillian said. 'He comes to me, too.'

A shiver crossed Perry's face, a painful twitch. 'He's going to hurt you. That's what he wants.'

'He'd be the first ghost on record,' said Marit, 'if he did that.'

'Does he come to you in Philadelphia?' Perry blasted her. 'Then shut up about it. What do you know about it?' He leaned closer to Lillian.

232

'Listen, he went right through me. I think he did some damage. Did he do that to you? Break pieces off?'

'Let's tell each other what we know, Perry, *please*. I saw them dig his bones out of my house. I know who he *is*.'

'If you stand in the snow,' said Perry, 'you get cold. If you go out in the desert you get sunburned. You stand where you stand and who's got a right to judge?'

Marit asked, 'You think you're being judged by him?'

'Sure, that's it. That's his big case. So it comes back at me now. They're all under the ground except me. Rupert and Elias. Old Samuel.' He lost his voice for a few seconds, not his concentration. 'Bartolotti, the father of the family, he came to the garage with his boy.'

'With Adamo?' Lillian said.

'He wanted to look at the cars. Of course. Just like an American kid. We didn't pay attention to the old wop. But his little boy, I liked him. He was playing on the chassis, making up some sing-song about cars, pretending he was driving it and what-all. Made believe it was a fighter plane.'

Perry leaned back, taking Lillian's gaze with him, holding onto it like a lover. In desperate attachment. A fact he wanted Marit to witness from her place outside the circle. After that only the occasional word or two rose clearly out of their low, intimate talk, but Marit gained more from the sight of Lillian and Perry together – crabby and cast off he may have been, plucking at her strength, heads bowed toward each other, both hands held, private language sizzled on the taut wires strung between them. This was happening to them both, they were together in their separation from the ordinary place inhabited by everybody else. It appeared to Marit that Perry was the frailer, in hungrier need, very likely because he was closer to death. He wanted allowances made for him, some responsibility lifted from his shoulders, and this might be what a sufferer needs to hear from his nurse: disease is the culprit, not my own faulty body, death comes from outside, I'm being preyed on. And the face of this death, for reasons Marit could only guess, was a lost child's, dead himself for most of this century.

One thing Perry had to say broke through his privacy, stronger than his whispering. 'He wants to murder me in my sleep. Who deserves that?'

'He's a little boy,' Lillian answered him. 'There's no harm in him, not in him.'

'Somebody put it there. Spite, see? You don't deserve it.' His grief, forced from him, was over the danger he'd called down on her and on himself. In the next second he disowned it. 'Who deserves it? Not us. I'm not doing this. I didn't do this to you,' shaking, Perry promised her.

He locked Lillian in a hug and they were knotted together like that when Mollo let himself in. The doctor was grateful Lillian was there, he said so. Then, as though it was the next item on his packed agenda, he delivered a hello to Marit. Lillian performed the introductions, leaving out Marit's professional title.

'I'm a friend of Hildy's,' Marit volunteered, a lie free of embarrassment either for her or Hildy's mother.

'They met in college,' Lillian said.

'Oh? Where?' asked Mollo.

Marit improvised, 'At Penn.'

'State or University?'

'University. She was in my ab psych class.'

'You teach? Or was Hildy a guest speaker?' Mischief from Dr Mollo. He said to Lillian, 'Your daughter's something else, isn't she?'

234

'I promised I'd look in on her folks,' Marit said, 'if I was anywhere in the area. I was in Boston, so . . .'

'What did it take you – two and a half hours to drive down?'

'Two,' she told him. 'It wasn't such a rough trip.'

'Get them to move their cocktail party to the cafeteria.' Perry wanted Lillian to himself. 'I'm suffering from stinkfoot and I need to discuss treatment with my nurse,' he made it wildly clear. 'It's very personal.'

'Marit,' Mollo said, 'why don't I show you around the unit? You two can meet up for coffee in . . .' – he checked with Lillian – 'ten-fifteen minutes?'

'I'd like to show Marit where I work, Doctor. It's not just the building she came to look at.' Lillian's glance traveled from Mollo to Marit and back to Perry. 'We won't be talking in here very long. Marit isn't bored yet. She'd say if she was.'

Perry grabbed back her attention. 'You don't know how long we'll be talking. As long as it takes, you'll stay with me. All right? Stay with me, I'm on my goddamn knees.'

Leaving the room Marit saw Perry's arms lifted to Lillian's shoulders, pulling himself closer to her, their faces almost touching. What he had to tell her he kept low but the necessity of it hissed into the air. It was like a view of the ocean from the dock, where the water is tamed and managed, the harmless fringe, while the real ocean with its bitterness, coldness, murderous moods, great swallowing distances and deep was shifting out beyond.

As they walked from the elevator and around the corridors of Molyneaux Wing, Dr Mollo talked about the years he had worked with and depended on Lillian, about her popularity in the unit with staff and clients, about her strength and sensitivity, a general summary which he ended by saying, a little provocatively, 'But you already know all this.' A vigorous walker and talker, Mollo guided Marit across the reception area, a few feet ahead of her, as smooth as a race car around a track, every gesture of his small tightly sprung body, every syllable he spoke, seemed meant to inform Marit of the kind of executive medical man she was dealing with. 'Mind if we make a quick stop at my office?'

Past his secretary they went without Mollo answering her wave or stopping to introduce Marit. He led the way into his private territory and made a beeline for the tall rack of magazines. He shuffled a stack of *The Journal of Neurophysiology*, pounced on an issue Marit recognised, thumbed through to the centerspread article and laid it open on the corner of his desk. He was on to her.

Marit's monograph, *Sensory Evocations of Unreality*, dealt with a young woman, Georgia, who reported that the apparitions she saw (an old man in a tweed suit; a dark-skinned girl) blocked objects behind them. 'I'll tell you why I remember it,' Mollo said. 'You published around the time I started working in the same area. I was – am – asking pretty much the same questions. In these people, where does the brain intercept the visual stimuli which they stop seeing when the apparition gets in the way?'

'How much time do they give you for research?'

'Plenty. It's a plus for the endowment committee. You know how that goes. My work attracts grants, receives attention. Kudos, even.'

'I'm twice as embarrassed I haven't read you, then.' Marit made an effort to be convincing, an effort she hoped she disguised with a spurt of interest. 'You're doing brain mapping? Cognition?'

'You know my work,' Mollo squinted, a teasing accusation. 'No? You don't?'

'If you've been reporting in the last year or so, well, I've missed a lot. I'm still catching up. My sabbatical—'

Mollo broke in, he was on another track altogether. Flapping the magazine limply in the air, he said, 'Was the retina at the back of her eye registering the stimuli?'

'There's a paragraph in my conclusion bit.'

'Remind me.'

Politely, performing, Marit said, 'The electroretinograph showed an apparition didn't affect the responses of Georgia's retina to light. Her evoked visual response to light—'

'Was blocked.'

'It was blocked after the light had been normally registered by the retina.'

He let her stand in dead silence before he sprang this on her: 'Dr Sonnenfeld, are you muscling in on my subject?'

Marit's tone was controlled, her balance steadied. 'Why would you think that?'

'Oh, I don't know.'

'Really, I'm in the dark.'

'Who's in the dark? Try harder.'

'In all honesty, I – you can take my word for it. Believe me, Doctor Milo, unless they overlap with NDEs I've got about zero interest in anomalous experience studies.'

'Who's Dr Milo?'

'I'm sorry. I must've misheard your name. I apologize if I've done that. It's – what is it, Doctor?'

'In all honesty. *You* give me honesty. How did you track Lillian down? At the Detroit conference I only referred to her by her initial.'

'Detroit? In September? I wasn't there.'

This he didn't accept. 'That's real interesting.'

'So Lillian was already working with you? On apparitions?'

'Please don't try to play me. It stands to reason you'd give up on *psi* and that wagonload of fruit salad. You'd climb out of that dry hole and climb into synaesthesia. Tell me the God's honest about something. Did Leo Kammelman tell you who Lillian was?'

'My relationship with Lillian, and with Leo Kammelman, as a matter of fact, is as private and privileged as yours.'

'But mine doesn't seem so safe. So why should yours be?'

'This is crazy. There's some kind of misunderstanding here.'

'All right. I don't want you to go away with the wrong idea: she's my subject. Stay away from her. We're scheduled for work on a graphic computer next week and I'd appreciate it very much if I didn't have to fly down to Philadelphia chasing after her.'

'I'm telling you the truth,' Marit reminded him. 'Lillian's synaesthesia is news to me.'

'Then what are you doing with her?'

'Ask Lillian. If she wants to tell you she will.'

'You know, I don't think you actually ever met her daughter.'

'She wrote to me. Lillian did.'

'Oh. So that was a lie about knowing Hildy.' Mollo shrugged, in tense reply to Marit's shrug. On his scorecard, she owed him. 'Has Lillian had a near-death experience?'

Marit had nothing to say on the subject.

'I'm fresh out of professional courtesy, Dr Sonnenfeld. Right now I think it'd be a tip-top plan if you found your way out of our psych unit.'

'Maybe you'd like to round up the boys and run me out of town,' Marit said, going.

'It's a free country.'

Among the nurses and orderlies and admin paper shufflers on their morning break, relatives of ailing or recovering patients killing time, and the bath-robed hospitalized in the cafeteria with her, Marit hoped

238

she was conspicuous. By sitting alone at one of the polished pine tables, at least – it wouldn't be her untroubled eyes that singled her out, because she *was* troubled and part of the subdued, birdcage commotion of the long room. She sat in front of the picture window, sealed in against the weather, lit by the gray-white snow-softened daylight; Marit's dark, massy hair and beatnik-black clothes made her almost a silhouette.

Already with her cup of tea, Lillian came to sit next to her as a stranger might, only sharing Marit's table. She was quiet as she stirred sugar into her cup, concentrating on the tiny whirlpool, folded in on her thoughts, which were not calm. She said, 'Did Dr Mollo get you to tell him why you were here?'

'Oh,' Marit said. 'Mollo.' She bit her lower lip. 'I called him Dr Milo.'

A nervous sip at her hot tea, then Lillian said, 'Bet he didn't appreciate that.'

'We're not going to be bestest friends, no.'

'But does he know now?'

'He's got his own theory about what I'm doing with you. I'm stealing you away from him, he's convinced. Grand larceny. He didn't believe me, just stopped listening to me, when I told him I didn't know a thing about your synaesthesia.'

This fell on Lillian as a judgment, a teacherly criticism. 'Should I have told you about it? My colors,' wiggling fingers in front of her eyes, 'my shapes and colors.'

'It's something I didn't know yesterday. Let's talk about it sometime.' Marit came up against the gloom that settled like an ashy film on Lillian's face, even her lips were colorless. 'Did your friend Perry have a lot to say to you?'

'I wish you'd met me a month ago. I wasn't such sad lump. Marit, you know,' she looked at Marit's face, full of bravery, 'I was

239

combing my hair in the bathroom this morning and in the mirror I saw how different I am. It's the same thing I see in old people. I'm not old.'

'You're not such a lump, either. Trust me on this.'

'No, but it's this ... drifting loose. Caring so much and yes, okay, caring is what you do: you do it if it makes a difference in the end or not. Sometimes it can't make a difference but you do it. For yourself, I think. Maybe it's a selfish thing, caring so much. That's what I feel. I don't remember feeling that way about it before.'

'I think you're being very tough on yourself. A strange thing is happening and you don't know why it's happening to you.'

Lillian nodded, looking away. 'Perry said – oh, it's all in bits and pieces. He'd say one thing and next thing he'd contradict it. I think he told me he knows who killed Adamo, and how he died.'

'He's saying he was there?'

'He was half-there, he said, or there for half the time. Then he said he heard the story after. He wants me to know and he doesn't. He said he's trying to protect me. And if I say a rosary every night for him, I can protect him too. But how can I do that? If it's your time to die what difference does a rosary make?'

'That must depend on who says it.'

With conviction, from experience, Lillian said, 'You never can know though. What happens after, I'm not sure about that anymore. But what was and what is both go on at the same time. The last hour or day of Adamo's life can be going on now. Can it or can't it? If it can then maybe what happens to us is already decided.' In the shadow of this certainty Lillian asked, 'What do you think is going to happen to me?'

The question could have come to her from Judith. It did, in her way, with her astral certainties. Judith and Lillian were facing in the same direction. This is what dying does, watching it or enduring it. You feel the startling distance open up between the ones who are here and the lost, the human and the ones who aren't human anymore. What was, who was, when was – Marit wanted to say at that moment to both of them, Lillian and Judith, that what's disappeared is more of a fabrication than your momentary view of me is. But she didn't say this, she offered more dependable objectivity. 'Only what's going to befall the rest of us. The same but different.'

'That's all you can tell me? Please, what do scientists say?' She insisted, 'Can time get mixed up?'

'I'm not really up on physics. When they talk about time going backwards, it's, they're talking about—' Marit abandoned the whole idea. 'I'm not really qualified.'

'Well, tell me what you *are* qualified to answer!' Then quickly, retreating, '*Please*. Please . . .'

'Lillian, I don't understand what you're asking me.'

She made herself ready to try to speak Marit's language. 'Being alive can't be just walking around, talking and forgetting. Human things . . . what we do . . . even if there's nothing left of them and no one who remembers . . . they really happened. Do you think so?'

'I think you're still trying to decide if you can trust me. Or how far.' Oh, for Judith to be at this table! To *accept* this, finally. In place of her mother, she had Lillian to convince. Marit started, 'Imagine walking through a doorway into a room that's two paces long and one pace wide. It ends at a door which you step toward to open. And as you open it the door behind you closes, seals shut, it turns into a wall. You go on through the next doorway into a room that's two paces long and one pace wide, which ends at a door that you step toward to open, so on and so on, one moment after the next.'

'*Can't you give me a direct answer?*' The paper napkin Lillian didn't use to wipe the brown droplets of tea from the corners of her mouth was tightly balled up in her hand. She passed it back and forth, left hand, right hand, while she kept on, 'You go away into theories and comparisons, anything so you don't have to say, "Yes, the evidence says it's possible," or, "No, the connections are too emotional – emotions aren't facts." What if emotions *are* facts?'

Chapter Twenty-three

ON THIS night, the sky empty and cold, at this hour buried in the dark, the Foys' bedroom was utterly still. The air lay almost solid around them and had a pressing weight, as the air weighs down in a cave or pit. Disjointed, insistent thoughts cartwheeled through Lillian's head: it's like this underground, I'm under the ground. She was headachy with it, this hammering in her head. My muscles are thinning, my skin is sinking away, I don't have a place in the world anymore – not like my chair or my bed. She reached out to run her fingers over the red silk of the chair beside her bed: it's here and I'm not.

From this her mind lurched to a picture of Perry Gillies in his box of a room, twinned with him. She saw him lying in his bed waiting for the final thing to happen. Waiting for Adamo to come to him one last time, with the truth about why he was there. This thing that was finishing had its own momentum and purpose which couldn't be calmed or softened by scientific explanations. Adamo was here to join in a death. He was owed a life, and more – owed a sacrifice for his unlived, massacred time, owed the telling of his secret drama. Lillian scrunched into another position, legs drawn up, knee resting on knee, tender bones, the soreness spreading out from there up and down her body, her knees grinding against each other, her hips twisted and aching, her skin the shell of a stale pain.

'What?' Freddy spoke to her, barely half-awake. 'What's the matter?'

'Did I wake you up?' whispered Lillian.

'Lil? No. I don't know why I did. What's wrong?'

Once the tears started Lillian knew that no word or act of will could stop them raining out of her. They throbbed in her throat. She used the strength she had to cover her eyes with her hands, that was all, a cracked dam that let the water trickle through.

Leaning over Lillian from the side of his bed, Freddy strained to see her face as though the cause of this sadness twisting through her might actually be breaking the surface, visible. 'I'm here, doll. Ssh, ssh, sweetheart. What is it?'

When he stretched out his hand to her Lillian took it, held it to her face. It was solid, she felt its warmth, his grip. Her shield against the questions, clues, rumors fluttering close. There might not be another chance to hear the truth (her fever said so), the need for clear facts was the need for air and if she was denied them she'd suffocate. Out of the spinning tumbling mess of uncertainties came, 'When Hildy said you hurt her and hurt me too, what did she mean?'

Patiently, doing his best, Freddy said, recalling, 'It must be how I wanted something for her that she didn't want. How I tried to help and I hurt her. Did that hurt you? Are you crying about Hildy?'

'There's so much I think I don't know. I want to know everything now. I'm afraid of it, Freddy, but I want to know. "He hurt me and he hurt you too." What does that *mean*?'

'I'd be guessing,' he said, rubbing his cheek. 'Since you told me she said that I've been racking my mind, going over that time, and

244

I can't settle on one thing. Unless it was the way I acted with her. Too strongarm. Too protective. She took any comment or suggestion as a judgment on her. I didn't judge. Can she still feel that way?'

'You did judge her.'

'Did I?' He truly wanted to be told. 'She had some pretty hard things to say to me. "You're a stranger. I don't know who you are." Hildy did her share of judging me. She said I wasn't like her at all and so I couldn't ever know her, you know, the way a father and daughter should know each other.'

'That was cruel of her. And not true. When did she say that?'

'Around that time. When she was going to have her baby. All that ruckus. She was different from me, all her made-up values and goals. All right, some things I didn't understand but I sure understood the situation. She had to live in the same world we all did. She couldn't make up her own rules as if nobody else deserved to be considered, and drift around on any breeze in any direction. Maybe I didn't know what kind of crazy thing made her happy, but the same things make everybody unhappy.' He let his eyes wander, and to the black square of the window he said, 'You tell me. Why did Hildy think it was her God-given assignment in life to make me admit she knows best? I broke my back for her sake.'

'For both of us.'

'You're the only one who thinks that's true.' He heard Lillian's crying open up again. 'Let go of it, Lil. If it's Hildy that's doing this to you. You came home upset. You've been so breakable. Worse since your Dr Sonnenfeld started grilling you.'

Between sniffs she said, 'Marit only wants what we want. To see where Adamo comes from.'

'And she doesn't care who she disturbs along the way. It's got nothing to do with her.' There was an edge of anger in Freddy's complaint. 'We were doing all right, finding things out. I get the feeling the Bartolotti boy doesn't like her or what she's trying to do. What she's doing to you. An outsider prying into our concerns.'

Lillian lay so still Freddy thought she had stopped listening to him. Which was true. She was in the silent grip of one overwhelming recognition. Her words brought it into the room. 'I think I'm dying.'

'No, doll,' he said, kneeling on the floor next to her bed, like a child saying his prayers, her face between his hands.

'I won't be here anymore. This house will be here without me in it. You'll look at my radio or this chair and I'll just be a memory around them.'

'No.'

'I won't be connected then, don't you understand?' Something like anger had rooted itself in her. 'When it's finished, oh God, Freddy, I know how it will feel. I'll *feel* it. The pain of all the unfinished things, what I didn't do and didn't know. Where will I be? In your imagination. And I'll see you but I won't be able to touch you. You won't be able to hear me or touch me while I'm trying to make you think of me and remember who I was to you.'

'Why are you talking like this?'

Exile was waiting for her, banishment into longing without end. 'Because I'm dying.'

'No, Lil. You're not leaving me. I won't let you go. Please, doll. Don't do this. I'll keep you here, with me. With me.'

He climbed into her bed, into Lillian's arms. His full belly pressed against hers, their legs touching. Clumsy and tender he lifted her nightgown and stroked the tops of her legs, brushing his fingertips over those long unvisited places. He cupped her narrow breasts then let them fall against his chest, keeping his protective weight close next to her. It was the same for him in that startling moment as it was decades ago – her hair threaded around his fingers, he clutched it at the back of her head and urged her toward him, her mouth to his. This is what young lovers dream about and unguarded pledge to each other, the future they want to arrive, every kiss, every stroke full of these shared years.

She felt Freddy untie his pyjamas and with his free hand scrumble them down to his knees and then she felt what love moved him to do. With his old sureness he was asking to be welcomed back. And they were together, the man and woman they had been at the beginning. Her arms around his neck kept him there; she opened to him, said his name and all her anger left her, the uncertainties stopped spinning and tumbling and in their place was the rhythm of his hips, his heavy strokes which beat like a loud noise blocking out every other sound. She kicked the blanket away to give him room with her, to feel only him, his wide back that had carried so much and was carrying her now. Alive, he was telling her, she was alive with him. She was here, feeling this. He moved quicker when he heard her say his name or let out a breath, all control gone, she clung on to his solidness on the loosely rocking bed, his motion and hers, alive together.

Freddy gasped once, twice, and seemed to fall through his exhaustion. She kept her arms around his shoulders, her hands splayed on the flesh of his back, gripping him there. Keeping him with her on the raft of her bed. As he slipped into sleep she pulled the blanket over him. But Lillian stayed awake, watching, eyes on the gaping empty dark outside the bedroom door. She wouldn't let sleep have her because the end of things might come tonight and this might be the last time she'd be with Freddy. So she didn't move and welcomed the cold air scraping her naked back.

Chapter Twenty-four

THE LILLIAN who opened her door to Marit wasn't the Lillian who had sat with her in the St Mount's cafeteria the morning before. Lillian wearing make-up was a startling sight. A soft pinkish cast lay on her face, the suggestion of a glaze, meant to put life into skin drained of color and strength, but it couldn't disguise the slackness there. She had also pulled back her dark gray hair, locked it behind her head with tortoiseshell barrettes, a younger style that added ten years to her age. Marit had seen women who had prettied themselves up like this in hospital rooms, other cancer patients plucked from the outside world at the same time as Judith, called in for chemotherapy and radiation treatments. Sickbed make-up, a little theatrical and vainly defiant – hair coiffed, eyelids daubed with eye shadow, bruises of rouge – a facsimile of health and optimism in faces where the real vigor was gone. Lillian's eyes weren't vacant but elsewhere; some sober knowledge had lodged in her and turned her into a floating spectator.

She held the screen door for Marit to trundle in with her two suitcases. 'I'm not moving in,' Marit assured her, 'I've got some equipment to set up in the bedroom. Where you saw the boy for the longest time. Have you seen him again?'

Lillian shook her head. 'I know he's coming back, though.'

'He's around, all right,' Freddy said from the foot of the stairs. He was in his navy cardigan, the sleeves baggy, the cuffs neatly, precisely turned. Next to Lillian's complexion his color was high and vibrant, rising out of a great settling satisfaction. He didn't offer to lend a hand with Marit's luggage, he just invited her to put it down anywhere.

'They're things she wants to put in the bedroom,' Lillian advised him, closing the door and standing with her arms folded.

'I've brought a video camera with me. A recorder and a motion detector. The highest tech tools I can afford.' Marit was aware of the atmosphere she had brought in with her. In the university they used to call it temple magic or sometimes rank scrutiny. Either way, there was an uncomfortable threshold to get across. 'I know the way,' she said, picking up the suitcases.

Freddy followed her upstairs and looked on from the bedroom door as Marit set up the camera on its tripod, connected it to its recorder and timer, found the wall sockets. She thought he probably did the same thing to any workman come to do a chore in his house; there he'd be at the bathroom door, overseeing the plumber who was unblocking the Foy toilet. She asked him to stand in the place where he'd seen Adamo.

'Here,' he said. 'But he's shorter than me. About this tall.' Freddy held the flat of his hand a few feet off the ground.

Marit framed him in the viewfinder and angled it to get in most of that part of the room: the foot of their beds, the door to the hallway, the lower half of the bathroom doorway. 'You won't mind this mess in your house for a night or two, will you?'

'I don't know if I like being filmed in bed.'

249

'This is a very discreet operation. Come look.'

Freddy checked the view through the camera. 'I just don't like the idea of a spy in our bedroom.'

Lightly, Marit said, 'You can't mean me.'

'Are ghosts supposed to show up on film? Or is this a special kind of camera. Infrared or something.'

'It would be a breakthrough if we got him on film.' It sounded like she meant it would be a surprise. 'But there are breakthroughs.' She swiveled the curved face of the motion detector. 'It registers tiny changes in air pressure. If this ghost is in the same world we're in, if it moves through the air, if it's a thing you can see then it's a thing you can record.'

'That's the theory, is it?'

Freddy was more annoyed by the disruption than she'd thought. He was being colonized by Marit with her gadgets. Inspected. Her object was to map out her doubt, not their certainty, he was sure of that. But if those were his nervous misgivings about her he couldn't have made a worse guess. Like a floorwalker or house detective Freddy escorted Marit downstairs into the kitchen where Lillian was arranging small sandwiches on a plain white platter, adding sprigs of parsley.

'I'm going to be busy for an hour or so,' Marit said. 'Re-checking those measurements I made.'

Lillian stopped fussing with the sandwiches. 'Don't you want to eat lunch first?'

'No, you two go ahead. The sooner I get through this the sooner I'll be out of your way.'

In the basement she knelt in front of the broken wall. It was still a burial place. She reached into it, touched the damp grainy soil; this same earth had covered him, the dead boy. A sensation traveled up through her fingers, not quite physical but a tugging emotion. It held her as her mind cleared of everything except a

250

sudden understanding of her first reason for being there: to get this ghost to show himself. This was how she used to search. In the belief the supernatural was nature, really, and there to be found. 'Oh, Mom,' she said out loud, because her argument with Judith, so many years of it, had chased her into womanhood and to the hard brink of her mother's death. Where was the most terrible danger? To see what isn't there, Marit said. No, it's worse, Judith was sure, not to see what is. A barrier had been raised. She could find Adamo, it was possible now, because Marit believed he was, somehow, in this house.

The Foys sat in the kitchen, sandwiches covered with tin foil, while Marit trooped through the rooms. She'd measure a space then sit at the dining-room table with her sheets of drawing paper, straight-edge and ballpoint pen, then get up again and disappear upstairs or into the backyard. Her footsteps came and went across the hardwood floors for an hour. Finally she sat with her diagrams and worked on them with fastened attention.

'May I see? Professional curiosity.' Freddy leaned over her with intense interest. 'You're getting into my territory.'

Marit said, remembering, 'That's right, you teach this stuff. How am I doing?' She tilted the page for him to see. The sub-division of his house, and of his private experience. The schematic drawings showed the three floors of the house and plot of ground it sat on. Each room was numbered. Dotted lines led between capital letters in a few of the rooms and outside, other places were marked with a letter only. On a separate piece of paper Marit had listed the descriptions. *1-A Basement room. Boy's remains found by Mr Foy ... B-C Line taken by apparition on first visit. Witnessed by Mrs Foy ... D-E Line taken by apparition on second visit. Witnessed by Mrs Foy ... X Marks position of figure seen by Mr and Mrs Foy from their beds.*

'You should use a mechanical pencil.' Freddy took one from his pocket to show her. 'This one's out of lead though.'

'What are those gangs of little kids roaming all over the place?' Marit was watching through the kitchen window as another gaggle of them passed the house, tightrope walking along the lip of the culvert.

'Selling immortelles,' said Freddy. 'It's a Lawford tradition.'

'And in Woodbridge. And Mistley,' Lillian told her. 'But Mistley's just since the war. They took it on from us. I don't think that counts.'

'Those dried flowers? The guy at the gas station practically forced a bunch of them on me. What tradition is that?'

'Well, the Immortelle.' Lillian took the lunch plates to the sink and let them soak in soapy water. 'I know the version that goes back to about 1810, around then.' Then as she sponged the dishes and Freddy dried them Lillian recited the story her mother had told her when she was seven or eight years old, the age Lydia Lenore Watson was when she was hauled into the bushes beside Church Hill and strangled to death by a Frenchman.

Lydia was born in Lawford on Christmas Day in 1802 or 1803. The talcum whiteness of her skin, the weightless nest of her flossy gold hair, the dimpled prettiness of her face, all disguised the little girl's prankish soul. She'd hide frogs in ladies' bonnets, spill lemon juice in the cream, steal her brother's clothes and pretend to be a boy, and befriend any stranger who would say hello to her. One of these gentlemen of the road tricked Lydia into showing him the way to St Mary's church. 'The Frenchy got her out on Church Hill,' Lillian came to the end of the story. 'The exact spot is about a mile from here, toward Hadleigh. There's a hollow oak tree where he supposedly hid her body after he killed her.'

Full of curiosity, Marit asked her, 'The dried flowers, what are they for?'

'Dried flowers – immortelles. Lydia comes back every year to show us poor mortals what it looks like, the place between life and death. She picks somebody who's suffering and takes their soul back with her. So people hang immortelles on their bedroom door for three nights. That sends her to somebody else's house.'

'Blood of the paschal lamb,' Marit commented.

'That's Hebrew. This is local.' Freddy knew his traditions.

Half-answering him, Marit said, 'A lost child. That's all I was thinking.'

'Adamo isn't a story. I didn't tell you a story about him.' Lillian raised her voice to say, 'Nobody knew about him, besides Perry.'

'You know, he wasn't the first thing that came into my mind,' said Marit, surprised about it herself. 'It made me think of your daughter.'

'What about Hildy?' Freddy treated this as out of bounds. He balanced himself on the window seat, crossed his thick leg, baring a piece of his hairless fish-white calf.

Marit continued, without softening the edge of her question. 'She sort of disappeared into the void for years, didn't you tell me that? What was it that pushed you so far apart?'

Freddy had nothing to say and showed he didn't by gazing out the window. But his tight jaw also said he wasn't happy to hear Lillian so willing to answer. 'When she was sixteen-seventeen,' she said, looking at him, 'Hildy was closer to Freddy. She's your generation, maybe you can remember what it was like. You had to show us we were the problem and you were the solution. She had to show me, and she was sure about how she wanted us to see her.'

'How was that?'

253

'Independent. Didn't need us. Except she did. And she could see things we couldn't about her life. Couldn't even imagine.'

Freddy chipped in, 'What kind of trouble did Dr Sonnenfeld bring home to Mom and Dad?'

'Nothing exotic,' Marit had to disappoint him. She asked Freddy, 'Was it all collisions or did you try to talk? Did talking ever make a difference?'

Lillian said, 'Oh, we collided over her boyfriends. One in particular.'

'Philip Fahey,' recalled Freddy.

'He called himself a musician. He played his guitar in the park. Hildy went with him, she said, because he was spontaneous.' Lillian frowned at that. 'He was just unreliable. So we collided over definitions. Hildy was tougher than I was at that age.'

'You were tough,' said Freddy, tickled, disagreeing, proud of her. 'I had to chase after her. Y'know, I had to *try*.'

But Lillian wouldn't let him sidetrack her. 'I tell myself this – well, one of the talks I have with myself is about why it went on for such a long time. I think she left before it was safe for her to be with me. Maybe you and your mother went through that too. When Hildy got to be a mother we weren't so foreign to each other. That's it, isn't it, the last thing you can say. That's when sympathy, *sympathy*, is the only necessary thing between you. She wasn't here though, so I couldn't say this to her.' An explanation, maybe, for why she was saying it to Marit. 'When there's no threat anymore, no risk of losing any bit of her she won for herself, oh I think about how we could have been together. Ten minutes of it, at the bus station: when I saw her there we had that peace between us. Late in the day, for ten minutes.'

Supporting her, Freddy said, 'You owe each other peace of mind. You watch out for children. Where's your choice? They think they can see the big picture, but they don't see the consequences.'

'The whole truth. Did she trust you with the truth about everything on her side?'

'She was slippery,' Freddy said. 'What she got up to. I was a step behind her. But Lillian—'

'She told me,' Lillian said. 'Anything she thought I could bear to hear. There are blank spots. But I told her I want to know what's really what. You know everything and accept everything and then you go on.' She spoke more to Freddy now. 'She didn't give me the chance to hold her, to say one word.'

'What was it, Lillian? What would you have said?' Marit waited, very still, with careful attention.

'I would have told her about my stillborn.'

'This is off the subject!' Freddy interrupted.

'It's all one subject,' Marit replied, 'your life here.'

'Stop examining our lives. You know enough about us now, don't you?' A redness came to Freddy's face, swelled it with heat. 'You know we aren't cheats or liars. Examine the Bartolotti boy's life. Or Perry Gillies', for Christ's sake. We're not the ghosts around here.'

'Marit isn't picking up gossip,' Lillian said to him. And to her, 'You're asking because you need to know. To help us.'

'It is helping. Yes.'

'I lost a baby boy,' Lillian went on, 'when Hildy was three. And after that we had our phantom pregancies,' she said with a warm, weak smile at the intimate memory, sharing it with her husband who stared down at the floor. 'Three of them in seven years. After that, I can't remember how long – anyway, we stopped trying. Didn't we, kiddo?'

'Lillian means stopped trying for babies. We're perfectly normal in the bed department.' The tightness and disapproval clung around Freddy's mouth. 'This personal business is a thousand miles off the subject.'

'Sometimes it figures in, the private side,' Marit told him. Lillian

255

asked her how it did. 'Depends who you ask. The fringe idea is it can attract *psi* activity. Apparitions connected with human tragedy, say. The conservative idea is that upheavals, oversensitive emotions, suppression, disturbances, these things can create supernatural events. Another idea is that you can be opened up by emotional storms and you're receptive then. You can be touched by spirits, souls, like a layer of your skin was stripped off.'

Still steaming, Freddy waited through this to say to Marit, 'Any stillborns in your family? Or was your mother fine in the pregnancy department?'

'Not any she told me about.'

No downcast warning look from Lillian could stop him. 'Maybe she doesn't tell you everything. You and your mother probably don't have the close relationship we have in our family.'

'Freddy, don't hound her.'

'Is that what I'm doing? Dr Sonnenfeld is pretty sure about what's going on in our house.'

'I'll tell you something about my mother,' Marit said, offering this to them. 'She made a beautiful meal for us. My father, my ex-husband, my two kids and me. Cooking all day. Bread, roast chicken, five kinds of vegetables, a big chocolate fudge cake. It was a kind of family ceremony. Mom arranged it all, with candles and her favorite music, to tell us she had cancer. It helped her. We were supposed to see it the way she did, it was just the end of her story. No suspense anymore: now we all knew. It didn't help me.'

Moved by this, Lillian asked, 'When?'

'Eleven months ago. She's still here, but she's going.' Slowly, Marit stood up and went into the dining room where she started gathering up her paperwork. Lillian stood behind her. 'Leave the video on. It'll operate by itself. And I'll pick it up on Monday morning.'

'What's your mother's name?'

Marit sat down and put the drawings aside. 'My grandfather named her for a great-aunt of his. Who he hated. He told Mom he always wanted to have a good reason to argue with her. Judith Rebekah. But she grew up with him calling her Bustballs Becky.'

Chapter Twenty-five

'STAY WITH us tonight.' The tumbling snow that had started to come down, clogging the streets and burying the roadside, might have been a good reason to accept Lillian's invitation. But Marit got in her car and drove through the flurries to the Bluebird Motel, packed her clothes, checked out and plowed back to the Foys' house for a reason with more force in it than the weather. Inside Lillian's trouble, someplace in the heart of it, a sense was shocked open and the dead boy's ghost climbed through into her life. Lillian could describe this place to her, the words were crowded just below the surface, not yet said, stopped (Marit was sure) by Freddy. Each time she combed through the Foys' account of events one fixed picture stood out against the background, no matter which angle Marit took as her approach. Adamo, Hildy, her stillborn boy, even in her way the Immortelle, all lost children beyond Lillian's reach but connected to her by coils of emotion unbreakable by death. And Marit felt the tug of a deeper intuition as this picture emerged. Her real sensitivity to it came whispering out of her own tangled, punch-drunk love for Judith. Soon (will she see New Year's Eve? her birthday in March? the summer flowers by the pool?) my mother will be erased from the world. It's, most of all, what Walter said: unreasonable, her death and persistence. Any woman's, any boy's.

After a winter dinner of vegetable soup, sourdough bread and cheese, Freddy asked Marit if she could tell them any real ghost stories. 'Ones the general public don't know anything about. You keep the most flabbergasting stories to yourselves, you professionals.'

She had gifts as a storyteller, bestowed on her by her father, the Sonnenfeld side packed with rabbis, lawyers and family historians. Marit could make distant events sound remembered, entrusted to her. Teaching in a classroom her voice had the same low pitch. It located whatever she was saying more in her dark-browed eyes and she unconsciously tilted her face forward when she came to forceful turns in a story, the glimpse of an admission that she could be amazed. Or she'd lower her head, almost sink behind her clumps of black corkscrew curls, preparing her audience for the next shock. Curled up and shoeless on the sofa with Lillian next to her and Freddy waiting in his green leather chair, Marit warmed the bowl of her wine glass between her hands and over it she told them about the Canadian abbot:

'I heard this happened in Québec in the 1940s.' A sip of wine. 'His name was St Cyr, a Benedictine. He was staying overnight in a nunnery outside of Rivière-du-Loup . . .' In his room (Marit told them, sipping her wine again), settled into bed, the light off, he heard the saddest sighing, gusts of real heartache, in the darkness around him. 'Who is it?' Silence, that was all he heard. He tried to sleep but, again, the sighing kept him awake and now the sadness was close to tears. 'Who's there? Sister?' Silence again. He switched on the bed table lamp, he was alone there. When the light was off St Cyr felt someone move close to his bed. Then he heard a woman's voice say, 'I'm in pain, Father.'

He sat up in bed and this time in the corner of the room he saw, he said, a concentration of darkness, a dense cloud of it that had a human shape. 'Who are you?' She said her name was Marie-Ange and she was in pain because of her lost virginity. 'Will you pray for me?' St Cyr told her he would if she let him see her face. Marit said, 'In his journal he described the dark shape lightening from inside. His exact words were, "It came up like the gray of early dawn." For a few seconds he saw Marie-Ange. She was about eighteen and she was wearing the habit of that nunnery's order. Before he left there he found out that a young novice called Marie-Ange had died eight years earlier in that room a month after she confessed she'd broken her vow of chastity with the local pharmacist. In the back of his drugstore. None of the other nuns prayed for her soul because they were so horrified, so Marie-Ange had to roam around Purgatory until St Cyr came along.'

Lillian softly asked, 'Did she take her own life?'

'Nobody there could answer that.'

'Either the girl killed herself or she didn't,' Lillian argued.

'She stopped eating. All the nuns swore they tried to feed her but she couldn't swallow. Or she'd swallow and then throw it up. If she chose to die, she got shamed into it.'

Freddy welcomed the pleasure Marit showed, obvious on her face, as she let them in on this professional secret. It was so unexpected to hear her talk about a ghost as anything plainly believable, as the simplest and final explanation. As long as the right elements were present she could accept it. In other words, about Adamo she was convincible. 'What happened to St Cyr?'

'He did say prayers for her. When he traveled, especially, wherever he stopped. A professor of mine at Penn found his journals in a box of books she picked up at an auction.'

A little dreamily Lillian said, 'Purgatory is just the Catholic name for it.'

'Maybe', Marit said, 'only Catholics are there.'

'Come on. Have you got another one to top St Cyr and Marie-Ange?' Freddy clapped his hands like a pasha, happy and ready to hear more from the archives.

The floor was Marit's. At Thanksgiving, say, after the pumpkin pie or while the Sonnenfeld clan sat digesting their Passover dinner, Marit usually stepped into the spotlight. When she was in school her audience would get a one-girl performance of The Most Fascinating Thing I Learned This Semester. Later on it could be the soap opera of a failed romance, complete with impersonations of her ex-boyfriend's feeble, vulnerable orgasms. Tonight, tucked into this family, she won their appreciation with ghost stories. 'I know about a murder case in South Carolina.'

If the Foys had ever heard of Tandi Flowers, Marit would have been astonished. They told her they had not. The crime and the eerie events around it weren't known very far outside the locality of Troy, NC, but down there, said Marit (her face tilted forward), you can still run into old people who'll tell you they remember the murder.

Tandi Flowers was living with her uncle Wheeler Flowers in a one-bedroom apartment over the shoe shop he owned. One night she went out with Jimmy Meakin, a clerk in Wheeler's store. Tandi never came back. The local doctor, who had just come home after a housecall at one in the morning, walked into his kitchen and found a woman covered in blood standing by the door. He asked who she was. 'She said, "Tandi Flowers."' (Marit held the name in her eyes). Tandi told the doctor she was pregnant and Uncle Wheeler did it. Wheeler sent her out with Jimmy Meakin, who was supposed to take her to some friends in Corinth where Tandi could have the baby without raising a stink. On the way there Meakin beat her head in with a ball-peen hammer, dumped her body in the woods across the border in Georgia. Then he went home to wash the blood out of his only pair

261

of overalls. The blood wouldn't rinse out, the overalls were too wet to burn so he hid them in a trunk in his attic. Then Tandi begged the doctor to tell the police. He blinked hard, rubbed his eyes and she was gone. He knew how tired he was, he didn't believe what he'd seen or heard, he always bought his shoes from Wheeler Flowers, so he didn't say anything to anybody.' (Marit took a slow breath, sank back into her curls. Her voice confidential and so low Freddy had to lean forward to hear.) The next night Tandi came back and threatened to keep coming back until the doctor went to the police, and finally he did. 'It was a rumor, he told them. Something he heard in Corinth, maybe, he couldn't remember where. The next day some picnickers found Tandi's corpse and after a search the police found Wheeler's hammer and Meakin's overalls. They went to trial, got convicted and died in the electric chair. The doctor put the story in his will.'

'Is it true?' Lillian said, turning her head to look at Marit.

'It's a story.' Marit shrugged, sensing the need for an apology. 'Are you asking me if I can swear it really happened?'

'It's imaginable,' Freddy urged her. 'You think it's imaginable, don't you?'

'You've got to ask yourself what are good reasons to doubt it. I trust the woman who found the St Cyr story. I trust her intentions,' Marit said. 'She didn't start out hoping it was real. But she went into it thinking it was just as likely as it was unlikely, and she's been investigating hauntings for forty years. Her standards are tough, she doesn't want to be fooled. St Cyr's story was imaginable to her.'

'That's what we'll be for you,' Lillian said, sinking into her own conclusions. 'A story for people you tell to guess about.' She lifted her eyes. 'If you trust your friend why can't you say if it's real or not?'

'I don't know if it is.'

'Then why didn't you say so? There's nothing amazing about

made-up stories. I hear them every day at the hospital. Tell me one you know is real. It really happened and it amazed you.'

'I don't know one like that,' Marit replied. 'Not personally, myself.'

Nights away from home were never easy for her, Marit never slept well in strange beds. Even with her eyes shut she felt on watch, waiting for the morning. In Hildy's room it was strange to be sleeping in a single bed. By the drizzling amber from the streetlight Marit saw places where Hildy's touches remained. Figures of seashells in pencil, soft pencil, dark as charcoal, drawn on the cream-colored wall next to the bed, and a triple portrait of a teenage girl smoking a cigarette, Hildy's face, floating among the scallops. A desk and a low dresser were still covered in black and white op-art contact paper. These protected remnants held the spirit of Hildy's bedroom against the removals and refurbishments. The tussle between Freddy and Lillian, between casting off and abiding, this was its courtroom.

There's the terror in the terrible: judgment ordering you to leave the whole monumental accumulation of memories, moments still unsettled, misunderstood. Adamo was this peril closing in on Lillian, as he was for the old man in the hospital, Perry. Both of them were in motion away, quicker than anyone else they knew, and all Lillian wanted now was the honest story. It was this way. It wasn't like that. You were right. You were wrong. Because to leave (we are all leaving) without knowing what was and what was not would condemn you to tragedy. To the worst kind of loneliness. Marit thought of Lillian shut into a lightless closet, asking whether it's day or night and being told it's six o'clock. Loneliness without escape.

You realize you are in motion, leaving, and this must cut you off as soon as the sensation hits you. You are already gone. The view from there will be the totality of your life, bordered by *that* beginning and *this* ending, a parcel of life shrinking into empty space. The sight

263

must strain your still-living eyes. One second Judith might see the ten-year-old she was in Stonehill, lugging her father's copy of *Gray's Anatomy* around the neighborhood, forcing the adults to take her *seriously*, lording it over her jump-roping playmates ... Then Judith at nineteen being courted by Walter, twenty-two and a law graduate. The afternoon he brought her arum lillies to draw ... Then Judith is twenty-five, painting her kitchen three shades of yellow ... All parts of a very long dream.

In motion away from it, Judith is watching it dissolve, silently explode, and the one certainty traveling with her is that the motion will stop. That's the acceptance she sees in our faces – Walter, Ben, Katy, Joel, mine, the living. Other things are waiting to happen to us and because of us, we will have other choices to make, we have more life and Judith has her cancer. Those black cells are closer to her than we can be, they are concretely true, doing their work, demanding her attention. 'Has it changed today?' 'How soon will it get worse?' 'How much worse before it's over?' Her oncologist has answers to these questions, but at heart they aren't questions for the doctor. It must be like living with the moon in her house, impossible to see around.

When Marit noticed the noises she realized they'd been going on for a while. Soft, labored grunts, pressing up through the walls or floor. Marit used her flashlight to see down to the end of the hall. The door to Lillian and Freddy's bedroom (bare of dried flowers) was closed. She was downstairs before she heard the noise again. It was hoarse and full of effort, the way a man might sound lifting a heavy weight by himself. Stepping slowly, listening for the next rise of sound, Marit followed the flashlight's beam through the kitchen. As she reached the door to the basement she heard it again, a cracked sigh, a brief, pained cry.

At the foot of the stairs Marit felt the cold wrap around her. From there she could see the crumbling hole chopped into the wall, which opened on heavy blackness. There was another raw-throated heave of breath. She was conscious of its closeness, and for the first time frightened – she was close to a revelation. The Maglite's sharp beam she swept ahead of her was an intrusion and she switched it off. In that second she saw a border of yellowish light along the edge of the broken brickwork, like the rim of roomlight that leaks under a closed door. Marit knelt and heard the hard breath behind her.

That fractured darkness showed Marit the shape of her fear. It wasn't fear at the break-up of reason, reason hadn't collapsed, it had led her to this. Reason said this wasn't the supernatural – it let her into the secret that nature includes this too. He was there, close to her, a moving strength, an intention. In jungle or cave darkness, Marit knew, a wild animal would circle in, and the fear rising in her chest would come too late to save her. An animal hunts with its purpose concealed. There was a wildness around her but with a human purpose pounding in it, he was there for Marit to see him, the boy wanted to be known.

She stood, her hand resting on one of the wide pipes connected to the boiler. A single cry broke out of her. Then she dragged in a lungful of air, let it go slowly and used the tail end of it to laugh at her own love of wonder. Marit could *feel* the breathing sound in the gullet of the pipe, feel the heat expanding inside it against the cold damp air. On her fingertips was a luminous powdery smudge, a smear of yellow light that glowed so palely against the wall. Where had she read about this mold? In Drexler's paper on the Brownsville haunting? Now she knew it for herself, touched it, smelled it, saw it bleed out its woeful phosphorescence. An earthly wonder.

Upstairs, Lillian blinked awake out of the first unbroken hour of sleep she'd found in many nights. The dream came back. In the kitchen that wasn't her kitchen she walked naked toward the pot-bellied stove and the small cries of animal pain. Unbearable pain, stronger than before, and this was the thing that had startled her awake – there was no monkey chained to the hot stove, it was Adamo. The skin of his wrists torn under the rope, his face flamed with pain, bewildered pain, hopeless surrender. Shaking and cold, dry-mouthed, Lillian carried these miseries with her into the bathroom where she drank from the faucet and wiped a handful of water over her face. 'You old woman,' she said to the hay-haired wreck in the mirror.

To keep from waking Freddy she turned off the bathroom light and then opened the door. For a second the dark was hard, opaque, but her eyes cleared and she saw something wrong with her bed. The folds and shadows of her scrambled sheet and blanket couldn't be doing this. It was a solid shape there. Two steps away from it Lillian thought that she was looking at her own body lying that way in bed, legs folded up, arms bent behind her back, that she only dreamed she'd woken from this sleep. A floating sensation took hold of her and led her to the sight that wrenched Lillian out of herself.

The brutality of Adamo's killing lay there. His neck broken, his skin mangled, the way an animal looks after it's been run over in the street. Thrown on her bed lay the ferocity of the end, which was not the end for him, but the beginning of Adamo's next agony . . . repeated out of time, brought back here for help . . . beyond anyone's help . . . to punish us for our unused, useless sympathy. Lillian couldn't hold herself up. She fell back against the windowsill and dropped slowly to the floor, conscious, crying, without the strength to look away from the beaten, dead boy, drenched in grief for them both.

Chapter Twenty-six

THE FIRST look at her lying on the bed, still in her clothes, pages of notes dropped around her pillow and onto the floor, desk lamp still on, told Lillian Marit's night had been long, her sleep unsheltered. Even so, Lillian couldn't wait for her to wake up, to tell Marit it was all right now, she knew the reason Adamo had come to her; the disturbance, the upwelling sadness, the horrific beauty, all of it made sense. She saw the clear reason in it, the perfect order around the reason, it made sense and because it did she had no doubt anymore that what was happening was real.

When Hildy was a little girl, in her elementary school years, Lillian came into her room like this and woke her this way. With a hand on her shoulder, gave her a gentle squeeze and said her name, quietly called it to her as if her voice were far away. 'Marit ... Marit ...' Marit's eyes opened, a question in them. Lillian answered her, 'I saw him last night. I know what he wants.'

The morning, especially the early hour, took on the mood of a special occasion – a family trip to the mountains or Christmas Day, the adults awake first and busy, still in pyjamas and slippers. Freddy wore his plaid bathrobe almost formally, neatly fit and snappily tied, dressed in it he could welcome the mayor. In her loose, functional red woollen robe Lillian moved with deliberate energy between kitchen and living room, brewing coffee, setting out cups and saucers. Both of them helped Marit bring the video equipment downstairs where Freddy hooked up the recorder to their television set.

Marit sat cross-legged on the floor, catching the Foys' excitement (which climbed another notch when she took the tape out of the camera and fed it into the VTR), while they placed themselves side by side on the sofa and sat as if they were posing for a photograph. When she saw Marit was ready to start Lillian said, 'He showed me how ugly it was when he died.' Her description of Adamo was calm and Marit noticed in that calmness an acceptance that had no use for outside support. 'To show me the difference between what he was,' Lillian plucked at her own flesh, the skin on her forearm, 'and what he is now. He's reaching through because he wants me to know what happened to him.'

'That has to be it,' Freddy agreed with her. 'A ghost isn't like a geyser that just erupts wherever it happens to be. He picked us.'

Marit said to Freddy, 'You saw him too, last night?'

'I woke up,' he said. 'I don't know why. I looked over at Lillian's bed but she wasn't there. I thought she was, but it wasn't her. Then I saw where she was, down on the floor.'

'Conscious? Were you awake, Lillian?'

'She was very shaken up,' Freddy explained. 'Seeing what she saw.'

Limply, Lillian gestured toward the video recorder. 'I don't mind if you see me on it.'

'That's not all you'll see.' Freddy sat forward, ready to see it too.

Marit hit the play button. The image intensifier gave a picture of bright patches in the grayness of the bedroom. Slowly she spooled through to the first sign of movement. The camera caught Lillian from the waist down as she got out of bed and crossed the screen into the bathroom. The white of her nightgown flared against the monochrome background. They watched Lillian come out of the bathroom, stop short of her bed, they saw all the strength go out of her body. She buckled and fell slowly into the picture, the hand that covered her mouth fled up to cover her eyes. Marit scribbled a note of the time, cold white digits running in tenths of seconds in the corner of the screen. Twelve minutes went by before Freddy woke to Lillian's crying and went to her, and for ten minutes more he huddled her in his arms, stroked her hair, kissed her head, her cheek, and led her back to bed.

Lillian asked Marit to rewind the tape, back through Freddy's consolation and her shattering powerlessness, back to the moment her questions ended in a staggering vision of the truth. 'There,' she said. 'Stop. I saw Adamo there. Look. At the corner of my bed.'

'What am I looking at?' Marit asked her.

'You can see his feet and his legs.' She joined Marit on the floor in front of the television and tapped the glass with her finger.

Behind them, Freddy said, 'It's obviously his foot. You've got it on film.'

There was a shape on top of the blanket, contours of light and shadow. Marit didn't raise an argument. She saw how much like a foot and lower leg the shape was. Her eyes went down to her notepad. 'Two-fifteen. I was in the basement around then. I heard noises. They were coming from down there.'

With a child's longing to be told, Lillian asked, 'What was it?'

'The sounds I heard, you'd think they were human sighs. Hard ones, hard work.'

'I heard them in here before,' Lillian said.

269

'And I saw the strangest light coming from the wall at the end of the room. Where it's broken up.'

'From his wall. Where he was buried,' Freddy specified.

'It's a kind of mold that gives off a glow. Like fireflies do,' Marit told them. 'And the sighing sounds, those come from your boiler pipes.'

Arms crossed on his chest, Freddy said in a controlled voice, 'The boiler. Maybe. Maybe not. But we never had those noises or that mold in our house before Adamo. He's causing those things by coming into the world. They're connected to his ghost. You've got it backwards.'

'I think I know where he comes from. Where he is now.' Marit spoke softly, straining out any emotion. It was an effort. Looking again at the frozen picture on the TV screen – Lillian crumpled against her bedroom wall – she was aware of adding a new cruelty. She glanced at her notes, then said, 'You're connected to him by a hundred threads. This house. A terrible thing happened here. A little boy was buried in this place, under your feet. Maybe he was killed here. And you found him. You brought it out. Perry Gillies. That old man is part of your house, too. He's the last surviving link to Adamo. He might have seen him on the last day of Adamo's life. Who knows what he saw!' Picking her way through the facts, she said to Lillian, 'He told you about Adamo, didn't he?'

'It's been coming out in scraps. I don't think he wants me to know anything about it, but it's too late now.' Lillian included herself in that regret. 'But whatever he said to me he said after the Adamo things started to happen. Not before, Marit – not before.'

Freddy jumped in on Lillian's side. Marit was in his sights. 'I know where you're going with this.'

'Let me finish first and let's see if you're right. Out of guilt or remorse, from fear, from shame, whatever it was, when this weird business started happening Perry was also whispering to you about—' Marit turned through her notes, landed on an early page. '"The dead boy." And pestering you to "say a special rosary" for him, "a double rosary". He's got Adamo buried in his life somewhere. I think the rumor of it leaked into yours. More than that. Perry's feelings about it all, too. Then', Marit said, almost as a concession, 'you found out Adamo was a boy who really was alive once. Freddy, these are just my sketchy thoughts on this, but listen to me. I think you've made Adamo yours because of Lillian. Please, wait a second.' He'd opened his mouth to interrupt her but Marit stopped him with a look that both offered and expected mature respect. 'You both lost a baby. And you lost Hildy for all those years. Time you can't call back. That's what's alive in this house. Loss, lack. Adamo is here, you both found him, and he fills in the old spaces. He has to be real to do that. So it's not so empty around here.'

Lillian dabbed her finger again at the TV screen. 'You've got his legs and feet right there. On your video tape.'

'I'm not sure that's what's there.'

Freddy was sure. 'You're not sensitive enough to see it.'

Marit answered, speaking to Lillian. 'You want to see things the way they are. You're not afraid to do that. Why else did I stay? What else am I doing here?'

'You're doing your damndest!' Freddy barked at her. 'You're the one who's afraid to see how it is.'

'And why would that be?'

'Because you're not like us. You're afraid to go back to your university and conferences and whatnot, your high and mighty colleagues, and get laughed at. Here – here's a breakthrough! A goddamned picture of a ghost and you won't do anything about it.'

'If I showed that to anyone in my department and told them that it was proof, that I was the first person in the history of the world to take a picture of a ghost, they'd pat me on the head and advise me to send it to the *National Enquirer*. An intelligent *eight-year-old* wouldn't be convinced by this.'

'Stop talking. Stop it right there,' Freddy said, kneeling next to Lillian, throwing his arm around her.

'She has a right to hear what I've got to say.'

'My wife's rights aren't your business.'

Lillian was quiet. She touched Freddy's hand, the hand that lay on her shoulder, and she held it there. Marit appealed to her, 'If it wasn't real you'd want to know. You'd want me to say so. That's right, isn't it?'

Her answer was this. 'Isn't there anything in the records like our case? In your experience,' speaking slowly, wanting to get her terms right, 'has a soul . . . has an apparition . . .'

'Lillian, I don't have any firsthand experience of ghosts.'

'I do,' Lillian said. 'A soul comes back to a person who can understand. A soul wants to show everything to somebody who can understand everything. Adamo wants me to know, he wants me to get the whole truth from him. Because I can understand him.' In that moment she looked to Marit for the same feat of understanding.

She tried. 'We're using different words to tell each other the same thing. You call it *soul* and I call it *psyche*. It's – I'll use your word, and it's the right one – all-out *sympathy*. Freddy's sympathy for you, yours for Perry, for Adamo, the way you've been with me. You live through sympathy, Lillian.'

'Dr Sonnenfeld will you *please listen* to what Lillian is *saying*!' In a seizure of outlandish anger Freddy paced to the mantle, grabbed up a glass vase and smashed it to pieces on the floor. Both women stared at him. A scrap of hair had twisted loose at the back of his head and jutted out at a ridiculous angle. His large face ballooned with ripe anger and his straight, small mustache underlined it. Hands on hips, bathrobe falling open, it was the stamping rage of a tin-pot dictator. Or a great one. 'That's something you can explain with psychology. I did that,' both hands circling over the calamity of scattered glass, 'because of X, Y, Z. Because of suppression, repression or because nobody *listens*, analyze it however you want. (I know you're going to.) I'm a serious man. We understand *psychology* in this house, Dr Sonnenfeld. Some things start in the mind. Do you think we're ignorant people? Unintelligent? This thing did not start in our minds. Adamo was here before we were; he came to us. I held his bones, they weren't imaginary. He's always been here. That's what we know. We found that out for ourselves. I've felt him here before, only then I didn't know what was affecting me that way. When I've been in the house by myself. Well, we feel him around here all the time now and when he's got a good reason for it he shows himself. Lillian explained that to you. He knows we understand what he went through. That's why – that's why.'

Lillian picked up the broken glass and then hugged Freddy. Her arms strapped around his chest, Marit thought, were there to keep him from flying apart. 'Kiddo, it's not Marit's fault.' Then, to Marit: 'It's not your fault. You didn't come here with any bad intentions. But it's just gone too far for you. It's all right,' she said with final conviction.

The Foys stood fastened together in this emergency. Marit was the emergency, her reasoning an undertow. They were protecting each other against her, walling her out. If she could have done it without stinking of hypocrisy or gutless insincerity she would have changed sides, right then. The real trouble was Marit suddenly, staggeringly, was overloaded with the sincerest need to tell them she was convinced: the ghost, the soul, the immortal part of a vanished boy was reaching out to them, walked with them in these rooms. Freddy was right. No ignorance, no gullibility or any failure of intelligence let Adamo in; he was the visible part of their embracing reality. The force in their embrace. What did Marit's careful method, her explanatory approach, amount to next to their love? She was there when a change overcame

Lillian and she caught the exact moment on video tape. Whatever Lillian saw that night drew a magic circle around her and Freddy, and outside it was Marit with her video camera and motion detector, her glow-in-the-dark mold, her notes and smart psychology. From Freddy and Lillian now she was further away than the afterlife. She didn't say another word, not even a reply (except to pack quickly), when Freddy politely suggested she leave. Lillian offered to make a sandwich for her drive to Boston. A few minutes later at the door, holding Marit's lunch in a brown paper bag, Lillian kissed her on the cheek, said nothing else, and left her with a disappointed, demolishing smile.

'It's good to get our privacy back again.' Privacy was a concept for Freddy that included more than being alone with Lillian. They were together, secured, cradled in each other's company. 'I'm going to make you some lunch.'

'I don't really have that big an appetite,' she said.

'How about tea and cinnamon toast?'

'That's all I want.'

'Should I turn the radio on?'

'You're spoiling me.'

'I'll take that for a yes,' he said and found a play, all English accents, on National Public Radio. He mimicked them, badly. 'Jolly good, eh what. A theatrical show.'

It occurred to Lillian, flickeringly, that she was physically in their kitchen, with Freddy, that she was looking through the window at the darkening afternoon, the bluegray light outside, the sawdust of falling snow. But the aroma of cinnamon toast bloomed and blew across her awareness as powerfully as the intense memory that flowed in and took its place. Of herself and Freddy unmarried. Twenty-year-old Freddy, and Lillian at seventeen, barefoot, walking the rumpled lawns of South St park, on the last day of August. With Hildy growing inside her. Nothing was growing there now except an emptying, a clearing out.

Cinnamon toast was Freddy's specialty of the house. It was the only recipe he knew and it was very fine. Twice toasted – lightly first and then again to melt the butter, dark brown sugar and cinnamon. He'd learned how to make it when he was in college, a waitress at Green's Diner taught him. Her name was Patté, she was from Winnipeg. 'Canadian-style cinnamon toast,' he announced and served it up with formal pride. The four aromatic slices were cut into eight triangles on a serving dish, a china plate for himself and one for Lillian, folded linen napkins. 'You know how much you'd have to pay for this in a restaurant?'

Lillian played along. 'How much?'

'You couldn't get this in a restaurant. Not cinnamon toast made to order.' His mood brought a vague light into Lillian's eyes, which left them just as quickly. 'I was proud of you today. Sticking to your guns. And with me.'

'Don't say that.'

'I mean it.' He shook his head, shaking out the disbelief. 'Breaking your mom's vase. Throwing a tantrum. It should've embarrassed you but it didn't.'

'You couldn't do anything that would do that.' Then, fondly, 'Your strongest feelings came out.'

'It's a twisted old root, isn't it.' He patted his chest. 'My heart,' then he took a bite of toast.

The look she gave him wouldn't let him go; a look of sweet surprise. 'Poetry, that's right out of a poem, Freddy.'

'I've got poetry in me. Of course. Didn't I ever write you a sonnet?'

'Nothing that phony.'

'What did I write?'

275

Lillian reached behind her and turned off the radio. 'When you decided you wanted to marry me, remember what you said? The first thing, not the big decision or the plans. When you kissed me.'

Freddy didn't need any more help. 'When I kissed you, that's right.'

'You said—'

'I said, "This will show you how I love my fate." The words just came out.'

'That was you this morning. When you broke the vase.' Then she asked him, 'Did you know what you were letting yourself in for with me?'

'I was cut out for it. You were a gift from above.'

'With Hildy?'

'Lil, it was the same for you. You make a choice. This, not that. There would have been good and bad with anybody. This happiness and whatever problems with you. That happiness and those problems with somebody else. There wasn't a contest. The man I could be with you, that's who I wanted to be.'

'My God, kiddo. The kind of trouble you got from us. Did you ever want to get out of it?'

'Leave you?' He saw it was her question. 'Not once. No matter how bad it got.'

'It was bad. I know it.'

'You don't know how bad it really was.'

Know everything, accept everything. Twice in the thirty-five years he'd known her Freddy let himself cry in front of Lillian. When she took his hand on that humid late summer day (he smelled the heat in the beech trees), and she said, 'I'm with *you* now,' he cried out of heartbreaking happiness. He believed his good luck. She saw the kind of man he was and she loved him for it. With one word she lifted him out of the crawling mass of other men, told him yes: I know who you are, an honest man, a loyal one, with a talent for love, you're not wrong about yourself, I'm the one who can prove it, by staying with you . . . And then, and then. So many *ambitions* sliding over and under each other, so much happens you can't even guess about, and the next time you look everything outside around you has changed. It hit Freddy that way the second time he cried to her. No private confirming joy then, only the absences between them. Those muddy bones spoke to him, the dead boy shamed him. When did he stop listening to her and trusting her? Also in late summer, fourteen years ago. Lillian would have known how to handle the facts, she was owed the truth and for her sake we lied. Lies from both sides, from her husband and her daughter, who only wanted to make it easy on her. Therefore easier on us. Can you ever love a person with a lie? It wasn't the way to love Lillian; he cried over that with the dirt from Adamo's bones on his hands.

This was Freddy's clemency. After this he wouldn't let them slide back into the fog. Everything known from the beginning, everything accepted: not a lesson learned in his head – every cell in Freddy's body had learned it, it was the way he *was* now. 'I thought I knew how the world worked. Well,' he said (he owed himself this much, at least), 'I knew how part of it did. Not the part where Hildy lived. I made a terrible mistake with her. I think it's why she didn't want to come back home.'

'She wasn't listening to either of us, Freddy. Hildy'd had it with my opinions just as much.'

'No, hear me out. I got her to listen to me. At the time – Lil, I should've told you all this then. There were chances I should've taken to tell you a month after, or a month after that. Each time though, it was the same. I thought if I told you I'd never see you again. Then I turned around and a year was gone. There weren't any more chances, not until today.'

Her eyes were almost expressionless as she let him talk. Lillian sat tensely, concentrating, undefended.

Freddy went on, 'You know Philip Fahey's old man told me Hildy was pregnant. Hildy told you a couple days later, I think. After I heard, anyway. Before she talked to you I went to that garbage dump she was living in with Phil. Hildy didn't want us to see it. It was trash. The boy she was with was trash. I just went to talk to her. To help.'

'She knew she didn't have to face it by herself,' Lillian said. 'We'd give her help with the baby.'

'That's right. Yes. I wanted her to know that. I said to her, Phil Fahey's going to take off. It looked that way to me. She didn't care. It was only one reason why her life was going to be messed up, maybe for the next eighteen years. Permanently, maybe. Then I came up with a dozen more, which wasn't too hard to do. My God, she was living in a leaking, bug-infested trailer in somebody's backyard. We didn't raise her to expect that kind of life, to settle for trash.'

'It's what she chose when she was seventeen. Hildy was going to climb out of it.'

'With a baby strapped to her back?' Freddy read the silent reply. 'You did it, that's right. With me. It wasn't a trailer I took you to live in.' His eyes closed, then opened on the real subject. 'It was going to be me, again. I loved her, I wanted life to be kind to her. So I started talking to her about going for an abortion.'

'Hildy wanted her baby. Remember how much? So you fought with her.'

'She gave me all the arguments. For two solid weeks, Lil. I was out there once a day. Did you know Phil used to hit her? One time I pulled in when he was zooming out of the driveway on his motorcycle. If I'd've known what he did, I swear to God, I would've run him off the road. Hildy had a bruise on her face as big as a baseball. She was confused, it was all messy in her mind. The baby would turn Phil into a man.

But there was real anger in her. Try to think about the big picture, I said to her. You don't have a child for revenge.'

'What else did you say?'

'She'd be going through every miserable hardship that would've landed on you if I hadn't been – if we hadn't found each other. I begged her, Lillian. "Don't do this to your mom. Don't hurt her. Don't let her watch this happen to you." Then she did a remarkable thing. I don't know, she just seemed to decide right there on the spot. It must have been like a dam bursting on her head. She decided I was right. Hildy let me drive her to a clinic in Boston early in the morning. I got Arthur to cover my classes. And I picked her up in the afternoon. Oh, Lil. She hated me. Hate like I never saw in anybody's face before. I was Hitler. She refused to get into the car with me. But she asked me for all the money I had in my wallet. She said it would be the last thing she'd ever ask me for. And she told me to tell you how I'd talked her into it. That was two days before she left.'

The force of his confession drove Lillian inward. As though she'd been shoved into an empty room where the missing things left their outlines in the dust on the floor. Her grandchild, gone; her daughter, gone. No accident swept them out of her life, no weakness in Hildy's body killed her baby, no kink in her mind kept her away from home – it started and ended with Freddy, his grim idea of the world. *Oh, two idealists!* Lillian thought. *All the time I was ready to do whatever had to be done! To face the hard realities: don't I always?* Now there was this one.

Weakness in her arms stiffened into strength when she hit him. The heel of her hand landed on the side of his face. 'All right,' he said, accepting punishment. She hit him again. Her fist skidded across his ear as he ducked, but not away from her. 'All right.' Freddy didn't try to protect his face but held still for another blow, which didn't come.

A wrenching revulsion gripped Lillian's stomach. Rigidly bent over she tottered to the sink, leaned down into it and vomited. Freddy called her name, reaching to touch her, and said, 'Do you want me to do anything? Do you want some mint tea?'

She waved him away, coughing out the last of her sickness. 'No, kiddo. It won't do me any good at all.'

The house was as dark and quiet as Marit expected it to be, a lifeless welcome home. Three days out of state and only one message was waiting for her on the answering machine. In the very still hardwood hallway the sounds of her homelife came straining through to her, grainy, from a distance. Katy and Ben were let down Marit wasn't there, wasn't there to be excited by all the civilized adventures they were getting into on their skiing trip. 'We're in a different time zone,' Ben adultly informed her, 'so when you call back you have to count backwards by two hours.' Then Joel, with that courtroom exactitude of his, read out the hotel's phone number and address, the kids' daily schedules and then, coming over all Papa Bear (loud enough for his cubs to hear), he did some bragging: what a talent Ben had for snowboarding, what a natural on the *après ski* scene Katy was, helping the cocktail waitress (Katy, in the background: 'Her name's *Elizabeth*!') ferry Irish coffees to the lounging guests. Marit left the machine in answer mode; she wasn't ready to tell her parents she was back.

Hours later she was grateful for the solitude. After a long bath, after half a bottle of wine, Marit wasn't much closer to knowing how to present the Foys' story to her mother. As she took an aerial view of the overlapping sheets of notes, facts and impressions, diagrams and photographs spread out on the coffee table (tea leaves at the bottom of a cup), at least one message was clear: leave nothing out. What Judith wants to hear is a firsthand report. Marit was in that house, spoke with the percipients. She'd show her mother the diagrams first, and the photographs of the site; walk her through the basement where they found Adamo Bartolotti's earthly remains, the dining room directly above where Lillian found an honest-to-God cold spot, the path Adamo took through the kitchen and upstairs, the bedroom where he came to Lillian, full of pain.

And there Marit would run up against the last question. Hidden somewhere in this nest of material was the answer to it, camouflaged, in pieces. What did Lillian see last night in her bedroom? This visitation – *this one* – changed her, it tortured her into certainty that this haunting was real. Lillian saw in a way she did not see before, *through* to something so powerful it broke her strength, folded her up on the floor, shivering, hemorrhaging tears. It made Marit's opinion worthless, blind and something to be pitied.

Half a dozen times Marit watched the video tape, pierced each time by the sight of Lillian's face caged in her hands, at the end of her courage. On the bed above her, cut out of the shadow of her twisted blanket, the shape put there for Marit to see, Adamo's feet bound together at the ankle. A human shape in half-shadow, invisible to her. She'd show this to her mother last of all. Judith would see Lillian's flailing despair in the face of – of what?

Lillian's purgatory, Judith's astral plane. My life may be momentary but I'm not only this – the invisible part of me is unkillable. Marit played the tape again and she thought, 'Knowing you will be dead someday isn't the same as dying. That separates us from them . . .' Lillian's compassion, Judith's cancer. Death is inside them, they know it is, it's awake, using their eyes to look out at us. And that changes everything.

The tape played on. Freddy lollopped into the picture, pyjamas askew, his walk a little clumsy, shaken out of sleep, led by the necessity of the moment: to go to Lillian. He held her until she was calm, he helped her stand up, he took her to his bed. Here we are at the heart of it. While you are alive, and they are, you owe them love as protection, love as influence, love as permission, as purpose, as remedy, love as presence and endurance, as witness, love as reflection, love as rationale, love as equity, testimony, confidence, as renunciation, love as origin, love as certainty. There's your realism. Marit thought, I can hear how she'll say it. 'Tre*men*dous. My girl made a scientific *break-through*. Show me what,' Mom will say. 'Look there,' I'll say. I'll point to it in the middle of the picture. 'See his feet? There. On the bed in front of Lillian.'

Chapter Twenty-seven

THE GLIMPSE she had of herself came to Lillian as she walked through the reception area at St Mount's on her first day back at work: she was divided like a Russian doll, with another Lillian cocooned inside. The outer Lillian, a thickness made of her face and body, met the ordinary world and performed ordinary functions, but the other Lillian, floating, encased, gazed on questions of final importance. The visible Lillian met Billy Cooke for the seven a.m. change-over, dealt with his report (Douglas Cottle's three-day grape soda and white toast protest against vitamin B-12, the readmittance of a twenty-two-year-old self-harmer who had scraped her thighs open with a fork, the sedation of Mrs Sweeney after a violent episode involving a wheelchair and a patio window), approved the morning medications and handed out shift assignments to her six nurses. Out of friendship more than anything else, Billy waited for Lillian to get through her morning meeting before he broke the news about Perry. Sometime on Saturday night he collapsed, probably on his way to the bathroom, Billy guessed, because the cleaner found him face down on the floor, half in his room and half in the hallway, wedged in the door.

Mollo's main business with Lillian when they caught up with each other was not Perry Gillies; he was anxious to lock down a date for their computer work on her synaesthesia, which Lillian gladly did. But the arrangement, even the idea of 'next week', had no meaning to her. How much life did he think Perry had left in him? Mollo was philosophic about Perry's hypertension, dehydration, pyelonephritis. 'His body's full of debris,' the doctor summed up. 'Abe Gertler's on the lookout for uremia.' Beyond the laws of medicine and biology there were always unpredictable influences, Mollo told her, and with Perry it had to be what a strong-willed wicked old bastard he was.

Seeing a stroke patient it's always your first thought, even if you had never known them when they were healthy: two seconds before the embolus sabotaged the blood vessel they were whole, and two seconds after they were stripped of their defenses, left with so little. Perry's collapse wasn't a stroke but Lillian found less of him lying in his bed. The only color his skin had was the same flat grayness of the cloudbound daylight that weakly pressed indoors. His body had gone bad. Loose flesh let the sharp angles of his chin and jaw push through, fiercely; in his bones Perry was untouched, unchanged.

'They stuck me in here with the poverty cases,' he called to Lillian across his new wide room.

Mr Kibbee in the next bed, offended, raised himself on one elbow to set Perry (and Lillian) straight. 'You don't know what the hell you're talking about. I'm on the GE medical plan.' He was a large man with densely freckled arms and a sheen of blondness clinging to his wavy white hair. A bowl of fruit still in its amber cellophane sat on his bedside table like a trophy on a mantel-piece.

Perry coughed out a dry laugh. 'If it's so A-1, why doesn't it cover diapers?'

'Nurse, he's mixing me up with McClure.' Kibbee's complaint went directly to Lillian. Dropping his voice, he said, with a secret nod at their roommate, 'Across over there.'

'I know who I mean, Frank. What beautiful sound woke me up at five o'clock? Was it raining in here?'

'You dreamed it, you crazy nut,' Kibbee fired back, and not caring anymore about anybody else's feelings he pointed at McClure. 'He's the incontinent. I'm not urinary. I'm osteo.'

Ancient Mr McClure, if he'd even heard a word of the argument, was numb to any insult. His one open eye stared distantly at the ceiling. For Lillian's sake Perry spelled out the problem. 'I caught him pissing into the water jug.'

'No – you didn't!' Kibbee flared. 'Because that's not what I was doing.'

'Then, to cover it up,' Perry's face filled with disgust, amazement, 'he drank out of it.'

'I didn't *do* that.'

Refereeing, planted between the two beds, Lillian said to Kibbee, 'May I have a drink of water?'

'Of course, yes.'

As Perry watched she put her lips to the rim of the metal jug and drank, finishing the few mouthfuls left in it. He said to her, 'It's the principle of it. If you got to live side by side you got to make rules.'

'Mr Kibbee didn't pee in the water jug.'

'You say. How do I know?'

The plastic cup sailed past Lillian and bounced off Perry's forehead. In another second she could have been in the middle of a bare knuckle fight, IV tubes flying, but she yanked the partition closed around Perry's bed, a reprimand that stopped and hushed them both. 'I don't have time for this garbage,' she said, only for Perry to hear. 'He came to you two nights ago. You saw him in your room.'

'Was I talking out loud when they carried me up?'

'Nobody said anything to me. I saw him too, Perry. The same way you did.'

'I've known happier times.' He turned his face away, birdlike, avoiding the look in Lillian's face that said she had too. 'I got out of bed. I was thirsty, hot and thirsty. Then I saw him on the floor right there, curled up. Scared holy hell out of me.' Kicked by the memory Perry's head jerked back. 'If he did anything to hurt you – did he? Are you all right?'

'No.' She sat close to him on the bed and in a low voice, an intimate whisper, Lillian said, 'You know what I want to know. I can't make a whole picture, it's all pieces, and I'm more afraid of not knowing. I get a hold of a tenth of it over here, then another tenth over here, but I don't know what came before or after. Nobody knows for sure. It's supposed to be enough for me, pieces and guesses. Don't you trust me? Don't you know me? What's going to happen?'

He felt her muted panic, it flowed into him and forced his words out. 'If I'd never said anything you'd be all right. This is my fault. Because I told you about him. It's one more mistake.'

'You're not telling me enough. And who else understands?'

'I'm the last one.'

'Then why is he killing me?'

'He isn't.' The reassurance was for himself, first. 'You shouldn't even say that. I'm the only guy in that boat.'

'I want to hear the rest. I want to understand.'

'God knows the score. Don't you think? A man gets punished for his mistakes. But you respect him when he tries to correct his life. It all balances out. Only there's no wall chart is there, on the wall, that states how much for what kind of mistake. It's not Hail Marys and Our Fathers for omission and commission, it's correcting your life *forever*. You know me, Mrs Foy. You know what I do. I *volunteer*. Years and years and years helping people not harming them. In a hospital, where else! If I notice somebody's too weak or whatnot I go get their food and bring it. I can't look at a suffering person and walk by. If I can do something then I do it. That deserves respect in God's book, doesn't it?'

'His forgiveness isn't automatic. He says first admit your wrongs.'

'Then I think. Think, think. Why doesn't God order Adamo to leave me alone? There always has to be a worm in my life. Why? I've been thinking that over very deeply. But I can't come up with it. What kind of good thing am I supposed to do? Suffer for him?'

'Maybe so. But as long as you're alive you've got a chance to stop it. Your soul has to be clean, going to God.'

Perry said, through his dry, long lips, 'He knows how the dirt got on me.'

'Then he knows how you're still piling it on. What you're doing to me is a muddy thing too.'

'What—? No, Mrs Foy! I love you! Out of everybody—'

'Yes, that's right,' she said. '*Yes*. You wanted *me*, you hounded me to say rosaries for you, and I did. It's always my help you want but I'm not allowed to know what for. I'm part of it and we're sinking into the mud together. So you help *me* now, Perry. Do something for *me*.'

'I am. Something good.'

'Holding back? No, Adamo's been bringing you to this. He's giving you this chance. There's a choice you've got to make, see? You can't protect yourself anymore by keeping your mouth closed. It's the wrong choice. If you go on doing that you double the harm.'

Emptying, thrown, he said, 'It's *bon voyage* for me.' But Lillian had broken through. 'It's what he's on me to do? That's why?'

287

She offered Perry her best guess. 'I think what's happening is what already happened. It's happening all over again, to us.'

'It is?' The notion flew around his bed, his eyes followed it to the ceiling, corner to corner, up down and back, until its sense settled in the air in front of him. Perry sat quietly with it.

Lillian touched him on the shoulder, with a guiding shake, as though she were waking him. 'What did you do to Adamo? You and Elias and Rupert. Tell me what you did to him.'

'Not one damn thing! I never hurt him *and he knows that*. Candyass little kid doesn't have any sense of fairness. Pray for that,' he raised himself to say. 'Fairness!'

'Was it Rupert Hoagland and Elias? Why did they want to hurt him? How did it happen?'

'I'm finished talking.'

'The three of you were working in the garage, and Adamo came down to see the cars.'

'No. I'm not saying.'

Lillian came close to pleading. 'He was a smart boy. Why didn't he get out of there? Or shout for help? Why couldn't he?'

'Oh, no – not this on top of it! I'm making sure you're safe. I'm not adding you to my bad conscience.' Perry pledged, 'You'll be safe if I don't talk. It's not a good thing for you to know.'

'Talk to me. *To me.*' Still in a whisper, strained, rough, hardly above a breath. 'Don't do this, please don't do this.'

Perry said, 'You didn't make any mistake. I see how you are with people. You've been a good friend to me and a good boss. It's not fair he's scaring you to death. You don't deserve such black trouble in your life.' Then he wouldn't look at her or say anything else.

Lillian's quietness at dinner didn't raise a suspicion in Freddy. If anything, it was a sign to him of agreement. The convulsion in

288

their lives had subsided, they'd ridden out the tremor and they were still standing here, together. This kind of silence between them was different; after all, he had another silence to compare with it. That one began growing when Hildy left, that sluggish reservoir of unsaid words, years deep, years wide. And then out they all poured, washing away all the dirt. What was waiting to be said we said, this was where we were heading all along, to this settled normality.

It went well, Freddy thought back – coming out with the fact about Hildy's abortion, his *mea culpa*. He expected Lillian to be harder on him. But her eruption – those stinging weak-armed jabs and slaps! – could any human reaction be more normal? And before that, her jagged moods, sinking into herself and away from him, all of that came clear in the one glimpse Freddy had of Adamo's spirit. In those few miraculous seconds he only had a temporary hint of the bludgeoning sadness Lillian bent under day and night. It was enough though (the boy must have known it would be), and he began to learn. His reward was this calm. In its freedom from questions it reminded Freddy of his earliest attraction to her. He imagined it, the first and real nature of their marriage, as a solid object, a pure polished cylinder of jade or amethyst he could close in his palm. He had forgotten the feel of it, or barnacled with waste it was scraped clean again; now he felt its new, old, smooth, solid weight. Yes, this silence was all right – their mutual unspoken declaration that they should be together and together they would be going on.

He refused to let her give him a hand with the dinner dishes. As soon as they were out of the way Freddy brewed Lillian a cup of tea and sat with her at the kitchen table. All the time he had been busy at the sink and with tea bag and kettle, she had hardly moved; her hands loose in her lap as if they'd fallen there, shoulders sloped forward, her narrow face emptied of anything expressible. After asking for the tea she put it aside without taking a single sip.

'I'm going to fall asleep sitting here if I don't get up.'

'Very understandable,' Freddy said. 'Your first day back in the saddle.'

'That must be it. I need my bed.'

'You want to take the radio with you?' He stretched across the length of the table to get it for her but she refused it with a shake of her head. 'You sure? I think WPNR's special anniversary show is tonight. They're playing all the golden songs from Broadway. Gershwin and Cole Porter.'

'Kiddo, I can't keep my eyes open.'

Forgettable otherwise, this small conversation only churned with meaning afterward. Over and over again Freddy combed it for signs and damned his ignorance or his lack of attention. He remembered every piece of it, with a thudding ache, because this was the last thing they said to each other that night.

Music from the radio played faintly downstairs. In the dark behind Lillian's eyes colors floated and tumbled, beads of rose red stuttered out of a clarinet melody across webs of bottle blue and bottle green, the breathing of violins, spindles of bright yellow flickering from the hectic upward sweep of piano chords. She knew this overture, she could sing the melody in her head; or was that what she was doing? The music wasn't in her ears anymore, it filled her, pulsing in its colors. Soon the rhythm faded, the colors clouded, they were clouds, eaten away at the edges, dimmed to dirty shades of gray, and finally blotted out by borderless dark space. Sleep quickly took hold of Lillian, spreading through her like black water. Water where her bones used to be, water for veins and skin, her whole body was black water sinking into the ground. Where she was wrapped in cold. The coldness took her shape and then melted around her. It let her go, she was weightless, rising into a stream of warmth. She rises up, up like heat in the air. The hiss of rushing wind follows her as the dark shreds away and brings her into a haze of white light. As the wind falls it tears through the whiteness too, with a soft rattling sound. Dry leaves blowing across the yard into the street. Day is almost gone from the sky. Lillian stands in fading winter sunlight on Church Hill near her house. Patches of mud rim the dirt lane where the morning's ice has melted and the puddles are glassing up again in the afternoon's chill.

He is walking toward her with his school books. Drab buckram covers, history, mathematics, English, slung in a leather strap Adamo carries over his shoulder. From behind Lillian three boys on bicycles shoot past, bunched together on that narrow stretch of the road. They're yelling at Adamo, who is crossing from the field side at the corner. Two bicycles in front of him, one at his back, and the boy on that one throws a punch at him. Lillian catches the force of the punch in her upper arm, sees their small mean faces circle her, they're making machine-gun noises, calling each other Flying Ace, laughing at their own joke, laughing all the way down Church Hill. Adamo is alone in the street, Lillian is nowhere to be seen. Though she's there. Adamo's brown brogues are on her feet, she's walking toward the Hoagland place, shifting the bulky weight of Adamo's books on her shoulder.

Along the culvert and cut across the back of Hoagland's garage then catty-corner through the orchard to Garrett St, one block down Appleby's alley and home. How many times home from school this way? One hundred and eighty days a year times four years equals. Subtract eleven days in third grade when I was sick and stayed home. I'll be eleven on my one thousandth time. He calls my name from the back door. Perry remembered my name. He stands there on the top step smoking a cigarette. 'Hey there, Adamo.' One of the older boys, doing a man's job. In rubber boots and overalls today, streaked with cakey white. 'Got a Nymph about done. How'd you like to drive it up into the yard?'

The light in the downstairs workshop is powdery. Under it the two-seater Nymph, all chassis and exposed drive shaft, looks like the skeleton of a crocodile. Rupert, the tall thin one, and Elias, stumpy, with corn-colored hair that keeps falling in his face, tighten the bolts that hold down the engine. Rupert moves the winch that lowered it out of his way so he can see. 'Look who's that,' he says. Elias stops turning his wrench, gives out a false smile. 'How's everything, Adamo?' Perry tells him, 'He wants to watch us poor bastards work,' and then gets back to the unfinished wall he's plastering. Either Rupert or Elias says, 'Yeah, I wish I could do that. Sit on my skinny butt and watch the workers work.'

Perry at work with bucket and trowel. He says to Rupert and Elias, 'Adamo asked me could he drive her up to the body shed.' 'Oh, we're not ready for that. Tomorrow, maybe,' says Rupert. 'We're done for today. Perry, close up those doors.' 'Yes, boss,' Perry salutes and lopes up the ramp and swings shut the big green doors. The slap of the wood against its frame makes Lillian jump. Elias sits on the front wheel of the Nymph, casts his hand over it and asks her, 'Any Red you know has the smarts to build a machine like this? Think your papa could?' 'Papa makes shoes,' Lillian answers him. Rupert pats her back, a little roughly. 'Did he make your shoes?' Lillian nods. Rupert kneels down for a closer look. 'They're pretty. Let's see.' He taps the shoe, wants her to take it off. 'I'm not going to eat it for supper,' he says and unlaces it. When it's off Lillian's foot he studies it from every angle. 'Doesn't look like Reds can make shoes, either,' and he throws it to Elias who sniffs it, makes a disgusted face then tosses it to Perry who fumbles it. The shoe lands in his bucket of plaster. He fishes it out and drops it on the floor.

'Do you know my daddy?' Rupert is angry, demands to know. Lillian doesn't know why he's asking. 'Well, your daddy doesn't know him any better than you do. He gave jobs to Elias and Perry, tell him that.' Elias jerks Lillian's arm, says, 'Maybe he'll give you a job sometime.' 'No, his daddy's teaching him the bosses are gonna do all the work. Workers don't have to work.' 'I heard that at Bartolotti's meeting,' says Elias, and, 'Your papa doesn't get it how we're thankful to Mr Hoagland. I *like it* he's my boss.'

Mama and Papa are waiting at home. And Marina, Tonio, Nicolo, and Donatella the baby. *Cannellini in brodo* on the stove. Lillian, in her one shoe, moves toward the ramp. 'You gotta go the other way,' Rupert tells her. She turns and heads for the stairs but Elias walks in front of her carrying a rear axel, blocking her. 'Pardon there, Adamo. Can't go this way.' From the other side of the room Perry tells them, 'You're just mixing him up.'

'We don't want him to go yet.' Rupert surges toward her and grabs her hands. They mean to hurt her and that's for sure. Elias uses the book strap to tie her hands behind her back. She shouts something about her shoe, the two men laugh at her helplessness. Elias kicks her behind the knees and Lillian folds up, lands hard on the floor. The first pinpoint of real pain and sudden center of fear stings her arm. She can't see what they're doing to her. She smells their cigarettes. On her neck another hot bite. Again on the back of her leg, on the small of her back, through the burnt fabric of her clothes. I have to tell somebody what's happening to me! Her shout is stopped with an oily rag screwed into her mouth. She'll tell somebody, even if she has to swear to them she never will, she'll tell everybody what they did to her. Unless the police blame her. Rupert Hoagland. Elias Corn Hair. Perry. They can say they caught her sneaking in, stealing. They won't believe me. I'll tell the truth when I get home, I'll tell what they did to me.

A rough grapple at the buttons on her knickerbockers. They're on top of her at the back of the Nymph, with a rope under her jaw. The loose loop fastens her to the rear of the chassis. Someone pulls her trousers down to her ankles and tears through her longjohns. On her naked legs and the cheeks of her ass she feels a blanket of heat from the open stove. Rupert calls over to Perry, 'Come on and get some of this.'

If she swivels her head a little she can see Perry on his step ladder looking down at her, at them, not moving, saying nothing, doing nothing. From behind they're making me dirty. Pushing something sticky between my cheeks, it's axel grease he's pushing up me. Rupert's skinny hands. Holding on to my hair. Rupert forces her legs apart with his knees, he's inside her, riding her, staying in whichever way she moves. The rag falls out of Lillian's mouth, her breaths are fast and shallow, not enough breath in her lungs to speak, but she tries to. She doesn't take her eyes off Perry and she says, with Adamo's voice in her throat, 'I'm just a little boy . . .' As if they were making a mistake, as if she could bargain her way out of this. Rupert can't hear her over his own noise, damning her, he won't stop, he won't let her up. She cries to Perry, in fierce panic, 'I'm just a little boy!'

Rupert climbs off her, rolls her over and lands a shattering punch on her breastbone. A monkey wrench is in his hand. The pain creases upward into her jaw, down into her twisted arm. No one knows where she is, only these three, who hate her. Elias pulls at the rope around her neck, which makes her cough and suck in the petroleum smell of the grease on it. Rupert and Elias are talking but they've moved away from her and Lillian can't hear what they're saying. The tinkling slap of chain and pulley against the metal frame of the winch. In one grab Elias has the rope collar hooked onto the chain. The first pull on it drags Lillian to her feet. The next one hoists her off the ground by her neck, legs kicking.

She isn't with them anymore, even though they're under her eyes. From someplace above the four Lillian sees them all – Adamo strangling on the winch, Rupert in command of the chain, Elias hugging Adamo's legs, adding his weight, killing him faster, and Perry up on the step ladder, dumbfounded, unblinking. She must be at the top of the ramp in the shadow of the doors. Rooted there. Without the strength to move down to them or back away or even to cry out, Lillian understands where she is: at the end of this, the death of the world. Life is outside this room. That's where Freddy is. She hears him through the storm doors, wanting her. 'Lillian! Can you hear me? Lil honey, Lillian . . .' Other men are with him, different voices. 'Is it her heart?' 'It's her heart.' The men are right. She looks down at the wound in her chest, where Rupert punched her. Blood is emptying out of it, blood and streams of sacred, failing light.

Chapter Twenty-eight

BLANKET-WRAPPED, oxygen mask greenly cupped over her nose and mouth, bundled on the stretcher in the ambulance: the shattering sight he had of Lillian almost annihilated by her convulsing heart, left Freddy weak. If the lamp hadn't fallen off her bedside table, or if he hadn't heard the crash . . . if he hadn't lunged upstairs to find her – barely breathing – on the floor between their beds . . . if the paramedics had been five minutes slower . . . Oh, this was the fruit of a fatal error of judgment, Freddy knew, the last mistake in a cavalcade of blind mistakes, his and his alone; he wasn't much good at doing good. As he rode with her, his face inches from hers, Freddy also held Lillian in his mind, already remembering her, as though he was peering down on her from a terrible height.

For the two days she lay unconscious in the hospital Freddy occupied the white plastic chair pulled close to her bed. Slumped back, arms crossed over the strained mound of his stomach, or curled forward, sleepless, unwashed, stubble mossing over his round heavy cheeks, his mustache frayed, he turned down the offer of an army cot, saying to Dr Mollo, 'I don't want to get too comfortable here.' He watched Lillian (others were in and out watching over her), and one minute he was positive she knew he was waiting there (her spirit knew), the next minute he was just as certain he was locked out.

In kindhearted conspiracy first Billy Cooke and then Dr Mollo asked Freddy to think about going home to rest; Lillian's signs were stable, more than his were – both of them cracked the same joke. He laughed both times, agreed with them and didn't move. Lillian must have been listening to the whole routine. When she woke for a few minutes on the Thursday, groggy, her speech slow, she ordered him home. 'I'm not going anywhere,' she said. Freddy replied, 'Neither am I.' But a little while after she sank into sleep again, he went.

Imagine this house with Lillian's ghost in it. Freddy did that sitting in his wing chair as the day's thin light drained away and early dark flooded in through the windows; it soaked into his bones. He'd see her in her favorite places, on the sofa listening to the radio or maybe the radio would start playing by itself; the ghost of her affection and touch, her habits and conversation, the smell of her hair might spring out at him from nowhere, trying to communicate. She'd have to work harder from her side to make up for his poor talent, she'd have to teach him . . . He tried and clumsily failed to make a real dinner for himself that night. Mim ended up bringing half a lasagne to him, which he heated in the microwave. That kindness hit Freddy as a peek into his widower's future – dinners with Mim and Arthur or else alone at a table in Giuliano's, Old Man Foy with his garlic bread and side salad and ravioli, reading a newspaper he's read through once already, to appear involved and content.

On Friday morning Freddy met Dr Mollo in his office and they went together to Lillian's room. The doctor floated on optimism. 'See that?' pointing with pride as if Lillian were his creation, even if she happened to be under another MD's care. She was sitting up but still looked like she'd been hauled from the sea. Dampness glued her hair to her forehead, her skin was colorless but some inner heat flickered with a will in the blueness of her eyes. It was the thing Mollo pointed at, the recovery he wanted Freddy to take in. Dr Bernstein, slope-shouldered, senior and cautious, examined her, was satisfied, ordered a string of tests and another string of medicines, and then on his way past Freddy he said, 'We're being careful with her. The Queen of England wouldn't get better treatment.'

'How careful do you have to be?' stooping a little to catch Bernstein's more serious meaning.

'She's out of the woods. Try to remember she's not superhuman.'

'All the signs are good, though?'

'We're going to keep an eye on her for another four-five days. But, yes,' Dr Bernstein said to him, with some warmth, 'she's come through it.'

They both had, Freddy recognized, permanently changed in ways he was finding hard to grasp. Where do you go for the necessary enlightenment? Straight-backed, he presented himself to Lillian, in his chair again as if it was a pew. 'We both look better,' he said, patting his shaved and cologned face, smoothing down his tie.

Her voice didn't have much power in it. 'Sore throat. Can't talk much.'

Freddy raised an understanding hand. 'Mim and Arthur came in twice on Tuesday and twice Wednesday. Did anybody tell you? Mim stayed with you while you were asleep. We didn't want you to wake up in an empty room.'

'Think they'll visit today?'

'Definitely, I know they will. Arthur won't be down until later. He's been babysitting my classes. The boys all want to know how you're feeling.'

'Says Arthur.'

'No, no, really. There's a card from my homeroom delinquents somewhere in that pile.'

'Tell them it cheered me up.' The effect must have faded; of course, Lillian had a good reason to sound flattened. 'I got one from Detective Early, too.'

'Yes, he was here,' passing over it, breezily. 'Your whole fan club has been buzzing around. Billy Cooke and all the nurses. I see one of your patients wrote you a poem. Maybe you can get more out of it than I can. It's about seaweed?' Freddy thumbed through the loose stack of cards to dig out Douglas Cottle's depressing free verse comparison of Lillian's insides and an oil-polluted kelp forest. 'Can't find it,' he said and gave up looking.

'I know. He said I'm not allowed to go home until he recites it to me.' She showed Freddy she was braced for the honor with her instant, First Lady smile. As it fell, she asked him, 'Did you get some rest?'

'Mim cooked dinner for me last night. A beautiful lasagne. Lil, I'm such a loss in the kitchen. Useless! I tried to make meatloaf the way you make it for me. All the right ingredients were in the refrigerator, you know, I was sure I knew how to make it. Oh, God, Lillian,' magnifying the disaster, 'I left out the egg and parsley, I chopped the onions wrong, I didn't even know what *temperature* to set the oven or how long to leave it in. The garbage disposal ate very well. What was I *doing*? It's just so stupid! Without you there, I thought – what's the point of this meatloaf?'

'The point is you have to eat.'

'Oh no,' he came back, 'it wasn't that. How many times have you cooked meatloaf for me in thirty-five years? I know what it's supposed to look like and how it tastes. Then when I try to do it for myself it's a mess, a ridiculous failure.'

It was more than she had the energy to hear. Still, she offered, 'Want to know something? You think you're worldly,' and this was more than she wanted to say.

'I disappointed you. Badly, badly.'

'I'll teach you how to make meatloaf.' Her sweet joke didn't reach him, he blocked it with a sharp look. Any fight had been wearied out of her. She said, 'Only once. Did you think I wanted to be married to a conquistador?'

'You had expectations. I wanted you to have them. Because I didn't have a doubt in my mind. Looking back, I think I tackled all the wrong subjects. I'm cloudy about everything now.'

'We don't have to look back anymore. Let's don't.'

Freddy's blood was shaking, he wanted to be heard out. 'It got to me finally in the ambulance. Jesus, Lillian, you were gone. My Midas touch. *I did this to you* – that's what I kept thinking. *The opposite of what I wanted*. How can you count on me anymore? I hit my limit a long time ago with Hildy. A wrong turn at every corner. Finally, I believe it's clear to me, the right thing to do, the good thing. We came through so much, we were safe. It was safe for you to know, so I gave you the truth about Hildy and her baby. What did that do? It almost killed you.'

'Stop it, honey.'

Downcast, he reminisced, 'Those three weeks when you couldn't stand to be around me. In a motel by yourself, and, Christ, in the Y in Boston. This time around you would've been where Adamo is.'

'We *aren't* going to *have* this discussion.' Now or anytime in the future – Lillian was finished with it, that was all she wanted Freddy to know. Yes, she was physically sapped, cushioned by drugs, pulped by her voyage back from myocardial infarction, but exhausted by another sickness – futility. Long ago she got used to the idea that ferocious human cruelty was a fact in the world. And there was also a healing reply to it. Adamo took her to a place where that faith was tormented and buried. What useful reply could she make to Elias Cobb's viciousness, his oily taunts, Rupert Hoagland's triumphant butchery, Perry's silent, frigid collusion. There was no reply to it, Lillian knew this now in her soul. And if all prayer was futile, then she was done with this tragedy, finished with Elias, Rupert, Perry and Adamo; she walled them off. Her reply was to Freddy. She said, 'I'm with *you* now.'

It was practically a vow, stark, intentional. It jarred Freddy and reclaimed him. 'I've been turning a plan over in my mind. Let's redecorate the bedroom. What's your opinion?'

'In favor,' Lillian said. 'A hundred percent.'

'Starting with the furniture. Give those beds the heave-ho. Donate them to the Salvation Army. What's your opinion?' He waited with a net, to capture it.

Did he realize he still could startle delicate thoughts out of her? 'If we find one we both like the look of. Nothing too old.'

'Danish Modern,' endorsed Freddy, pink as a lottery winner.

'That was a long time ago. We'd have to go to an antique store, God knows where, to find it today.'

'Belgian Modern, then. Armenian Modern.'

'They had one in the window at Haisfield's. It was there last summer, a beautiful bed. With reading lights built into little niches in the headboard.'

'I'll go over there before they close today,' he said. 'We'll find one we both want to sleep in.'

Freddy's expedition wound through six stores in Lawford, Mistley and Woodbridge. He returned to St Mount's the next afternoon, an hour behind schedule, with snapshots of thirty beds for Lillian to look over. Home is the hunter, home from the hill. Here it was, the thing Freddy could provide for her, a piece of furniture, solid in its being and its meaning alike. As the elevator doors opened he was fishing in his heavy coat's pocket for the envelope of photographs, wording the apology for arriving late he was going to make to Lillian. He had completely forgotten the real reason he'd arranged to be at the hospital before noon; seeing Detective Early at the reception desk, waiting for him, Freddy felt a cold weight drop into his stomach.

'There you are.' Early registered the fact, merely.

'That one-hour developing place at Greendale Plaza,' Freddy winced, flapping the blue envelope in his hand. 'They shouldn't get people's hopes up. Two hours and twenty minutes to get these done.'

'Time's pressing on me a little too, Freddy.'

'Did you already go in and talk to her? Without me being there? I know you're working on a tight schedule, and you want to do it correctly, but we had an agreement about this.'

'We did, yes sir. There's no problem,' Early said and started to walk with Freddy toward Lillian's room. 'I talked to Dr Mollo this morning and he told me she's in very good shape.'

'He means she's strong.' Freddy stopped and said, 'But it won't help if she's agitated.'

'As far as I know, nobody's mentioned the subject around her. I don't think anyone really wants to talk about it much. At least, not to me.'

If talking to Det Early meant Lillian had to take any more punishment, then procedure or no procedure, Freddy was on hand to stop it. 'Her strength isn't back yet. It's coming, but it's not back. You have to remember that. Lillian's recovery is what matters here.'

They were outside the door of her room, heads bowed together, whispering. 'She'll have to be a little stronger today. Do you want to let her know what happened? Let her hear it from you.'

'No, no.' Freddy's eyes blinked shut, his refusal was firm. 'It's not my territory.'

During that week the St Mount's staff had got used to Det Early's official presence in the hospital. He wore his authority loosely, it settled

302

around him in the casual folds of his suit, draping his grasshopper arms and legs. The security guards and staff nurses, orderlies, consultants, all answered and reanswered his questions with the same patience he brought to his work. They were his work. And because every day they sat with the ailing, the victims, they saw behind Early's even temper, they knew this bedside trick; it contained his outrage.

'I've written to my congressman. This isn't fair, Lillian,' Early said from the foot of her bed. 'Things like this shouldn't happen to people like you.'

She answered, 'My mother used to think sinning attracted diseases.'

'Didn't she believe in microbes?'

'Sure she did. Sin attracted them. The sicker you were the blacker your sin was. That's why the Reaper is so grim.'

'Your mother told you that? That's frightening. Man, that's a scary thing to tell a child.'

'Massachusetts got another RN out of it. Temporarily out of order.' Lillian lifted both forearms, an IV drip running into each. 'It can still frighten me a little bit.'

'I know you don't believe that bull.'

'No, she's kidding you,' said Freddy.

Any joke that was in it had seeped away. 'We've got other names for it now.'

'Did Freddy tell you I've been coming around to see you? I was by on Thursday, the minute I heard you were awake.'

'I told her, yes.'

'You were only up for a little while.' Early's mood turned serious. 'It took a bite out of me, that's the truth. I'm real happy that you're going to be okay.' Then, 'Hey, are you tough enough to take in some news?'

'You mean there's still a world outside?'

'My cousin is on the St Mary's parish council. She's pushing to get them to give Adamo a churchyard gravesite. Louise has half the council on her side, but Father Tim is fighting it every step. Finances and square footage, it's unbelievable, but that's his argument.'

Lillian spoke from inside herself, with granite certainty. 'Adamo would rather be with his family.'

'Understood. But it's a long complicated process.' Early summed up the problem by saying, 'The State Department is just slow and confused, but the Italian bureaucracy! Sister, they are something *else*. It could take years. They've got to trace the right Bartolottis, so on and so forth. We should bury the boy,' he said, and he was weighed down by the pity of it. 'I'd give a lot to know what exactly happened to him.'

Her business was among the living. She was not, after everything, going to be loaded onto a gurney and lowered to the basement, rolled through the underground passageways, over the disinfected green linoleum ramps, left like an order of medical supplies on a stainless steel table. Freddy did not have the bitter duty of signing papers to allow her autopsy, there was no funeral for him to arrange. Lillian's secret knowledge was this: she was released – from the havoc of crime and the expiation of crime; the icy memory of Adamo's fate lodged in her without any force of blame or regret. It belonged to Perry Gillies who didn't save him. In the dirt and heat and mayhem Adamo begged Perry to tell what happened, for both their sakes. He was still begging him. 'You should talk to Perry,' she encouraged Early. 'Ask him.'

Early's attention hardened. 'I know he had a connection. He saw our boy outside Hoagland's. Wasn't that the last time anybody saw Adamo?'

'The report in the *Intelligencer* had that. They got that part of the story from Perry, they must have.'

'It sounds like you think there was more to it.'

'He's careful about what he says to me.'

'You had a conversation with Perry on Monday, is that right? After the quarrel he had with Mr Kibbee.'

'Perry gets under everybody's skin,' Lillian had to say. 'Mine, too. I didn't blame Mr Kibbee.'

The slow glance from Early, like the sweep of a beam from a lighthouse, warned Freddy not to interrupt. 'There's no way I can make it easy on you,' he said to Lillian. 'Perry died on Monday night.'

She didn't die, he did. She was a passenger, a witness, and Perry's death set her free. 'He knew he was dying,' she said in the quiet white room. 'It's finished, so that's good. It's over for him.'

'That old man got helped along in that direction.' Early went on, 'I understand from Dr Gertler that Frank Kibbee is an osteo patient. He was into his second month of physiotherapy. Lillian, did you notice how well he could use his hands? Would you say he had much strength in them?'

'To do what?'

'Monday night, the nurse went in with Perry's medication and he was on the floor. Craziness,' was the next word that came to Early's mind. 'Somebody choked him with a rope. He's in the morgue with a vicious rope burn on his neck. Who had that kind of feeling against Perry, to want to hurt him like that?' Lillian shook her head. 'Did you see anybody around the geriatric unit on Monday who shouldn't have been in there?'

Again, slowly, Lillian shook her head.

'She didn't see anybody,' Freddy made it clear, and in an undertone made it clearer. 'Don't push her.'

Lillian's muteness wasn't empty. She looked past Early, tuned him out, absented herself. He won't find anyone. She'll tell what she knows if he asks the right questions; if he lands on an innocent suspect; if it helps anything. 'Can you think back for me? I'm just wondering if anybody from your psychiatric unit, a patient or ex-patient, might've had a grudge against Perry.'

'Don't ask her any more. You're pushing her.' A spasm of worry jerked Freddy out of his chair. 'It's not good for her to think about those things. She was feeling sick all day, she shouldn't have gone into work at all. You could see it in her face when she got home on Monday night. It must have been building up all day, affecting her, tiring her out. What do you expect from her? She hardly noticed *me* sitting next to her at the dinner table.' He stood in front of Early, screening Lillian off from him, a plump physical barrier, tough as a nightclub bouncer.

The kingsize bed attracted Freddy with its clean geometry, Art Deco planes and angles clad in bird's-eye maple the color of pale whiskey in a glass. It fit exactly into the space their twin beds used to occupy. He had trusted his eye, estimating the width and depth, so this neatness struck him as another sign of the upswing in his life. A border had been crossed. It was almost a physical relief he felt, as though he'd waded and torn through a tangled acre of briar to stride into an open field. Normality returned as a reward.

After the clearing out, the calm. Silent arguments with Lillian and with himself were settled, put away, and bed-buying meatloaf-cooking dish-washing early-night normality ruled. As an example to Lillian he kept up his night-time exercises. On each downward bend Freddy's hands dipped toward his toes and stopped short just below his kneecaps, his stomach doubled and squashed. Between loud breaths he counted out his progress. On each upward stretch the peaceful view was waiting for him: Lillian cozily reading her *People* magazine on her side of the big square bed.

He said, 'The movers almost knocked a hole in the paneling when they carried the headboard upstairs. They scuffed the varnish.'

'I wish you waited till I was here.'

'What could you have done?' He heard her turn the pages of her magazine.

'Don't know,' she said. 'Directed traffic.'

'I wanted it to be here for you.'

'You didn't have to do it in such a big rush. We could've waited for the other one.'

Freddy quit bending and stretching. He was panting slightly, which made him sound overexcited. 'This one's custom-built. You can't compare it to anything else. It's better in every imaginable way.'

'For the extra two hundred dollars you'd think they would've built in reading lights.' The bed was here, it weighed hundreds of pounds, it was not going to be moved again. So Lillian hopped off the subject. 'I need a stronger bulb in this lamp. It's a strain on my eyes.'

'If you set your heart on the factory model, we'll exchange it. Compared to this one, believe me, Lil, the construction's flimsy. We've got a handmade piece of furniture.'

'Why didn't they want it?'

'Who?'

'The people who sold it back to Haisfield's.'

Untroubled, Freddy said, 'Oh, for some goddamned reason. The headboard was a quarter-inch too high or the corners weren't square enough. We would've had to wait six weeks for the other one.'

'I'm just getting used to it.'

'Haisfield's has got to have a return policy. If we're not satisfied. Whatever you want, that's what we'll do. Should I call up the movers tomorrow to take it back? It's for the two of us, after all.'

'When you described it to me I thought the wood was darker. Not so yellowish.'

'Maybe Haisfield's will pick it up.' Then, sincerely, if she didn't think he was trying hard enough, 'Lil, say what you think. This isn't – we're not having an argument here.'

307

Well, did she want that? 'I'll get used to it.'

'That's the ticket.'

Normal existence for Freddy, though, was a grace period; sometimes long, sometimes short, but always coiled inside it was the danger of falling backward. No structure was completely safe – (they received an early Christmas card from Hildy with her address in London, a spur to Freddy to write to her and drag himself again through his wanting judgment, his parental felonies) – an obstruction was building up somewhere or a support was coming loose somewhere else, a weak spot was ready to give. Normal life required steady maintenance.

'That's the ticket.' His voice caught, in hesitation, and kept Lillian listening but Freddy said nothing else. Instead, his quietness held her as it held him. In his slippers and clean blue-striped pyjamas, arms crooked, standing motionless, staring straight ahead for a long moment, he had the look of a men's store dummy. Whatever he was looking at had to be as fragile as a soap bubble or panicky as a wild bird because he acted as if a sneeze would startle it away. 'Him,' he said.

Lillian looked where Freddy looked. She saw his eyes were fixed in mild wonder on the empty air.

'He's welcoming you home,' said Freddy.

First, a warm wave folded over Lillian: he was doing this for *her*, testifying to his love. Freddy's broad face showed off its welcome, unfrightened, unbewildered, as innocent as a drunk. This sweet demonstration was for her and he watched for a response. A coldness poured into Lillian. He didn't see Adamo. Or if he did Freddy only saw the unmarked schoolboy in the newspaper picture, Adamo as happy and green as he was until that day, before he was chained up, beaten, burned, smeared with filth, raped, deserted, hanged, buried. The agony of it would cover Freddy's face if he knew and he'd know how Lillian carried real horror in her heart. He smiled at the shadow of the bedroom door and lowered his hands to his sides, slowly, harmlessly. He didn't know. So he couldn't know how this pretending lacerated her.

'Will you come and lie down? Freddy, you're so far away.'

'Talk to him, Lil.'

'No.'

'Why won't you? Adamo's one of the family.'

'What you're doing is frightening me to death.'

'He doesn't understand why you don't want him here.' Helpless in the face of it Freddy said, 'I don't either.'

Nausea flushed through Lillian's stomach and its heat was on her skin. Tell him. Or else this is what she'll have with Freddy – the illusion of life together, days and nights piling up blankly, meeting him in the kitchen where they'll talk about the food they're eating, in the bedroom they'll talk about the furniture they own, she'll live without an effect on him, disconnected, transparent, untouched. It's the sadness of the dead as they witness the living. Adamo saw Lillian this way, in this room, and reached across the same silent distance. Tell Freddy all of it. Or hang in a kind of damnation. Longing with no answer, the labor of separation, the suffocated cry . . . unless she can touch him now it will be her fate as it was the murdered boy's. Lillian felt the reality of this at the very edge of her senses, as a soft concussion in the air. It was the opening between two worlds.

He stood at the foot of the bed, brought back – in his knickerbockers, white shirt and polished brown shoes, with his heavy black hair oiled and combed off his forehead, Adamo rotated his face into the light. Serious eyes, dark and tear-coated, found Lillian. He raised his arm and stiffly pointed at her. Here was his ultimate purpose, it was with her: tonight. Only Lillian, in the whole great living river of souls, knew how he had been obliterated. To know such a thing alone (the pointing finger said) is cold exile. So tell it.

Tell it. Adamo's need lived inside her, beating in her pulse. To tell

309

Freddy, tonight, and mix this into his memory: a greasy rag in the mouth, a rope cinched under the jaw. Another little killing. Tell him, Lillian, be unsparing. Be the cause of brutal sadness. If his sleep is racked and molten murderous dreams take him into the basement, when he wakes up beside you in this bed you'll be the source of his comfort, also unsparing.